NAMELE

SHADOWS OF ASH

ADRIAN J SMITH

Shadows of Ash

Copyright © 2021 all rights reserved.

This is a work of fiction. Names, characters, organizations, places, events, and incidents are either products of the author's imagination or are used fictitiously. Any resemblance to actual events locales or persons, living or dead, is purely coincidental. No part of this publication may be reproduced, distributed, or transmitted in any form or by any means, including photocopying, recording, or other electronic or mechanical methods, without the prior written permission of the publisher.

For Wu-zy. The cat that changed my heart.

*Depart from me, you cursed, into the eternal fire
prepared for the devil and his angels.*

—Matthew 25:41 KJV

ACKNOWLEDGEMENTS

This series wouldn't be possible without the following wonderful people:

Lisa Omstead, Nathan Yokoyama, Nicholas Sansbury Smith, Karin De Vries, Daniel Arenson, Frances Liontakis, Sam Sisavath, Jacob Toye, Lee Murray, Brandon Swanson, Mark Campbell, Bill Holder.

I'm sure there are some people I'm missing. Those who I pestered about life in the Armed Forces. I thank you all.

The friendly people of Japan.

The team at Deranged Doctor Design

My family for encouraging me along the way.

Edited by: Laurel C Kriegler, Alison Robertson, Nikki Crutchley

ALSO BY ADRIAN J SMITH

EXTINCTION NZ SERIES:
THE RULE OF THREE
THE FOURTH PHASE
THE FIVE PILLARS

NAMELESS SERIES:
WHISPERS OF ASH
SHADOWS OF ASH
MASKS OF ASH (COMING SOON)
SILENCE OF ASH (COMING SOON)

ABOUT SHADOWS OF ASH

The enemy of my enemy is my friend...

All retired operative Ryan Connors wanted was to live a life of solitude in Japan. He wanted to leave LK3, the extraction and espionage agency and hoped to find peace in the thriving city of Tokyo. But nothing is ever easy. His old team – The Nameless – seek him out to use his skills to find the missing daughter of one of his dearest friends – Sofia. The yakuza attack and kidnap Sofia, thrusting Ryan back into the life he'd tried to leave behind.

While following a lead near Osaka, a worldwide catastrophic event occurs. Humans, cats, and dogs self-combust, and turn to ash. Even though he is desperate to get home to his daughter, Zanzi, Ryan tracks down his missing friends only to face the yakuza and a new foe – OPIS, a sinister organization whose motives are unclear. Two sides battling it out with Ryan and his team in the middle.

To survive, and desperate for answers, Ryan makes a deal with the head of the Yamada clan – Touma Yamada.

Ryan and The Nameless thought they were finished. They had held up their end of the bargain and stopped

Yamada's enemy from taking control of Japan. They were heading home to America. But Ryan will learn that making deals with the devil is never simple. His life and his friends' lives are about to get even more complicated with new enemies swarming from every direction.

Ryan is tired of playing games. He's not only defending his adopted country, but all of humanity.

PROLOGUE

SHINJUKU, TOKYO
DECEMBER 31ST, 1999

The heavy bass of the dance music blasted from the speakers, so loud it vibrated the wooden floor.

It reverberated through the legs of two hundred sweaty people as they moved to the rhythmic music. Arms waved, twirling, glo-sticks clenched in fists. Feet stomped and shuffled with the rising beat, and the dancers' faces were locked in expressions of joy and contentment.

Most of the dancers were dressed in fluorescent yellow, blue, or pink. Plastic beads covered their wrists and arms. A few had beads and chokers clasped around their necks. One had flying goggles pushed back over his spiked hair, another had a gas mask on, while others sucked on baby dummies. Men and women ground their bodies against each other, lost in a moment of time when nothing else mattered. Nothing but the music. The feeling. The people you were with. It was the eve of a new millennium and they were alive to usher it in.

In the seating area next to the dance floor, Ebony looked on, envious of the dancers' freedom. She cringed inwardly as the Japanese man ran his hand from her knee up her inner thigh. She had become adept at hiding her true feelings. Keeping a poker face. Not that he was ugly or being too rough. Or that he was drunk. He, like nearly everyone else in here, was probably on cocaine or ecstasy, or some other form of narcotic. It was part of the dance culture. Expected and encouraged.

Above the DJ was a large digital clock, red and glowing bright. It flashed *11:55 PM*.

Five minutes until the new millennium. One more client and Ebony would be free. Her debt paid. A new millennium meant a new life for her. Something she had yearned for these last three years.

Ebony smiled at her client before taking his hand and kissing it. She had teased him all night, saying she wanted to wait until the new millennium before sleeping with him.

"I want you to be the first. My first of the new era, Ando. We're all virgins again, didn't you know?"

"All right, my red-haired beauty," he'd said.

Ando tugged on her top, groping her.

Ebony gently pushed his hand away. "I have to use the Ladies."

Shadows of Ash

"Hurry back. I want to kiss you at midnight."

"Of course, darling."

Ebony ignored the other men staring at her. Standing at six foot with an athletic body, pale skin, red hair, and large breasts, she was used to the stares, the whistles, the vulgar gestures. Drugs lowered people's inhibitions. Though slightly more respectful than drunks, the drugs gave them courage they otherwise didn't have.

She fended off two Westerners wearing Australian flags and screaming "Oi! Oi! Oi!" and ducked into the VIP section. The bouncer acknowledged her and lifted the velvet rope aside. The VIP section was luxurious. Thick carpet and leather chairs. Waitstaff, to serve the guests their every desire, buzzed around. Guards stood ready, weapons tucked away but easy to spot if you looked. Like most clubs in Shinjuku, this one was operated by a yakuza clan.

Ebony closed the toilet stall door behind her and quickly removed the lid from the cistern. She reached in and extracted the watertight bag. She smiled at her passport and the bundle of cash. A friend at the bar had agreed to hide it there, a move that could get them both beaten. Even though she was supposedly free tomorrow morning, Ebony knew that the yakuza didn't let prized property leave so easily. They would invent a new debt. Not for the last time, Ebony cursed her naivety. She should never have let her friend Angela talk her into being a hostess in Tokyo. Great money? Yes. Like a fool, she had believed it and become entrenched in the lifestyle, using cocaine to dull the self-disgust as man after man moved on top of her.

"You have only yourself to blame, girl," she said into the mirror.

There was banging on the door.

"Ebony! Get back out there."

She was always being watched. Monitored. Her time was their money.

"Ebony!"

"All right!"

She secured the cash and passport under her dress and opened the door. Her yakuza handler growled and shoved her back into the club.

The DJ was now playing a dreamy trance song as the clock ticked down. Thirty seconds to go. Ebony pushed her way through the crowd. She blew Ando a kiss and sank down into the curved loveseat.

"Miss me?" she said, winking.

"Always." Ando pecked her cheek and fondled her again. He had snowy white hair, meticulously combed with a side part, and was dressed in an old-style suit. Maybe from the '50s or '60s. Nothing like the garish clothes people wore today. Bright colors and wide ties. Ando wore a finely tailored three-piece, complete with pocket watch.

She was perplexed by Ando. They had spent a few nights together and she still couldn't read him. He was a master at controlling his emotions. He had the white hair of an elderly person, but his skin was smooth as marble. His mannerisms and speech were old fashioned like his suit. He used phrases and words Ebony had never heard before. Ando was an enigma. He disappeared for months, only to reappear again and pay her for days at a time. He gave the impression that he was perhaps in his mid-fifties, but the way his eyes observed everything told a different story. Like he had been there and done that and now he was bored.

The crowd erupted into cheers as the clock counted down.

10...

9...

8...

7...

Gunfire exploded across the room from the direction of the bar.

6...

5...

4...

More gunshots followed by a woman's high-pitched scream. Yakuza guards scrambled and swarmed, tackling someone to the ground. Ebony's attention was caught by the out-of-place noise and the movement, but her mind struggled to grasp what was happening. She had been around enough of the yakuza to see violence. Probably just a scuffle.

3...

2...

1...

"Happy New Year!"

Ebony was assaulted by a cacophony of sounds. Glitter cannons exploded. Dry ice flooded the dance floor. The partygoers shrieked, hugged, and kissed. The music thundered in a pulsating drumbeat. The laser and strobe lights flicked on and off in a seizure-inducing cadence. Ebony was flooded by emotion at the same time. Hadn't anyone heard the shots?

Pop! Pop! Pop!

That was definitely gunfire. Ando yanked her down underneath the table and shielded her with his body.

"Stay down!" he shouted, his eyes scanning the club. Dozens of suited men rushed toward the entry foyer, hands on their holstered weapons as the crowd dispersed. Some screamed and some stood frozen, unsure what to do, while others barged people out of the way in their desperation to get clear of the danger.

"Ebony. Doctor Ando. Come with me." The same guard who had knocked on the toilet door leaned into the booth with his hand out. He had a machine gun of some sort hanging across his front.

"Hurry," he urged as he pushed Ebony and Ando before him, his eyes on the dance floor. He guided them past the private booths and toilets and opened a back door.

"What's going on?" Ando said.

"A rival clan," the guard answered, swinging his weapon up and pointing it down the brightly lit hallway. He raised a radio to his lips. "Property and client ready."

"Get them..." The voice was replaced by gunshots and grunts. *"...next door."*

The yakuza guard hesitated, shifting from one foot to the other.

Ebony could guess what he was concerned about. This hallway led to either the front entrance or to a side alley

Shadows of Ash

as a fire escape. He would be weighing up the risks. The club they were in – Shinjuku Palace – was operated by the Akoshi Clan. Fights for territory were common amongst the yakuza.

"This way." He tugged on Ebony's hand, guiding her and Ando toward the alley.

The door groaned as the guard nudged it open with his gun before poking his head out. Crisp air filtered through, sending shivers up Ebony's spine.

The trio exited the club and hugged the shadows. The gunfire was sporadic now. Police sirens wailed in the distance, growing louder. A black limo, its engine running, waited at the exit.

"Where to, Dr. Ando?"

"Hotel Gracery."

The guard tapped the driver's side window of the limo. He turned and held open the door for Ebony and Ando.

Crack! Crack!

Ebony flinched. The guard gasped and looked at his chest. Two blood flowers bloomed as he slumped to the ground. Ebony went to scream but Ando's surprisingly strong hand clamped over her mouth.

"Don't struggle. This will all be over soon." He shoved her into the limo and slammed the door behind him.

Ebony kicked and screamed, lashing out with every bit of fight she had, smashing her fists and feet against the doctor. Her worst fears of being kidnapped and killed by some creep had become reality.

"I said, don't struggle!"

Ebony gasped as something jabbed in her neck. Ice-cold liquid flowed into her bloodstream. She laughed, her anger instantly replaced by euphoria.

"Why are you doing this?" she said, giggling.

"You are very special." Ando smiled.

"Aw, you think I'm special. How?"

"No more questions."

"Where are you taking me?"

"Sleep. We have a long journey ahead."

"I want to go home."

"You are. Now sleep."

Ebony couldn't help but grin. Whatever drug he had given her, it was fantastic. She had never felt so warm. So content. Like she had nothing to worry about, that she was perfectly in tune with the world and she would be okay. But still, a coal-sized lump of doubt gnawed in the back of her mind, and it was only the overpowering happiness that kept it back there. Wherever Ando was taking her, it would be all right. Everything was fine. She closed her eyes and let sleep's warm embrace envelope her.

ONE

TOKYO, JAPAN
PRESENT DAY

"That's absurd. That song is not about sex." Ryan shook his head at his oldest friend.

"Sure, it is. Every song is about sex," Booth said.

"Like what?"

"'Baby Got Back.'"

"Nope. It's about his love of female derrieres."

"Okay. 'Alive.'"

"'Alive' by Pearl Jam?"

"Yeah. It's totally about Eddie Veder wanting to bang some chick."

Ryan, Booth, Cal, and Allie sat in a grouping of four seats, eating and drinking as the train cruised through the night. Sofia sat across the aisle, tapping away on her tablet, while Keiko and Hogai slept in the other group of four seats.

"How is 'Alive' about sex?" Allie said, raising her eyebrows.

"It's all there in the lyrics. You just have to listen," Booth said.

"No way."

"Sure it is."

"No way. That song is about a teenager who finds out the man he thought was his father is in fact not. His real dad was dying of cancer or drug abuse or something," Allie said.

"Okay. But 'Born To Run' is definitely about Bruce Springsteen cruising around New Jersey hooking up with girls," Booth said.

Ryan glanced at Cal. She sipped her water, watching them.

"What do you think?" he said.

"I think Booth is as deluded as always. 'Born To Run' is about the hot-rod cruising culture of the sixties. Yes, there are elements of sex in the song, but if you listen, it's about cars. Dumbass."

"Can't be. He says they're tramps, because .... Now hear me out." Booth shifted forward and put his elbows on the table.

After the crazy events of the last few days, the enormity of what had happened had hit them all hard. The Nameless needed this. To feel normal. Forget for a while.

"So the main guy in the song is a bit of a nerd. A Poindexter," Booth said. "He gets himself a sweet ride so he can hook up with chicks. As the months go by, he gets a bit of a reputation because of it. Poindexter gets an ego. Starts preying on girls. But then he falls in love with this goody-two-shoes, like Sandy in *Grease*. And the dad forbids her from seeing him. The dad calls him a tramp and he speaks the famous line at her from his car. So the song is about sex."

Ryan shook his head and chortled. Allie and Cal joined him, their laughter high-pitched.

"You guys are idiots," Sofia said as she closed her tablet and leaned over. "Music and songs mean different things to each listener. The artist is trying to get you to tap into the desire or the sadness. Or, in the case of 'Born To Run,' the nostalgia of a more innocent time before the reality of adulthood takes over. It's what they were feeling at the time. That's why you can get so much out of music. The performer puts raw emotion into the piece. You take what you want, what it means to you. Idiots."

Cal reached out and high-fived Sofia. "That, ladies and gents, is why we love Sofia Ortiz. Insightful and brilliant." She looked at Booth. "You have to admit it. She's right."

Booth sighed. "Maybe. But 'Killing in the Name' is for sure about sex."

Everyone groaned. Ryan looked out the window. Streetlights blinked in the darkness. With every station they sped through, he witnessed the same scene. Groups of survivors, shouting and waving as the train rushed past. At one station, the train had stopped so Yamada's men could clear the tracks of bodies, both human and Siphon—people enraged by the nanites, strangely drawn to spinal fluid.

The door to their carriage whooshed open. Goro bowed and his gaze met Ryan's. "Grandfather wants to see you."

"About what?"

"Please. He will discuss it with you."

Ryan shrugged and followed Goro through the Shinkansen.

Touma Yamada's private carriage, toward the back of the bullet train, was luxurious. The first section was an office, complete with a large mahogany desk and leather chairs. Hundreds of books lined floor-to-ceiling shelves.

"Sit, Mr Connors," Yamada said.

"What's this about?" Ryan said. He still couldn't believe how old this man was. Yamada must be full of these nanites. Ryan raised his arm and looked at it. It was hard to comprehend that, right now, there were thousands of microscopic robots inside his own body. Changing him. Regenerating his cells.

Yamada cleared his throat.

"What I told you about the two factions within OPIS is true. Offenheim does want to build a utopia. Myself..." Yamada paused. The train rocked gently as it moved through another station. Tokyo flowed by. "My followers and I don't want that. I'm sure you know your history, Mr Connors. Under Hirohito we entered the war, allied with Germany and Italy. We swept south at an exceptional pace. Because of my education, I oversaw a project. We were looking for technological advancement. Anything and everything. We found something in the Philippines. A plant with remarkable healing properties. Because of the scorpius plant, because of that one plant, my family

Shadows of Ash

regained its honor. It brought me wealth and power. But all along, I wanted something else. Wealth gave me freedom to do what I most desired, but it never brought me true happiness. Everywhere I looked, I saw the disease. The disease of Western influence, and I wanted it gone."

Yamada turned to gaze at Ryan. He saw a sadness in the old man's eyes he had never seen before. If you lived for a long time, like Yamada had, maybe you witnessed too much. Saw too much hate. Too much heartbreak. Watched loved ones wilt and die. Saw a thousand changes. After 1945, technology and the Western world set off into a new era that science fiction writers had only dreamed of. Within seven years, commercial jets made world travel faster. Televisions began to appear in people's lounges.

Yamada had been alive for it all. Birth. Death. Destruction. Peace.

"Thanks for the history lesson, but you still haven't answered my question," Ryan said.

"I need you to rescue my son."

"Your son?"

"Yes. Takeshi. Offenheim's soldiers have him surrounded. Takeshi managed to seal himself away, but without assistance, he and the others will not survive for more than a week."

"Where?"

"Tomari Nuclear Power Plant."

"I thought the nuclear program was suspended after the tsunami?"

"Not quite. The public was in fear because of Fukushima. Inspections were carried out. Tomari was the first brought back online, but it continued to have problems, so the decision was made to decommission it slowly. One reactor still runs at low capacity. However, our target is a building complex behind the plant. Our research facility. That is where Takeshi and Doctor Ando are trapped. It is vital we extract them and our research. I can't let Offenheim get his hands on it."

Ryan mulled over what Yamada was asking of him. He shook his head. "I'm sorry, Touma. Cal and I want to get home to our daughter. Find her."

"How do you know she's even alive?"

"That's not the point. There's been too much delay as it is. We helped you fix your computer breach. Now we're going home."

"And I thank you, but I need your skills."

"Again, I ask, why don't you send your own men in? I'm sure you could overwhelm Offenheim's soldiers."

"Too risky within a nuclear reactor. I need The Nameless. Sneaky and silent, not loud and careless. Offenheim's men will be expecting us to attack. I'll provide the diversion while you secure Takeshi and my chief scientist, Ando."

"Can't do it. You're on your own."

"Will you at least consider it?"

"Look, all we want to do is get back to America." Ryan took a couple of deep breaths doing his best to keep his temper in check.

"Mr Connors. Believe me when I say that I want you all gone. For over two hundred years Japan was closed to outsiders. That is all I wish. All I have ever wanted. To

Shadows of Ash

become emperor and rule Japan as it should be. Glorious and independent. Closed off from the world."

"I want all our names on the safe list, permanently. Or, better yet, switch off these damn bugs."

"If you are successful in rescuing my son, I will, and I'll give you that plane."

"And if we refuse?" Ryan asked.

Yamada ignored his question and ushered Ryan from his office toward the back of the train. They walked through what was clearly his private cabin and down a long narrow corridor. Exquisite paintings hung at regular intervals, softly lit. Most works were by Japanese artists, and some by well-known European painters. Degas, Gauguin and Picasso.

Yamada nodded to the two steely eyed guards and pushed through the door.

The carriage beyond was bare and brightly lit with white halogens. Five naked men were shackled to the ceiling and floor with iron chains.

"These men conspired with Offenheim to overthrow me," Yamada said.

He took a gray wand from one of the guards and pressed a red button on its handle. He held it up to the neck of the first prisoner. Almost immediately the prisoner gasped and went rigid before letting out an agonized shriek through his gag. He arched his back and his eyes bulged. His arms and legs contorted. Seconds later, the man was a pile of ash on the floor. The other prisoners thrashed in their bindings. Even though their mouths were gagged, their muted screams were enough. Yamada passed the wand back to the guard and gestured at the struggling traitors. The guard kicked out viciously, booting the nearest prisoner in the groin. He then held the wand up to the man's neck. That traitor too contorted and his eyes bulged before his body deconstructed into dust.

"We can activate anyone's alpha nanite using this wand. Except the elites, of course; theirs are encrypted. I'm sure you don't want this fate for yourself and your friends. Like these traitors here."

Ryan pushed past Yamada, back into the cleaner air of the next cabin. He glared at him. "It appears that you have left me with no choice but to accept."

Yamada smiled. "I knew you would see it from my point of view." He signaled for the two armed-guards and Goro to take Ryan back to his team. No one spoke as they shuffled through the rocking train.

Goro bowed in the doorway of the carriage. "Apologies, Mr Connors. Grandfather said to take Keiko and Hogai."

"What. Why?"

"To ensure that you complete the mission."

Cal and Sofia bolted up. "What's he talking about? What mission?"

Ryan waved them back down, holding his palms flat. He glared at Goro. "That wasn't part of the deal."

The guards pushed their way past The Nameless and yanked Keiko and Hogai to their feet. Guns were raised and everyone began shouting at once.

Ryan whistled, loud and shrill. "Quiet. We don't want anyone to get hurt."

Shadows of Ash

Goro left with the guards, Keiko and Hogai in tow.

"What the hell is going on, Ryan?" Sofia said. "If that had been Zanzi, you wouldn't have let her go."

"I'm with Sofia. What gives?" Cal said, her lips pulled tight.

"Yamada wants our help again," Ryan said.

"Well, duh. We figured that." Sofia rolled her eyes and sat on the armrest of the chair, staring, waiting for Ryan to explain.

"Yamada wants us to rescue his son, Takeshi. Offenheim has him trapped in one of his research labs. Get him and a doctor out, and our original deal stays."

"And you agreed. Without consulting us?" Sofia said.

"He left me no choice."

Sofia jumped up and pushed her face into Ryan's. "Explain it and make it real clear so I can understand."

"These Alpha nanites that we have here." He touched the base of his skull. "Yamada has one of those scanners, but this one's different. He demonstrated it on some traitors he caught. It triggered the self-destruct. The men suffered dreadfully as they died. Turned to ash. Like all the victims we saw."

Sofia sank back into her seat. "They can trigger a localized pulse?" She shivered. "I thought we were on the safe list."

Cal began to pace the aisle, muttering. "Again, we only know fragments. I can see why you agreed. You don't think he's bluffing to get us to accept?"

Ryan shrugged. "Sofia?"

"It's possible. The scanner could read the Alpha code, then send a signal causing it to destruct, but I'd have to see the code to know for sure. Ideally, I need one of those scanners."

Booth stretched and flexed his arms. "Well, let's steal one. That's what we're good at. Where's this rescue meant to take place?"

"Tomari Nuclear Power Plant on Hokkaido," Ryan said.

"So we have plenty of time. I say we steal one of those scanners. Sofia can reprogram it, or whatever, and then I vote for rescuing Keiko and Hogai, ditching this train and getting the hell out of Dodge."

Booth was answered with murmurs of agreement. Ryan grasped his shoulder in appreciation. A couple of moments ago he'd been at a loss. Like he was cornered into an impossible situation. Yamada held all the cards, but Booth had given him the pep talk he needed. The Nameless were not ones to lie down and roll over. Ryan should have known that. Normally it was his job to keep everyone's spirits up.

"If everyone's on board, let's start probing. Test how far we can go before Yamada's men push back. Use the bathrooms, look for the usual crawlspaces. Sofia, see what you can do with the computer system."

"What can I do?" Allie said.

Ryan handed her a pen and paper. "List all the airports and airfields that you know in this country. Any of them. Private or commercial bases, anything we can fly out of."

"On it," Allie said.

Ryan clasped his hands behind his back and watched The Nameless break apart and go about their tasks. His mind turned to Zanzi once more, and he whispered a quick prayer for her safety.

TWO

THE EYRIE
SIERRA NEVADA MOUNTAINS, CALIFORNIA

Zanzi's mind was in turmoil. Could she kill someone? Not because she had to, like the Black Skulls, but more like a murder. Get up in the morning after planning it. Eat her breakfast and drink her coffee. Perhaps watch some TV. Then set off, kill the target, dispose of the body, just like she'd planned, and afterwards, carry on as if nothing happened.

What is murder? Is it only when you go out with the intention of killing someone? Was it murder when she had killed the Black Skulls? She hadn't woken up that morning and thought, "Today is a good day to kill some commandos." No, that was self-defense.

Zanzi ran these thoughts over and over in her head. Milo had been clear: kill Alba and I'll get you out. She could even take Tilly and Harriet with her.

Alba. The sadist. Her constant questions. She'd use her taser on Zanzi, electricity coursing through her body, over and over. The surging agony through every fiber. Every cell. Motivation to murder wasn't the problem. Alba was insane. The only time Zanzi had seen any semblance of fear in Alba was in Devil's Falls when the Rabids attacked. The millions of nanites in her system may have made her nearly immortal, but the nanites didn't take away her emotions.

Zanzi sighed, sat up and kicked off her blankets.

"Is it time?" Tilly whispered.

"Yes. Are you ready?"

"I was born that way. That's a song. I don't know by who. I heard Imogen say it was a baby lady. But that's strange. How can you be a baby lady? Maybe she meant she was a lady who looked like a baby. But then why would she sing. I mean, why would you be a singer and call yourself lady baby? Imogen used to say the most peculiar things."

Zanzi kissed Tilly on her forehead and hugged her. "The singer's name is Lady Gaga."

"Gaga. That was it. Must have been what I was thinking."

"She named herself after the Queen song 'Radio Gaga.'"

"The Queen sings?" Tilly said wide eyed.

"Not *the* Queen. A band called Queen."

"Oh. I wish everyone explained things to me like you do."

Shadows of Ash

"I'm happy to because you have an inquisitive mind," Zanzi said as she guided Tilly out of their sleeping quarters.

"That's all I ever wanted. Someone to explain things to me. Not tell me to shut up. Stop talking. They called me a retard or stupid." Tilly wiped a tear away. "One of the nice nurses said my brain is just wired differently. I just need to learn how to slow down and separate my thoughts."

Zanzi stopped in front of a window that looked down over the satellite dishes and radio telescopes. Dozens of them. In various sizes.

"You stay the way you are, Tilly. You're unique, that's all. You're kind and smart. Funny and full of love. I'll take that any day over someone who is cold and vile. Being a chatterbox is part of your personality. Don't let people with their callous words influence you. Embrace what you have and live with it. Wear it proudly."

Zanzi stared at the helicopter on the landing zone then glanced at the clock in the guard room. She had forty-five minutes to kill Alba and sneak herself and Tilly on board.

Milo had planned it all down to the last detail. Which doors to use, how to avoid the cameras, when Alba was in her lab. If that was what that crazy woman called a lab, then she was more deluded than anyone else here. It was more like a torture chamber.

Zanzi pushed herself into the corner of the hallway and counted to ten. Right on schedule, the guards left their desk and came through the doors. So far so good.

Milo had told her that this part of the building was empty. The guards didn't bother to patrol it.

"This is where we used to come to read and paint," Tilly whispered, pointing.

Through the large panels of glass on the doors it was evident that the room was designed like a relaxation room in a public library. Chairs and desks with lamps. Bean bags on the floor. Paint easels in one corner. Shelf after shelf lined with books. It had been abandoned for some time.

"When did you last come here?" Zanzi said.

"A while ago. Maybe a year. I remember there being a lot of snow on the mountains. There weren't many of us left by then."

They went past more abandoned rooms. A few sleeping cells. A kitchen, and even a small gymnasium with a basketball court.

One room had a strange looking chair, like a dentist chair. It was rigged up to a hydraulic lift. The opposite wall was filled with monitors, now dead, gathering dust. It was like the floor they'd explored the other day. At one stage, this place must have been filled with children.

Tilly whimpered as she walked past but said nothing. Zanzi could only imagine the thoughts and images running through the young girl's head. What horrors she had been subjected to. She had meant what she'd said earlier. Tilly was kind and smart. Funny and full of love. She didn't deserve what had happened to her and neither did any of the other children who'd been housed here. It amazed her that Tilly had survived it all and still come out of it with her head held high and full of questions.

Shadows of Ash

Zanzi pulled free the taser baton that Milo had given her and gripped it tight. She peeked through the next set of doors, looking for the camera. Milo, true to his word, had shifted it so it was pointing away from the stairwell.

"This is the tricky part. We must be fast, okay?" Zanzi said.

"Three flights?"

"Yes. Three."

"Why do they call them flights of stairs? They don't fly."

"You know what? I'm not sure. Once we get out of here, we'll find out."

Zanzi took a moment to steady her building nerves. The question that had raged in her mind all night still nagged her. Could she kill Alba in cold blood?

She pushed the thought aside, dashed down the stairs two at a time, burst through the doors on the third floor and into the guard room. A man with oily slicked-back hair, the same man who had smiled at her with glee as Alba tortured her, swung around.

"What the fuck! What are you doing here?"

Zanzi lashed out, jamming the taser baton into his chest. Oily went rigid, slid off his chair and landed on the floor with a thump. Like they had practiced, Tilly rolled him up against the wall so that if Alba happened to look, it would appear that Oily had left. Zanzi shocked him again on the neck for good measure and glanced up at the screens. She wasn't prepared for what she saw.

In a thousand scenarios, she never would have guessed this. Alba was dressed from head to toe in white PVC. A long apron covered her pants and jacket. Crisp white boots went up to her knees. She had a face mask on – like a welder's helmet, but this one was clear – and it was covered in blood splatter and fragments of bone.

Alba was bent over Harriet, who was laying on a stainless-steel table, a bone saw in her hand. She had just finished sawing around the top of Harriet's skull and, as Zanzi watched, pried it off with a pop to expose the grayish brain underneath.

Zanzi couldn't look away. The scientist in her was morbidly fascinated by the procedure. Was Alba studying Harriet's brain? Was Harriet alive?

A glance lower down Harriet's body answered that question. Her chest was cracked open, ribs splayed. Her organs had been removed and lay, dripping blood, on trays. This was an autopsy.

Tilly gasped next to her and buried her head in her hands.

"Don't watch," Zanzi said. She grabbed the guard's HK VP9 pistol and clicked off the safety. She didn't need to check if it was loaded; she could tell by its weight. It was heavier than she was used to, being more familiar with Glocks and Sig Sauers. She took the guard's spare magazine and hustled to the door leading to Butcher Alba. If Zanzi had lacked motivation to kill her before, she didn't anymore. Now she had the image of Harriet's desecrated body lying on a metal table.

Zanzi caressed the VP9 and nodded at Tilly to push the button that opened the door.

She burst into the room, her pistol directly in her line of sight. She squeezed the trigger and Alba spun, a shiny metal instrument in her hand. Zanzi's first bullet pinged off the instrument, deflecting the bullet. Her second hit Alba in the shoulder and her third in the neck. Alba toppled over the instrument tray, sending the metal objects flying.

Growling at the sight of Harriet peeled open, Zanzi shot Alba twice more, this time in the head. She dropped her arm to her side. Harriet didn't deserve this. She deserved some sort of farewell. Zanzi put Harriet's organs back in her chest and replaced the top of her skull. If she couldn't bury Harriet, she would burn her.

Cleaning alcohol. Great as a disinfectant, and flammable. Zanzi spilled it around the room, over the floor, the walls, and the beeping machines. Over Harriet, and lastly, over Alba.

As she splashed it on Alba's face, the woman gasped, blinked, and sat up, holding her head.

"You bitch. You shot me."

Zanzi went for her gun, but Alba's superhuman speed caught her off guard. The ivory-colored woman smashed into her, tackling her to the ground. Zanzi twisted and her hip slammed onto the concrete floor. Sharp pain flooded up her back. Zanzi ignored it and brought her arms up in front of her face.

Alba straddled her and, with surprising strength, began to pummel her. Over and over. Blows rained down, her rage never quitting. "Bitch!" she screamed with every blow.

Most punches connected with Zanzi's arms, each contact sending jabs of agony into her body. Alba could hit hard. Some found their way through with concussive force, exploding against her chest, her sides, and glancing off her head.

Stars swam in Zanzi's vision, little firework bursts of red and orange, as if each punch came with an explosion of color.

She wanted her gun but had no way of reaching it. Likewise, she wanted to light the alcohol. Burn it all, herself included. At least Alba wouldn't be alive to harm anyone else.

Zanzi tried to bring her legs up and throw Alba off, but the woman was too strong. Then a scream of agony rang in her ears, and Alba suddenly went stiff, fell to the side, and convulsed on the floor.

Tilly, taser baton in hand, stood over them. She jabbed Alba once more, under her chin. "Leave her alone you bitch!" she screamed then dropped the baton and pulled Zanzi to her feet.

Zanzi wobbled for a few seconds as her head cleared. Retrieving the baton, she zapped Alba again, holding it against the woman's temple as she counted to ten. She turned and looked at Harriet's body.

Gritting her teeth, she wedged the pistol under Alba's jaw. "Survive this," she muttered, and she pulled the trigger.

Alba's body jerked as the bullet exited the top of her skull, coating the wall behind with blood and brain matter.

"Thanks Tilly. You saved me."

"Is she dead?"

"I hope so."

Shadows of Ash

"I always wanted to do that to her. She hurt me so much, and my friends. I couldn't stand there any longer, watching her hit you."

Tilly tore her eyes away from Alba. Her face appeared to relax, like a mask she had worn for a long time had finally been taken off.

"Thank you. We have to go, before the guards come." Zanzi picked up the electric bone saw and, without looking at Alba's corpse, ran it across the metal cabinet, sending sparks into the alcohol, igniting it. She threw the saw across the room, grabbed Tilly's hand, and dashed back to the stairwell.

THREE

NORTH OF TOKYO, JAPAN

Dawn broke over the distant mountains, painting the sky with pinks, purples, and hints of yellow and orange. Allie hadn't been able to sleep much, her mind too full of questions. Too full of doubts, whispering anxiety-laced jibes.

You're not one of them...
Your name isn't on the safe list.
Why don't you just run?

It had always been like this for her. Self-loathing and doubt, never thinking she was good enough to achieve anything. Having famous parents did that to a child. Her father had been a test pilot for NASA, but he'd never made it into space – though he'd been on standby a few times. He'd been scheduled for the space shuttle flight following *Columbia*'s disastrous reentry in 2003. By the time the two-year flight suspension was lifted, he'd retired and joined the ground crew. Her mother was a paramedic, training recruits on combat triage. The Army flew her around the country, schooling the special forces.

"Can't sleep either?" Booth said, stretching.

"Too many questions buzzing around," Allie said, tapping her temple.

"Like what?"

"You really want to know or are you just making conversation?"

"A bit of both. More the first one."

Allie looked around the carriage. Ryan, Cal, and Sofia were sleeping soundly. She wouldn't be overheard.

"I suppose this is normal for you guys?" she said quietly.

"What? Trying to save the world?"

"No. I meant, being in dicey situations. You seem relaxed. Calm, even."

"Part of our training. 'Panic never solves anything, Mr Booth.' That's what one of our instructors would say all the time."

"That would be a good start. Who are you guys?"

Booth sighed. "I guess there's no harm in telling you. We work for a small agency: LK3. Don't ask me what it means, no one has ever explained it to me. I think maybe it was its original designated number and they just left it. I've known Connors for over twenty years. The others we met during training, became friends, and eventually a team."

"LK3. Are you a government agency, like the CIA or NSA?"

Booth laughed and shook his head. "We kind of work for the State Department – not just looking out for America, but any of our allies too. We keep a low profile. Sneak in and out. Our specialty is extraction."

"Extraction. Like kidnapping?"

"C'mon, really?" Booth shook his head.

"I've heard rumors of black ops kidnapping terrorists and wanted criminals, taking them to Guantanamo."

"Definitely not us. I'll give you an example. Let's say you're the daughter of a senator or governor. You're a good girl and go off to college, but afterward you want to travel. Same as everyone, right? Not for them; too much of a target. But let's say you're determined and, against your parents' wishes, you go anyway. You go to Thailand and on to Myanmar, where some rebel group kidnaps you. That's where The Nameless come in. We sneak in and get you out. Take you home. No medals, nothing. Barely a thank you."

"So you are black ops," Allie said.

"I suppose in a way we are. But we try really hard not to kill anyone."

"Really?"

"Well, only the bad guys."

"And ReinCorp?"

"Ugh. Where do I start?" said Booth. "We have friends in all the agencies. They alert us to strange, out-of-the-ordinary things. Not red alerts like terrorists. More odd things. ReinCorp came up all the time but we couldn't get anything on them. Apart from a few unethical practices, they were clean. We kept an eye on them, which is why we knew about the satellites and codes. If it wasn't ReinCorp, it was YamTech or Zizer Pharmaceuticals. We pulled Ryan in once Keiko, Sofia's daughter, went missing. Now, here we are."

Allie nodded, taking it all in. As far as she could determine, The Nameless – LK3 – were the good guys. They'd been trying to stop this sort of madness from happening. She gazed out the carriage window. Sunlight flooded the countryside, revealing fields of rice, broccoli, and kabocha squash. Quaint villages dotted the hillsides and bunting fluttered in the light breeze.

"What made you decide to become a pilot?" Booth said.

"Dad took me up when I was about four years old, and I loved the feeling of freedom. It feels like it's just you up there." Allie winked and said, "Plus, I was an Air Force brat. Had to show the boys how to do it."

"Yeah. That would do it."

"You? Did you always want to be a spy?"

Booth let the jibe pass. "Stuff happened so I couldn't go to college. So I joined the Army, I kind of fell into this. Glad I did."

"Because you help people?"

"Sort of," he said.

"It's hard to put it into words, I know. When I flew aid into war-torn countries, I'd get the same feeling."

Shadows of Ash

"Exactly. It just feels right. Your purpose?" Booth raised an eyebrow.

"I suppose destiny, purpose. Fate."

The train shook violently, starting small before rocking from side to side. Allie and Booth grabbed their armrests and hung on. She frowned and looked at him. Booth had his eyes squeezed shut as the carriage rattled again, listing and tilting to the left. It took her a moment to recognize the motion as an earthquake.

Metal screeched.

Glass shattered.

The train's dampeners tried to engage, but the motion of the rolling ground was too strong. In seconds, their carriage capsized and screamed along the tracks, bucking wildly. Allie was flung against the windows and Booth crashed on top of her, knocking the wind from her lungs. Something sliced her upper thigh.

The carriage seemed to grind along the ground for hours, throwing stones and soil into the air. Allie reached out and held onto the seat's upright. At long last, the train ground to a stop.

Booth rolled off Allie. He shook his head and sat up. "You okay?"

Allie couldn't speak. She gasped. Coughs and groans sounded from across the aisle. Allie managed to push herself upright and began combing the glass from her hair. Tiny fragments of silicon and dirt fell to the floor.

"Nameless. Sound off," Ryan croaked. The futon mattress he'd been sleeping on had acted as an airbag, cushioning Cal, Sofia, and him as the train derailed.

"Booth."

"Cal."

"Sofia. I think."

"Allie."

"Check yourselves over for injuries and be ready to move. I'll scope out what's happened."

"The kids," Sofia said.

"Our safety first. Then we'll go get them," Ryan said.

The force of the crash had buckled the main train door and popped it open. Allie hobbled after Ryan. He hadn't heard an explosion, so death squads couldn't have attacked. One minute they'd been cruising northward, and the next, the train had thrown a tantrum.

Yamada's private bullet train lay in pieces like a toddler had kicked a toy one off its tracks. The white and blue carriages were scattered, some on the rails, some down the embankment, entangled in trees and scrub. Others, like theirs, were half on and half off the track. Several Yamada guards lay prone, unmoving. The stench of burning oil and hydraulic fluid hung in the air. Exposed electrical cables sparked and hissed.

Farther out, huge landslides had cascaded down hillsides, swamping villages and farms, long cracks disappeared into the distance. Trees and power poles had snapped in half. Houses were aflame. Roads had buckled and split apart.

The ground shook again. Not as violently but still strong. Allie clutched the handle next to the door and rode it out. A Californian native, she understood with complete clarity what had happened. A powerful earthquake had struck

Japan. She shivered, remembering footage of the tsunami that had followed the last big one.

Were they far enough inland?

Once the aftershock had subsided, Ryan grabbed her shoulder. "Get your things. This is our chance."

The other members of The Nameless were picking up their belongings and wriggling into backpacks. Booth handed hers to her.

"Thanks."

"All good?"

"A little sore but I'll live."

Booth nodded. "I still prefer coffee in the morning."

"No arguments from me." She liked the well-mannered agent. He had an easiness about him. She'd found herself talking to Booth like they'd been friends for years. She made a mental note to continue their conversation. She wanted to know more about The Nameless.

FOUR

NORTHWEST OF TOKYO, JAPAN

Apart from the sounds of metal groaning, of liquids dripping and electricity humming, there was nothing else. No human sounds. No screams or shouts. No cries for help. No calls from survivors. Ryan mapped out the Shinkansen in his mind. They were in the second carriage from the front. Yamada's suite was near the back of the train. Was that where Keiko and Hogai were? Or had they been taken to the carriage with the traitors? He flinched. That was the one place he hoped they weren't. First, they needed weapons, and for once luck was on their side. The guards who'd been stationed at their doors were now dead, the force of the crash too great for even the nanites to repair. Ryan signaled to Booth and Cal, jogged to the nearest guard, and scanned the vicinity. Still no sign of the Yamadas. The guard was armed with an HK VP9 and an SP5K. An odd choice of weapons, Ryan thought, but beggars can't be choosers. He pulled them free, rifled through the dead man's pockets and grabbed the extra magazines.

He handed the VP9 to Cal, scanning for threats again, ever fearful of either Yamada or any Siphons showing their faces.

"Ready?" Ryan said, checking everyone over. Apart from a few scrapes and bruises, The Nameless appeared mostly unharmed, a few cuts and bruises that were already beginning to heal. His question was answered with nods and murmurs.

"Keep it slow and smooth."

The Nameless crept through the wreckage, searching for survivors as they went. Ryan led them, methodically hunting. Eyes and ears alert. They had to shimmy down a slight bank to reach the last two carriages, which had rolled into the short trees and twisted scrub. Apart from broken windows, they were both intact. A few scrapes and gouges, bumps and dents. The train's integrity had held.

Ryan raised his fist, stopping the group. They had reached the carriage that held the traitors. "Booth, with me. Everyone else, watch our backs."

He gripped the SP5K and thumbed off the safety. Booth swung open the door and ducked back. The overpowering scent of misery and death leaked out. Ryan crouched and risked a peek. Apart from ash remains, the carriage was empty.

"Clear," he said, returning to The Nameless.

"I'll check this one," Cal said, pointing to the rear carriage. Allie went with her.

Sofia waved Ryan over. "The train's still giving off a Wi-Fi signal." She showed him her tablet. "I've got a map of where we are."

Ryan spent a few moments thumbing through the map. As fate would have it, they were close – well, close-ish – to the airport used by the wealthy to access Japan's ski resorts such as Nagano, host city for the 1998 Winter Olympics. He ran the numbers through his head. The airport was at least a two-day hike through the mountains and into the next valley. Maybe three, depending on what assholes they ran into along the way.

"See what the closest village is. Once we have Keiko and Hogai, we'll find a car," he said.

"Already have," Sofia said. "Five kilometers southwest."

Ryan's gaze turned in the direction Sofia indicated. He could just make out the roof tops in the distance.

Cal and Allie exited the carriage. "Clear."

"Eyes sharp, everyone," Ryan said, pivoting. He raised the machine pistol and picked his way through the carnage.

They reached Yamada's carriage and split into two groups, each taking a side. Ryan stopped in his tracks at the sight of three heavily armed guards in black suits. The lead goon had his shirt sleeves rolled up, exposing his tattoos.

Adrian J Smith

"Drop your weapons," Tattoo said. He grinned and gestured with his head. Ryan watched as Hogai was frog-marched around the corner. He had a bloody wound across his scalp. His eyes met Ryan's. He blinked as he shook his head, as if to say, "Don't do it."

"Where's Keiko?" Ryan asked.

The goon smirked and pulled Keiko out from behind the train.

Ryan hated losing. Hated it more than anything. Growing up, he'd played soccer. Loved it. Was obsessed with it. It was all he'd thought about before puberty struck. While he hadn't been the most naturally gifted or technical player, he could read the game. His favorite coach had said something that had stuck with him: *You don't have to be the best to win. Just the most determined. Leave it all out there, on the field.*

Ryan gritted his teeth. He was determined to keep everyone safe. Right now, that meant not getting anyone shot. Slowly, with his free hand raised in surrender, he lowered the SP5K, signaling for Cal to do the same. Once they were unarmed, the guards took them to the back of the derailed carriage. There, Touma Yamada and his grandson Goro waited. Goro stood with his hands in his pockets. Yamada, arms crossed in front. Both men had slight smiles, as if they were amused by the situation.

"Ah, The Nameless. For a moment I thought you had run off without your children," Yamada said.

Ryan stayed silent.

Yamada rocked on his heels. "Despite the interruption, we are still going to rescue Takeshi. Ueda is a few hours walk from our location. I trust you will honor our agreement."

"And then what?" Booth said.

"We'll take one of my helicopters."

Ryan tilted his head. Now was not the time to test the yakuza. The city of Ueda would provide a better opportunity to escape. They would be closer to that private airport in Nagano for one. He flashed a series of quick hand signals for The Nameless to stand down for now.

Yamada's armed guards split up. Four covered the rear while two took up point and led the group away from the derailed train. The extent of the wreckage astounded Ryan. How had they survived that? Now that their nanites had been activated, the little robots were healing them all. The aches and pains he'd had moments ago had vanished. Not for the first time, he wished he had an expert who could explain several things to him: Why did some people swell or shrink? What caused the Siphons? Why did Yamada and Goro have ivory-colored skin?

Cal nudged his arm. "We can take these idiots."

The guards were too close together in a bunch, almost crowding. Professionals would be more spaced and cover more angles. Ryan or Booth or Cal would only have to drop a shoulder and charge the middle guard to knock them all down.

"Now's not the time. We don't know what's out there," Ryan said.

"The sooner we do it, the better."

"Stay cool. Wait until the city."

Cal nodded, but the scowl that flashed across her face gave away her thoughts.

Ryan breathed deeply as he walked. He had always enjoyed mountain air. Crisp, laced with the scent of pine and fir. Earth and water. Up here, it was free of pollution. If it wasn't for the fact that they were surrounded by armed guards, he could have been forgiven thinking he was on a hike with Cal, enjoying the early spring.

After an hour, the tracks bent around a gradual corner and disappeared into the side of the mountain. Thick slabs of granite soared to the top, the peaks covered in snow.

Yamada's men brought them to a halt at a tunnel entrance. They seemed reluctant to enter but began handing out headlamps and flashlights from a sports bag one of them carried.

Yamada grinned at Ryan. "You're on point, Connors."

"Don't I get a gun at least?"

"What, so you can shoot us?"

"The thought never crossed my mind."

"Get going." Yamada turned and spoke to one of his armed men. "Itsuki. Watch him."

The tunnel was made from concrete, its walls smooth and painted white. Running along the right-hand side was a raised platform for walking on. Soft orange lights glowed from the ceiling at intervals. Cal and Booth dropped in behind Itsuki, followed by another two guards, the Yamadas, and the rest of The Nameless. The remaining four guards brought up the rear.

Their boots clunked as they walked along the platform, their echoes bouncing off the walls. So much for being sneaky. The Yamadas and the guards sounded like a herd of buffalo.

Conveniently, the builders of the railway had stenciled hundred-meter markings on the wall, with a sign indicating how far to the end of the tunnel.

As they reached the halfway mark, Ryan stopped and held up his fist. The group halted. He clicked off his light and crouched down.

"What is it?" Yamada said.

Ryan shushed him. He pointed down the tunnel and held up six fingers and gestured at his eyes. "Siphons. Up ahead."

"Siphons?"

"The people that have mutated. Suck your spines dry."

Yamada's eyes widened. He beckoned over one of the guards and whispered something. The guard bowed and ran past, shining his light.

Cal looked at Ryan and rolled her eyes.

Protect the kids, he signed to her, using American Sign language.

The Siphons howled in chorus, a garbled sound that sent a shiver up Ryan's spine. At the same time, the guard's weapon burst into life. More howls erupted from farther down the tunnel, followed by more shots. Itsuki pushed Ryan out of the way. "Protect the boss!" he yelled to the other guards and sprinted toward the Siphons.

Cal and Booth sprang into action. They dropped and swept out, knocking the remaining guards to the ground.

Sofia and Allie pulled Keiko and Hogai off the walking platform and onto the tracks.

Ryan pivoted, launched himself across the walkway and tackled Yamada to the ground, knocking Goro off balance so that he fumbled as he tried to unholster his side arm. In moments, Cal and Booth had disarmed the goons and stood over them. Cal threw Ryan a pistol and he switched off the safety. Farther down the tunnel, Itsuki and the guards' gunfire grew in intensity, the noise echoing off the walls.

The creatures' shrieks became louder as dozens ran toward them.

Ryan looked back at the way they had come. It was clear. He lifted Yamada to his feet and pushed him ahead. "Move. Now!"

Goro froze. A survival situation was something new for this long-pampered man.

Ryan grasped his shoulder and shook him. "Move!" Goro stumbled forward, obeying Ryan's urging.

The Nameless hustled the Yamada clan back outside, the inhuman sounds of the Siphons chasing them. Itsuki's and the guards' guns fell silent, replaced with groans and shrieks as the creatures fought over their spinal fluid.

Ryan spotted a hiking trail rising steeply between giant pillars of rocks. A Shinto altar wrapped in red ribbons was carved into one side. In the steeper section of the trail, steps had been hacked into the sides of the mountain, making for a precarious climb.

The howls blaring from the tunnel made up his mind.

Shadows of Ash

"Incoming!" Booth began to shoot, unloading the machine pistol. He slapped in another magazine and unloaded that too. Dozens of the Siphons poured from the rail tunnel.

"Leave it. C'mon!" Ryan screamed. He waved the others past him and, grabbing an SP5K, covered Booth's retreat. He backed away up the steep stairs, Cal's strong hands on his shoulder, guiding him.

He didn't need to shout any more instructions. The Nameless knew what to do. Cover everyone. Force the Siphons into a bottleneck. Ryan went into battle mode. Controlled bursts. Aim for the center mass. Cal fired over his right shoulder while Booth fired over his left.

In a weird tight knot, The Nameless advanced up the mountain side. Some of the creatures broke away and ran into the forest but the rough terrain made it difficult for them to get any sort of foothold. Siphon after Siphon tumbled to their deaths. The remaining guards used their taser batons to zap any creature that managed to get through.

The Nameless were now in control. Yamada needed them to survive. *Screw Takeshi*, Ryan's mind screamed as he shot another Siphon, a young woman dressed in a bright yellow tracksuit. Her body tumbled down a few steps, knocking more Siphons off the mountain. Yamada could rescue his son with his own men. Ryan was taking The Nameless and going home. Home to Zanzi.

"Keep going. Don't let them flank us."

"We've got it covered," Cal said.

Ryan's legs burned from the effort of climbing the steep stairs at such a relentless pace.

Adrian J Smith

Cal blew a hole through the skull of a Siphon still wearing the uniform of a policeman. The policeman was replaced by a teenage girl. She still had a clump of hair above her left ear. She snarled at Ryan and lashed out, clawing at his backpedaling leg. He gritted his teeth and shot her in the head, kicking her backwards.

At the top of the hiking trail, the ground leveled out and cleared. A small temple with a high raking roof sat nestled between a stone boulder and a copse of conifer trees. Moss covered statues of Buddha flanked the front entrance, incense burning at their feet. The temple was a welcome sight. The Nameless and the Yamada clan had decimated the chasing Siphons. Only a few still gave pursuit.

"Booth and I will take out the dregs. Everyone else inside," Ryan said.

Once the thick wooden doors thumped closed, he turned to his old friend. "Go left and do a quick recce at the same time."

"On it," Booth said.

The temple was largely unscathed from the recent earthquake, though a few trees had toppled over, and some shingles had fallen off the roof. As he scanned the area, Ryan spotted a couple of monks quietly watching. He held up his hand in greeting and smiled.

Booth whistled for his attention. The remaining Siphons had scrambled their way over the landslides, broken rocks and mounds of mud and roots.

Ryan observed them over the sight.

"Mercy," he whispered as he squeezed the trigger.

Shadows of Ash

He and Booth took out the surviving Siphons with several well-placed shots. Some crawled, dragging broken legs behind them. Some staggered from the loss of blood from other bullet wounds. All of them had been normal, everyday citizens before OPIS unleashed their nefarious plans. Lives cut short and, adding to the insult, instead of dying, these people had become something worse. Something inhuman.

"Didn't see much of use," Booth said. "A couple of vehicles. One van and a motorbike."

"Road?" Ryan asked.

"Narrow but clear of damage, not that I could see far."

"Okay. Stay alert."

"Expecting trouble?" Booth flashed a lopsided grin.

"Always."

Before heading to the temple Ryan and Booth waited for five minutes, checking that no Siphons remained.

The heavy oak doors creaked open as Ryan entered the small temple. He had left Booth keeping an eye on the path and the road. Inside, he found several monks deep in meditation, with incense burning. Hundreds of small candles were lit, causing flickering shadows to dance on the walls. Here the monks were carrying on as they had for the last thousand years. Finding solace in prayer, reflection, and kindness.

Yamada and The Nameless sat cross-legged against the wall, snacking on fresh rock melon provided by a monk. The guards, out of respect, had tucked away their weapons.

"We're all clear for now," Ryan said, lowering his voice.

"For what it's worth, Connors, thank you," Yamada said. He bowed his head in respect.

Cal and Sofia glanced at Ryan, with Cal gesturing outside with her head. He nodded.

The Nameless stood, pulling up Hogai and Keiko.

"We're leaving," Ryan said to Yamada. "I could say it's been an honor, but it hasn't. You and OPIS are the worst kind of people."

Yamada frowned. "What happened to our agreement? To rescue my son."

"Off the table. You forced it on me. I'm taking it away."

The guards bristled and snarled as they pulled out their guns. Both Goro and Yamada waved them down.

"Listen," Yamada said. "There's an airport in Nagano. I happen to own a heli skiing company. We should have several helicopters available."

"So?" Ryan said.

Yamada's eyes flashed pure hatred, just for a second. Then he quickly regained his composure.

"My offer still stands. Rescue Takeshi and I'll give you a private jet to fly home."

"No deal."

"Remember the traitors, Connors?" Yamada snarled. "We can still do that." He pulled out the wand to emphasize his point.

"You need us more than we need you," Ryan said.

Yamada smirked and pressed the button on the wand. Immediately Hogai groaned, dropped to her knees and held her head in her hands. Yamada pressed the button a second time. Keiko slid to the floor and curled up in the fetal position.

Sofia ran to her daughter. "We'll do it. Just stop. Please."

"Well, Mr. Connors?" Yamada said. "It's your call."

Ryan cursed himself. He was playing Chinese checkers while Yamada was two steps ahead, playing chess.

"The agreement stands," Ryan said.

"Very well." Yamada pressed the buttons again, releasing Keiko and Hogai from their agony. He approached one of the monks and spoke to him for a few moments.

"The monks have kindly lent us their van. We leave for Nagano in five minutes."

FIVE

HOOD RIVER, OREGON

Director Lisa Omstead pulled her shoulders back, working out the stiffness. The problem with retiring from active duty was that she had lost that edge, that point she had honed to perfection, when all her senses were in tune with one another. For too long she had been organizing and directing, overseeing the training of new agents. Planning operations and playing the political game. She lacked the edge constant combat situations engendered.

She crouched low and peered around the side of the brick fire station. Black Skulls were fast approaching, only a hundred meters out. "Any luck with that door?" She glanced over her shoulder at Doctor Monica Johnson.

"Almost there. Just a little farther," Johnson said. She had the roller door open a few centimeters, not enough to squeeze under. The roller door had been damaged at some point by a vehicle and the bend in the metal gave them a chance.

Lisa checked behind her. The Black Skulls were only coming from the one direction. Earlier she'd considered running. Finding a vehicle and leaving the area. But with her injury and Johnson's advanced age, she had to dismiss that option.

"Got it." Johnson rolled under the door and used the chain pulley to open it a few more centimeters.

Lisa pointed to one of the fire trucks. "Get in." She banged a large red button on the wall next to an office. Immediately the alarm rang out, filling the station with its deafening clangs. The doors shot up as if a giant had grabbed them and flung them open.

Lisa jumped into the truck and gunned the engine, tearing out of the building. The Black Skulls gawked as she flashed by. They recovered their shock in a split second and started shooting. Bullets pinged into the red and white metal and off the retractable ladder. Lisa swung the big steering wheel, scattering the commandos, and bumped onto the road.

"Take my rifle. Know how to fire it?" she said to Johnson.

"Point and shoot, yeah?"

Shadows of Ash

"See that selector on the side. Switch it to semi. They're going to come after us. Rest the barrel on the window. When you see one of those pricks, fire. Got it?"

Johnson nodded. "Spares?"

"Rucksack."

The road looped around so it joined the street Johnson lived on. Lisa spotted one of the Humvees burning in the middle of the road, and Cordwell's still form lying alongside. His last act had been to toss a grenade, scoring a direct hit, giving them the time they needed to escape.

Lisa was going to miss the grumpy old bastard. When she'd joined the Marines all those years ago, Cordwell had been the first to give her an ounce of respect. A lot of the time he'd acted as a buffer to the constant teasing and pranks that were played on her.

"They're just threatened, Omstead. Rise above it and show them who's the badass."

They'd shared a love for hunting and fishing, often spending what little leave they had on trips into the wild. The other members of their platoon had sworn they were a couple, but she and Cordwell had always been friends. It horrified her that she had to leave him out there on the street and not give him a proper send-off.

Safe journey, old friend.

She kept her speed up and squealed around the corner, aiming for the interstate. The fire truck was by no means the fastest vehicle, but what it lacked in speed it made up in sheer strength and power. The Black Skulls gave chase in their 4X4s and Humvees, content to hang back for now. Lisa ignored them for the time being. She cruised down the main street of Hood River, shoving stalled cars out of the way.

A flash of silver careened from her right, screeching. An SUV slid next to the fire truck. Johnson fired a burst and squealed in surprise at the rifle's retort. Another SUV moved from the left. Frantic, Lisa looked over the dozens of switches and buttons. She spotted the one she was hunting for.

Ladder release.

There was a clanking sound, followed by metal grinding against metal. The ladder released and swung free. She followed its trajectory in her wing mirrors, then yanked down on the steering wheel, slamming the big vehicle into the SUV.

The fire truck shuddered as its now-swinging ladder smashed into lamp posts and power poles, showering the pursuing Black Skulls in debris, hunks of concrete and plastic.

Lisa swung the other way, crunching the silver SUV into parked cars. Its front wheels caught the bumper of a Chevy, spinning it into the path of the fire truck.

Metal screeched.

Tires popped.

Gunfire erupted.

The truck jerked as the SUV crunched under her back wheels. Lisa gripped the steering wheel tighter, wrestling with it. More gunfire pinged off the bodywork, stitching along its flank. Ahead, the interstate that followed the Columbia River was closing in fast. Johnson fired another burst and screamed. Bullets peppered the windshield.

Using one hand to steer and the other to control the extendable ladder, Lisa swung the fire truck onto the sidewalk, tearing into the huge plate-glass windows of a furniture store. The SUV, attempting to evade the carnage, slid and fishtailed around before flipping onto its side, sparking as it slid into a bodega car park and bounced off a F350 like a pinball.

"Watch out!" Johnson warned. One of the Black Skulls had jumped onto the driver's side footplate and was pulling his handgun free. Lisa groaned in frustration and plowed the fire truck into more parked cars, attempting to shake him free. The commando lifted his legs, holding on. Another swung down from the rooftop, firing blindly into the cab.

"Hold onto something." Lisa shouted.

She slammed the brakes on and yanked hard on the steering wheel. The truck tilted but maintained its grip on the concrete street. The commando on the roof flew off and thumped onto the road, just in front of the truck. His body barely made the truck jolt as it crunched over. The other commando clung on.

"Duck," Johnson said. She shot him point blank in the face. Brains and blood sprayed out as the bullet left his head.

The fire engine fled down the freeway, crunching through any vehicles stalled on the road. Lisa didn't care. All she cared about was escaping Black Skulls. For now they appeared to have given up.

Johnson gripped the M4, neck craned to watch their retreat.

"You okay?" Lisa asked.

"Not really, no."

Lisa flashed a smile, trying to calm the doctor's nerves. "Any ideas on what could cause this?"

"This in general?"

"The suckers. Those infected."

Johnson sighed and shook her head. "The infected's behavior is like rabies. The aggression and irritability. The excessive movements and confusion. But that's where the similarities end. I can't explain the pale skin covered in red slashes or the cloudy eyes. I really need a test subject to take samples from."

"I had one in the truck. But I know where we can get another. I have some blood for you as well. Comes from a girl we picked up. One of my scientists found something odd in it," Lisa said. "We'll ditch this and try to find a less conspicuous vehicle."

"And after that? I'll need to get to a research center or a hospital. Any place I can run some tests."

"How about Lewis McChord Base up by Tacoma? General Munroe has suitable facilities and manpower."

"That should do," Johnson said. "You know, when I worked for the CDC, our biggest fear was somebody weaponizing a virus and releasing it. In your line of work, I'm sure you're aware of a few close calls?"

"That Ebola weapon scare in 2015?" Lisa said.

"Among others, yes. But I'm certain this isn't a pathogen. Nothing can act instantaneously like that. Not even something weaponized. You need an incubation period, time for it to spread."

Shadows of Ash

Lisa slowed the big truck and scraped past a semi-trailer tipped on its side. "I've heard about these ancient pathogens coming to light with the perma-frost melting."

"Still no. They may be ancient, and we may have no cures for them, but they would still have to act like a virus. This was like a switch had been flicked."

Lisa nodded, rubbing her left temple with her thumb. The pain had been so intense she had considered shooting herself.

"I think *Mortis* has something to do with it." Johnson's eyes glistening with tears. "I was having lunch with my friend Jean before we headed off to play cards when the agony started. I don't remember much, only thinking how badly I wanted it to stop. Through the pain, I saw Jean wither and contort. Her howls of pain will give me nightmares until I die. And how she blackened and just wilted, as if her cells had suddenly lost all their structure. It reminds me of those samples you brought back from Romania; we never did solve it. They were put into storage in Atlanta. If I'd figured it out then, I could have prevented this."

"You can't blame yourself, Monica. No one can. Whatever happened, it's organized. Highly. All we can do now is find out how and catch those responsible."

They drove on in silence for the next twenty minutes as the route followed the surging Columbia River. Lisa kept her speed to thirty mph, not wanting to miss the place where she and Cordwell had shot the Rabid.

The road, like the sky, was still as Lisa brought the fire engine to a halt. She recognized the two crashed minivans with their belongings strewn across the concrete. The overweight man wearing the Seattle Seahawks jersey still stared into the forest, his head all but severed from his body. Lisa took the M4 and slapped in a fresh magazine. Her last one. She had left the ammo bag in Cordwell's Chevy.

Johnson gasped at the sight. "What the hell did that? An infected?"

"Yes. If I hadn't seen it with my own eyes, I wouldn't have believed it."

Lisa scanned the area, wary of threats. Since the explosion at LK3 headquarters she had been on the run. Fumbling and guessing. Black Skulls hampering her every step of the way.

"The dead infected are up there. I'll take one of these minivans," Lisa said, pointing.

It only took them a few minutes to heave the dead Siphon into the back of the van. She was a woman wearing active wear. Lisa draped some blankets over the body, half to keep the smell down and half to hide the blank, cloudy eyes. Despite what she had become, she had been a human being and Lisa wanted to treat her with some respect.

Johnson was silent through it all, keeping her thoughts to herself. Lisa had known Monica for a long time and had seen the frown she now carried plenty of times before. It was her thinking look. That intelligent brain was whizzing around, putting all the pieces of the puzzle into place.

Shadows of Ash

Now that she had time to breathe, Lisa pulled her smartphone from her pocket and called Avondale.

He answered immediately. *"Director."*

"Avondale. We ran into some trouble. The same Black Skulls. They've disguised themselves as FEMA. Cordwell is dead, but I have the doctor with me. We've obtained a dead Siphon, and we need to get up to Munroe so we can try to figure out what the hell is going on. I need you to guide us. Use back roads, et cetera."

"No problem. Bringing up your location now. Oh, and Director?"

"What is it?"

"Sofia pinged me. It was brief. Two letters only. AA. Do you know what that means?"

Lisa grinned. "Yeah, it's an old code. It means they're alive. All of them." Trust The Nameless to be alive. If Sofia could have sent a longer message, she would have. "AA" was all Lisa needed. They would be doing their best to get back stateside. "Any luck with a location?"

"Just a general area. Three hundred kilometers northwest of Tokyo."

"Weird."

"That's what I thought."

"Keep trying. Have FEMA or the National Guard shown up in Portland?"

"Sure have. They're setting up a base in the Convention Center. They're driving around telling everyone to report in. Anyone injured is to go to the nearest hospital. The National Guard is going street to street,

looking for those suckers. Also, the Secretary of State is going to do another address at 8 p.m."

"All right. Keep hidden."

"Don't worry about me, Boss. You ready to drive? Next river crossing is the Bridge of the Gods."

"I know it," Lisa said. She liked the nerdy computer genius. He had an affable manner. He was loyal and kind. Sure, he was socially inept, but she didn't care about that. He got the job done.

"It's clear. The Washington side of the river too. No sign of any authorities or Black Skulls."

She scraped against the other minivan as she reversed hers and headed east, her sense of helplessness gone now that she had a plan again.

SIX

SIERRA NEVADA MOUNTAINS, CALIFORNIA

"What the hell did you guys do?" Milo shouted over the noise of the alarms.

Zanzi evaded his glare and hustled into the wooden crate. Tilly was already inside. The crate was filled with two stacks of water and electrolyte drinks. A gap had been cleared in the middle, just enough room for the two of them. As Milo had explained to her earlier, part of the second phase was to spread the nanites into the surviving population through medical and food supplies. This load was designated for Portland after some tweaks by the scientist here in The Eyrie.

"Just a little fire," Zanzi said.

"A little fire? Half the bloody floor is burning. What happened to being stealthy?" Milo said, covering the crate with a fine plastic mesh.

"Alba deserved it. She had Harriet cracked open like a lobster."

Milo's eyes widened. "I'm sorry. I didn't know. That explains why I couldn't find her. Doctor Lahm will let you out in Portland. After that, you're on your own."

"Good. You know I'm going to come after you guys, don't you?"

"Zanzi Connors, I wouldn't expect anything less."

"Then why are you letting us go?" she asked.

"You may think I'm a monster, but I keep my word." He slammed the crate shut, tied off the lashing and hopped back down to the helipad.

A few minutes later, the crate lifted off the ground and slid into place inside the hold of the helicopter, its rotors already thumping.

Tilly shifted closer to Zanzi and clutched her hand as the chopper took off and banked away. It was loud inside the hold. There was no point in speaking to comfort Tilly, so Zanzi kept hold of her hand while she let her own mind wander. Memories of happier times came flooding back. Times with her family, watching live music performances. They all loved them. She and Liam loved thrash metal. Bands like Sepultura, Amon Amarth, and Megadeth. Her parents preferred more classic rock, like the Eagles, Led Zeppelin, and Deep Purple. But they always went to the American and Bluegrass Festival in Portland as a family;

late summer evenings spent with a picnic, enjoying the music and the laughter of friends.

Zanzi shut her eyes. Friends she may never see again, wiped out by madmen. She had no way of knowing. She clenched her fists tight, her nails cutting into her palms. Once she and Tilly were free, she was going to get to Avondale. He would have a way, some way, of knowing. For now, she would just have to be content with her memories. She vowed that if she survived, she would erect a memorial to her friends.

***

The helicopter reached Portland and bumped to the ground.

"Keep quiet, okay?" Zanzi said.

Tilly smiled, for once not verbalizing her thoughts.

The doors to the hold were yanked open amid shouted instructions. "Take all these crates to the loading dock. The next load will be here in thirty minutes."

"All of them?"

"What did I just say? Do I have to repeat everything? Seriously?"

"Sorry, sir."

Boots stomped away to be replaced by the chug of a forklift. Zanzi held her breath as their crate was lifted out and they bounced along rutted ground. She breathed in and from the scents around them tried to figure out exactly where they were. Propane and oil were all she could detect, and a hint of Avgas. Portland didn't have too many large, flat, open areas to set up a camp; the most logical place was down by the river, or a school sportsground, close to the main hospital and the freeway.

The forklift dropped the crate onto a hard surface and screeched it against something hard.

Tilly stiffened as the tines of the forklift clanged against concrete.

"It's okay," Zanzi whispered. She hated being stuck inside the crate as much as Tilly did.

They had to wait another couple of hours before finally, they heard a whisper. "Zanzi?"

Zanzi banged on the side of the crate, making as much noise as she dared. "In here."

The latches pinged as they sprang open and the lid was pushed off. Glorious cool night air brushed Zanzi's face. She helped Tilly out and into a large canvas tent pitched over a concrete pad. They were surrounded by stacks of supplies. Food, water, and medicine.

Zanzi smiled. "You're Doctor Lahm?" she said. Standing to one side of the crate was the same scientist that had flown to Devil's Falls with Alba a couple of days before.

"Yes. Call me Josie."

Doctor Josie Lahm had long, straight black hair, twisted into a bun and held with a red pencil. Her skin was pale, the whites of her eyes were red with dark, puffy bags underneath. Zanzi had seen the same look when she was at university. It came from hours and hours of study and work.

Zanzi smiled again. "Where to now?"

"Back to my trailer. Once it's safe, we can move you out. Security is lax once you're inside the camp. They want everyone to have the supplies. I'm sure you're hungry, and I've organized some clothes for you. Army fatigues, I'm sorry."

"Anything is better than these gray overalls," Zanzi said.

They followed Josie past tent after tent filled with supplies. Mostly water and electrolyte drinks, like the crate they had been smuggled in. There were pallets of basic food as well. Rice, wheat, flour, sugar, dried fruits, and piles of canned goods. There was even a tent full of beer and wine. The camp was well organized. Electrified high fences kept the Rabids at bay. It was set up like a drive-through. Citizens could come and show their identification. After being checked over by the medical staff, they were given a ration booklet and a map to where supplies were. The camp was quiet for now. Zanzi suspected it would be a few days before survivors started to come in large numbers.

After a disaster or catastrophic event, most people went through three stages: impact, rescue, recovery. Folks normally had a few days of food on hand, maybe a couple of weeks at a stretch.

Power. How long would that stay on?

The staff manning the facility had living quarters set up at the back. Josie led Zanzi and Tilly to the last trailer on the row, facing a copse of trees and, beyond that, the interstate. They were close to the river and main roads. Once they were rested and supplied, Zanzi wanted to get out of there. Find Avondale and seek the answers to her questions.

Josie waved Zanzi and Tilly inside the trailer, shutting the door with a click. She shoved a pile of clothing into their arms. "You can get dressed back there." She gestured to the bedroom at the back. "There's a bathroom if you want to freshen up."

"You go first, Tilly," Zanzi said. She waited until she could hear the shower running before looking at Doctor Josie Lahm. "Why are you helping? Aren't you one of them?"

Josie's eyes flashed angrily. "At first, yes. Now, no." She pointed outside. "If I had known what they had planned, I would never have agreed to work with them. I tried many times to leave. I did for a few months..." She went silent. She pulled a bottle of wine from a cupboard, offering a glass to Zanzi.

"No thanks. I'm good. Need to keep my mind sharp."

Josie poured herself a large glass, her hand shaking. "I'm helping you because your mother helped me. I left ReinCorp for a few months, tired of all the politics and the toxic work environment. But ReinCorp grew tired of asking nicely for me to return and forced the issue. They knew of my research, trying to help my daughter. So they took her, leaving me a message: come back and she's safe."

"What research?" Zanzi's interest was piqued.

"Nanotechnology. Specifically, how nanomaterials interact with cells, what materials are safe to use. How we can use nanites for biomedical advancement."

Shadows of Ash

"You helped do this? Surely you had to wonder what all that research and development was for?" Zanzi slammed her fist on the bench. "Do you know how many people have suffered? Do you want to know what Offenheim showed me?"

Josie cast her eyes to the floor, refusing to meet Zanzi's stare. "I'm sorry. But I was one person, part of a large team. We were given goals and problems to solve. I didn't know about this until the day it happened. As a scientist yourself, I thought you would understand. I, like many others, suffer from obsessive behavior. Each step, I was closer and closer. My daughter had cauda equina syndrome. All I wanted was for her to have a normal life. To not have to use a colostomy bag. To have children. That's all I wanted. Not this." Josie gulped down her wine and poured herself another glass.

"Did you try surgery?" Zanzi said.

"We tried everything. It became too much for my husband, seeing our child go through so much pain. After a while, he left. I vowed to find a cure, threw everything into my research. When ReinCorp offered me all the money and materials I needed, I jumped at the chance. Then they took Harriet and used her as a guinea pig. They cured her and made her stronger than she had ever been, but I saw the tragedy in her. Thanks to Cal, we got her out."

"Harriet's your daughter?"

"Yes. Why?"

Zanzi bolted up and reached for the wine bottle. Her heart thumped at a thousand miles an hour. A lump the size of a watermelon formed in her throat. How do you tell a mother her daughter is dead? Sliced open. Experimented on by the demented Alba. She gulped down the glass of pinot gris, her mind whirring.

She looked back up at Josie, her eyes filled with tears. There were no words.

"What is it? What happened?"

"I'm sorry. Harriet's dead," was all Zanzi could say.

Josie dropped to her knees and howled, her sobs deep and painful. She curled into a ball and hugged her legs.

Zanzi slouched back down. She didn't know what to do. Comfort her or leave her to her grief?

The bathroom door slid open. Tilly was dressed in gray fatigues, her hair wet. "What happened?"

"Harriet was her daughter."

"Oh." Tilly blinked. "Oh," she said again. "We had a dog once when I was young. Sparkles. She was black and had floppy ears that would cover her eyes when she ran. I don't know why she was called Sparkles. I didn't name her. I mean, that's a weird name for a dog. Even my dad said so. Dogs should have a strong name like Rex or Max, or something else with X in it…. I came home from school one day and Dad…"

"Tilly," Zanzi said, keeping her voice soft, "not now." She looked at Josie. She was sitting on the floor with her back against the kitchen counter, head in her hands.

"Who did it?" Josie said.

"Alba."

"I should have guessed." Josie leapt up, gripping the edge of the countertop, whitening her knuckles. "I'm going to kill her."

"She's dead. Zanzi shot her under her chin." Tilly mimed the motion using her fingers.

"Is that true?" Josie said.

Zanzi's stomach lurched. "Yes. It's true." She was suddenly overcome by guilt at what she had done.

"Because of Harriet?"

"Mostly, yes."

Josie sniffed and wiped away her tears with the back of her hand. You remind me so much of Cal, Zanzi. She was always willing to help too. I'm going back to The Eyric to end this madness. It has to stop. Offenheim, Killian. All of them have to die."

"Aren't they impervious? I had to electrocute Alba before she died."

"I have to try. They'll never stop otherwise."

"Let's think this through. Why are you here in Portland?" Zanzi said.

"To test the survivors. To see if they have nanites in their systems. And why some of them want the spinal fluid."

"So. If you suddenly show back up at The Eyrie, they're going to be suspicious?"

"Not if I take back a subject. Say I've made a breakthrough and need my lab."

"What are you using here?"

"Nothing yet. It's still being set up at the hospital." Josie gestured outside. "Not far from here."

"Can you smuggle me back?"

"I don't see how. Nothing's going back."

"What if I looked like a victim? Cover me in blood. We'd still need a Rabid, like we saw in Devil's Falls." Zanzi clapped her hands. "The guards will never check."

"That could work. It's extremely risky, though. We don't even have weapons."

"True, but I know where we can get some."

"There could be another way…" Josie trailed off and poured herself another large glass of wine and opened a fresh bottle, offering a glass to each of them.

Tilly giggled as she sipped hers. "I feel like one of those ladies in that Abbey TV show."

Zanzi clinked her glass with Tilly and said, "That would be nice, sitting in the sun drinking wine." She took a sip. "What other way, Josie?"

"A possibility. The nanites are programable. In theory we could activate the self-destruct sequence to those in The Eyrie, but we'll need a coder at the very least, and that could take months."

"What about security. How many?"

"I don't know. I'm sorry. It's hopeless," Josie said, tears falling down her cheeks.

Zanzi let go of her awkwardness and hugged Josie, letting her cry. She understood the pain of losing someone close all too well. Her brother was never far from her thoughts.

SEVEN

NAGANO, JAPAN

The trip down from the temple was uneventful. The mountain road was in bad shape but there had only been a few minor rockslides from the earthquake. Most of the damage was centered on the opposite side of the valley. There, large landslides had taken out swathes of trees, cascading down the steep hills and filling the river below with rocks and stone.

The Nameless sat in the middle row of seats in the white Toyota van, squished together, the Yamada clan gunmen in front and behind. They snarled at Ryan and Booth and openly leered at Cal, Allie and Sofia, occasionally making lewd comments in Japanese.

Sofia nudged Ryan in the ribs. "I messaged Avondale."

"When?"

"Back on the train."

"What?"

"AA."

That was a code they had established years before, meaning "All Alive," letting HQ know the team was safe but couldn't speak. One of the yakuza jabbed his pistol into Ryan's leg.

"No talking."

Cal rolled her eyes. "Dickhead."

The valley below was densely populated. Cities merged into one another, forming one long expanse of habitation. Ryan's eyes followed the railway as it swept past the river before disappearing into another tunnel. The tracks were twisted and buckled like a can of silly string had exploded. Large boulders and trees had slid down covering roads, houses, and temples. Bridges had cracked and shifted. The whole area was devastated from Mother Nature's fury.

The driver slowed as an army truck appeared around the next corner. Yamada snapped his head around. "Keep your mouths shut. Let me do the talking." He held up one of the nano wands. "Don't make me press the button."

They were waved to a stop by a soldier wearing a white helmet, its chin strap pulled tight. "Where are you going?"

"Nagano."

"What about them?" The soldier pointed at The Nameless.

"We picked them up. The train they were on couldn't go any farther."

Shadows of Ash

"All foreigners are to report to the tourist office."

"We'll get them there," said Yamada.

"Identification?"

"Listen to me very carefully. I'm going to tell you my name. Then, if that doesn't make a difference, I'll show you my ID."

The soldier stepped back and raised his rifle. "All of you. Out of the vehicle."

"Hey. Calm down," Yamada said.

A sergeant with a pistol at his hip walked over. "What's the hold-up, private?"

"They aren't cooperating, sir. And those men are armed."

"Armed?"

"Sergeant. My name is Yamada. Touma Yamada."

The sergeant's eyes widened, and he bowed deeply before shoving the private away. "Please forgive me. I will personally deal with him. Can I assist you in any way?"

"We need better transport," said Yamada.

"Certainly."

The sergeant turned and shouted instructions. Soldiers dashed from the truck and ran up the street, looking into stalled vehicles.

"How's the road up ahead, Sergeant?" Yamada asked.

"Good through to Nagano. We're still clearing it to the coast."

"And the other preparations?"

"On schedule, sir."

Yamada exited the van and pulled the sergeant away. They conversed out of earshot. Ryan kept an eye on the pair, hoping for any indication of their discussion. He'd learned that one could tell a lot from watching someone's body language, but all he could gather from the pair was the power that Yamada exuded.

After a few minutes, one of the soldiers drove up in a Toyota 4X4. The yakuza jostled The Nameless inside, shoving Sofia, Keiko and Hogai onto the floor and pulled away, leaving the Army to deal with the growing crowd of survivors. After the events on Wednesday in Koyasan, Ryan had seen few people; only small groups here and there. In Tokyo there had been hundreds, trying to get into the train station. Here in Ueda, there were thousands – and not as many Siphons. Did it have to do with the way the signal was broadcast? Did the mountains interrupt it somehow? Here the Army was responding, setting up roadblocks to stop people from traveling. Handing out essential food and medical supplies. Maybe the major cities were slower to respond due to the enormity of the task.

Cal leaned into Ryan and laced her fingers in his. He was looking at the passing landscape. Steep, forested mountains surrounded the valley, their peaks capped with snow. Dozens of villages alternated with lakes and rivers. Bright greens of new spring growth shone on the maple trees.

Ryan sighed. Despite the chaotic events, nature was moving along as if nothing had happened.

***

They made it to Nagano and the driver brought the 4X4 to a sliding stop outside the train station. When the earthquake hit, two trains had been pulling into the station. They had clearly been tossed about, leaving the carriages skewed at odd angles. One carriage had mounted the raised platform and slammed into the ticket booth and concourse, showering bricks and glass across the road. But that wasn't what stopped the Toyota. Siphons were desperately trying to get at a group of people who had barricaded themselves inside the station and were poking at the creatures with umbrellas and chairs, anything they could get their hands on.

"We have to help them," Cal said, gasping at the sheer number of Siphons.

Yamada shook his head. "Go around," he instructed his driver.

"C'mon. We can at least draw some of the Siphons away?" Ryan said.

"Go around," Yamada spat. "Now!"

The driver did as he was instructed, skirting the knot of Siphons and ducking down a side street. Apart from a few wrecked cars, it was clear.

Ryan ground his jaw, angry at Yamada's disregard for the lives of his fellow countrymen. They were expendable to him, nothing more than an annoyance.

"You're not going to have much of a country left to be emperor of," he muttered.

"And you, Mr Connors, are a self-righteous bore. All of you Nameless are. Flying around, trying to save the world. Where did that get you, huh?"

Ryan glared at Yamada. One of the yakuza gunmen made a show of checking the magazine in his weapon.

"The problem with people like you, Connors, is that you never see the big picture. You think too narrowly. Too afraid to look outside the box. Let me ask you something. Did you ever question your orders when you rescued some idiot politician or some drug baron because he had amnesty for giving information?"

"Of course I questioned them."

"But you always obeyed the director's orders, did you not?"

Ryan said nothing.

"Huh. I thought so. Your team is good at what they do, but you are a bunch of sanctimonious fools."

"We'd rather be that than some megalomaniac asshole with an emperor complex," Sofia muttered.

The yakuza guards cocked their weapons.

"Everyone, let's all take a breath," Goro said.

Ryan raised his eyebrows. Goro had spoken out of turn, talking over his grandfather. He half expected Yamada to reprimand him, but nothing further was said as the yakuza holstered their weapons. Yamada ignored his grandson perhaps bored by the argument, or more likely it was beneath him. He was the Oyabun – the head of the Yamada clan and that always demanded respect. His kobun, his followers, would never act without his permission.

As they pulled into the airport, Cal let out a low whistle. Several planes had smashed into each other, wrecking across the runway and into the terminal. Ryan counted three burned-out wrecks. Siphons turned when they heard the noise of the Toyota 4X4 pulling into the narrow slipway, but thanks to the security fencing, they had no way of reaching the group. The helicopter pads and hangers were located at the back of the airport, away from the terminal and runways.

A Bell 212, painted bright orange, had been pulled from the hanger and towed to the pad. More of the Yamada clan surrounded it. They bowed when Yamada and Goro exited the 4X4. Everyone climbed into the chopper. Ryan was pleased to see supply crates strapped against the walls. Four of the new yakuza jumped in and they lifted off the ground, banking away.

It was five hours since the train crash. Five hours of torture. So many times Ryan had wanted to shoot Yamada and his goons, but the opportunity had never arisen – plus the fact Yamada had activated something in Hogai and Keiko. All Goro or Yamada had to do was push a button and they would turn to ash. Better to wait at least until Takeshi had been secured.

The chopper turned north and flew high over the mountains. Everywhere Ryan looked, he could see evidence of the earthquake. Towns washed away in landslides and rockfalls. Cracks splitting highways in half. Bridges collapsed and buildings toppled over.

He settled back, holding Cal's hand. Maybe tomorrow would provide the opportunity to even the score.

EIGHT

HOKKAIDO, JAPAN

"This is crazy," Allie said.

"I know," Booth agreed. He smiled at her. It was crazy because they were heading into an unknown situation in a country they had little intel on. They had no business being here. Yamada had made it their problem; the old "help me help you" cliché.

They had flown north and landed in the small coastal town of Yoichi. A light dusting of snow coated the ground as if someone had shaken icing sugar over everything.

From there they took taking an RHIB – rigid-hulled inflatable boat – and headed west around the rocky headland, cruising slowly to avoid making noise.

Ryan brought the RHIB to a stop two hundred meters offshore. He and Cal observed the Tomari Nuclear Power Plant through night vision binoculars, thanks to Yamada. He had provided the team with everything they needed.

Allie was sure everyone had the same question. What did the Black Skulls want so badly? Yamada's kid? The target wasn't the plant itself. Rather, it was the seemingly innocuous rectangular building behind it. To the casual observer, it looked like a separate business altogether. The building was low and squat. Six floors, with the first-floor windows blacked out. Surrounding the structure were acres of open space – carefully mowed lawns. Not a shrub or tree within a hundred meters. Beyond that was a two-meter-high chain-link fence. There was one access road in, gated, with a guardhouse. No signage. Anonymous and nondescript.

"Seeing anything?" Booth said.

"Hostiles have the place surrounded. Humvees with .50s. Thirty commandos so far. Road is barricaded but the oceanside is clear," Ryan said.

"Five snipers on the power plant roof. Fifteen soldiers in the plant grounds, stationed at every corner. What are they waiting around for?" Cal said.

"Heavy equipment?" Allie said. "Yamada said the blast doors were three meters thick. Ain't nothing getting through there."

"Not that I can see," Ryan said. "Sofia? Any movement in the abandoned seafood factory?"

"Negative."

"Remember what's at stake. We're here for Takeshi and a Doctor Ando only," Ryan said. "We row to shore."

They had planned it out once they'd reached Yoichi. The Nameless and the Yamada clan, like they were old friends, planning a raid. Allie had watched Ryan and Cal struggle with what they had to do. Touma Yamada had them, played on their emotions by threatening the kids. She doubted he would let them go once they had rescued Takeshi.

The Yamada clan were to provide a diversion, attacking from the road and the air, while The Nameless, dressed in the same black fatigues, were to sneak into the building, punch in the access code to get through the blast doors, grab their targets, and get out again. Easy. Nice and smooth. Thank you. Goodbye. No plan survived first contact with the enemy though, did it?

Allie understood why the team looked up to Ryan. He had a knack for figuring out ways into buildings. He had pored over the blueprints, firing question after question at Goro and Yamada. He'd even grilled one of the heavily tattooed goons.

Yamada wouldn't disclose exactly what the building was used for, but it was secret enough to warrant an off-site data storage server, hidden in the abandoned seafood factory. Normally data was stored far away by a specific company specializing in storage. Yamada had explained that their research was too secret and kept off-site for security. Ryan had smiled; that was their way in, squeezing three hundred meters along the cable trench and into the building. Undetected. It was going to be a tight fit and hard work. Cal had suggested using skateboards: lie down and slowly wheel yourself along.

The RHIB bumped against the mussel-encrusted rocks just below a rickety dock. The timber was split and filled with worms and insects. Seagulls nested on the posts. Allie helped pull the boat under the factory and followed Booth to a side door. Inside the factory the old machinery had been covered in plastic sheeting, now painted with years of dust. No one spoke as they threaded their way through the rooms and down into the basement. Ryan entered the code he'd been given and ducked in, sweeping the room with his Glock.

Allie shivered. The server room was clean and painted stark white. Soft blue lights glowed, illuminating enough to see by.

Ryan lifted the access panel to the cable trench and turned toward The Nameless. "Let's go over the plan. Sofia?"

"I'm staying here. Watching. Providing mission control."

"Allie?"

"Guard duty. Watching our backs."

"Booth?"

"Keeping our escape open."

"Good. Cal and I will access the lab, get our targets, and we all backtrack to the next bay over from where Yamada will extract us."

"I don't like it," Allie said. "What's to stop him from shooting us once he's got his son? Or turning us into ash?"

Booth, Cal, and Sofia murmured in agreement.

"That's the sixty-four-thousand-dollar question, isn't it?" Booth said.

Ryan checked his watch and looked at Allie. "I've been thinking about that since Nagano. Unfortunately, he has Keiko and Hogai. We can't risk it. We must carry out this mission. If Sofia had one of those wand gizmos, then we could scan Takeshi and Ando, give ourselves a little insurance. But we don't."

"I'm not positive that even if I did, I could get the nanites to activate like he can. That's days if not months of work. If I can even make sense of it," Sofia said.

"All Yamada has to do is believe we can. Find something that looks like the wand, pretend we scanned Takeshi, and we do an old-fashioned prisoner exchange. Then go our separate ways," Booth said.

Sofia exchanged a look with Ryan. He shook his head slightly. "All right. Nice idea, but we have no way of obtaining a wand. Complete the mission. Cal and I are Alpha team. Everyone clear?"

"Affirmative."

"Positions. Wait for the diversion," Ryan instructed. He unzipped a large duffle bag and grabbed three skateboards. "Comms check."

Allie used her throat mic to check after everyone else. Not for the first time, she wondered why she'd agreed to assist them. Okay, not so much that she'd agreed, more like wondering if she was good enough. Flying planes, yeah, she was confident. Small firefights, okay. Killing the Siphons, not a problem. But an actual operation, like she was a Navy Seal or something? Insane. Confidence had always been an issue for her; it was a miracle she had succeeded in the Air Force. She sighed and waited until Ryan and Cal had rolled down the narrow space. She shivered. Tight spaces? No thanks.

Sofia left the basement and headed upstairs to the main office. It provided a three hundred and sixty-degree view, thanks to the windows on every wall.

"In position," she said over the comms.

Booth stayed behind with Allie. He looked at his watch before stretching. "How are you going?"

"Going? What do you mean?"

Booth grinned. "I've hung around Ryan too much. It means the same as "How are you doing?"

"Coping. So far. I'll feel better once we're back on American soil."

"Heck yeah. Nothing like home. The sweet fields of Iowa."

"I can't help but think about what kind of hellfire we're flying into. If this Offenheim joker has managed this in Japan, what's home going to look like? Are we going to have a home to go to? After nine-eleven, airlines came up with protocols for terrorist attacks. Procedures, stuff like that. It's all I've ever known. I was still in high school in 2001. Surely the government had something, a shit-hitting-the-fan response."

"Connors told me he asked Yamada the same thing. Yamada said they had OPIS members in positions of power all over the world. Assurances that their plans went undetected. LK3 only caught wind of it by chance, and then only a hint. We had no idea what the hell was going on."

Allie frowned. "Still, it's an awfully big conspiracy to hide for so long. You'd think someone would have found out. What about Cal? Do you trust her?"

"Do you have kids?" said Booth.

"Nope. Not interested. Little demons."

"Love for children is a powerful thing."

"That's why you trust Cal?"

"Yes. Cal may be a lot of things but she loves her children. Plus I trust Ryan's judgement wholeheartedly."

"You have kids?" Allie asked, smirking.

"Two. I'm not with the mother, so I see them when I can." Booth looked away. "I've been thinking about them a lot since this clusterfuck went down."

"Where do they live?"

"Seattle. I'll check in on them on the way. I tried phoning before but couldn't get through. I was like you a few years ago. Not interested in the noisy little tykes. I had better things to do with my time. If I wasn't on an operation, I was surfing or hunting in the wilderness. Partying, hopping from one bed to the other, never settling down. The only way I could cope with some of the things I saw and did was to numb the feelings. It wasn't a good way to live. Connors tried to get me to chill out, but not everyone is lucky, finding that special person to love. Then there was Rita. I was in Bora Bora, surfing the pipeline, when she phoned me with the news: I'm pregnant. Like you, I thought, "Shit, I'm not the parent type!" But let me tell you, the second they're born, crying, and covered in mucus and blood, you love them with every fiber of your being. Your whole outlook on life switches. Before, it was all about you. Now it's about them. Providing for them and keeping them safe."

Allie nodded. She checked her watch as Sofia's voice came over the comms.

"Alpha team. SITREP?"

There was a humming noise, followed by hissing static. *"Two hundred meters in. Over."*

"Twenty minutes to diversion. Hostiles no change." Sofia said. "Booth. Move up."

"Wilco," Booth said, grabbing his skateboard. He dropped into the tunnel and popped back up to look at Allie. "Hey. What's your favorite movie?"

"Why?"

"Just curious."

"Huh. Probably *Last of the Mohicans*."

"How about when this is all over, we have dinner and watch it?"

"Are you asking me on a date?"

"Most definitely."

"I'd love to. Thanks."

Booth pumped the air with his fist. "See you on the other side, kid." He dropped back into the hole and disappeared.

Allie shook her head. *If we make it out of this.*

NINE

HOKKAIDO, JAPAN

The concrete was smooth and cool under the wheels of his skateboard. The cable tunnel had a slight musty smell, like socks mixed with garden lime – or maybe more like an old basement that hadn't been opened for years. That dusty whiff you get when the mites are disturbed. The tunnel was about the scale of a packing box, an old tea chest, and divided into three sections with a metal grid shelf running the entire length of the walls. Thick spools of cable had been encased in cooling insulation – probably waterproof too – and above and below the shelves were gaps just large enough to allow Ryan and Cal to move.

They rolled forward meter by meter, listening and watching for any sound or movement. When Yamada had built the lab, he had left this little detail off the submitted plans. So far, it appeared the Black Skulls had no clue of its existence.

After another five minutes, they reached the end. A solid metal door painted glossy black barred the way.

Ryan nudged his comms. "Alpha team at location. Over."

"Copy. Booth?" Sofia said.

"In location. Over."

"Allie. Status?"

"In position. Over."

Ryan glanced at his watch; they had made it with minutes to spare. It was nearing 3 a.m., their agreed-upon time. Yamada's yakuza were to attack from the ground while his surviving security forces would strike from the air.

What do you think we'll find in there? Cal signed.

Who knows? We've seen some bad stuff over the years. I just hope I don't get any more traumatic memories. What I have is enough to last a lifetime.

Ryan turned away as he recalled some of the atrocities he'd witnessed over the years. Children kept in flea-ridden hovels, forced to work. Men and women tricked into thinking they were moving to the West, only to find themselves trapped in a life of prostitution. But one memory always surged to the forefront of his mind: Bangladesh, and Zizer Pharmaceuticals using the poor and the downtrodden for drug testing. He gritted his teeth and checked his magazine to stop the thought going any further.

I hope there are no abnormalities, Ryan signed.

Like we saw in Manila? Cal signed back.

I was thinking about Bangladesh, but Manila was bad too.

For months after, all I could see were those little bodies and those eyes, Cal hesitated.

Staring at us?

Staring, pleading, questioning. I've never figured out how someone could do things like that to innocent children.

I like to think that is why we do this job. Help the innocent.

Of course. Cal patted his arm and glanced away.

Ryan shivered, thinking of it. That had all been before the twins had come along. Having children had strengthened his resolve to stop any exploitation.

Sofia's voice came over the comms, loud and clear. *"Heads up, Nameless. Show time."*

Ryan unlocked the metal door using the key Goro had provided. It swung open, smooth and quiet. He strained his ears, waiting for the sounds of battle.

"Hold location, Alpha team," Sofia said.

There was a muffled boom, followed by sporadic gunfire. Ryan calmed his breathing and focused on what he had to do, running through the directions that Yamada had explained to him and what locked doors he could expect.

A louder boom echoed, vibrating the concrete under him as rapid gunfire exploded from somewhere deeper in the building.

"*Alpha. Proceed.*"

"Wilco," Ryan said, giving Cal's hand a squeeze.

"*Booth. Move up.*"

"Wilco."

Ryan placed the skateboard to one side and shuffled his feet in front of him. He looked back at Cal, nodded, and slid through the open door, dropping into the corridor. It was brightly lit, almost gleaming like a ski slope. He went down on one knee, drew his Glock 17 and swept the vicinity. Cal followed him out and protected their eastern flank. The access door swung shut.

Yamada had disguised the access door as a fire alarm panel, complete with blinking lights. Ryan made a note of the serial number before rechecking his immediate vicinity. The gunshots were coming from outside the building, over the roar of SUV engines and the soft pops of the yakuza's preferred weapon, the MP5s. Cal tapped him on the shoulder and leap-frogged past him, moving twenty meters away. She stopped and crouched before pivoting back toward him. Ryan trained his Glock east, covering that position. Next, he leap-frogged Cal, and they repeated the procedure all the way to the first junction. They had expected little resistance at this end of the building. To get to the blast doors and their targets they needed to go down one floor at the far eastern end of the lab.

Ryan glanced in each door he passed, just a quick look, making mental notes, more out of habit, recording

Shadows of Ash

items and equipment in case he needed it in the future. Most of the labs were filled with typical medical equipment: microscopes, beakers, test tubes. Each had a small room attached for the scientists' computers and pegs for clothing. Like in Koya, forms of ash from the workers littered the floor, chairs, and desks. From what Ryan could see, there was nothing dangerous being experimented on up here.

Was this the legitimate business to cover what really happened down below?

They made it to the end of the corridor without any contacts. After checking the door to the stairwell, Ryan whispered to Cal, "Eyes sharp. Something's off."

"Alpha at the doors," Ryan said into his throat mic.

"Standby."

"Booth. Move up."

The battle outside the building intensified. Ryan and Cal waited for Sofia to give them the green light. The easy part was over. This next phase was the critical part, where they expected to meet fierce opposition from Offenheim's Black Skulls.

Four muffled booms rattled the darkened windows. Humvees with machine guns roared into action.

"Go, Alpha."

Sofia had been waiting for the main attack. It was insane, attacking head-on, but the goal was their task, not success for the frontal attack.

Ryan cracked open the fire door and peered through. No movement, not even a fragment. He looked up and side to side. Nothing. All quiet.

Cal brushed past him and waited until he was inside. The stairwell was gray and boring, built for a purpose and a function, not for aesthetics. Using the same leap-frogging method, they hustled down to the next floor.

Here, a small, secondary set of thick doors had been smashed open. Two Black Skulls, necks broken, were slumped against the wall. Their weapons, HK416s, lay discarded on the floor. Not Ryan's favorite rifle, but he grabbed it all the same.

He tossed one to Cal, who caught it and checked the magazine.

"What happened here?" she said. "No wounds. Just broken necks."

Ryan shrugged. Something strong had torn the doors off their hinges. Thick-cast steel bolt hinges, no less.

The corridor ahead carried on for another fifty meters before ending in a T-intersection. Lining each wall were thick steel doors, each with a tiny window in the center at eye level. Ryan jogged over to the first one and peered inside. A large male stared back at him, snarling and showing yellow teeth. Eyes brown, but bright as if the whites were illuminated from behind. He was huge, nearly two meters tall, with muscles like an action movie hero. His skin was dark brown with patches of gray and calloused into ridges and troughs like the bark on a pine tree. The man snarled again and thumped his meaty fist against the door.

Ryan moved on. The next room held another man. He was curled up on the bed under a filthy blanket. His fingers were long and spider-like. Lumps, some as large as apples, bulged from his skull. Webbed feet with long toes poked out at the end of the bed. Another cell held a thin man, sitting cross-legged as if deep in meditation, his hair long and snowy white. His ivory skin was covered in scars, some delicate and small, others angry and ragged. The next room held a woman covered in incandescent scales, shimmering in the pale light. She glared at Ryan but remained stationary.

Cal watched from the opposite side of the corridor, tears in her eyes. "This is sick. Heartbreaking even. What the hell is going on down here?"

"Nothing like this in The Eyrie?"

"Not that I saw. There's a dog in this cell."

Ryan frowned and gestured for her to cover him. The dog was a golden labrador. It sat in the middle of the room, wagging its tail. It saw Ryan and whined and wiggled its butt.

Cal jolted her head back from the corner and held up a closed fist. Heavy footsteps clomped toward them. The footsteps stopped and were replaced by hushed orders. Ryan was a firm believer in taking control. Shoot the other guys first. In situations like these, conversations didn't work. Arguments were settled with bullets. He went high, Cal low. He flicked off the safety and let off a three-shot burst at the first target he saw, scoring a hit in the chest and neck. Cal shot a second target, while the third dove to one side.

More shots came at them from farther down the corridor. Chips of concrete flew at Ryan's head. He ducked and pivoted. Four more Black Skulls had caught them napping from behind. Ryan cursed himself for acting like an amateur and returned fire. The two he had shot sat back up, shaking their heads. With everyone flooded with nanites, he shouldn't have been surprised they didn't stay down. Still, he chided himself. Too long out of the game and rusty as hell.

Ryan had no time for answers as he scanned for a way out. If he couldn't go out, maybe he could get in? Beside the cell with the dog was a large red button, and next to that were door-release switches. Each cell was numbered. He reached up and flicked all the switches.

Klaxons blared.

Speakers boomed out warnings in Japanese and English, so loud they rattled Ryan's teeth. He grabbed Cal's arm and dove into the dog's cell. The golden labrador wagged its tail and started licking Ryan's face and hands until he gently pushed it away.

The dog switched its attention to Cal. "Down boy," she said.

As quickly as the alarms sounded, they switched off.

Cal grimaced as she turned and continued to fire her weapon. Blood dripped from several wounds on her legs and torso. They may have made it into the cell, but now they had another problem. For the Black Skulls, it would be like bobbing for apples, or was it shooting fish in a barrel? Either way, they were screwed. And no one stayed down.

Ryan skipped through the files of his mind, trying to figure out a way to get the Black Skulls permanently dead. His mind flashed back to the guards with the broken necks. Maybe like that? Or head shots, destroy the brain.

Shadows of Ash

The dog licked Ryan's face and hands before barking at the noise in the corridor.

The commandos kept firing at the inhabitants of the cells Ryan had unlocked. Their shouts became filled with terror.

Ryan checked on Cal. "All good?"

She nodded, lifting her top. A bullet had punched through her side, taking a hunk of flesh with it. Already the bleeding had stopped, and the wound had begun to heal. Not for the first time, Ryan wished he had a better explanation than just nanites. Sure, he knew what they were and the basic principle, but, like most technology, how it worked stumped him. It was something he was going to rectify if he ever got out of here.

A roar, like a note sung by a tenor, rumbled into their cell. The dog raced around in a circle and licked their hands again. The man with the bark-like skin stood in the doorway. He was huge, blocking out the light. The dog ran straight to him and bounced in circles.

"Who are you?" he said. His voice sounded garbled, as though the words were gurgled through a mouth of water.

Gunshots boomed up the corridor.

"Who?" he gurgled again, stepping into the room.

Ryan glanced at Cal before answering. "LK3 operatives. We're looking for Takeshi Yamada."

"Why?"

"We were sent to extract him, by his father."

More bullets pinged off the man's thickened skin, as if they were nothing more than slugs fired from a BB gun.

"Let them pass, Yuri," a voice called out from the next cell. "Can't you see they're friendly."

"Down there," Yuri said, gesturing deeper into the complex. He turned away and growled at the Black Skulls. "Stay with them, dog."

The dog growled again, much louder this time, and lumbered into the corridor, facing the men. The Black Skulls continued to fire their weapons.

Cal sighed as she stood up and checked her magazine. "What's that saying about insanity?"

"You can't expect a fish to climb a tree?" Ryan said.

"No. Insanity is doing the same thing over and over and expecting different results. How many rounds have they fired? A thousand?"

"Yuri is scaring them, that's all."

The woman covered in incandescent scales slipped into the room. Her nictitating membrane blinking. Next, the last occupant of a cell stood in their doorway. His fingers freakishly long, almost three times the normal length, and his feet resembled flippers.

They both stared at Ryan and Cal, said "thank you," and darted from the room.

"In here," the voice called out again. It was the thin man who had been meditating. He held up a bony hand and waved. "I don't see nowadays, but I hear you well enough."

"We're operatives from LK3. Gather your belongings. Once we have Takeshi, we'll come back for you," Ryan said.

The thin man stared at them with unblinking eyes. A small chuckle sounded in his throat. "I thought I heard your accent. It's there, barely, but there. New Zealand?"

"Yes. Originally."

"How is it these days? Like I remember? Bush-clad mountains. Rolling green fields. Turquoise water that shimmers in the summer heat?"

"More or less. Who are you?"

"That I remember. I've held onto it all these years. I'm not sure how much time has passed exactly, but Ando could never take that from me. Corporal Bruno Muir." Bruno wheezed and lay down on the narrow bed. He coughed a few times and rummaged under his pillow. When his hand emerged, he held out dog tags faded with age. "I'm afraid I've reached the end. Pity. I would have liked to have seen the *pohutukawa* flowering one last time. Can you get these to my family? Let them know that I never gave up hope of seeing them."

Ryan took the tags, feeling the weight in his hand. Not the physical weight, but the years of hopelessness Bruno must have felt. He tucked them inside his combat vest. "I'll make it my personal mission, sir."

Bruno chuckled again. "They caught me in Singapore during the war, taking me first to the Philippines. Gave me medicine. Cut me, shot me, broke my bones. Over and over. I heard the battle, the heavy artillery, and thought I was going home. But no. They brought me to Japan. I heard the guards say that we had won the war, and again I thought I was going home. Years went by. More prisoners joined the experiment, and Ando was never satisfied. Always wanting something else." Bruno coughed again, wet and full of mucus. "The other prisoners will leave you alone."

"Thank you," Ryan said.

"It was nice to hear a friendly voice before I died."

Cal knelt and held Bruno's hand as his breathing became ragged. He gasped one last time. Cal placed his hands over his chest and pulled up the blanket. "This place isn't a lab. It's a chamber of death."

They left Bruno and darted back into the corridor.

Ryan listened to the shrieks of the commandos as the former prisoners tore into the Black Skulls. He didn't look; he didn't need to. More to the point, he didn't want to. He turned back to Cal. "Let's move."

"What about the dog?"

In response, the golden lab wriggled its butt, happy to be included. Ryan had always had a soft spot for dogs and cats. They were completely different as pets but brought so much joy to the family.

"Fine, we'll take him. But we can't call him dog."

"What about Sam?"

"Sam it is." Ryan smiled and bumped his throat mic. "Sofia. Resistance met. Proceeding to blast doors. Over."

"Copy. Speed it up. Yamada's men are losing."

"Wilco."

They paused at the door and peered out. The former prisoners had disappeared, leaving a trail of carnage in their wake. The commandos all had their necks broken, like the first two they'd encountered. In addition, their arms were missing, and their intestines were pooled on the floor like a major operation had been underway before being disturbed. Blood coated the floor in thick puddles, and splashes of the plasma had flicked up the walls in long, arch-like spatters. The air was heavy with the stench of iron and excrement.

Shadows of Ash

It didn't take long to reach the blast doors. All they had to do was follow the line of dead commandos. Some had their heads bashed in, brains and skulls crushed from huge blows. Some had their necks snapped, like they'd seen before. Some had been impaled on their weapons, usually the rifle entering beneath their genitals and exiting through their mouths. These ones were still alive and gasping for air, desperately trying to remove the guns with feeble swipes of their hands. Others had been sliced open with nice clean cuts from navel to sternum, their organs removed and crushed. As horrific as the scene was, Ryan took notes. The prisoners they had freed had been experimented on for God only knew how long. Treated as mere playthings. He didn't blame them for exacting vengeance.

"Where did they go?" Cal said, swinging from left to right. The semi-circular blast doors – to fit the corridor – were directly ahead of them, with nowhere else to go. They were gray, like everything else, apart from the painted red stripe in the center.

"Not our problem. We're here for Takeshi and Ando." Ryan flicked the cover off the security panel and pulled the key Yamada had given him from his pocket. It was a weird-looking key. Long and cylindrical, made from gold, and when you pressed the button on top of the grip, tiny SIM-card-like panels opened.

Ryan inserted the key into the slot and waited for the beep before pressing the button. The panel hummed and the lights changed color from yellow to red. Next, he entered the four-digit code three times. Once forward in sequence, followed by twice backward. The panel changed color from red to green.

Deep inside the door mechanism, reinforced steel bolts, each the size of an average human – so he had been told – slid back with a clank.

"Alpha team inside," Ryan said into his comms.

"Copy. Booth. Move up. Alpha, advance."

"Wilco."

The blast doors opened painfully slowly, inching their way across the corridor as if they had all the time in the world. The passage beyond was silent and dark. Cal slid past Ryan and went left.

Ryan didn't like it. Silent and dark wasn't good. A bad feeling began to gnaw at the back of his brain. The warning part. The part honed over thousands of generations, passed down through the years.

Danger.

TEN

WASHINGTON, USA

Avondale had been true to his word and led Director Lisa Omstead and Doctor Monica Johnson to Fort Lewis, now known as Joint Base Lewis McChord. Part Army, part Air Force, it was the most-requested duty base in the Army. Lisa could see why. Mount Rainier towered above like a lonely sentinel.

The last few miles had been a tortuous drive through checkpoint after checkpoint. Black Skulls had attacked and attempted to bomb the airfield only to be chased away and annihilated by Munroe's men, but it put everyone on edge. Lisa and Monica were waved through each time with curt nods.

Most of the soldiers were wearing protection suits and gas masks and made the two women don their own. "General's orders, ma'am" was the only explanation given.

Once they were inside the base proper, they were directed far to the right and back. Here, bodies of the Rabids had been stacked into piles and were being burnt. Munroe had acted fast, setting up a perimeter and keeping it secure. They passed the hangars and equipment warehouses. Trucks were parked up, the drivers milling about. They seemed to be waiting for something. Orders?

Munroe was waiting outside the small lab building, arms folded across his broad chest. He wore a protection suit but had pulled the hood and mask off. The late afternoon sun glistened off his shaved head.

"Director Omstead," Munroe said with a nod. "When this shit went down, I thought if anyone had survived it would be you. Stubborn, fortuitous. Smart as a whip. Cordwell?"

"He didn't make it, sir," Lisa said.

"Pity. Good soldier that one. What happened?"

"Black Skulls attacked us. He protected our retreat."

"Black skulls?" Munroe frowned.

"The soldiers wearing black. They have a skull sigil."

"We fought some men wearing black fatigues, but they had no markings. These had a skull sigil?"

"On the right shoulder, yes."

"Special ops?"

"That's what I want to find out."

Shadows of Ash

"A real shame about Cordwell," Munroe said. He turned to the sergeant on his left and gestured at Lisa. "This woman here, Sergeant. Take a good look. One of the toughest sons of bitches I've ever known. She and her team slogged for over two hundred clicks through camel shit-encrusted sand. Scorpions, spiders the size of your head. All the way chased by Iraqi bastards wanting revenge. You take a good look, son. That's a leader. That's a soldier."

"Nice to see you too, General. This is Doctor Monica Johnson, formerly of the CDC," Lisa said.

Munroe beckoned them inside and shut the door. It locked with a hiss, leaving the sergeant and another soldier outside standing guard.

"Nice to have you on board. What do you make of all this, doctor?" Munroe said as he led them deeper into the building, down a short hallway and into a lunchroom. The building housed two small labs for running blood, urine and stool samples, and a few exam rooms like those found in a doctor's office. Obvious signs of struggle were evident: equipment knocked over, and a couple of the tables still had an ashy residue. The general pulled out three chairs and they sat down.

"Doctor?"

Monica shook her head, removed her mask, and took a deep breath. "I've been a virologist my entire working life. What's happened isn't acting like any virus I've ever seen or studied. It had no incubation period, no start. It just happened." She clicked her fingers. "Like that. Bang."

"What can you tell me of this *Mortis* virus in Africa and Europe?"

"Not much. *Mortis* is neither viral nor bacterial. I know that."

"Nothing weaponized?" Munroe glanced around, his eyes flicking to the door. "Like that Ebola scare in fifteen."

Again, Monica shook her head. "Thanks to LK3, we managed to get some samples of *Mortis* a few years back in Romania. I was at the CDC then. The best minds couldn't work it out. We found no trace of either a virus or bacteria. No trace of anything toxic at all."

"So what killed the victims in Romania?"

"No idea. For that, we needed to perform an autopsy."

"Best guess. In your professional opinion?"

"In my opinion? Okay. Strictly speaking, I would need my notes to refresh my memory, but the tissue samples I did examine looked frozen. Like they do to peas to keep them fresh. Snap frozen. It was like that. The cells had been snap frozen, killing the tissue, turning it gray and black. I would say the victim died as a result of his whole body freezing suddenly."

Munroe stood and paced around, his hand on his chin, rubbing over the stubble of his three-day-old beard.

"What's your take, Omstead? From what you've seen."

"Sir. I've seen some strange events in my time, both in the Army and with LK3, but the events of the last few days..." Lisa sighed. "I don't know. People driven insane and sucking the fluid from the spine. Militia dressed in black, killing innocent civilians. Foreign fighter jets flying in American airspace. I've been involved in disaster prep teams, brainstorming scenarios on what could happen. Ways the world could end. How to ensure the survival of humanity. But not in our wildest nightmares did we ever come up with this."

The general nodded. "You think this was organized?"

"It sounds bat-shit crazy, but it's the only logical explanation. Like Monica said, it can't be a virus. Too instantaneous. Victims dying and turning to ash. Others swelling and some shrinking. Those rabid freaks, maybe? That's why we brought a specimen. No way it's a virus. No. This is something else."

Munroe stopped his pacing and looked from Lisa to Monica, smiling. "Good. Come with me."

They followed the general outside, down a concrete path and into a larger brick building. Guards were posted at the outside entrance and a further pair stood at an internal set of doors. Munroe waved them aside.

The Joint Operations center was full of activity. Desks with computer monitors crowded the central space, with staff in uniforms glued to their screens. The far wall was covered in screens, all showing different camera views and computer graphics. Field positions of active operations. The sergeant on duty saluted.

"At ease," Munroe said.

He took Lisa and Monica toward the back of the room and onto a raised level. Even here there were signs of fighting. And though it had been cleaned away, grime from the ash remains was scattered about.

Munroe turned. "After the event, and when we'd finished off the suckers, I followed protocol and reported in. As you know, we found nothing. No one answered at the Pentagon, Langley or the White House. Slowly, forts and bases reported in. Sporadic, but at least they were coming in. Heavy casualties from all reports. We're getting drones in the air now and starting sweeps of the state. We have no access to satellites presently. Radio communication is all we have left, and you know how glitchy that can be." He grimaced. "Corporal, play them the Beale recording."

There was a short belch of static over the speakers next to the monitor.

"...Munroe. What the hell is going on? I've got heavily armed unknown hostiles attacking. Ground and air. Black fatigues, German weapons. They're bombing us to shit. Caught us completely by surprise. Radar is down, everything..."

Lisa breathed deep. Beale Air Force Base was an obvious target. Home to reconnaissance and intelligence squadrons, Air Defense Command, missile warning systems, refueling. It was exactly the right play by whomever the enemy was. Take out the main command posts and cut communications. There was no need to ask Munroe what he thought, the creases in his forehead told her.

"Corporal, play the others," Munroe said.

More recordings from bases and forts across the continental United States. Same panicked calls. Same sounds of fighting before everything went quiet.

"Anything from overseas?" Lisa asked.

"We're dark. Someone flipped a switch and it's not coming back on for the moment. I have my best technicians working on it as we speak."

"Not even on the military satellites?"

Munroe shook his head. "We're locked out. None of our codes are working. I've appealed to Secretary Ward for assistance. You know his response?"

"They're working on it. Which means…"

"Don't ask," Lisa and Munroe said together, smiling at each other. They knew the drill. Been there, done that. Seen it all.

What little staff were left at the Pentagon would be scrambling to secure Ward and anyone else left there. Keep them safe. Establish a chain of command, organize civilians, maintain law and order.

"We're all agreed that it was a coordinated attack?" Lisa said.

Munroe and the corporal nodded. Monica stared around the room, watching the buzz of activity.

"Doctor Johnson?"

"I'm just thinking all this through," Monica said. "If it was planned and coordinated, the level of organization is astounding. First, they had to invent whatever it was that caused the combusting. Distribute it. Move everyone into position. Know which bases to attack and execute the plan – all without a hitch. Maybe the suckers were not foreseen. But that level of organization means a lot of people – hundreds if not thousands. And they all managed to keep their mouths shut? Without any agencies finding out. That's why the 'moon landings were a faked conspiracy' is so ridiculous. As if four hundred people conspired together to fake it. Fifty years on and no one has spilt the beans. It's absurd."

Adrian J Smith

Lisa grimaced. Normally, at this point, she would nod her head and offer some form of agreement. Play the game, keeping her aces up her sleeve. But now, there was no game to play. Someone had entered and killed nearly everyone. The game was over, or was it? She couldn't be certain of anything anymore. Her father's voice echoed in her mind. *Find one solution and move on, step by step until you defeat the problem.*

She pulled back her shoulders and looked at General Munroe and Monica. "I can fill you in on what little I know – but not here."

Munroe stayed silent for a few seconds before he waved them outside, along a concrete path to the medical facilities and back into the lunchroom.

"What is it, Omstead?"

Lisa shuffled in her seat and stretched her tired legs. "Six months ago a NASA deputy director died while visiting a dominatrix. Nothing suspicious – a heart attack. It was kept out of the press by the White House as a matter of national security. Again, nothing unusual there. This happens a lot more than you think. There are staff to deal with this kind of problem. A couple of weeks later, an anonymous person claims they have government secrets to sell to the highest bidder. Once again, as I'm sure you realize, this sort of thing happens all the time. It turns out the deputy director had his laptop with him, and the dominatrix decided to remove the hard drive to try to make some cash. I was asked to investigate it and fix the problem, which my team did. No sooner did we secure the hard drive the CIA swooped in and took it. No harm, no foul. We did our job, pat on the back, on to the next mission. Like you're thinking now, so what? I thought the same. My computer guy saw some of what the dominatrix was offering. She had no idea, but he did. Satellite codes. A few, not many."

"Huh?" Munroe said.

Monica was frowning but said nothing.

"Right. Naturally, the back of my brain is screaming, something isn't right. Something was nagging me. Three years ago LK3 received a tip-off about a satellite installation, telling us it was being used for other reasons. So I put my best team on it. I lost a valued member that day and another retired because of it. But both the police and FBI could find no evidence of wrongdoing. The official line was that my team member died in a hiking accident. The other members of that team kept on investigating, ears open, that kind of thing. Then a couple of months ago we hit the jackpot. A general was selling satellite codes, and last week the FBI intercepted a truck filled with girls destined for some perverted sex ring. One girl, Harriet, told stories of a place high in the mountains where she had been experimented on. She described the same satellite installation. Naturally, we were set to investigate, but our HQ was attacked. A few days later, bang."

"Huh," Munroe said again. He stood up and began pacing, his hands clenched into fists. "Omstead, I'm recalling you to active duty. Secretary Ward has ordered me to coordinate recovery operations for Washington State. I'm sure you saw the trucks. Select a small team from what few soldiers I have. I can spare you three."

"General?"

"Recon. Find out who these Black Skull bastards are and where they're operating from. I'll provide you with whatever gear you need, but I want you in mufti. Take as much as you can because you can't be seen returning. You report only to me. Understand?"

"Got it."

"Doctor, the specimen you brought is waiting for you in Exam Room Two. I want an autopsy report on my desk by zero-nine-hundred. I want to know what the bloody hell is going on with those suckers."

"Okay. I'll need some staff."

"I'll see what's available. I have two medics for the whole base. There are sleeping quarters in the back. Guards are on the doors."

General Munroe left Lisa and Monica in the small lunchroom.

Monica stood and smoothed down her clothes. "I better get started then."

Lisa handed her the vial of Harriet's blood. "Test this, but don't say anything to anyone."

"All right." Monica sighed. She left, her shoes squeaking on the linoleum.

Lisa glanced down at her hands. She had retired from the Army a long time ago and had long thought those days behind her. She should be exploring the country in an RV with her husband, not chasing bad guys. Guilt washed over her for not telling Munroe everything, but old habits die hard. She headed for the sleeping quarters, a million problems buzzing in her mind.

ELEVEN

PORTLAND, OREGON

Where do you see yourself in five years? One of the most cringe-worthy questions interviewers liked to ask, from school administrators to prospective employers. Zanzi hated it the same way some people flinched when they heard the words *moist* or *panties*.

Where do you see yourself in five years? How does one answer that? In a big house with kids and a husband? Working here at this amazing company while you slowly suck all the joy from my life?

She and her friends used to tease each other with that question in college. Answering it became a game: who could come up with the most outlandish response? Like the four Yorkshiremen skit Monty Python did.

Zanzi, where do you see yourself in five years? *"Running a tattoo parlor that secretly draws supernatural symbols into the tattoo so the dark lord can take his rightful place on the earth."*

That had won her the Best Response Award at the end of the year. She smiled, thinking of it. Looking out at the rising sun, knowing what was out there, she couldn't help but wonder if perhaps the devil had come. Never would she have imagined this five years ago.

She shivered and sipped her green tea. She loved this time of day. It was almost sacred to her. Like her mother, Cal, she was an early riser. Up with the birds. In happier times they had often sat on the porch, drinking tea, silent, just watching the world wake up.

"Mind if I join you?" It was Josie.

Zanzi moved over on the step and patted the space. "How are you?"

"Okay. I guess. Mentally I feel fine. My stomach is in twists. I don't think I can cry anymore. Now I feel determined to make ReinCorp pay."

They sat in silence for a few minutes. Zanzi was lost in thought. Like Josie, she wanted to go back and destroy the satellite installation called The Eyrie, but it was heavily guarded, and she had no means to do so.

"Can I ask you something?" Zanzi said.

"About?"

"These nanites. How do they work? Milo said we have billions of them in our bloodstream and in our brain, but

Shadows of Ash

how do they know who to trigger? To, you know, turn to ash?"

"It will be easier to show you." Josie stood and moved back inside the trailer.

The scientist booted up her laptop and zipped open a black rucksack. From it she grabbed a flat baton, about the size of a 27-ounce water bottle. She clicked a red button on the side and swiped it over Zanzi's neck. It emitted a sharp beep.

"Attached to the back of the brain is the alpha nanite. Actually, it's thousands of them bonded together to form the CPU. It receives signals telling the worker nanites what to do. In my research, I was looking at ways to repair damaged cells in the spine."

Josie turned her laptop around. On the screen were streams of green numbers, with one sequence in a larger font, also colored green.

"That large number is your alpha. It's showing green, so it's safe. If it was flashing red, then I'd be worried."

"Can Offenheim make it flash red?"

"Not likely. I reprogrammed yours to act like theirs. Elite, having the same fail safes. Tilly too."

"When did you do that?"

"While you were sleeping. Milo asked me to do it a couple of days ago."

"I don't understand."

"Milo came to me asking if I knew who had taken Amelia off the list. Which I found strange, as he knows full well that only two people are capable of that. Killian and Daniel Kummerow."

"That's when you agreed to help us?"

"Yes. Milo offered me and Harriet a way out for good. All I had to do was update your alphas and assist you once you reached Portland."

"But how did you update it?"

"Using the Wi-Fi. The alpha receives data packets like a cell phone." Josie brushed a tear from her cheek and murmured, "Did Milo know about Harriet?"

"Only after I told him. Can we trust him?"

"He's one of the better ones. After his wife Amelia died, his demeanor changed. Like he doesn't want any part of it anymore and wants to leave."

Zanzi bit the inside of her bottom lip, thinking of all the things she wanted to do to Offenheim. Getting to him was going to be the challenge. "Essentially, the nanites are a small computer?" she said.

"In a nutshell, yes. Extremely small. With only one specific task. Some are shaped like ticks to interact with blood cells, give them the proteins and enzymes needed for healing."

"A tick?" Zanzi shook her head. "I knew I wasn't seeing things."

"You saw one?"

"Yeah, I was examining Harriet's blood..." Zanzi paused, unsure how to continue. The last few days had been a whirlwind of adrenaline-inducing situations. Part of her wanted to sugar coat it all for Josie but she'd always favored honesty.

"I'm sorry. That's how I became involved in all this. I saw one of the nanites in a blood sample of your daughter.

Shadows of Ash

I didn't know what I saw, so I asked Doctor Kohli to look. Half an hour later the lab blew up and those commandos were attacking us."

"It's okay. It's not your fault. ReinCorp, and only them, are to blame."

Zanzi nodded. It all came back to Offenheim. During the flight to Portland she had run through a dozen ideas of how she could destroy the satellite installation. But she was just one desperate person, not a soldier. She thought of Devil's Falls and the corpse of the elderly man they had seen, his spine licked clean as if it held the elixir of youth.

"There's something that I'm curious about," she said. "The rabid humans, with the cloudy eyes – any ideas as to why they suck the spine?"

Josie took a sip of her tea before answering. "I'm sure that in your studies you touched on cerebrospinal fluid. What is does, et cetera. At first I thought the suckers wanted it for the chloride or sodium, maybe the electrolytes, but those can be found in blood plasma. Different levels, of course."

"And now, you're not so sure?"

"It can't be that simple. It doesn't make sense. What I need is a fresh sample. That's today's mission. Working will help take my mind off Harriet."

"Occam's razor?"

"Exactly. The simplest explanation is usually the right one, I know. Perhaps you're right."

Zanzi mulled it over. Josie's theory, or her conclusion, at least, closely mirrored her own. The Rabids – suckers, berserkers, whatever you wanted to call them – must want the spinal fluid for another reason. In this case, there was no simple solution.

Her eyes widened as an idea popped in her head. "What about stem cells?" she said, her voice filled with excitement. "Doesn't marrow contain hematopoietic? Maybe they want that, suck it right out of the vertebrae." She made a sucking sound like a kid finishing the last drops of a soda.

"I don't think so. Wouldn't they just crack open a femur or a radius? There's plenty of red marrow in those."

The two scientists watched the sun creep above the horizon. It felt good to talk on an intellectual level with Josie. The past few days had been hell. Zanzi had barely escaped being blown sky high, then been chased by Black Skulls. Tortured by Alba. Made to witness the end of the world.

Now she had a chance to get back. To do what her parents did. Fight for the freedoms of the many.

"We need to figure out a plan," Zanzi said, "to take down ReinCorp."

Josie sat up a bit straighter. "I was thinking about that as I lay awake. About your idea of playing possum. It could work, but the helicopter ride in a body bag, I'm not so sure. And once we reach The Eyrie you'd be taken straight to the lab where an autopsy would be performed by other scientists. I'd be given samples and a report, but at no stage can I be present. It's not my job. They'd know if I try. I can't risk your life too."

"Okay. But you can get back to The Eyrie?"

Josie nodded and drained her cup.

Shadows of Ash

"Run me through what your orders are. See if we can figure out another way," said Zanzi.

"Once the lab is ready at Legacy Emanuel Medical Center, I'm to take samples and run diagnostics, figure out why the victims behaved the way they did. There will be a team. We all have our specialties." Josie looked at her watch. "I'm to meet a field team at zero-nine-hundred to go over the mission."

"Can you get us on that team?"

"Possible, but risky."

"Won't you be wearing protective suits?" Zanzi said.

"Yes, but our hoods will be open."

Zanzi took another sip of her green tea, swirling the gritty dregs in her mouth to savor the bitter taste. "What if Tilly and I come to the hospital? I know my way around a lab. I can help. It might take us a few weeks, but we could get back up there that way."

"Not with Tilly. She's too recognizable, even if you dye her hair." Josie stood. "I need to head to the mess hall. I'll bring you back something."

"Any chance you can bring back a working radio or, better yet, a phone?"

"I'll see what I can do."

Josie Lahm left the trailer, closing the door with a click.

Zanzi made herself comfortable, envious of Tilly, who still slept. Back in The Eyrie, Zanzi's only thoughts had been to destroy ReinCorp from the inside. But there was no way she could gain the level of trust she needed. Milo could be an option, but he was a believer, only wanting revenge because of what they had done to his wife. He still believed, as far as she knew, in ReinCorp's mission, their end game: to recreate the world the way they wanted.

Zanzi needed another way. Brute force? Sneak attack? She knew some of the layout. Maybe it was possible to blow some of the satellite dishes and radio equipment. She was desperate to find Lisa and any patriotic military left standing.

Tilly woke yawning then stretched. "Breakfast?"

"Josie is going to bring us something."

"Breakfast is a funny word, don't you think? I mean, why is it called that? Lunch and dinner too, those are weird enough. My mum used to call dinner tea, but I thought that was a drink. Like those fancy people do, you know – tea and cakes in the afternoon. She would call us, *'Tea is ready.'* My sister and I would look at each other and laugh."

Zanzi smiled. Tilly had a way of making her forget all her anxiety.

"Was your mum English?"

"Nah, she came from Jamaica when she was a little girl. Her and Dad worked together before they had us."

"That explains it. Sometimes the English call dinner tea. It's just their word for it. Even though lots of countries speak English as a language, each country has its own lingo – words that are only used there. Breakfast literally means break your fast. Meaning, you are breaking your fast since you last ate."

"Oh. Yeah. That makes sense," Tilly said.

***

Time dragged on. Josie had been gone for over two hours. Zanzi hated being stuck inside. All she and Tilly could do was peer out the window and watch the camp. She had to give it to ReinCorp; it was well organized. Tents and supplies in neat rows. Personnel with clipboards and tablets, keeping track of everyone. Medical staff giving free consultations. The medication, like everything, would be laced with nanites.

Tilly yelped from the other side of the trailer and jumped away from the curtain.

"What is it?" Zanzi said.

"A man, like that old lady. Cloudy eyes."

A Rabid was pressed against the chain link fence, the mesh digging into its pale flesh, adding to the red slashes. It still wore jeans, though they were torn and dirty. A white T-shirt clung to its bony frame, hanging on by threads. Zanzi craned her neck and looked farther out. Dozens more were advancing toward them, unhurried, slow and steady. Like they didn't have a care in the world, other than the promise of fresh spinal fluid on display.

Shots rang out. Singles at first, followed by rapid gunfire as klaxons rang out through the camp. Boots thumped on the ground.

Trailer doors opened and slammed.

Engines revved.

Rifles barked.

Zanzi shrugged into her rucksack. "We need to go. Stay close to me, okay?"

They eased their way from the trailer. The Rabids had blocked off the best escape route, out over the back fence and into the trees. Louder gunfire erupted from the front of the camp as SUVs and smaller cars tore out. Soldiers ran to the perimeter, looking to a bearded man for directions. Zanzi ducked down between the accommodations and pulled Tilly behind her. Surely this camp would have an armory. Most likely in a plain tent, out of the way. Next to something else so it could be easily guarded, but far enough away that if it went boom no one would be injured or killed. She mapped out the small fraction of the camp she had seen. Next to where the crates had been unloaded had been an odd grouping of five tents, four at each compass point with one in the middle, like the tents themselves were keeping guard. It was worth a shot.

"Stay close to me," she repeated to Tilly.

They zig-zagged their way past RVs. Past trailers and food trucks lined up in rows. Armed men and women ran to the perimeter, ignoring them. Even so, Zanzi dragged Tilly under a caravan and they crawled along on their stomachs, pausing and checking every few meters.

Louder, higher caliber guns rang out, controlled and precise. Then, as quick as the shooting and shouting started, it stopped.

Zanzi cursed. The armory was only a few meters away. Now the same armed men and women walked back down the rows. Some were laughing, others slapping their friends on the back. A couple walked past, bragging at the kill shots they'd executed.

"Did you see its head explode? Like a fucking watermelon. Dumb fuckers."

Shadows of Ash

"Now Juno's going to up the defenses. I don't fancy shivering my ass off on fucking guard duty. Who were those idiots anyhow?"

"Raiders. Lots of reports coming in from the stations. The cleanup crews aren't doing a good enough job."

Their voices faded out of earshot. Tilly sighed and rolled onto her back to stare at the underfloor of the caravan "Dad took us on this trip to Mexico in one of these. He and Mum wanted to look at the Aztec ruins and at the Temple of the Sun, or the moon or something. But all my sister and I wanted to do was eat tacos and try chilies. We camped on the side of the road at the beach, wherever. Dad got so angry at me for picking up stray dogs and smuggling them into the RV. So mad. The whole time I was on that holiday, I hated it. I wanted to spend the summer with my friends at camp, not stuck with my parents and my kid sister." Tilly's eyes glistened with tears. "Now I want nothing more than to be on that holiday again. Then I could warn them about the bad men. The ones that shot Mum and Dad." She wrapped her arms around Zanzi, nestling her face into the nape of Zanzi's neck.

Zanzi held her. Life could be so cruel. She knew all about it. Lives torn apart by greed. By lust and power. Maybe Offenheim was right. Maybe this was necessary. Maybe the planet needed a restart. She shuddered. No, not like this. Fighting fire with fire left the world a pile of ash, like ReinCorp's attempt had. She couldn't accept it as the answer. She had always believed in brilliant minds coming together to solve issues. Not death and destruction. Pain and war.

"Zanzi?" a low voice called out. Legs appeared, slowly walking between the trailers.

"Here," she answered, recognizing Josie's voice. She crawled out, pulling Tilly after her.

TWELVE

TOMARI NUCLEAR POWER PLANT
HOKKAIDO, JAPAN

Bulbs still flickered on and off. Ryan kept his back pressed against the concrete wall, all his senses on high alert. Sliding along, he strained his eyes to peer into the strobing light. Other than that, it was dark and quiet. Not ideal. Not the conditions he wanted. Not when he had to guess what was waiting for him. The Nameless were successful for a lot of reasons, one being that they planned everything. But the old saying held true: no plan survives first contact with the enemy. Coming here should have been easy. In and out, silent and silky. Disappear into the night while Offenheim's and Yamada's soldiers battled it out above.

Someone, or something, had left a trail of destruction. Lights smashed. Doors torn off hinges. Smears of blood leading to Japanese guards who had their heads crushed, brains oozing out onto the floor. Ryan grabbed any spare magazines he could. Cal mirrored his actions on the opposite side of the passageway, with Sam the dog padding silently beside them.

They stopped when the passageway ended in a T-intersection with Sam standing silently next to them.

"Left or right?" Ryan said.

"Left."

The plan – that word again – had been that Ando and Takeshi would be waiting at the blast doors. The air was heavy with moisture and the stench of cleaning alcohol. Deeper they walked, coming level with a row of blue doors made from thick metal, like those in a maximum-security prison. Ryan slid the viewing panel of the first door across and peered in. Like the other cells, these held captives, victims of experiments. Failed, if he had to speculate. Since they were behind the blast doors, these victims must be more dangerous. This cell contained a man with sharp, bony protrusions covering his back and arms. His eyes were staring but vacant, his skin sallow.

The next cell held a woman, her epidermis flaky like she had bad eczema. She hung upside down from the light fixture, clutching it with elongated toes. She laughed maniacally as Ryan and Cal walked past.

Cal whistled softly to get Ryan's attention. In the next cell, a tall, skinny man smiled at Ryan. He was pale, ivory-colored, and covered in scars. Some small, some long, and others angry and raised. Exactly like the other prisoner, Bruno.

Skinny smiled again. "English?"

"Yes," Ryan whispered.

"It's all right, mate. She's got them trapped down in the back. You're safe."

"She?"

"Ebony. The teacher's bloody pet. The queen herself." The man tilted his head back and cackled.

"Who's the queen?"

"You don't work for him, do you?"

"Not permanently, no."

"Good. Good." The man smiled, showing dark-stained teeth. "Name's Gaz, from what I can remember." His accent was twangy. Australian.

"I'm Ryan. This is Cal. How long have you been down here?"

"I don't know mate. Been here so long I've lost track of time. I don't even know what year it is."

"It's 2021."

Gaz's eyes flared and his mouth dropped open. "You're bloody pulling my leg, ain't ya?"

"I'm afraid not. Why?"

Faint screams and shouts filtered down the long corridor, followed by booms and cracks from above. Cal glanced at Gaz but kept her Glock pointed at the doorway. Gaz sat back down on his bed. The cell was grimy but pleasantly furnished. He had a chair, a TV, a writing desk, and a shelf filled with books. A second smaller room was partly partitioned off. The bowl of a toilet peeked around the wall. Nothing like the other cells.

"Sofia. Targets are not at the rendezvous point. Proceeding with caution. Over," Ryan said, nudging his throat mic. He kept his voice low, not knowing what was down here. What exactly had caused all this damage.

"Copy. Yamada is losing ground fast. Get a move on."
"Wilco."

Ryan looked around for a door-release button like in the previous cell block. He spied a board next to a destroyed guard station.

"You're going to need a guide, mate," Gaz said, "someone who can pacify the queen."

"What about the other prisoners? Are they dangerous?"
"Hardly. Most of them are sick anyway."

Cal raised her eyebrows, as if to say, *"It's your rodeo."*

The key to the board was attached to a retractable keyring on the guard's corpse. Like the other victims, his neck was broken, and his skull crushed. The neck was otherwise untouched, telling Ryan that Siphons hadn't killed him.

The thick blue doors screeched as the locking mechanisms released. All but Gaz fled back the way they had entered. Gaz stretched his back and strolled over.

"Thanks mate, ma'am," he said nodding at Ryan and Cal.

"No worries. Which way?" Ryan said.

"Down there." Gaz pointed deeper into the gloom.

He led them on, his pace slow but steady, like he was just taking his dog for a reluctant walk in the park. After another hundred meters the corridor ended at a pair of double doors, painted in the same blue as the cell doors. Bright light flared from beyond the doors. A keypad once attached to the wall had been smashed off, and one of the doors was twisted and warped. Scratches and dents covered the middle. Gaz squeezed through and helped Cal.

Ryan blinked a few times, waiting for his eyes to adjust to the glare. All the surrounding surfaces had been painted white, apart from a solid black line in the middle of the wall. Maybe painted to stop the illusion of a whiteout.

The damage was less in here. Some internal windows had cracks; some had been broken altogether. But even down here there was evidence of people combusting. Ash silhouettes lay on the floor, on chairs, and over workstations.

Gaz didn't pause. He strolled on, seemingly unperturbed by the pervasive deaths. Ryan stared at the back of his head as they walked. Perhaps he had seen too much, become accustomed to it. Desensitized.

They walked past more labs. These were clean rooms with large fans, equipped with hazmat suits with an oxygen supply hanging on hooks. In other rooms, a large window overlooked a small space. Long rubber gloves reached into it so the scientists could perform tasks without coming into contact with it directly. Ryan had seen it before in research facilities that tested viruses.

Farther along they walked past robotics labs and rooms filled with computer equipment.

Gaz stopped outside another doorway. The door had been torn from its hinges and hurled across the room. It was embedded in the sheetrock. Fear gripped Ryan. What on earth had the strength to do that? Gaz grinned and pointed. Ryan followed his gesture.

The room was the size of two basketball courts. At the far end, naked and squatting on a table, was a red-haired woman. Beyond her was a separate room with a large viewing window in which stood two Japanese men, staring. The red-haired woman turned and eyeballed Ryan, cocking her head to the side. Sam whimpered and bounded over to her. She hugged the dog tight and ruffled his ears. Was she responsible for all the damage and the dead security forces?

"Who're your friends, Gaz?" she said.

"They're here for them."

"Of course they are." The red-haired woman turned back and continued her vigil.

Cal stepped into the room and nudged her comms. "Targets located. Over."

"Copy that, Alpha. Booth. Allie. Status?" Sofia said.

"In position." Booth and Allie confirmed.

"Standby," Cal said.

Gaz flicked on a light switch, bathing the front half of the room in light. Glass tanks three meters tall and a meter deep lined each wall like an avenue. Cal gasped and held her hand to her mouth. Ryan still had his weapon trained on the naked woman. He turned his head.

The tanks were filled with deformed humans, preserved in some type of liquid. Some looked like Egyptian mummies, their skin pulled tight over their bones. A couple of tanks held skeletons, twisted and warped, with spiky protrusions like the man Ryan had seen in the cell. Several tanks held bloated remains, covered in boils, and another held a body with a second head growing from its shoulder.

The last few tanks held failed experiments, showcasing the same traits as the prisoners Ryan and Cal had released. A man with freakishly long fingers, but not only that, his ribs had broken through his skin, so it looked like he had two ribcages, external and internal. A woman with misshapen legs, contorted to strange angles. Her top half was covered in incandescent scales and her face was frozen in agony. The final tank held a man. He had thick rolls of skin so large they folded back on themselves, forming clusters of waves that seemed to have suffocated the life out of him.

Ryan clenched his fist at his side but kept his gun trained on the two Japanese men. They were responsible for this building of tragedy. Of Moreau-like research. Part of the sick quest of OPIS, fueled by a desire to reform planet Earth as they wanted.

He ignored the appalling contents of the tanks and, with Cal, strode up to the glass. One of the Japanese men stood clasping his hands behind his back. He was the spitting image of Touma Yamada, right down to the steely gaze. Ryan spotted an intercom and pressed the talk button.

"Your father sent us," he said, addressing Takeshi. "After seeing those prisoners and these tanks, I'm not sure I want to release you."

Takeshi remained silent, as if he knew his father would have the upper hand – the edge.

The other occupant stood and showed Ryan a small, remote-like device. "Hi, I'm Doctor Ando. This opens the door over there. If you subdue A-three, we can come out."

The red-haired woman smiled, then glared at Ando.

"I'm guessing you want him?" Ryan said.

"Oh yeah. The doc and I go way back. He took so much from me, but not my memories. I was Ebony in those days."

"It would appear we have an issue. Yamada has friends of ours. If we don't return his son to him, he'll kill them. I can't let that happen. I swore to protect them, and I hate breaking promises."

Ebony pursed her lips. "When I was young, my father took me to the county fair. I loved it. The smell of corn dogs and cotton candy, and those little roasted nuts with caramel. We played carnival games and rode on the rides. I swore I was going to puke but I never did. While my father was in the toilet, a nice man talked to me. Asked me how my night had been, asked if I wanted the large teddy bear he'd won. I said, 'What about your kids?' He said he wanted me to have it, to just follow him, and it was mine. What kid wouldn't, right? I followed that man. If it wasn't for my schoolteacher seeing me, I would've ended up just another missing girl. A statistic on a milk carton. Years later, and you would've thought I'd learnt my lesson. Nope. Like an idiot, I followed Ando. Who are you to deny me my revenge?"

She unfolded her legs and stood up, her eyes glowing. She had no fear. She took five steps to one side and dressed slowly in a pair of loose cotton pants and a top that hung on a row of hooks. Lastly, she tied her hair into a ponytail.

Shadows of Ash

"That was your handiwork back there?" Ryan said.

"They created the soldier. Now they must do battle with it," Ebony said. "You can take Takeshi, but Ando is mine."

Ryan's finger rubbed the trigger guard. He had seen the empty shell casings, the snapped necks. The crushed skulls. Could he take her out?

"I need both. We can take you with us. Take you home." He crouched slowly to get close to her face, keeping his back to Takeshi and Ando. "Listen. I don't give two shits about the doctor, but I'm guessing he must press that remote to get out. He's never going to do that with you here. Let us go with Takeshi. You can circle back, and Ando is all yours."

"I need him to stay in that room."

"Why?"

"Stay and you'll see."

"Alpha team. Incoming. Multiple hostiles." Booth's voice crackled over the radio.

Cal ducked back into the room. "Incoming," she said.

Ryan acknowledged that he'd heard the warning by flashing the okay sign.

Ebony's head snapped up. She snarled and sprinted from the room in an incredible burst of speed. A barrage of gunfire rattled the lab windows.

Ryan pivoted and waved to Ando and Takeshi. The side door hissed and clicked open. Takeshi shoved past the doctor to stand before Ryan.

"Where is my father?" he said in heavily accented English.

"Waiting with a helicopter."

"Let's go, then. What are you waiting for? The crazy bitch is gone."

Ryan rolled around Takeshi, using his body like an NFL defenseman. He drove his fist into Ando's solar plexus, knocking the wind from the doctor. As expected, the doctor dropped the remote and Ryan drew back his hand to catch it in one swift motion. Using his forward momentum, he crushed his knee into Ando's ribs, pushed him back into the room and slammed the door shut.

Takeshi watched it all with a bemused expression on his face, as if he couldn't care less.

Gunfire from rifles and handguns rattled down the corridors. The battle outside had moved indoors. Yamada had promised a lengthy diversion and he was coming through. Behind the plant were steep hills. The nearest town was miles away, making an attack difficult. A kamikaze mission. The Black Skulls had set their defenses well, digging in and guarding the road and perimeter. What was in here that was so valuable to Offenheim and Yamada? Takeshi?

The screams and shrieks from the hallway grew in intensity.

Carbines barked.

Orders were shouted and the released prisoners howled.

"Booth. What's happening?" Cal said from the doorway that led back into the corridor.

"Ahhh, it's not good. Soldiers and Siphons everywhere. Suggest a different exit."

"Copy that. Keep eyes on."

"Wilco."

Ryan grimaced and turned to Takeshi Yamada. "Is there another way out of the building?"

"There's a small tunnel where the cables run."

"That's how we came in and it's blocked. Any others?"

"On the ground floor. There's an executive exit. In case of a fire."

Ryan nodded and gestured to Cal. "I'll take point." He nudged his throat mic. "We're going to try another exit."

"Copy that."

Cal had her head turned toward him as a blur of reddish pink sprinted past her and skidded to a stop. Ebony. Blood was splashed across her white clothes. She grinned when she saw Ando trapped in the room. She picked up the remote Ryan had left.

Gaz laughed and turned to Ryan. "Have fun out there. Think I'll stay with the queen and watch the show."

Ando's mouth opened in a silent scream as Ebony clicked the remote. As Ryan watched, ports opened on the wall behind him. Bright orange flames shot out as Ryan and Cal hustled Takeshi from the lab, away from its tanks of twisted torture. Away from the years of torment in the name of progress and science. In their time with LK3 they had seen the depths of depravity some were capable of. He hoped Ebony would find her peace.

THIRTEEN

JOINT BASE LEWIS MCCHORD, WASHINGTON

So much of Lisa's work relied on her instincts. Whether it was pursuing hunches or connecting dots. Some she learnt as she navigated her way through the corridors of power. But like everyone she owed a lot to her cavemen ancestors.

Lisa snapped awake. It was 5.01 a.m. The hairs on the back of her neck and on her forearms were standing up, tingling. She strained her ears, listening for any sounds out of place. Nothing. Just the usual sounds of an active base during a crisis. She blinked, letting her eyes adjust. In wasn't particularly dark in the sleeping quarters; the early morning light was enough to see by. The other bunk remained empty. Nothing moved in the room and everything was in place. She sat up and pulled her Glock from under her pillow, comforted by its familiar feel. She breathed deep and detected a faint scent of smoke. Wood smoke, maybe pine or fir, mixed with a chemical smell.

Lisa whipped back the covers and peered through the curtains. The trench the Army had dug for the dead Rabids was ablaze. She sighed and dressed in khaki cargo pants and a black hiking top. She belted a holster with a sheathed Ka-Bar knife to her hip. As she was lacing up her boots, she heard light footsteps in the hallway. Moments later, Monica knocked softly.

"You awake?"

Lisa opened the door. "Morning."

Doctor Monica Johnson's eyes were red and puffy. "You'll want to see this," she said.

***

The lab had a sickly scent of death as Lisa walked in. She took shallow breaths and tried to ignore the unpleasant odor. A white sheet stained with blood covered the specimen they had taken from the highway. Monica had removed his organs and brain and placed them in metal dishes. She pointed to the microscope. "Look in there."

Lisa frowned. She could identify blood cells in plasma, but not the little insect-like creatures swimming around.

"What are those?" she asked.

"No idea. But I can tell you that I found something similar in the blood sample you gave me."

"And?"

"They're not a virus or bacteria, and they're certainly not any pathogen I've ever encountered."

"So what can they be? You must have a theory?"

Lisa stepped back from the microscope, her mind whirring through memories she hadn't accessed in years. It filtered through conferences she had attended, TED Talks on scientific developments – in America and overseas.

"I've spent all my life looking at viruses, microbiology," said Monica. "This is something out of science fiction. Something I never thought possible in my lifetime." She picked up a clipboard of notes. "I've run every test I know, that I *can* here. I really need better equipment. An electron microscope, or even better, a scanning probe microscope. Those babies can see on a molecular nano scale."

Lisa's eyes widened. Nano. Was it possible? She had listened to a talk by an Australian team developing nano-technology to treat degenerative brain disorders. The lady giving the speech had clearly stated that they were years away from trials. But she had shown slides of the most practical shapes the nanites could take. Lisa squinted and looked at the blood sample again. Yes. One of the slides had shown a tick-like shape. Nanotechnology?

"I took a holiday to Hong Kong, once," she said "Spent my days sweating my body weight as I trudged around the streets and up Mount Victoria. Fascinating city. Filled with lights and noise. Old and new. Tradition mixed with futuristic gadgets. By the end of the week, my husband and I had grown bored, so we attended a TED Talk. Extremely smart people. One of the talks was on nanotechnology and its uses in the medical field. They showed graphics of the best possible shapes to use. Shapes like that ... if only we could see it more clearly."

"Huh." Monica scrunched her eyes together. "I need a coffee. Three coffees. I suppose they could be nanites. I'm definitely going to need better equipment."

"Get some sleep. I'll chat to Munroe; he'll send a team out to get you what you need. Make a list."

"You heading back out there?"

"With a small group, yes. It's what I do."

"Even at your age?" Monica said, grinning.

Lisa had always enjoyed Monica's quips and returned the smile. They hugged.

"Take care," Lisa said. "Figure it out and keep me informed. Go through the general only."

She left Monica to her notes and her recent discovery of the possible nanites. Was it true? Had someone used nanites to cause all this?

She didn't have time to ponder the problem further. She exited the building, acknowledging the two guards. Three soldiers saluted as she took the last step. One had sun-bleached blond hair, buzz-cut on the sides and longer on top. His bright blue eyes held her gaze. He was tall, his muscles taut but not bulging like a bodybuilder's. More the physique of a rock climber or gymnast. The other two men were shorter and Hispanic. Their dark eyes stared, but not in a rude way. Like they were assessing her.

"Staff Sergeant Joe Reid, and corporals Clough and Torres reporting, Major Omstead, ma'am."

"On whose orders?"

Shadows of Ash

"General Munroe's, ma'am."

She looked them over again. Like herself, they were dressed in a mixture of fatigues and civilian clothes. Cargo pants, T-shirts, and jackets.

"Well, let's go and get briefed."

"This way, ma'am," Reid said. He brushed a hand through his blond hair then gestured toward a grouping of buildings. Behind them the morning sun crept over the towering presence of Mount Rainier.

Seagulls squawked in the distance. A lone dog barked. Birds sang. On any other day, the morning would be one to savor.

Reid led them inside a small classroom-like office space. It had a whiteboard on a stand at one end, and twenty chairs, all recently cleaned. The stench of the industrial cleaner still hung strong in the air.

Reid, Clough, and Torres took the front three seats while Lisa stood in front of the board. She didn't pick up the marker. She'd agreed with Munroe to keep the mission off the record. Verbal briefing only.

"Let's start with what you know of me."

"Ma'am?" came the reply.

"I realize that this is unconventional, but I'm sure you're aware there's some unconventional shit going on. So what do you know about me? Reid?"

"Nothing, ma'am. Munroe told me to report to you and follow your orders as if he gave them."

"I was in the Marines. FORECON. Green operations. Served in the Gulf wars and 'Stan. Since leaving the corps I've served as a liaison officer for a private company specializing in rescue and locating kidnap victims. Any questions so far?"

Three heads shook.

"Very good. Any of you have recon experience?"

Reid raised his hand. "Ma'am, we all do. We were long-range surveillance before the pencil heads nipped it in the butt back in seventeen. Now we're part of the Battlefield Surveillance brigade. Two hundred and first."

"Two hundred and first," Clough and Torres said together.

Lisa snorted. That wily old bastard Munroe had told her she could choose her team, all the while knowing he had these boys on base.

"It's bud."

"What is ma'am?" Reid said.

"The saying is nipped in the bud not butt. A common eggcorn."

"A what ma'am?" Torres stared at Lisa like a deer in headlights. Reid was grinning at her.

"Never mind. Back to the mission. I'm sure you all felt and witnessed what some are calling the Combusting. I know, stupid name, but whatever it was, it was terrifying. It's even worse out there. The highways and roads are clogged with crashed vehicles and burning wrecks. Trains have derailed. Planes slammed into mountains. Packs of the Rabids roaming the streets. Let me be clear. It's chaos, pure and simple. On top of all that, we have an organization executing survivors. Their uniforms are all black. They have a Black Skull insignia, and they seem to favor Austrian weapons. Our mission is to locate these traitors, find their Forward Operating Base, and, if possible, their headquarters. They must be operating from somewhere close by. So we'll start local and circle out. This is a green operation. In case you don't know what that means, if we must fire our weapons on the enemy, it's a failure. Recon and intelligence gathering only. If the enemy engages, then by all means we will defend ourselves. Am I making myself clear?"

"Yes, ma'am."

"Get some grub. We move out at zero-eight-hundred. On foot."

One raised his hand.

"Yes, Clough is it?"

"Torres, ma'am."

"What is it, Corporal? And let's drop the ma'am. I feel like I'm in the South. Omstead is fine."

"Are we expected to wear those Hazmat suits out there?"

"Only until we're clear of the base."

"Ma'am?"

"That will be all. Zero-eight-hundred. Load up."

Lisa walked briskly away from the briefing and quickened her pace toward Munroe's office. She needed to clear up a few points before she left.

FOURTEEN

TOMARI NUCLEAR POWER PLANT
HOKKAIDO, JAPAN

Ryan groaned. What else could go wrong? They had made it past the cells and the blast doors, and then the doors had slammed shut – either Ebony's doing or some sort of security protocol.

There had been a battle between the former occupants of the cells and the Black Skulls. Most of the cell occupants lay dead, their bodies riddled with bullets. Offenheim's men hadn't fared much better. Several were torn apart, arms, legs, and entrails splattered all over the floor. The man with the thick, bark-like skin stomped up and down the corridor, punching any commando foolish enough to get close to him and swatting away bullets as if they were annoying insects. Ryan noted that he never strayed farther than twenty meters from the blast doors. Was he protecting the place?

"Booth. Status?"

"In position at the access door."

"Give us a minute. Might need you."

"Copy. Holding."

Ryan reached back to his rucksack and unzipped a second, smaller radio.

"Yamada. This is Connors. Target acquired. Need immediate back up."

Hissing and static hummed. *"Stand by. Position?"*

"Pinned down at the blast doors."

"Can you make it to the roof?"

"Negative. It's too hot. Execute the back-up plan."

"Hold tight. We're having trouble amplifying the signal from the wand devices. Are you sure you want to do this?"

"Affirmative."

In truth, no, Ryan didn't want to go through with the back-up plan. It was insane and risky, if not near impossible, given the time constraints. Sofia had come up with it as a failsafe: use the handheld wands to broadcast the kill signal to Offenheim's men. They had debated most of the flight whether to attempt this before sending men into the fray, but without scanning everyone, there was no way of knowing their codes. Instead, they had scanned everyone on the mission and put their codes onto a separate safe list. It had been a painstaking task, with Goro assisting Sofia.

"Sofia. Yamada's going to initiate the back-up plan. Are we in the clear?" Ryan said.

"Confirmed. We are safe. I found something you need to know while trawling through his servers. I got access to a YamTech satellite."

"What is it?"

"It's a countdown. Wave two is happening in a little less than four days."

"What?" Ryan said. He pushed his back harder against the concrete, sweat suddenly beading on his forehead.

Cal flashed a stunned look at him, eyes wide. She mouthed, "What the fuck?"

"You have to be kidding me?" Booth said.

This changed everything. Here they were, helping one of the men responsible for the events of the last few days, and wave two was happening in less than four days. Not enough time to destroy the satellite installation – nowhere near.

"Stay focused. Allie, we need you here," Ryan said.

"Copy. On my way," she said. Her voice was strained but calm.

A pained howl broke through the cacophony of battle sounds. Ryan raised his rifle to scan the corridor for targets. He spotted eight. Four Black Skulls on either side. Two high-fived as the man with the thick bark-skin howled once more before falling silent, bleeding from a plethora of wounds. Ryan steeled himself for battle.

They had tried and failed to get back into the facility through the blast doors. Takeshi had attempted his personal code to no avail. Simply put, they were trapped. Trapped and relying on an untested theory.

"Heads up, guys. Sending you a gift," Booth said over the comms.

"What?"

"Siphons. About ten. Hungry-looking too."

"Copy."

Ryan checked if Cal had heard. She nodded and slid her finger onto the trigger. He turned and handed Takeshi his Glock.

"Know how to use this?"

"More or less."

"Good. Only use it as a last resort. Always stay behind us. When we move, you do. Understand?"

Takeshi responded by gripping the handgun.

The Black Skulls made no attempt to advance on their position as the concrete pillars supporting the blast doors gave ample protection. The commandos were less protected, but anytime Ryan or Cal tried to fire on them, they responded in kind. It was a stand-off. The Nameless couldn't go anywhere.

The first Siphon reached them a few minutes later, stumbling and groaning, saliva drooling from its mouth. Its head snapped around. It was quickly followed by a second and a third, moaning and gnashing their teeth.

The Black Skulls split into two groups, four firing on the Siphons while the other four kept their rifles trained on The Nameless.

More Siphons arrived and were greeted with callous gunfire. They fell to the floor, landing on the dead prisoners. Still more Siphons came, groaning at the promise of the meal they desired. Far more than the ten Booth had mentioned. There had to be at least thirty converging on Ryan and Cal's position.

"Connors," Booth said

"Go ahead."

"On our way to assist. There might be a few more than I thought."

"No kidding," Ryan said. He checked the safety was off, breathed out and burst from behind the pillar. He squeezed the trigger and placed three bullets into the chest of the first commando.

Pain rocketed up Ryan's leg and he stumbled, caught his balance then adjusted his aim to the next Black Skull, hitting him in the arm and chest.

The other commandos were too busy shooting at the Siphons crowding into the corridor to realize what was happening behind them. Ryan and Cal shot them without a second thought. Then they put a bullet in each of their heads to be sure. Ryan had seen what these men were capable of. He killed them with a clear conscience.

"You're bleeding," Cal said as she reloaded her rifle.

"I'm fine. Just a scratch."

With no time to check the wound, he hoped the nanites would do their job and stop the bleeding before closing the wound as if it had never happened.

"Booth?"

"Almost there."

Ryan grabbed the handheld. "Yamada. Any progress?"

Adrian J Smith

"Some. Another ten minutes." His voice filtered through as a whisper.

A Siphon shrieked, breaking up the radio communication. Cal silenced it with a three-round burst before swinging to her left and dropping two more. These Siphons moved slower than others they'd encountered. Back on Koya, the monks and workers had sprinted toward them. These walked. Fast walking, sure, but it made them easier targets.

"Let's move. Cal, take point," Ryan said. He signaled for Takeshi to stay behind him.

Pops of handgun fire echoed down the corridor, dispersing a knot of Siphons. Booth and Allie burst through before turning and firing at the Siphons.

Ryan took down three more and urged the others on. They had to make the cable tunnel. It was the only way out.

"We got more Black Skulls incoming," Booth said.

"Understood. Keep moving."

Ryan adjusted the shot selector to single. He was down to his last magazine.

Slowly, The Nameless and Takeshi advanced along the wide corridor, shooting any Siphon that hindered their advance. They passed the cells and stepped over and around the guards with their broken necks. Necks that had now been fed upon. Dead Siphons with gaping holes in their skulls lay next to them.

Allie shrugged. "I had to give them mercy."

They made it to seventy meters from the tunnel entry without any further resistance, only to be greeted by Siphons and Black Skulls leapfrogging each other along the corridor. The commandos would shoot a Siphon, then spin and rake the walls with rounds.

Bullets slammed into the concrete walls, sending chips and fine dust into Ryan's face. He pivoted and released a couple of rounds in the commandos' direction. They scattered but kept firing.

A new and chilling howl sounded from the front of the building. It was joined by a chorus of others, filling the early morning. Ryan flinched. He'd never heard anything like it. It was like a wolf but not quite. More a cross between a wolf and a howler monkey. Whatever it was, it was loud. Within a few seconds the howl was nearby and coming up fast, echoing from the way they'd come. Ryan renewed his efforts to make it to the tunnel, but the Siphons and commandos still blocked their way, and there was still fifty meters to go.

"I'm running low. Cal?"

She tossed him a spare magazine and jammed in a fresh one herself. "Last two. Make it count."

"Any idea what's coming, Takeshi?" said Ryan.

Takeshi Yamada was slumped forward, his eyes downcast. He held the Glock loosely at his side.

"Takeshi!" Ryan said again, snapping his fingers.

Yamada's son looked up and frowned. He listened to the growing howls. "Horkew Kamuy has returned for his revenge."

Cal took down a Siphon that had ambled too close. "What's he saying?"

"He said Horkew someone is coming for his revenge," Ryan said.

"Who's Horkew, Takeshi?"

"A wolf spirit. Angry."

The howls grew louder. The Black Skulls and Siphons stopped fighting and turned toward the noise. Booth and Allie snapped their heads around searching for the source of the noise. Ryan pressed his rifle against his shoulder and peered through the scope. At first they were just blurs of white. Then their shapes slowly came into focus. It was difficult to count them, they were moving so fast. Maybe half a dozen, but no more than ten. They had thick white fur and red eyes, and their skulls were deformed, their foreheads squished back and their jawlines long. Each creature had a mouth full of threatening jagged teeth. Ryan shook his head in disbelief. It was like a bad '80s horror movie come to life. Being attacked by werewolves. Not quite. More like a beast trapped between a wolf and a human. They ran on four legs, but those legs were elongated, twisted and sinewy.

"What the actual fuck are these things. Satan's hounds?" Cal cursed.

The Hounds barreled into Black Skulls and Siphons alike, tearing into them. Cal opened fire, sweeping her carbine from side to side. Ryan followed suit. As they fired, he advanced toward the tunnel entrance. It was tantalizingly close at just ten meters away. A quick jog and they would be in and away.

"I'm out!" Ryan shouted, patting his combat vest in case he had missed a magazine.

"Me too," Cal said.

Shadows of Ash

Allie and Booth were still firing. Commandos, Siphons, Hounds. A chaotic mess of fighting bodies. Using her foot, Allie kicked a dead commando's rifle over. Cal grabbed it, reloaded her own and moved forward slowly until she was above the commando. She grabbed two more magazines and threw one to Ryan.

The Hounds howled, tearing into the Siphons' flesh. One broke through the knot and sprinted toward Allie. Cal shouted a warning and managed to score a shot to its torso. It barely flinched. The bullet only seemed to anger it more. It swiped at Allie with a clawed fist, its fingers abnormally long. She took a hit in the shoulder and spun into the tunnel door.

"Allie!" Booth shouted. He released a full burst into the creature's chest. The Hound stumbled and fell to its stomach, blood flowing from its open wounds. It snarled and swiped at Booth as he drew his pistol and shot it in the head.

Ryan grabbed Takeshi and yanked him toward the tunnel. This was their chance. "Let's go!"

Booth reached the cable tunnel first and helped the still-dazed Allie inside. Ryan took up a covering position, laying down suppressing fire. The Hounds sensed that some of their prey was escaping. Several leant back and let out ear-splitting shrieks. Then, with almost supernatural speed, they attacked.

"Hurry!" Ryan shouted. He didn't bother aiming, he just fired. The mass of white fur staggered. Two Hounds broke away and scampered up to the ceiling, sharp claws digging into the concrete as if it were soft clay.

Cal yanked Ryan back. "Get in."

A klaxon blared, so loud it drowned out the cracks of the rifles. It wailed three times, then blared once before repeating. Ryan ignored it and went to slam the door home. The Hounds, snarling, baring their ferocious teeth and paws, covered in matted white fur, gripped the door.

Cal grabbed Ryan's collar. "C'mon. Move. Forget about them." She thumbed her throat mic.

"Sofia. We're coming in hot."

A monotone voice replaced the blaring alarm. *"Attention. Please evacuate."*

The voice repeated the same three words over and over. It didn't give any indication as to why. Just that they should. Was it the nuclear power plant? It shouldn't be. That had been offline for years, running at minimal power to keep the last remaining reactor cool.

"Takeshi. What's that alarm for?" Ryan said.

"Self-destruct. Ando must have activated it."

Takeshi continued to roll down the tunnel, offering no further explanation.

As Ryan predicted, the wolf-like creatures crawled into the tunnel. Barking, and letting out the occasional howl, they moved steadily forward on their bellies and knees, sniffing and gnashing their teeth.

Ryan retrieved his Glock and tossed the HK aside. He was out of ammo, its .22 caliber incompatible with his pistol. Plus, he didn't want the extra weight.

One of the Hounds got within a few meters. He shot it. Immediately two more crawled over the dead creature. The tunnel gave the escaping humans a slight advantage;

though the Hounds were fast and strong, they were big, their limbs long, like they had been stretched to almost breaking point. Out in the open with room to maneuver, they were formidable, but down here in this cramped space they had to slide along on their stomachs, dragging their tall frames. If the infiltration team kept away from the sharp teeth and claws, the Hounds were just a hindrance.

A Hound crawled onto the metal grating the cables were tied to and pulled itself along, long nails latching onto the holes. Ryan leant back on his skateboard to face up. When there was a gap in the rack, he fired a quick burst. His first couple of attempts were mistimed, the bullets pinged harmlessly off the metal. The Hound gained momentum and was soon above him, slashing its claws and spitting through its teeth. The cable shelf saved Ryan. The creature couldn't get around it. The creature howled and burst ahead. Ryan rolled onto his stomach and emptied his magazine into the creature's back. It cried and shrieked one last time before becoming still.

The other Hounds fell back, keeping their distance – for now.

After twenty minutes, Cal and Takeshi, quickly followed by Allie and Booth, exited the cable tunnel. Ryan scrambled under the trapdoor and accepted Booth's firm grip as he hauled him through. Then slammed the trapdoor back into place and locked it shut.

"Everyone okay?" Ryan said.

The Nameless and Takeshi grimaced in reply. Cal alone met his eyes. Hers looked haunted by what they'd seen down in Ando's lab. The cells with imprisoned experiments.

The tanks filled with mutants. And now the Hounds. Horrifying killing machines. Had they been dogs once? All those humans and animals, treated so cruelly, mere test subjects, not beings full of life, love, laughter, and potential. Objects to be discarded when they no longer had any use.

The team had hardly caught their breath when the ground shook beneath them and a split second later an explosion rolled out over the bay.

Ryan ran up the stairs two at a time and saw orange plumes of flames reaching into the early morning sky as if seeking the sun, wishing to rejoin the molten star. The ground shook again, and three more explosions rocked the squat building above the lab. The trapdoor thumped as flames shot out of the ventilation shafts along the length of the tunnel they'd just traversed. Black Skulls sped away in their Humvees and SUVs.

Ryan's radio crackled to life. *"Are the doctor and Takeshi safe?"*

Ryan gritted his teeth. He glanced at Sofia; she gave a barely noticeable twitch to tell him she had made sure her daughter Keiko and Hogai were safely off any kill list.

"Takeshi is safe, but Ando didn't make it. I'm sorry," Ryan said.

There was a long pause filled with squelching. *"That wasn't part of the agreement."*

"The agreement was for Takeshi. Later, you added Ando. I'm sorry, but we barely got your son out."

"This is a disaster. Years of research blown sky high. I hope for your sakes that the backup server has done its jo—"

Shadows of Ash

Sudden bursts of gunfire echoed over the airwaves.

"Shit. We got incoming!" Booth warned. "Six groups of hostiles, approaching fast. Three from the north and three from west. And more of those Hounds." Booth was peering out the window into the car park.

Ryan pulled Takeshi behind the main bank of servers, next to the trapdoor. He pressed the talk button. "Yamada?"

"We're pinned down at the cell phone tower."

"We have incoming hostiles. Initiate back-up plan. Now!"

Ryan didn't wait for a reply. Instead, he kept low and glanced out the corner of the window. He spotted the approaching commandos, their dark uniforms silhouetted against the dawn.

As before, the pain started behind Ryan's ear. To be more specific, inside his ear. It reached out like a poltergeist squeezing his brain. He gritted his teeth as a quick flash of doubt struck him. Had Sofia stuffed up the code?

As quick as it began, the pain vanished. He looked around. Allie, Cal, and Sofia were huddled together, holding hands. Booth had his knees drawn up to his chest, a faraway look in his eyes. Takeshi stared blankly, his mouth open in shock.

Screams and howls came from outside as the kill code took effect. The Black Skulls contorted and twisted on the ground, Heckler and Koch rifles forgotten, backs arched, convulsing. As Ryan watched, their skin first turned gray, then black. Their flesh lost density and crumbled into ash.

The Hounds were unaffected apart from sinking to the ground, tails between their legs, letting out long howls.

Cal laced her fingers into Ryan's. He knew what she was thinking. Had Keiko and Hogai survived?

FIFTEEN

PORTLAND, OREGON

"Quick. Put these on," Josie said. She handed Tilly and Zanzi two Hazmat suits.

"What was all that shooting?" Zanzi asked as she struggled to do up the zip.

"We've been having problems with raiders since yesterday. They like to test the defenses periodically. This group herded the Rabids as a distraction." Josie shook her head. "Idiots. We're heavily armed. Now Juno's going to electrify the fence, and he's posting double guards. So this is our only chance to get you out of here."

"Juno?" Zanzi said.

"Guy in charge."

Zanzi made sure all her hair was tucked into the hood of the suit before resting the mask on top of her head, ready to drop into place. Then she helped Tilly. For once, the young woman remained silent. She was probably still thinking of the last vacation she went on with her family to Mexico when her parents were killed. For as long as she'd known her, Zanzi had wanted to ask Tilly how she'd ended up at The Eyrie, but she could never draw up the courage.

How did you ask someone how they became an orphan? Was it rude?

Shaking off her questions, she followed Josie between the trailers and tents filled with supplies, with Tilly close behind. Armed men and women rushed to the perimeter, rifles clasped.

Josie slid back the door of a white Ford Transit van and ushered them into the back seat.

"If anyone asks, you're my assistants. Okay?"

"Sure. What's the plan?" Zanzi asked.

"One of the patrols spotted a group of survivors that had been picked off by the Rabids. They managed to shoot a couple of the Rabids. It was early this morning, so the specimens will be fresh."

"How far?"

"Across town, maybe ten miles. You can sneak away while we're taking samples."

"What about you?"

"I'd better stay put for now," Josie said as she checked that their suits were fitted correctly. "There's a park near the hospital. Give me two days, then meet me there at midnight."

"Two days from now?" Zanzi said. Already she was trying to figure out where to hide for those forty-eight hours.

"Yes. I need time to learn more, gather some things."

They didn't have to wait long before more personnel arrived. Two more scientists, both wearing glasses, and three armed men dressed in black uniforms. One of the armed men slid behind the wheel and gunned the engine. The van was waved through the gate without having to slow down. They turned left and headed into the city center. Zanzi stared out the window at the abandoned buildings. Most had doors open to the elements and piles of ash were still present. Some buildings had been looted.

They'd only driven a couple of miles when the driver cursed and swung the wheel a fraction before something slammed into the Ford Transit sending it spinning, tires screeching. The driver strained, determined to keep the vehicle upright, but they were hit for a second time. The tires hit the curb and the van toppled onto its side before grinding to a halt. The passengers' grunts and cries of pain were drowned out by gunfire.

Pop ... Pop ... Pop.

Looking out the broken window, Zanzi spotted several pairs of legs, leather-clad and wearing boots. She checked on Tilly; the young woman blinked but was alert. The driver and armed men returned fire as they all scrambled from the crashed van. Rounds pinged off the vehicle, adding to the noise that thumped inside Zanzi's skull.

Whoever had crashed into the van had given them an opportunity to escape in the confusion.

Zanzi glanced at Josie, noticing the doctor was clutching her left shoulder. "Okay?"

The doctor shook her head. "Broken something."

"We have to go. This is our best chance."

"I'm not going to make it far. Go. Good luck."

"You're coming with us. You're our ticket inside The Eyrie," Zanzi insisted.

"I can't, Zanzi. ReinCorp will come looking for me. You're better off on your own."

She shuffled over to Josie, ignoring the doctor's protests. "Tilly, give me a hand."

Together, they managed to drag Josie free of the wreckage. The Black Skulls were exchanging periodic shots with a motorcycle gang. Five, wearing leather pants and denim jackets and leather vests covered in patches. The gang members had taken shelter behind an overturned car, occasionally popping up to fire. The commandos had overcome their shock at being blindsided and had regrouped, flashing hand signals. One commando popped up and lay down covering fire as two others sprinted in opposite directions in a flanking maneuver. The fight would be over in another few minutes. If Zanzi, Josie, and Tilly were going to go, it had to be now.

Zanzi scanned the vicinity. The Transit had come to rest against the bank of a shallow culvert. She followed the culvert to where it emptied into a stormwater system. Up ahead was a street lined with shops. She recognized a narrow entrance to the Docklands mall. With the Black

Skulls distracted, the trio ducked into the drain. The gunfire faded as they crouched low and moved away. Zanzi ignored the other shops and buildings, instead focusing on the mall. With dozens of shops, there was a better chance for them to hide until the firefight ended.

They entered the mall through its wide sliding doors, which whisked open and closed behind them with only a slight bump. Countless piles of ash littered the floor, the seats surrounding the fountain and the still-humming escalators. Next to a hot dog stand were three frozen ash forms. Two short figures huddled together, and a taller form stretched out as if reaching for the hot dog that had fallen out of his hand to land, half eaten, a yard away. The short couple had a bag of heavy metal T-shirts. One had been pulled out and lay in a crumpled heap next to them.

Zanzi played the scene out in her head. The couple had been showing the taller figure their purchases as they ate hot dogs. Perhaps they were all going to a concert that night. She kicked the crumpled T-shirt with her foot. Ghost was the name of the band.

Tilly and Josie flinched as throaty motorcycle engines echoed through the mall.

"Up there," Zanzi said.

"They could help," Josie said.

"They were the ones fighting."

"Really?"

"Yes. I saw bikers."

Josie shrugged and peered deeper into the mall. The roar of the engines grew, rebounding off the glass and tiles. It sounded like dozens of bikes.

Zanzi paused on the escalator. "Josie!"

Josie jerked her head around as three Harley Davidsons roared into the foyer and squealed to a stop next to the fountain. The riders laughed and hopped off their bikes before grasping their AR-15s.

"Let those wankers come to us," the tallest of the three said. A snake tattoo coiled up his arm, its head poking up above his vest collar. He turned away from the women. On the back of his jacket, the words "Outcast Mongrels" surrounded an emblem of a bulldog wearing a top hat and monocle.

"I told you smashing their fucking vehicle wouldn't work, Grub. They're armed."

"Shut your piehole, Mutton, or I'll shove this gun up your ass," Grub snarled as he shoved the barrel of his carbine into Mutton's face. "I'm president now, so do as you're fucking told. Now spread out and find those three hot chicks I saw running away."

"How do you know they were chicks? All I saw was bomb suits."

"'Coz I saw their heads. Now fucking look for them."

Mutton grumbled something inaudible and ambled away, his rifle held casually by his side.

Zanzi ducked down and hustled into the nearest shop, waving Tilly and Josie on. From the looks on their faces, they'd also heard the conversation.

They passed rack after rack of clothing. Suits and dresses. Shelves of shoes, handbags, and wallets. Zanzi headed for the back of the store and flicked off light switches as she found them. With the power still on, it was too damn bright inside the shop. The mall hadn't changed when everyone's lives had stopped in one way or another. Either you were dead, a Rabid, or living in the nightmare that was now. Zanzi clung to Tilly's hand and flicked her eyes from side to side, searching for a hiding place or, better yet, an exit. Surely these stores had back entrances, where the goods were delivered? She pushed through a door marked *Staff Only*. A long corridor stretched in both directions, the air here cool. Directly across the corridor was an open lunchroom. Josie was already making her way there and started to strip off the bulky Hazmat suit.

"Lock that door. Give us some time," she said, "I might need some help getting this off."

Tilly gently rolled back Josie's suit.

Josie groaned and stomped her foot. "Find something to cut it off."

Tilly found a pair of scissors in a drawer and sliced through the fabric. Once she'd cut the suit off the doctor, she laid it on the table and cut a large triangle, making a sling for Josie's injured arm.

Josie sighed in appreciation. "How'd you learn to do that?"

"Girl Scouts. Mum took me." Tilly smiled, unzipping her own suit.

The door leading to the clothing store thumped and rattled in its frame. Grunts came from the other side. Zanzi quickly grabbed the discarded suits and shoved them in a cupboard. She kept the gas masks though, knowing how useful they could be. The trio glanced at the door as they crept past and down the corridor.

Zanzi instinctively headed north, back the way they had come. She hoped the corridor led to a loading dock of some kind. She wanted to avoid elevators and fire escapes. Each door they went by was conveniently labeled with a store name. Most were clothing stores or gift shops, though one or two were food places selling frozen yogurt and candy. She stopped at one marked *Adventure Sports*.

She tried the handle. The door swung open with silent ease.

"Zanzi," Josie whispered. "C'mon."

Zanzi pointed through the open doorway. It was too tempting not to investigate the store. It could have weapons. Guns. Knives. Food like MREs. All the supplies they needed.

"Zanzi," Josie whispered again, more urgently this time.

"We need supplies. This is our best bet."

"The bikers?"

Since they'd thumped on the door, there hadn't been any further indication of the Outcast Mongrels' whereabouts. Was it worth the risk?

Yes. "We need weapons," Zanzi said. "Without them, people like them will kill us." She stepped into the store and Tilly followed. A door crashed open farther down the hallway. Josie yelped and bolted inside.

"I see you, bitch!" one yelled.

Zanzi recognized Grub's voice. He whooped and sprinted down the corridor, his boots thumping on the concrete. Bullets thudded into the sheetrock, sending pieces of plaster flying.

Shadows of Ash

***

Lisa waited patiently outside General Munroe's office. It reminded her of her Army days. Waiting. Waiting for orders. Waiting for food. Waiting for something to happen. Anything. When it did, it was normally zero to a hundred in an instant.

The door opened and two sergeants left the office, hats grasped in their hands. Neither made eye contact nor acknowledged Lisa in any way.

"Omstead," Munroe's voice boomed from inside.

"Sir."

"Come in. Shut that door."

He waited until she was standing in front of his desk before sitting. Lisa cast her eyes over his décor, or lack thereof. Only one painting adorned the walls. A print of Edward Hopper's *Nighthawks*. Munroe's dark timber desk was just as bare, save a framed photo of his family.

"I've been on the horn to Secretary Ward. Now President Ward. Sworn in this morning."

"President?"

"Exactly. He was the most senior politician left. President Jackson. Vice-President Roberts. Cohen. Hudson, all gone. They're still completing a census but are operating on a skeleton crew. Reports are coming in from every major city. The black-uniformed soldiers you reported are sweeping through. Mass casualties confirmed. All turned to ash. FEMA camps are being set up. We don't know which are the real deal and which are fake. It's a shit storm out there. I have a report of heavy fighting at the camp in Portland. We'll take care of anyone we find up here. I want you and your team down in Oregon for now." Munroe glanced up at Lisa and slid a printed piece of paper across the desk to her. "This came in. Direct from the president."

Lisa spent a few moments scanning the paper. It contained a list of names. Hers was third. Ryan and Cal's names were there too. There were fifteen in total, and she recognized them all from various agencies and private security companies. Agencies like LK3. Retired special forces who had started up firms specializing in kidnap resolution. Finding people. Tracking down smugglers and criminals hiding in countries with no extradition agreement. She smiled at the last name on the list: Brandon Taylor. Needed to locate someone and solve a problem? Brandon was your man. He was ex-LK5 and worked solo. He was all but a ghost. A wraith. No one had physically seen him in years. Her last intel placed him in South East Asia.

"What's this?" Lisa said.

"The president's main suspects. Traitors, apparently."

Lisa coughed and almost choked. "Traitors? All these men and women have served. Bled for this country. Done things that would make even your skin crawl. Those brown-nosers on Capitol Hill should be giving them medals, not adding them to a list. They may be a lot of things but traitors they are not. I'm on that list. When have I ever done anything but serve America?"

"I agree with you, Omstead."

"What are your orders from the president?"

Shadows of Ash

"Locate and, if alive, neutralize any persons on this list."

Lisa gave a humorless chuckle. "Good luck finding Taylor or Connors."

Munroe stood up, shredded the list and sat back down. "Take your team and get out of here. Find out exactly what's going on. It's like we're driving at night, blindfolded. We have a few operational satellites, with more coming online, and nothing but conflicting reports. Avoid civilians but give me locations and numbers."

"Understood. Do I have any support? Drones, men?"

"Negative. You're on your own for now."

"I don't like it, Munroe. Watch your back. Oh, and Doctor Johnson needs some medical equipment. She found something strange in the specimen but needs to test her theory further."

"I'll give her everything she needs."

"Thank you, sir."

Lisa hurried from the office building and went straight to the armory and the quartermaster. With the general's orders, she could take whatever she needed. Knowing their mission was recon and stealth, she opted for small and light arms. She selected a Glock 17 and an MP5, and five extra magazines for both. Next, she grabbed a dozen MREs, water, field kit, spotting scope and NVGs, and shoved them all into a tactical pack.

After securing all the gear, she met Reid, Torres, and Clough in the forecourt. She nodded a greeting. "Munroe has issued new orders. We're taking my vehicle south. I'll fill you in on the way."

"Ma'am," was the only response.

SIXTEEN

TOMARI NUCLEAR POWER PLANT
HOKKAIDO, JAPAN

The Nameless still had a few magazines of ammo for their handguns. Sofia handed out what little they had as they prepared for the Hounds sniffing around outside. The RHIB was tied to the end of the jetty. Close, but so far.

The trapdoor to the cable access tunnel thumped, and muffled howls broke through in the hushed silence. Ryan turned and looked at Takeshi Yamada. He still hadn't moved. His face still wore the same expression.

"Takeshi?" Ryan said, giving him a nudge

Takeshi slumped over like a drunk falling off a barstool and collapsed to the floor.

Booth crouched and felt his neck for a pulse. He shook his head and looked at Ryan.

"Sorry, Connors. He's dead."

"Are you sure?"

"One hundred percent."

Sofia groaned, checked for a pulse herself and groaned again. "Damn it all the hell." She stood, shook her head, and shoved her laptop and tablet into a rucksack. "He was our ticket home. Keiko and Hogai's survival depended on him."

Ryan searched Takeshi's body, looking for wounds or any other indication as to what had killed him. He hadn't turned to ash or bones like the Black Skulls outside. So what then?

"I'm sorry, Sofia. We'll figure something out."

"What, Connors? What?" Sofia said, her dark Columbian eyes flaring. "What have we got left? Are you going to pull a rabbit out of your ass?"

"Hey, Sofia. C'mon. We all risked our lives to get him out."

"Don't 'c'mon' me, Cal. You... You disappeared for three bloody years. We all thought you were dead. I buried your fucking coffin, for Pete's sake. Held Zanzi while she cried her eyes out at your wake as your mother and father berated Ryan for putting you in a dangerous situation. We cried for you, Cal. It tore our hearts out, and then you come walking back like some savior. Well, look around. You didn't save shit!"

Cal pulled her lips back tight and her face turned red. "Don't you think I know that! It wasn't like I had a choice.

Shadows of Ash

It was that or everyone died. Everyone. You, Eddie, Keiko. Booth and his family, and especially mine. Offenheim gave me a choice. My service for your lives. I spent every night lying awake knowing the pain I must've been causing. But do you know what got me through? Knowing that you were alive and breathing. If you were all still alive, then we had a chance. A tiny sliver of a chance, sure, but it was all I had."

Cal sat back down and pinched the bridge of her nose. The two women glared at each other, but nothing more was said. It was out there now, the emotions that had been simmering just beneath the remains of their friendship. The Nameless were professionals. They had done their job to the best of their abilities. Sometimes, despite their best efforts, things didn't work out well. Sofia had said what they had all thought at one time or another.

Ryan jumped up. "Allie, what's happening out there?"

"The wolf things are sniffing at the ash remains."

"Keep watching. Anything changes, give us a heads up." He grasped Cal's shoulder and turned to Sofia and Booth. "Listen up. I know emotions are high. Our mission failed, putting the kids in danger, but we are The Nameless. This is what we do. We get out of tough situations, think on our feet. We still have a greater mission. Stopping Offenheim. Now, as we have done before, it's time to put aside our differences and do our jobs. For the many."

"For the many," Cal, Sofia, and Booth murmured in response.

"Sofia. You know the frequency for the wand devices. Can we jam it, deny Yamada access to our nanites? If it comes to that..."

"It's possible yes. I'll need something powerful to broadcast the signal, and all the time you can give me."

"Something like what's on top of this building?" Ryan said.

Sofia grunted. "Yeah. That'll do. I need to find the right server. Could take some time."

"Good. Cal, you help Sofia. Your computer skills are sharp. Allie, Booth, we're on guard duty."

The Nameless clicked into job mode, the emotion and argument isolated, to be discussed at a more opportune time. As he walked up the stairs to the first floor, Ryan's radio hummed to life.

"Connors. Do you copy?" Yamada said.

"Go ahead."

"We're on our way. Did the plan work at your end? Everyone accounted for?"

"Affirmative. All safe. Hostiles neutralized. But we have some wolf-like creatures sniffing around. Would advise to keep clear until we've taken care of it. Keiko and Hogai? Over."

"Safe. Say again. Wolf creatures?"

"I don't know how else to explain it. Dr. Ando was into some weird shit. Think werewolves. Takeshi called them Horkew something."

"Horkew Kamuy? Ando, what have you done?" Touma Yamada's voice trailed off. He barked orders to someone before speaking back to Ryan.

"I have a few men left after our skirmish with the Black Skulls. We'll come to you."

"ETA?"

"Twenty minutes."

"Copy."

Ryan switched the radio off and thumbed his throat mic. "Nameless. We have twenty minutes. Make it count. Give me a SITREP."

"We found the server that broadcasts the data. I'm attempting to utilize it. It'll be close. Over."

"Booth?" Ryan said.

"Hound creatures are sniffing around."

"Copy. Allie, keep watching. Booth, I need you back down in the server room. Bring an office chair."

Ryan had a plan in mind for the exchange. It was absurd, but it was their only shot. He met Booth on the stairs and helped him lift the wheeled office chair down into the server room. Without a word, they lugged Takeshi onto the chair. Using duct tape from Ryan's satchel, they taped him upright.

"This isn't going to work," Booth said.

"It only has to give us a few minutes. Enough time to take Keiko and Hogai while Sofia jams the wand frequency."

He let Booth wheel Takeshi's body to the foot of the stairs. He was curious about how he had died. As far as he could ascertain, he had no visible wounds. It had to be the back-up plan. When Yamada had activated the nanites in the soldiers, something had happened to Takeshi as well. Maybe his alpha nanite was faulty? Whatever it was, it had put them in a sticky position.

"Sofia," he said, pivoting back. She looked up from her tablet. Blue and yellow cables ran from her device into the server.

"Is there any chance you can activate the alpha nanites in Touma and Goro as well as the yakuza?"

"The yakuza, that's definitely possible. Yamada, nope. Their Alpha nanites are heavily encrypted. It would take me weeks to figure out, if at all. It's the same reason he can't turn us into ash now, but I like how you're thinking."

Ryan grunted as they hefted Takeshi's body up the stairs and placed him amongst the old seafood factory equipment. The factory looked like it hadn't been used in some years. Heavy plastic sheeting now covered the abandoned machinery. Despite this, the air was heavy with scents of the sea. Fish, oil, and salt.

"I still don't think your *Weekend at Bernie's* idea is going to work," Booth said.

"That's why Allie and you are going to flank the yakuza. Plenty of buildings out there to hide behind."

Ryan snapped his head up at the faint sound of an engine whining along the coast road. His comms sparked to life.

"Silver SUV heading our way," Allie said.

Ryan cursed. "Sofia. Cal?" he called down the stairs.

"Ready. But I haven't tested it," said Sofia.

Ryan's ears pricked; there were howls and shrieks nearby. He took a quick look out the window and saw the Hounds sprinting up the road toward the oncoming SUV.

"Booth, Allie. This is our chance. Keep out of sight. Once Yamada arrives, keep your weapons on his yakuza until we can activate their nanites. As soon as you see them twitching, secure Keiko and Hogai. Understand?"

"Got it," Booth said. Allie smiled but remained silent. She slipped out into the chilly morning.

Shadows of Ash

The others rushed into position. Tires squealed on the road as the vehicle swung from side to side, trying to shake off the Hounds. Small arms fire exploded from the yakuza inside. The pops of handguns and the rapid fire of the submachine guns the gangsters favored. Metal screeched and the SUV spun out, skidding as the driver fought to keep it under control. It clipped an ancestor temple on the side of the road and tilted, thumping onto its side. Some Hounds clung to it while others were thrown off, slamming into the asphalt. They didn't move again. A second SUV tore up the road, killing any of the remaining wolf creatures. They looked vicious and were fearless and fast, but that was their downfall as they charged into the direct line of fire with no sense of self preservation.

Cal squeezed Ryan's shoulder. "I hope this works."

"Marginal at best."

"Marginal? Better than nothing," Cal said. "Touma's not going to be happy."

"I don't understand how Takeshi died. He was fine, no injuries, no bullet wounds. Nothing."

"Maybe the signal that killed the Black Skulls fried his alpha nanite?" Cal mused.

"I hate this." Ryan sighed. He checked his magazine before holstering it. "We really need someone who knows about nanotechnology. We're making assumption after assumption. It's not how we do things. We've always gone in with all the information. Every time. Remember that operation we called off in Cali because we had the wrong blueprints? And here we are, stumbling in the dark like a couple of drunks coming home, trying to be quiet."

"Agreed. We need to contact Zanzi, Lisa, and Avondale – if they're still alive. Find experts so we can bring down OPIS. Fight fire with fire," Cal said.

"First let's deal with Yamada," Ryan said.

Cal helped wheel Takeshi to the front door. "This better work."

They walked outside and Yamada drove up in a third SUV, black with dark windows.

"Why is my son in an office chair?" Yamada said.

"He passed out during the back-up plan. We haven't been able to wake him yet."

Yamada signaled one of his yakuza to check on Takeshi. Ryan flicked his gaze behind the Yamadas. There was still no sign of Booth and Allie. The yakuza checked Takeshi's pulse, shaking his head when he didn't find one. Goro hissed and lurched forward, only to be held back by the elder Yamada. Goro hissed again, fighting his grandfather, but he was no match for Touma.

"Sit down, Goro," he instructed.

Ryan spotted Booth and Allie creeping along the road. Five meters out. Maybe six. He just needed a little time. "I'm sorry, Touma. It was beyond our control."

"You disappoint me, Connors. Not only did we lose all that research and equipment. Dr. Ando is dead. Now my son too."

"It must have been the signal. Give us Keiko and Hogai and we'll be on our way."

"But you failed. The deal was to get Ando and Takeshi out. That hasn't transpired."

"What about Offenheim?"

"I can deal with him." Yamada raised the same gray wands as before. Ryan caught another glimpse of Booth and muttered under his breath. *"C'mon, Sofia. Anytime now."*

He never got to see if she triggered the signal. Like before, the pain erupted behind his left ear before spreading across his brain. He dropped to his knees and looked back at Sofia. He gritted his teeth. "What's happening?"

Sofia was shaking, trying to type something into her tablet. "I don't know. My signal isn't getting through." She gasped and held her head in her hands.

Cal groaned and fired a couple of rounds at the parked SUVs. Three yakuza stood guard, cradling weapons.

The pain in Ryan's head increased tenfold, erupting behind his eyes in an explosion of fireworks.

He managed to fire his Glock at a couple of the Japanese gangsters before his world faded to black.

SEVENTEEN

Ryan slowly became aware of his surroundings. The first thing he felt was the damp and cold seeping through his clothes. Next, the silence. It was complete and unnerving. No clocks ticking. No humming of electronics. No sounds of animals. Just the steady breathing of others around him.

He forced himself to remain calm and keep his heart rate steady. He flexed his feet, stretched out his toes, and slowly worked his way up his body, checking for any injuries. Apart from his throbbing head and dry throat, he was unscathed. Gently, he sat up and looked around. Cal lay next to him on one side, Sofia on the other. Keiko,

Booth, and Allie were a couple of meters away, against a wall. Hogai was nowhere to be seen. The room was made of concrete. Walls, floor, and ceiling. Dim lights were evenly spaced at intervals. A few wires poked out of the wall, with no indication as to what they were for. Their gear was piled next to a table, minus their guns. The only other objects in the room were a desk with a TV on it, and a stack of crates.

Ryan rose and checked that everyone was breathing and uninjured. The crates held water and food: cans and MREs, a few candy bars and boxes of crackers. He ran his fingers along the smooth concrete walls, pressing and prodding, looking for a door. He found it after ten minutes of searching. Tiny seams indicated the entrance, but there was no handle, no buttons. No way of opening it.

He walked back to Cal and shook her awake. "Hey."

"Hey." Cal pinched the bridge of her nose with her finger and thumb. "Where are we?"

"A concrete room of some sort."

Cal sat up. "A room?"

"Yup. You feel okay?"

"You mean apart from the pounding head? Yes."

"I'm going to wake the others," Ryan said.

It took some time to rouse everyone. Booth grumbled and belched, muttering that he wanted another ten minutes. Keiko groaned and swatted Ryan's hand away.

**

Sometime later The Nameless stood in a huddle next to the TV, sipping on the provided water. They were weaponless but had all their other gear. Rucksacks and bags. Tablet and food.

"How long were we out for?" Booth said.

Sofia brought her tablet to life, the glow from the screen illuminating her face. "Eight hours, twenty-two minutes."

"Any theories, Connors?" Booth said.

"Yamada, a step ahead of us again. I'm beginning to wonder if he even wanted Takeshi rescued. He asked more questions about Ando, like he needed the doctor for something. Takeshi was the edge. The pull on our heartstrings."

Cal, Sofia, and Booth mumbled their agreement.

Keiko picked up the remote and switched on the TV. Immediately, Touma Yamada's face came into focus and what was obviously a pre-recorded video played. His voice came through, deep and commanding.

"By now you are wondering why you are in the concrete room with no way out. What is going on? We had a deal? First, I don't accept failure. You failed. Both Ando and Takeshi are dead. All Ando's decades of work, destroyed. That is unacceptable. After we triggered your Alpha nanites, knocking you out, Goro and I debated about what to do with you all. He and the yakuza wanted to shoot you execution-style, leave your bodies for the wildlife. You may have encrypted your alpha nanites, but that doesn't stop us from giving you an electric shock before putting a bullet in your skulls. You see, the electricity temporarily knocks out the nanites' capabilities. Iro, my yakuza chief, wanted the women, but I said no. You needed something worse. Something much worse. Then it dawned on me as I looked at the power plant. One reactor still operates. Radiation, Connors. That room you are in is radioactive – or soon will be. Small amounts, but enough to kill you slowly. Smart people like you will know how it starts. Vomiting. Diarrhea. Fever. Then it gets serious. Weakness and fatigue. Hair loss and bloody vomiting. The food and water are so you don't starve to death before the fun begins. If you somehow survive, remember, you don't only have to take down Offenheim. He is but one of four. You need to take them all out." Touma Yamada smiled, his face barely creasing. "The TV has an internet connection so you can watch as the world is reborn. Instead of being emperor of Japan, maybe I'll be emperor of the world." He smiled again. "Oh, and the boy you had with you, Hogai? He's with me, where he belongs, in Japan. Good luck."

The screen went black. Keiko cycled through the channels, looking for anything else. Sofia took the remote from her and switched the TV off.

"What a douche," she said.

Ryan was stunned. So many feelings and thoughts rushed through his mind, he wasn't sure how to prioritize them into anything resembling a plan. For once in his professional life, he was stumped. The only way out of this room was the door, which had to be opened from the other side. No one, other than Yamada, knew where they were. They had no back up. No cavalry. Nothing. Overriding all this was his deep guilt. He had led his family and friends into danger. Now they were going to die in an excruciating, painful way. For three years he had prayed for a miracle. Prayed that somehow Cal was alive, and they could be a family again. Drink tea and watch the sunset over the Pacific Ocean. Not much to ask for, was it?

"I'm sorry, everyone. It was my plan and it failed," Ryan said.

"We all agreed to it," Sofia said. "If anyone is at fault, it's me. I should have figured out the programming quicker. We knew Yamada couldn't be trusted. But Yamada, OPIS, they've always had the upper hand. They wrote the code. They know the code. I'm working with scraps." She hugged Keiko and kissed her on the forehead.

Booth picked up the TV and threw it against the wall, shattering the screen into a million pieces. He stomped on the electronic parts, grinding the circuitry into the floor. No one stopped him. They watched and waited for his anger to subside.

"You know something?" Booth said, kicking the larger pieces across the room. "Rita made me promise that after the kids were born, I'd take a desk job. File paperwork or run mission control. You know, a safe job. I played that role for what – two months? It sucked. Boring as hell. I belonged out here, with you guys. I was good at it. The Nameless, a team of individuals coming together to achieve something. I felt like I was doing something useful for the world. Never in a billion years would I have imagined this madness. Now, because of those pricks, I'm never going to see my kids again. I'm going to die a slow and painful death? Now I'm wondering if I made a huge mistake not keeping that desk job."

Allie, who had remained silent till now, sat on the desk. Booth embraced her.

"Did I ever tell you guys about my first flight instructor in the Air Force?" she said.

Ryan and the others shook their heads.

"Total hard ass. Ground me down into a weeping mess on the floor, then built me back up, molding me into the pilot I am today. We trained in the worst storms you could imagine, flying through rain so hard the window wipers were bystanders. Lightning fizzled all around. In commercial jets we fly over that shit. This guy wanted us to fly into it. He trained me for every possible catastrophic failure. Like your debriefing on the train the other day, after every session we went through it. What went right? What went wrong? Why? What did we learn? How can we improve?"

"Nice story," Booth said, scuffing his shoes on the concrete floor.

"C'mon, guys," Allie pressed on. "I thought you were this kick-ass team. The Nameless. So-called because you were whispered about. No one ever saw you. In, out, job done."

Cal sat up. "She's right. Yes, we are down. Really down. Fucked. Sofia, who was that blonde lady that taught us at the Lodge?"

"Which one? De Vries?"

"Yes, that's her. She used to tell us that there is always a way out. We just need to figure it out. Think outside the box." She turned and looked at Ryan. At Booth and Sofia. At Keiko and Allie. "We are all intelligent and resourceful. Surely we can figure a way out of here. We're no good to anyone in here, dying. If we want any chance of stopping

Shadows of Ash

Offenheim, we need to be out there." As Cal pointed to the ceiling, the scar on the side of her head pulsed.

The room fell silent as Cal's words echoed inside Ryan's head. He was tired. Not only physically, but mentally too. A week had passed since that night in Shinjuku. One hell of a week. But Cal was right. Allie was right. There had to be a way out. He sighed and stretched his aching back. His earlier search of the room had only revealed the door. Had he given up his search too soon?

"You're right. There's six of us. Split up and search the room. Note everything you find. Any hole, any crack. What are those wires for over there? Even if there used to be a door or window, tell me. Sofia, Yamada said the TV was connected to the internet. See if you can connect." He paused, remembering Sofia's words from the mission. *It's a countdown. Wave two is happening in a little less than four days.* "That countdown you found. Are you certain?"

"Definitely."

"All right. See what you can do with the connection. We'll figure out how to get out of here, then come up with a plan."

"On it," Sofia said. She was already plugging the blue ethernet cable into her tablet. Ryan picked up a piece of broken circuit board and marked where the outline of the door was. Then he walked to the opposite wall and stared, running his fingers along the smooth surface. It didn't take him long to find another door. He shoved at it with all his weight, but it didn't budge. Next, he scanned the room and noticed small holes where cameras had been mounted.

"Over here," Allie said.

"Something here too," Booth and Cal both called out. Ryan went first to Allie, as she was closer. She pointed to more holes in the concrete. Maybe ten or a dozen. There was a slight depression where clothes hooks had once been. Booth had found a similar set of holes, while Cal had located square markings and scrapes on the floor.

"This must have been some sort of suit-up room," Cal said. "You know, for putting on those radiation suits before heading into the reactor area. Something like that."

"Logically, you would have a dressing room and some sort of washing room, wouldn't you?" Allie said. "Then, once the suits were clean and safe, they'd be hung back here. So maybe through there is the washroom, and through that is a corridor."

"Controlled by cameras and monitored with sensors?" Booth asked.

"Probably. They're not going to let someone out who has higher than normal radiation levels," Allie said. "Ryan?"

"Umm. It all sounds plausible. Something Yamada said is bothering me."

"What?" Cal asked.

"He said we were going to die from radiation exposure, right? But if this is a dressing room where the workers donned the suits, it would be designed to keep radiation out. So how is it getting in?"

Booth screwed his face into a deep frown. "I hate it when you point things like that out. Makes me feel like an idiot."

"Guys," Sofia called.

Shadows of Ash

As Ryan and the others walked toward Sofia, muffled klaxons blared out, their high decibels filtering through the concrete walls.

"I'm linked into the plant security cameras," Sofia said.

On her tablet screen was an image of abandoned rooms, red alarm lights flashing. A loud clanking sound echoed through the room as the door opposite them hissed open. On instinct, The Nameless spread out, hugging the walls. Ryan crouched, wishing he had a gun or even a knife. Unarmed, he felt naked.

As they'd suspected the door led to a washroom. The floor was covered in shiny metal grates, and large shower heads hung from above. On the opposite wall, another door creaked open to reveal a small ante chamber.

"What's going on?" Cal said.

Ryan shrugged. He was just as confused. "Sofia. Any luck opening the exterior door yet?"

"Nope."

"What were those wires for?"

"The door release that just opened."

"Could you use them to open the other door?"

"Maybe."

"Okay. Split up. Cal, you're with me. Booth and Allie. Sofia and Keiko. It's a big power plant. We'll see if he's left anything unlocked. Look everywhere." Ryan checked his watch. "Meet back here in two hours."

Touma Yamada was a smart man. Old and wise. Everything he did had a reason, sometimes two. Forever moving chess pieces. There had to be a way out. Sure, he'd said he wanted them dead, but it didn't strike Ryan as true.

The Nameless filed through the washroom and separated out into the vast expanse of the containment building. Glancing to his left, Ryan spotted a yellow box – a Geiger counter, used for measuring the level of ionizing radiation. Switching it on, he checked the readout. It was hovering around eighty counts per second. Nothing too bad now, but Yamada had said he wanted them to have a slow, painful death, gradually growing sicker, or starving, whichever came first. Ryan took the Geiger counter.

Cal turned and shook her head. "Nothing. Not a damn thing."

"Keep searching. There has to be something. Tools, anything."

They searched for another thirty minutes but came up short. Booth, Allie, Sofia, and Keiko joined them back in the bare concrete room. Allie moved the crates against the wall so they could all sit down.

"Anyone?" Ryan asked.

Booth slammed down a thick binder. "Just this." Ryan could see it was clearly marked *Maintenance*.

He cupped his hands together. He was at a loss. There was no apparent way out. Was Yamada toying with them?

EIGHTEEN

PORTLAND, OREGON

Zanzi dove behind a shelf filled with football apparel and flinched as the door splintered and broke off its hinges. Grub the biker burst through, his AR-15 held out in front of him. His eyes were wide, pupils dilated. Was that from the thrill of the chase? Or was he high? Whatever the case, Zanzi didn't care. She slithered farther down the aisle on her elbows and knees. Tilly had the injured Josie somewhere deeper in the store.

Grub kicked out at the shelves, scattering clothing. The clanging metal reverberated around the store. "There's nowhere to hide!"

Bang! Bang!

He kicked the shelf again before running to the next aisle. Zanzi rose in a crouch and crab-walked, joining Tilly and Josie behind the service counter. She'd spotted the hunting crossbows and knives when she'd seen Tilly's and Josie's reflections in the display case. She grabbed a crossbow and a dozen bolts, and loaded it, straining with the mechanism. She handed it to Tilly and set about preparing another.

"Pretty ladies! Come out and play!" Grub shouted. He was close.

Zanzi stayed low and looked for his feet. She turned back to Tilly and whispered. "Lie flat like this and point the crossbow in that direction. When I say, squeeze that trigger. Okay? Aim for his legs."

"What if he starts firing?"

"Let's hope we get him before that happens."

"Are you going to kill him like Alba?"

Zanzi blinked. She had shoved a pistol under the woman's chin and pulled the trigger. Even the elites with their high-grade nanites couldn't survive that. To be sure, she had set the lab on fire. She had done it for Josie's daughter – for Harriet.

"I have to, Tilly. If I don't, they'll do bad things to us."

Deep laughter rang out, chilling Zanzi. "There you are." Grub had spotted them. He unleashed a volley of bullets. The glass display cabinets above them shattered. Tiny shards rained down, pricking into the women's skin, and getting tangled in their hair. Tilly screamed and dropped her crossbow. She covered her ears and kept screaming as the bullets tore into the woodwork.

Shadows of Ash

Grub stopped firing and reloaded. "You hot bitches had enough?" His boots thumped on the linoleum floor. "Mutton! Dean! Get in here!"

More boots stamped into view.

"Where are they?" one of the bikers said.

"Behind that counter," Grub said.

"Well, what're we waiting for? Christmas?"

The three bikers chortled.

"If you're so eager, Dean, go fetch."

Dean grunted and advanced. Zanzi clutched her crossbow and waited until he was a few steps closer. She rolled and pulled the trigger as soon as he came within range. The bolt thunked into his thigh. Dean shrieked and jumped back, releasing a three-round burst into the ceiling. Chunks of sheetrock and dust rained down over the injured biker.

Grub and Mutton guffawed. "You fucking moron! What did you think was going to happen?"

"Bitch shot me with a crossbow."

"No kidding."

The bikers lowered their voices.

Zanzi knew when to surrender. Her father's words spoke in her mind: *Live to fight another day.* She dropped the crossbow and slid next to Tilly and Josie. She took one of the bolts and jammed it behind her bra strap.

Bullets rang out, peppering the walls behind them. It only lasted a few seconds. Enough time for Grub to advance and point his rifle at them.

"Game over, bitches."

Zanzi gritted her teeth but didn't struggle as Grub hauled to her feet and frisked her, missing the crossbow bolt. Josie yelped as Mutton tugged on her injured arm.

"Careful. She's injured," Zanzi said.

"Not where it counts." Mutton grabbed Josie's breast and kissed her cheek.

"All right. Leave it. There'll be plenty of time for that at the party tonight," Grub said.

"Where are you taking us?" Josie said.

"You'll see soon enough." Grub bound each of them in turn with yellow cable ties.

The Outcast Mongrels shoved the women back down the escalators, past the ash forms and the discarded, unused shopping bags. Dean hobbled alongside, a black bandana secured around the crossbow bolt still sticking out of his leg.

The bikers, taking one woman each, cut the cable ties and ordered them to sit on the pillion seats of their Harley-Davidsons. They roared back down the empty concourse and exited the delivery ramp into Portland.

Out of habit, Zanzi took note of where they were going, ticking off landmarks and committing them to memory. It was an old impulse, one she had picked up from her parents.

Always know where you are and how you got there.

***

There were no signs of the Black Skulls as the motorcycle gang left the business district behind and wound their way through the suburban streets of Portland. Their Harleys were so loud, it wouldn't have been much of a challenge to track them.

They roared down another street lined with several industrial buildings. A metal fabrication shop, panel beaters, sign writers. The Outcast Mongrels' pad consisted of four houses surrounded by an eight-foot solid fence. The gates rolled back, and Grub led the way inside. Between the houses, an open-sided shed housed a bar, tables, couches, and pool tables, and right smack bang in the middle was a caged fighting ring like ones used in mixed martial arts.

Zanzi shook her head at the setup. The bikers suited their name.

They were greeted by a dozen or so men and a few other women. Grub roughly pulled Zanzi off the bike and stood her in front of the gathered members.

"Brought you all a treat," he said, pushing Zanzi in front of him. "She's a feisty one."

He was answered by a chorus of jeers and vulgar gestures.

"Show us your tits!" one of the members shouted.

"All right, Axl." Grub laughed. "Leave it for later. Is the first match ready?"

"Fuck yeah."

"Well, get it started, then!"

Grub dragged Zanzi to a stadium seat and shoved her onto the bottom terrace. He leant down and licked her ear before speaking. "You're going to want to see this." He chuckled. "We used to use the cage for dog fights and to settle any disagreements."

Zanzi pulled away. "Dog fights? That's disgusting," she spat. She flicked her eyes to the cage and spotted smears of blood and feces. She shivered. How anyone could harm a dog was beyond her comprehension. They were beautiful and loyal and only deserved the best care, love, and attention.

"They're just dogs." Grub chuckled again and looked up at the gathering members. "Traci, where's my beer?"

Traci had stringy, unwashed brown hair and the strung-out look of a drug addict: dark bags under red eyes, sallow skin covered with sores, and so thin her bones stuck out.

"Coming," she murmured.

"Traci." She turned. "Give us a smile," Grub taunted.

Traci half-smiled, showing chipped and rotten teeth.

"Ugh. On second thought, just bring my fucking beer, you junkie bitch."

Traci melted into the group. Zanzi turned to check on Tilly and Josie. They were up on the next level of seating, wedged between their captors. Josie was being groped but was ignoring Mutton. Tilly stared at the cage.

Zanzi used the time to get a better look at the motorcycle gang's HQ. The layout and design were for two things: parties and keeping the law on the other side of their fence. The barrier was well constructed, with welded metal posts and thick bars locking the gates. Nothing a bit of C4 couldn't take care of.

The bikers began to whoop and holler as Axl and three others brought some prisoners into the yard. They had four Rabids in chains and were moving them with animal control poles. As Zanzi watched, the bikers unchained the Rabids and shoved them into the cage. Immediately they spun and tried to grab the bikers, who only laughed and bashed them with pipes. The cheering and whooping rose in decibels as four human captives were brought out next: three men and a woman. They were dressed in mechanic's overalls, but barefoot. Two dropped to their knees and begged to be released.

"Please don't do this. I don't want to die," the Asian man said. He had a nasty gash on his head, crusty with dried blood.

"Please. No!" the woman with red hair pleaded.

This only made the bikers more excited. They slammed their beer bottles on the table and began to chant.

"Make them fight! Make them fight! Make them fight!"

Zanzi shook her head. Was this what it meant to lose all sense of morality? Of empathy? To stop caring? To be so obsessed with giving in to your desires that you stop being human and become something else? Tears welled in her eyes. To think these people had survived the combusting only to come to this. Milo had told her that not everyone had the nanites; that was why wave two was happening. To mop up the rest. Like these degenerate bikers.

The captives were thrown into the cage, the bikers using tasers to keep the Rabids at bay in a corner. Mutton moved to stand before a board and gathered bets like a bookie at a racetrack.

"All right, you mongrel bastards!" Grub shouted as he raised his hands. "As your president, I promised you girls and entertainment. So here you are!"

The bikers cheered. Several threw bottles of beer at the cage.

"Let the fight begin!" Grub said. He sat back down. "Take notes," he whispered in Zanzi's ear. "I'll give you two choices. Mistress, or that." He gestured at the cage.

Zanzi pulled back from his breath. It stank of old beer and rotting meat. She tugged her arm away. "How about one on one? You and me, in that cage. Or are you a wuss?" she said.

"Watch the fight, bitch." He slapped her hard across the face.

Zanzi gritted her teeth and lifted her tear-filled eyes to the cage.

NINETEEN

TOMARI NUCLEAR POWER PLANT
HOKKAIDO, JAPAN

It was late. At least, Ryan's body clock was telling him it was nearing midnight. He and The Nameless had been stuck in the power plant for six hours, with no apparent way out. They had explored both the washroom and the large containment room that led to the reactor itself. It was sealed up tight with only one other access door. Ryan and Booth had attempted to remove the hinges to no avail. It was like they had been welded shut. There was no way out. No one to rescue them. No one even knew they were there except the men who'd imprisoned them. Sofia had tried to communicate with the outside world, but apart from access to the power station's cameras, she had nothing. Yamada had The Nameless trapped like bugs in a Venus fly trap. Ryan grunted. The Nameless, experts at sneaking in, extracting. Experts at recon and getting out of sticky situations. Trapped with nowhere to go. Pathetic.

"Another drink, Connors?" Booth offered him the bottle of Mars Iwai, a traditional Japanese whiskey. They had found the alcohol after a more thorough search of the crates.

Strangely, Yamada had supplied them with whiskey, sake, beer, and wine, as well as water and electrolyte drinks. In another crate, they had found bedding. Futon mattresses. Camping stoves. Tea and coffee. It was all there. Everything needed for a long stay. They had set the futon beds up in a circle after eating a meal of MREs and cookies.

"Yeah, why not," Ryan said, holding out his glass. Booth poured two fingers' worth, then poured more for Allie, Sofia, and Cal. Keiko smiled and wriggled her glass.

"You've had enough," Booth grinned. "You don't want a hangover down here."

Keiko giggled. "Just a little more."

Booth looked at Sofia for approval.

"She's twenty-one," she said, shrugging her shoulders.

Ryan took a deep breath and looked at his team. Cal, his wife, her eyes alert as always. He was still getting used to her buzz cut and the fact that she was still alive. Her brow was creased in concentration. He knew, without asking, what she was thinking. How were they going to get out of this mess? She would also be thinking that they needed to lift their morale. The Nameless did it best when they shared stories. Stories of childhood. Of university, stolen kisses, and lost loves. Of hopes and dreams. When one had hope, one had determination. Determination was a great motivator. It could be your desire to see a loved one, to be reunited. It could be to stop someone evil, or to fight for a cause you believe in.

Ryan glanced at Booth. "Whatever happened to weird Kevin?"

"Weird Kevin?" Booth laughed. "Now that's a name I haven't heard in a while."

"Why did you guys call him weird Kevin?" Allie said.

"It wasn't meant in a mean way. The guy was a machine – never complained. We could trek through the desert for hours on end and he always had a smile or a joke. He was great for morale, that Kevin." Booth paused and refilled his glass. "One of the lads caught him sniffing his belt like it was covered in catnip and called him weird Kevin. It kind of stuck, like names do in the Army."

Ryan raised his glass. "To Kevin. Wherever you are."

Allie shrugged and took a sip of her whiskey.

"Tell them about Rodney MacLeod," Booth said, nudging Ryan.

"No way."

"Go on. It's not that embarrassing."

"Rodney MacLeod?" Cal asked. "I haven't heard this story."

The ensuing chorus of pleading jolted the memory from Ryan. He cringed. Booth was correct to a point – it wasn't really embarrassing.

"C'mon, Connors," Booth pressed. His speech was slightly slurred now.

"There's nothing to tell. In any case, it was a long time ago." Ryan sipped his whiskey, enjoying the amber liquid.

Allie and Cal groaned. "C'mon," they both said.

"All right. Fine. Now keep in mind, this happened before I met Cal. I was still young and full of myself. I'm sure you can attest to the allure of the Army uniform, or Air Force. Any uniform, really. Girls loved it. In school, no one paid me an ounce of attention. Suddenly I was in the Army and girls noticed me. All we had to do was walk into a bar in uniform and snap—" Ryan clicked his fingers. "We had girls around us wanting photos, asking us questions. Wanting to ride in our trucks or tanks. Fire a gun."

"Get a bit of an ego?" Cal laughed.

"You could say that, yeah. There was an older guy, a corporal. Rodney MacLeod. I knew his family from back home. Notorious, they were. Fighters, scrappers, troublemakers. Always looking for a fight. My little group did everything to avoid visiting the same bars as Rodney. For some reason, the ladies were attracted to his bad-boy status. So this time we found ourselves in Honolulu and met up with Booth and his crowd. They took us to a few bars. We were having a good time. Jonesy – one of my mates –loved Polynesian women. We were sitting at a table, chatting up some locals, when who walks in? Rodney bloody MacLeod."

Ryan looked at Booth, then the others. Even Keiko was listening. "He strode over — though I should say he swaggered over like he owned the place — squeezed between Jonesy and me, looked the two beautiful Hawaiian girls dead in the eye and said..."

"'All right, lads. I'll take over from here,'" Ryan and Booth said in unison.

Booth laughed, a deep chortle at first, and before long he was clutching his side and snorting through his nose. In between gasps, he said, "Connors came over to me with his tail between his legs like the school bully had taken his lunch money."

Cal, Allie, Sofia, and Keiko chuckled and shook their heads.

"What happened with the girls?" Allie asked. "Did they go off with this Rodney?"

"Like he was the last man on Earth," Booth said, still laughing.

The group fell silent as everyone escaped into their own memories. Cal took his hand and kissed it. "I'm glad you weren't like that when I met you. I probably wouldn't have gone on a date with you."

"I wouldn't have gone on a date with me back then. Arrogant as heck."

"Weren't we all, at that age. Remember Liam?"

Ryan groaned. "Ugh. That's right." He blinked away the tears forming in his eyes. Five years had passed since his death and it was still raw. Still too much emotion. Life could be so cruel at times. It could fill you with so much joy and love, and in an instant, take it away. He pulled Cal into a hug and held her, enjoying the warmth of the woman who shared his grief.

"If we get out of here, I have an idea for stopping wave two," Sofia said.

"You mean other than nuking Offenheim to hell?" Cal said.

"That would be a sight to see." Sofia leant forward and looked at everyone in turn. "Weather stations use satellites to gather information. They have powerful radios and communication equipment. We can use one to send a signal using the codes. Stop wave two from happening everywhere."

Was it possible? Ryan dared to hope. "All you need is that station and you can send the signal?"

"With a bit of tweaking, yes. I mean, I need to write some code, with Avondale's help. Work out a few algos."

"Confident?"

"About eighty percent."

Ryan looked at Cal. "You've been inside the satellite installation. Do you think it'll work?"

His wife brought her fingertips together, forming a steeple. "Possible. I never saw the control room. But I must play devil's advocate here. Why would OPIS go to all this trouble only to be vulnerable to a single beam of code? It's not logical. Like a huge flaw in a meticulously thought-out plan. I do know they've worked toward this for over forty years, and The Eyrie has an array of powerful radio telescopes."

Ryan paced back and forth. Cal was right. It was too simple. Sofia was a computer genius. She could hack into nearly anything. Even if they had Avondale, they would struggle to stop the second wave. They had to kill the source. Destroy The Eyrie. Or...

"Is The Eyrie their HQ?" he said.

"It's their communication hub, yes. But Offenheim will be expecting us. He wants us to attack. Killing you isn't enough. Because it's a game – the end goal is to torment you for as long as possible," Cal said.

"Be that as it may, we must. If he wants to kill us, then at least we do it fighting. We die knowing we saved at least a few people."

Ryan continued to pace, an idea forming. Destroying The Eyrie would be difficult. *If* – and it was a big *if* – they had military help, then yes, it was possible. He pivoted. "Sofia. What if we took out their satellites instead? Is that a possibility?"

"With missiles?"

"Not what I was thinking. With other satellites. Is that possible?"

"Huh. I mean, yeah, it is." Sofia's fingers tapped the screen of her tablet. "Satellites have propulsion systems, and LK3 has satellites. In theory, we could use one of ours to hit one of theirs, but there's a ton of variables. First, I would need to find the right satellite, track its trajectory, calculate a collision course – if that's even possible." She sighed and rubbed her eyes. "I don't know, Ryan. We would need to transmit signals to our satellites, and I'd need Avondale's help and lots of time."

"So it's possible. That's what I'm asking?"

"In short, yes."

Ryan turned in a semi-circle, looking at each of The Nameless. "Think about it. It's better than attacking The Eyrie on a maybe. We're not soldiers. We were trained to infiltrate, to observe, to sneak out. To get assets out of sticky situations, keep it quiet. This is more our style. OPIS and Offenheim won't see it coming."

The Nameless agreed with nods and smiles. Cal draped her arms around his shoulders.

Booth grunted. "All right, Connors. Just where can we do this?"

Ryan broke away from the embrace and looked at Booth and Allie. "Dutch Harbor in the Aleutian Islands. Remember that North Korean agent we tracked?"

"The NSA weather station?"

"The very same."

"Of course. I remember all the fancy equipment everywhere."

"*The* NSA?" Allie asked.

"It's a listening post disguised as a weather data station, near Dutch Harbor. Cold, miserable place," Ryan said. He began pacing again, re-energized by the plan forming in his head, making him all the more determined to escape this prison.

They had a mission. Get out. Get to Dutch Harbor. Stop wave two.

The Geiger counter sat on one of the crates, and Ryan spent a few minutes taking readings. It was still hovering around eighty counts per second, no increase. No one had shown any signs of sickness yet. He racked his brain, trying to think of the time it took. What dosage was fatal? But he had to try to forget the radiation for now and focus on getting out.

He grabbed a couple of water bottles and sat back down on a futon bed. "Reading is still eighty counts per second."

Shadows of Ash

Sofia grunted and looked up from her tablet. "I've been thinking about our idea for destroying their satellites. I know where LK3s are, and I could possibly figure out where the OPIS satellites are, but I really need to contact Avondale. I need his help and expertise." Her fingers flew over the screen as she flicked through the pages of data. "Allie. Do you know of any airports around here?"

"Why? What's the point?" She drained whiskey and reached for the bottle. Booth moved it out of reach.

"Give it," Allie said, her tone stern. Booth handed it to her, and she filled her glass. "Yes, I know where the nearest airport is. Yes, I could find an airplane, refuel it. Fly us home. But—" She stared at Sofia. "How the bloody hell can I do that when we're stuck in here, our only company radiation that is slowly but surely killing us?"

Allie shook her head and walked from the room, her gait off balance as her angry footsteps faded out of earshot.

Sofia raised her hands, palms facing the ceiling. "What did I do?"

Booth stood. "She's not one of us. Not used to our endearing optimism." He jogged to catch up with Allie.

TWENTY

TOMARI NUCLEAR POWER PLANT
HOKKAIDO, JAPAN

Allie fumed as she stomped from the room. Her decision to join The Nameless and their mission had been stupid. Yes, she liked the idea of doing something positive, and their success at Yamada Tower had felt good. Really good. Great, even. It was the same feeling she got when she delivered aid to those in need. Flood victims. Famine victims, or innocent civilians caught up in a civil war. Helping those in need was what had attracted her to enlisting. In anything, there was a level of risk, sure, but this? This was insanity. She would never have guessed she'd find herself trapped inside a nuclear power plant that was slowly leaking radiation to kill them. If they didn't kill each other first. She clenched her fists at her side and battled to regain control of her emotions. She made a mental note to apologize to Sofia.

"Hey, wait up," Booth called after her.

"Not now, Booth. I just want to be alone."

"I have chocolate."

Allie stopped walking and pivoted. "You think chocolate is the answer? Is chocolate going to cure the radiation?"

"Well, no. But it tastes good," Booth said, his smile lopsided.

She stared at him. His hair was a little messy, but stylish. His clothes were dusty from the night's exertions. His blue eyes shone with youthful vigor despite the creases in his face betraying his advancing age. Much to her disdain, she liked him. Liked him a lot. He was cheeky and carefree, at times reckless. He seemed to operate on a whim. She had seen him totally focused and serious when on a mission, and she had seen him cracking jokes and being spontaneous. Not at all like the guys she usually dated.

She sighed and took the chocolate. "Fine. But only because I'm hungry."

"Of course." Booth smiled again. They sat on the floor with their backs up against metal cupboards, staying silent while munching on the sugary treat.

"You know, I never wanted to be a commercial pilot. It sort of just happened. Did you ever think you would end up where you did?"

"No."

"What made you become an operative then?"

"Much like Connors, I lost someone close to me to an act of terrorism." Booth looked away, staying silent. Allie let it go, not wanting to press him. She knew of many others still raw from such events. "I'm guessing you were a jock at school.

Booth chuckled, his face growing red. "I dreamed of playing for the Vikings as a quarterback."

"What, so you could lose in the play-offs every year?"

"Who's your team then?"

"None."

"That's a cop out. You must have a team. What about your father?"

"Cowboys."

Booth chuckled again. "What did you want to be, then?"

"I wanted to fly relief planes for the UN. Do something worthwhile."

"Flying commercial isn't worthwhile? You take people to exotic locations, broaden their horizons."

Allie laughed. It was a giggle at first, but it didn't take long before she was guffawing and holding her side. "Have you flown commercial recently?"

"Yeah. It's horrible."

They fell silent again, and the machinery behind them hummed.

"So why didn't you?" Booth asked.

Allie shifted her weight and leant against Booth. "Like I was saying on the train, I was an Air Force brat before Dad got his gig with NASA. We moved around a lot. Base to base. I never felt at home anywhere, always just the temporary visitor. As I got into my teens, I realized I could get into all sorts of trouble because we were always on the move and I could run away from it. I've always run instead of facing my problems. Did it in the Air Force. Something happens that I don't like, I put in a transfer. Problem solved. After I left, I enrolled in the UN program. I ran into a doctor and his wife. I had been his mistress at one time. So, as always, I ran. As far as I could. To Chicago. Because of my father's contacts, United asked me to fly for them. Good money, and they look after us. And best of all, I'm always in the air, running – well, flying – from my problems."

Allie stood and stretched her back before sitting back down. "What about you? How did you end up with this lot?" She nodded toward the washroom.

"Well, it became ever apparent that I wasn't any good at football. As my dad said, 'You have the quarterback looks, son, just not the arm.' Mom got sick, so I gave her my college fund to pay for her medication. I didn't fancy working in construction, so I enlisted. It was hard at first, but little by little I got better. They put me in recon, and I excelled. LK3 came knocking a few months before I was due to be honorably discharged and offered me a place at the Lodge – where they train new recruits. I knew Ryan from before, but that was where I met Cal and Sofia. We formed an immediate bond and were soon working together."

"Well, if there's one shining light to this madness, it was meeting you," Allie said. They stared at each other for a few moments. There was that awkward silence where neither party is sure about making the first move. It feels natural, but anxiety gets in the way. Allie leant closer, breathed out and kissed Booth on the lips. He smiled and kissed her back, softly at first, then growing in passion.

Allie pulled out of the embrace. "Wait a minute. Aren't you married?"

"Divorced," he said before kissing her again and squeezing her leg.

"Kids too?"

"Yeah. My son's going to play for the Vikings for sure."

Allie punched him lightly on the arm and kissed him again.

***

Ryan didn't fault Allie for being upset. Hell, anyone would be in this situation. The Nameless had years of experience. Years to adopt the mindset of never giving up, no matter how bad the odds were stacked against them.

"Keiko, how did you end up in the cells where we found you?" Ryan said. "We saw no evidence of you entering the way we did."

Sofia's daughter cast her eyes down. "I wandered around down there and gave up. As a last resort, I asked the head librarian. He got upset – really upset – that I had been down in the archives without permission. Told me to wait in his office while he got the dean. But it wasn't the dean who showed up. Two security men arrived and took me through an entry by the librarian's office. Down through a long tunnel and into those labs, through a lot of locked doors. The strange thing was, they never harmed me in any way. They were nice and kind. Gave me food, drinks. Let me watch TV. They said not to worry. It would be all over soon, and I would be free to go."

Ryan glanced at Cal. "Your doing?"

"Sorry, Keiko. I needed you to get your mum, Ryan, and Booth out in the open. It was the best way to keep you safe." She grimaced. "Sofia, I never said it, but I'm sorry they tortured you. Yamada had promised your safety. I didn't know he would do that."

The two women eyed each other for a few moments. They had been friends for over fifteen years. What Cal had done was hard to comprehend. Ryan thought back to their time in the submarine, how he had agonized over the situation. He asked himself again: How well do you really know someone?

Cal seemed genuine. She was displaying all the traits. Warmth. Compassion. Sorrow. Her actions since had shown no indication of betrayal. Ryan shook away his doubts. He had to trust his heart. He believed her. He had to. If he didn't have that, what did he have?

"I know," Sofia said. "Let's move on. Do our jobs. Get the hell out of here and stop Yamada and Offenheim."

Ryan picked up the maintenance manual and flicked through it again, stopping on the page detailing the intake pipes and condenser tanks.

"You have that look in your eye," Cal said.

"What look?"

"Like the Tetris pieces don't fit."

"It's the crates. There are too many. We're too well supplied. Yamada said he doesn't want us to starve before we die of radiation poisoning. He wants us to die slowly.

Sure, but we have weeks of food and water. One can survive three weeks without food. Three days without water."

"Yeah, yeah. The rule of three. So?"

"So, it's still too much. And why the whiskey?"

"Maybe he wants us to drown our sorrows."

Ryan jumped up and paced in front of the door. He had ripped out a couple of pages of the manual and was holding them up to the light.

"The more I think about it, the more I realize Yamada wasn't upset at his son's death. He seemed amused – relieved, maybe. Like we did him a favor. Think about it. Why was Takeshi way out here?"

"You saw what was down in that lab. Touma would have wanted someone important overseeing it," Cal said.

"Maybe. It got me thinking. Something I overlooked before."

"A way out?" Cal said.

"Yes. A possibility, at least. This plant draws seawater in for cooling. We get out through there."

Ryan looked down at the plans. Was he right? Whatever the case, it was risky and would mean a swim for someone. A long swim.

"Find Booth and Allie," he said.

TWENTY-ONE

"Are you crazy?" Booth said. "That's the most insane thing you've ever come up with."

The Nameless were gathered around the maintenance plans, listening to Ryan.

"Someone has to swim sixty meters down this intake pipe, then come back inside and open the door," Ryan said.

"Exactly. Insane."

"I'm out. Last time I was in water, I nearly drowned," Cal said.

"I don't think I'd make it that far underwater," Sofia said.

"It's okay. I'll go," Ryan said. "See if you can find some rope as a safety line."

Allie let out a deep sigh. "I'll go."

"Out of the question. You're our only pilot. We need you."

"If we don't get out of here, it won't matter. Besides, I'm the only one capable. I used to swim competitively. Sixty meters underwater is nothing."

"It'll be dark."

"I can make it."

Ryan didn't like the idea, but he could see the sense in it. If Allie had indeed swum competitively, then she was best suited for the job. "All right. If you're confident. Do you think you can find your way back here?"

"I'll work it out." She pointed into the large containment room. "That big dome is a giveaway."

"Fine."

"Fine," Booth, Sofia, and Cal echoed.

The Nameless broke apart and gathered supplies for Allie. Ryan tipped out the contents of a plastic bag for Allie to put her clothes in. They all filed out of the room, through the small chambers and across the gangway. It took a few minutes to find the tank. The water was sky blue and had a tangy, metallic scent.

Allie took the plans from him and scanned them. "We can't drain the tank or reverse the flow of water?"

"I couldn't find anything about that in the manual. Maybe they don't risk it. I'm more worried about the water being contaminated, but the Geiger counter readings match what we have already." He waved the counter over the tank. "If you feel sick at any stage, come back. We'll figure something else out."

"Okay. Wouldn't these pipes have grates or something to stop fish coming up?"

"Nothing's marked."

"What's this?" Allie jabbed her finger at the page.

Ryan frowned. "Literally translated, it says *Draw off instalment*." He smacked the heel of his palm against his head. "I'm an idiot. It's a pumping station. To control the flow of water. You can exit through there after a thirty-meter swim."

"Good. I'll still do it," Allie said.

Ryan grasped her shoulder. "Thank you. I'm glad it was you I met on Koya. I wouldn't have made it off that mountain otherwise." He handed her the relevant pages of the manual.

Allie pulled off her top layer of clothes and raised an eyebrow at Booth. "Don't get any ideas. You still have to buy me dinner."

"I can't help it. Here you are, stripping in front of me."

"Turn around, then."

"And miss the show," Booth quipped as he placed her clothing in the plastic bag and tied the top.

Allie took one last look at the plans and dove into the cool water of the tank. She saluted, took a deep breath and kicked toward the bottom.

***

She began cramping after twenty meters. Up until then it had been easy going. Her heart thumped, pounding in her ears as, fighting the current all the while, she felt along the smooth metal above her head for the large access panel to the pumping station. The farther she traveled along the pipe, the stronger the pull toward the sea.

At last she located the access panel. Clinging to it, she strained with her fingers to grip the hatch. The opening mechanism gave without much resistance as she broke the surface and gasped in lungful's of air.

The pumping station was well lit, and there were no immediate threats visible. Allie squeezed the water from her underwear and wriggled into her dry clothes from the bag. The air outside was cool, and a slight breeze carried the scents of battle and fire. A chemical odor hung around, scratching the inside of her nostrils. She slowly turned, getting her bearings. The big dome loomed above her.

She set off toward the dome, pausing every few moments to listen, sniff the air, and stare into the semi-darkness. Nothing moved in the power plant, but the twisting maze of pipes made it difficult to see.

As she walked, Allie wondered if they would ever make it back to the United States. She had come to Japan seeking an escape. Seeking solitude, time away from her life, somewhere to figure out the next step. Instead, she had found horror and chaos, got tangled up in the machinations of a megalomaniac group. She smiled. She had also found Booth. Where that was going, she didn't know. Could it go anywhere?

Allie flinched as a gray powder dusted her exposed forearm. Glancing up, she spotted its source. A rifle with a long barrel was caught on some railings. Dog tags dangled below. Ash coated the area, swirled around by the breeze.

Howls broke through the silence, raising the hairs on her neck. They were out there somewhere. The Hounds. Allie had seen them. Evil-looking abominations created in the lab that now burned just out of view. A creature howled again, closer this time. Several others replied in rapid succession.

Had they picked up her scent?

Not wanting to hang around and find out, she climbed up the railings like she was in a child's playground and crouched down next to the scattered ash. She lifted the sniper rifle to her shoulder and peered through the scope. Immediately she spotted five of the wolf-like creatures. White fur. Long heads and weird, stretched-out limbs. They stopped and nuzzled one another, then sniffed the air and pawed the ground. That they could smell her was certain, but perhaps their eyesight was poor. Allie shrugged and, working the bolt action, loaded a round into the chamber. The scope had clear optics and she lined up one of the Hounds with ease. Her finger caressed the trigger. Allie had always found it hard killing animals. Even though these looked like something out of hell, they had to have been majestic wolves at some stage.

She stared through the scope. The Hound swiveled its head to look directly at her, as if it knew. It snarled, showing its teeth.

"Sorry," Allie whispered. She tugged the trigger. The Hound dropped as the kick of the rifle slammed into her shoulder. The boom of the supersonic bullet echoed around the plant. She slid the bolt and repeated the action, killing another of the Hounds and scattering the rest. They shrieked and howled, disappearing into the jungle of pipes and buildings. And sure enough, the howls were replaced by groans. Groans of workers. Workers who, instead of turning into ash or surviving, had become something else entirely. Not human. Siphons.

Allie looked around. The gangway she was on led to the roof. She could either go up or down. Down meant the dome and the trapped Nameless. Down also meant the Hounds and Siphons. Allie let out a groan of her own and rested the rifle on the railings. She loaded another round and picked her next target, and the next, saying a prayer for each one she killed. Once her path was clear. She stood up, and as she did so, her foot kicked an object amongst the remains. A Sig Sauer P365, still in its holster.

New howls interrupted her celebrations. The Hounds were back, and they'd brought friends. Lots of friends.

Allie groaned again and dashed down the stairs two at a time. Faster she ran, aiming for the big dome structure. She ducked under pipes and around sharp corners, ignoring the chasing pack. The noise they made as they yelped and howled was enough to wake the dead. On she ran, leaping down stairs and trying every door she came across. Locked. Faster, the sniper rifle banging against her bum. A shriek from above caused her to look up. Three Hounds had scaled to the roof of a square flat building and were tracking her. Allie grimaced and slipped the handgun free.

Shadows of Ash

Up ahead she spotted another door, larger than the rest, painted dull black with white Japanese writing. She urged her exhausted legs faster. The Hounds above her shrieked and leapt off the roof. Allie barely had enough time to swing the sniper rifle round in front to block the creatures' attack. Teeth smashed together centimeters from her face, and clawed feet scratched her legs. Somehow, she found the strength from deep down inside to fight back. It wasn't only the thought of dying that gave her the energy; it was also the thought of Booth and The Nameless dying from either starvation or radiation sickness. Allie let out a garbled howl of her own and pulled the trigger of the P365, silencing the beast on top of her. The second Hound attacked, and the third. Allie shot them in turn, and they fell, quivering and whimpering as they died.

Their pain tore at her soul. More Hounds slunk out of the shadows. Five? Six? Nine? It was difficult to judge their numbers. Allie rolled back her shoulders and eyed the door. So close but so far.

***

"You have that look again," Cal said.

Ryan grunted, low and guttural. "It's the can of Natto – fermented soybeans."

"So? What about it?"

"It tastes nasty. Only Japanese people eat it. People born here. Brought up on it."

"Like Vegemite?"

"That's delicious and good for you. But why would Yamada give us that?"

"I hardly think he'd care what food we ate."

Ryan shook his head and picked up the can, feeling its weight. He turned it over and chuckled. Showed Cal the object taped to the bottom: a pair of alligator clips used for making temporary electrical connections, and a small USB stick. "Sofia. Can you use these?" he said, throwing her the clips.

Sofia caught the clips and frowned. "The wires. That's what they're for."

Ryan stared at the USB before giving it to Sofia as well. He knew what it was – information on Offenheim. "Check what's on there too."

"We made Allie swim thirty meters, putting her in danger," Booth said. He banged on the concrete door. "C'mon. It's been ages."

Sofia deftly connected the clips to a cable from her tablet. She banged the side with her hand and muttered in Spanish under her breath. A few minutes later there was a clicking sound, followed by a groan as the door swung inward.

***

The Hounds attacked with an abrupt burst of speed, shrieking, saliva drooling, eyes red and wide. But amongst the rolling mass of white, Allie glimpsed a flash of gold. It sped past and skidded to a halt in front of Allie. A golden labrador. A split second later, another flash fought its way through the pack. Allie blinked at what she was witnessing and emptied her magazine at the creatures, firing until the gun clicked empty. She pocketed it, unslung the sniper rifle, and shot bullet after bullet until that clicked empty as well.

Carnage greeted her. The flash, she could now see, was a woman, and Allie watched her break the neck of the last Hound and spin toward her. Dressed in white, splashes of blood soaked her garments, blending with her mess of red hair. The woman gazed at Allie, nose twitching as if she was inhaling her scent. She smiled, making the freckles above her lip dance.

"Who are you?" the woman said.

"Allie."

"What are you doing out here?"

"My friends and I were trapped inside there." Allie gestured at the dome. "Where did you come from?"

The woman grinned and tilted her head. The dog wagged its tail, sniffed Allie, and licked her hand. "Dog likes you. I'm Ebony."

"You called your dog 'Dog?'"

"It's not my dog. I'll think of a better name soon."

"Thanks for fighting off those creatures."

"We'd better move. There are more out there." Ebony brushed past Allie and tried the handle. Locked, like all the others. She grunted, leant back, and kicked it open. "Let's go find your friends."

TWENTY-TWO

CASTLE ROCK, WASHINGTON

"What are they doing?" Reid said, lifting the NVGs that were mounted to his helmet.

"It's certainly odd behavior," Lisa whispered. She lifted her own NVGs, pivoted, and sat back down behind the low hill.

Lisa, Staff Sergeant Joe Reid, and corporals Clough and Torres had made it as far as Castle Rock before holing up for the night. They had spent the day driving back roads at a slow pace to avoid detection. Along the way, they had taken notes of any human survivors and any Black Skull operations. So far, both had been minimal.

Reid had suggested they stop in Castle Rock as it had ample high ground to observe both the interstate and secondary roads.

Lisa turned around and adjusted her NVGs. The Rabids were congregated around a cell phone tower like moths to a flame, silent, unmoving, their heads tilted back as if watching a fireworks display. She cast her mind back to her conversation with Dr. Johnson, Monica, and her discovery of nanites in the victim's blood. Though unconfirmed at this stage, did it have something to do with the odd behavior of these Rabids?

"Keep watching. Two hours each. Torres, you're up first," Lisa said.

The corporal moved into position without uttering a word. Lisa tapped Reid on the arm and, along with Clough, moved a few meters down the slope. They sat down and ate a quick meal.

"Any ideas?" Reid asked.

Clough shrugged. "Way above my pay grade."

"Forget about it for now." Lisa said. "Remember, our main goal is the commandos roaming around like they own the place. I've had a couple of run-ins with them already. The sooner we take them down the better. Clough, watch our backs. Same deal – two-hour shifts."

"Yes, ma'am."

Lisa pulled a small tarp from her backpack and checked her weapons. She leant back and gazed at the stars, running through all that had happened since the explosion and subsequent attack on LK3. It had to be connected to the satellite codes. To ReinCorp. All the strange events had begun when they had discovered the codes.

She sat up and grabbed the field radio. "I'm going to report to Munroe."

Clough and Reid barely responded as she made her way to the minivan. It was time to check in with Avondale too. Once in the van, it only took a few moments to dial up the correct frequency.

"Avondale."

"Director."

"It's good to hear your voice again. What have you got for me?"

"Black Skulls are sweeping through the smaller towns, rounding people up. A lot of them are wearing FEMA jackets. At this point, I haven't seen anything bad happening. Once the citizens have been given supplies and checked medically, they can return home. They are, however, shooting the Rabids on sight, and I watched a team take a few captive, hauling them away."

"Captive? That's weird. Have you seen any congregating around cell phone towers?"

Avondale coughed. *"No. Let me see."* The computer genius stopped talking and tapped on his keyboard, stopping only to click his mouse while muttering to himself.

"Yeah. I can see them. There's a group up in Longview. Hillsboro. Clackamas as well. What the actual flip?"

Lisa sighed. "Just another mystery to add to the list. Any luck locating The Nameless?"

"Yes. Their trackers show they're on the island of Hokkaido. The signal is weak, making it hard to pinpoint their precise location."

"Any other way?"

"Director?"

Lisa hesitated. Avondale's voice had a nervous tone she wasn't used to. "What is it?"

"Ever since the combusting event, I've been watching cellular networks for any spikes in activity. Mainly keeping an eye on ours here in the States, and in Japan – since that's where The Nameless are. There were two spikes, forty-five minutes apart, fourteen hours ago. Both the same frequency and strength. The strange thing is, it was on Hokkaido, closest point of interest, Tomari Nuclear Power Plant. I ran some checks and tried to access the network, but since I don't have any backdoors into their systems, that proved fruitless."

"You think its them?"

"I'd put money on it. I'm tracking any flights or shipping leaving the island just in case."

Lisa stared out the window. It was a crisp, clear night. The streetlights of Castle Rock blinked below. Could it be The Nameless were still alive?

She had hoped, even had confidence, that they were. Connors was one of the stubbornest sons of bitches she'd ever met.

"Thanks, Avondale. Keep up the good work. Out."

Lisa turned the detent dial and contacted Munroe. She didn't have long to wait, as she made contact at the same time every night.

Shadows of Ash

"Omstead. Good."

She made her report, filling the general in on what she had seen. He grunted a few times in reply.

"Johnson's here and wants to talk to you. I want your opinion after you hear what she has to say."

"Hi Lisa. This is going to sound bizarre, but you were right. Those were nanites we found in the dead sucker. His bloodstream and tissue were flooded with them. None were present in his cerebrospinal fluid though, or in his bone marrow. I found a half-formed cluster around his cerebellum and brain stem. The best way to explain it is that it looked like half a spider. Legs were pierced deep into his temporal and occipital lobes. I'm going to dissect the brain fully in the morning to see how far the strands go."

"Does that explain their ... their non-human behavior?"

"I would hazard a guess at yes. The temporal lobe controls speech, behavior, memory, your vision and hearing. The cerebellum and brain stem together control balance and coordination, your fine muscle controls, breathing, blood pressure. It makes sense. My hypothesis is yes. This half-formed cluster is causing these survivors to attack unaffected humans. But don't ask me how the nanites caused the combusting. We need a nanotechnology expert or similar for that."

"Huh." Lisa didn't know what else to say. She was used to dealing with enemies using conventional methods to cause harm. Weapons – both ordnance and chemical. During the Cold War, other methods were explored, such as psychology and manipulation, but this was a whole new level – hell, several levels above. She suspected ReinCorp. Had they developed nanotechnology, kept it secret, and used it to wipe out most of humanity?

"I think you're right, Monica," Lisa said. "It's the most logical explanation. What did you find in Harriet's blood?"

"Ah, yes. Now that is interesting. I found nanites too. Different. Older models. Primitive, even. But I can see the progression."

"That makes sense. The poor girl was their guinea pig. Keep investigating. If you need more subjects, get them."

"Okay. Stay safe out there."

Munroe came back on. *"You really think this is the cause?"*

"I do, sir. I've seen some weird shit in the field. I can't help but think that we've been played for fools. For a long time. I suspect ReinCorp is behind it all."

"The tech company?"

"Not only a tech company, but yes, them."

"Do you have any proof?"

"No, but I intend to get it."

"Where are their headquarters?"

"Berlin is their HQ, but they have offices all around the world. Denver is the American HQ."

"Damn. All right. Keep tracking those Black Skulls. Find their Forward Operating Base."

"Wilco, General. I think it's time you talked to my special operations officer. His name is Avondale. I'll get him to contact you."

"He has intel?"

"Yes, and he'll assist you with anything else. In return, I need your help bringing home one of my teams, from Japan. If we're going to get through this unscathed, we need each other's backs."

"Make it happen, Omstead. I'll see what I can do." The radio went silent.

Lisa hesitated before turning the detent dial back and calling up Avondale once more.

"Director."

"It's nanites. Nanites caused it all."

She was met with a whistle at the other end, followed by the sound of fingers tapping on the desk. *"Clever. It's the most logical explanation."*

"You thought of this?"

"I suspected, but thought we were years away from that kind of tech. Remember those streams of numbers Sofia and I found?"

"Yeah."

"IP addresses, like I thought. Now that you have confirmed it was nanotechnology, it makes perfect sense."

"How could they pull something like this off?" Lisa said. "I mean, it would've been a huge undertaking to keep it quiet."

"I'll leave those theories up to you, Director. That's more your field."

"How could they execute the combusting event? That's your mission. Figure it out for me."

"Gotcha."

"I also want you to contact Munroe. Assist him with anything he needs and see if you can track down The

Nameless. I want to know *if* they are alive and *what* they're up to. We've been in the dark for too long. Get in contact with them. Munroe's going to assist in bringing them home."

"As you wish," Avondale said, his voice fading away to be replaced with static.

Lisa signed off before making her way back to her team. She handed Torres a GoPro.

"Film the Rabids. Anything we see now, we film. General wants evidence."

Torres grunted and turned the high-definition camera toward the Rabids clustered around the cell tower.

Reid was fast asleep, breathing deeply.

As Lisa settled in for another night camping out under the stars, like she had done a thousand times before, her head spun with the same doubts and questions. Was it just ReinCorp behind it all, or was it bigger, more widespread? Avondale had been right; theories were more her field. Misdirection and lies. Smoke and mirrors. She smiled, thinking of her father's stories of the planning of D-Day. The Allies had even gone as far as to load a satchel with false information, place it on a dead soldier and float it to shore in Nazi-occupied Europe. They had constructed inflatable airplanes and tanks, massing them on the east coast of England to make the Germans think they were attacking at Calais.

It was all about misdirection. Occupy the enemy in one place while the real trick took place elsewhere.

***

Shadows of Ash

The first two captives, cowering in one corner of the cage, had been quickly overrun by the Rabids. They'd screamed when the suckers tore into their flesh and fallen silent when their spines were snapped and the fluid sucked out. Thick pools of blood now coated the floor of the cage. The Asian man who'd pleaded for his life, and another younger man, maybe twenty years of age, clung to the roof, watching the gory feast below.

To Zanzi, this was the wrong move. It would have been smarter to attack the Rabids while they were preoccupied with their meal. The bikers had set down an assortment of weapons just outside the bars. A couple of hammers, a hatchet, a mechanic's wrench. A couple of savage blows to the backs of their heads and they would have won.

"Give them a jolt," Grub demanded.

Axl jeered and zapped the two captives clinging to the roof with a cattle prod. The Asian guy howled as he fell and crawled toward a hammer, using his elbows to pull himself over the blood-soaked canvas. As he reached for the hammer, the younger man let go and crashed down on top of him, knocking the wind from his lungs. The bikers cheered and threw beer bottles and glasses at the cage, showering the battling occupants. Two of the Rabids looked up and spied the fresh meal. They shrieked, ear-splitting howls so shrill Zanzi wouldn't have thought it possible. The Rabids scrambled up and leapt toward the two men. The gang members cheered at this turn of events.

Zanzi pulled her eyes away from the carnage to observe the bikers. Their eyes were wide in a bloodlust she'd never seen before. These men and women liked what they saw.

Wanted more, demanded more. She glanced at Tilly and Josie. Both had their eyes squeezed shut, refusing to watch.

Grub tugged Zanzi closer and groped her breast. "You better watch. It's your turn in a few days." He licked the side of her face and exhaled cigar smoke into her eyes.

In the cage, the Rabids were tearing into the young man who had landed on the Asian. To Zanzi's relief, the Asian had managed to grab the hammer and pull himself up to stand. Tears streamed down his face as his chest heaved with sobs. He raised the hammer above his shoulder and brought it down onto the skull of the nearest Rabid in a frenzied attack. Pieces of skull bone and tissue flew into the air. The first Rabid down, he moved on to the next.

The two remaining Rabids finished their meal, leapt across the cage, and barreled into the Asian man. Within seconds he was buried beneath flailing arms and kicking feet.

Zanzi blanched as his screams for help were drowned out by the whooping bikers who were incited by their bloodlust and gladiatorial display. Their world had changed forever, and these men and women had chosen to embrace their most primitive desires.

"Keep watching, girly," Grub said. There was an audible crunch when the Asian man's spine broke. The Outcast Mongrels threw more bottles of beer and glasses at the cage. Some high-fived while others kicked barstools at the result of the fight. The biker who had taken bets and written them up on a whiteboard was writing up the results for all to see.

Grub stood and cheered. "Pay up, worthless assholes!"

Shadows of Ash

The bikers began handing him wads of money.

Once the frenzy had died down, Grub and Mutton led Zanzi, Tilly, and Josie deeper into their headquarters. Zanzi could see the gang had certainly been busy, collecting motorcycles, looting gun stores, and acquiring electronic goods. The goods were piled up on tables and stacked against walls in a haphazard manner.

The three women were shoved into a bedroom at the back of one of the houses. The room had a musty stench, mixed with the sour aromas of sweat and beer. The windows had plywood screwed over them like they were preparing for a hurricane, making the bedroom dingy.

"Get some rest," Grub said. "As a favor from me, I'll keep the boys off you tonight. From tomorrow onward, you're fair game." He chuckled, blew each of them a kiss, and shut the door.

Josie clutched her broken collar bone. "Why would they do something like that? And enjoy it?"

"People have always enjoyed watching others' misery," Zanzi said. "Look at reality TV."

She sat on one of the two beds against the far wall. A small bathroom was the only other exit. From the darkness inside, she could tell that window was blocked as well. Tilly sat next to her and hugged her.

"What are they going to do to us?" Tilly whispered. "What did he mean by fair game?"

"Don't worry about that. We're going to get out of here before we find out."

Josie sat on the other bed and drew her legs up to her chest. "Can you help me reset this collarbone?"

"Sure. Let me find something for you to bite down on." She left Tilly and scanned the room, her mind whirring with thoughts of escape.

The door banged back open. Grub took two steps into the room and yanked Tilly off the bed. "I changed my mind, bitches."

Tilly slammed her hands into the biker, but this only made him laugh more. "Oh, a fighter? Even better."

Zanzi launched herself at Grub. All the frustration at their seemingly hopeless situation came out in a rage-filled explosion and she landed a couple of blows to the side of Grub's head. He wheeled back but kept hold of Tilly. He shoved a Glock against Zanzi's temple.

"Calm down, bitch. You'll get your turn."

Zanzi could do nothing more. Without a weapon, the biker could do as he pleased. But she did have a weapon. The crossbow bolt tucked into the back of her bra. She took a step back. Grub followed her, his handgun still trained at her head. She weighed up the options. There was no way she could reach the bolt and stab Grub before he pulled that trigger. Then Tilly would be at their mercy forever. Zanzi took another step back and held her hands up. Grub smirked and kicked the door shut.

Stay strong, Tilly. I'll come for you.

The thought felt empty, even though she meant it. Her parents had never told her and Liam exactly what they did, but Zanzi was smart. She'd worked it out. She saw the cuts. The bruises. The faraway looks in their eyes, even if just for a fleeting second. In unguarded moments, she would see it in her father's eyes as he sipped his favorite lemon green tea. Or as her mom brushed her hair, getting ready for work. It was the look of someone who had seen true horror. Like they were putting on a brave face, determined that they were fighting the good fight. That their side was right.

Zanzi had chosen to pursue science, to better people's lives through medicine and technology. Despite her survival training, she had stayed on target until this nightmare had begun.

She sighed and looked around the shabby room. No, she hadn't trained to kill, but after what she'd witnessed these last few days, it was time to put her parents' training to the test. She didn't know if she could defeat the bikers, let alone ReinCorp and the Black Skulls, but as Ryan and Cal had often said. *"A slim chance is better than no chance at all."*

TWENTY-THREE

TOMARI NUCLEAR POWER PLANT
HOKKAIDO, JAPAN

Ryan clutched his hands behind his back and stared at the bank of monitors showing a plethora of camera views. The Nameless had found the control room within a few minutes of searching. He frowned, scanning the screens again. Allie had been gone too long. Hundreds of thoughts and doubts chipped away at his mind.

Had she made it?
Did I choose the right option?
Should I have insisted on going?

"She'll be okay," Booth said, voicing his concerns. "We can only hope."

"Got her," Sofia said. She jabbed her finger at one of the screens. Allie strode down the wide corridor, followed by Ebony and Sam – the dog they'd rescued in the lab.

"Yes!" Ryan pumped his fist. Finally, something was going right.

The Nameless ran from the room and waved as Allie came around the corner.

Sam, whimpering with excitement, his plumy tail wagging, bounded up to Ryan, bringing a smile as he hugged the dog.

"How did you get out?" Allie asked.

"Found some alligator clips under a can of beans. Sofia used them to hotwire the door open," Ryan said.

"They wanted us to get out after all?"

"I believe so. I think this OPIS organization is fractured; the four families are fighting for power. Yamada wants us alive to finish Offenheim."

"So I got wet for nothing. Nearly eaten..." Allie said. She smirked.

"Sorry about that. I should have found the clips earlier. We thought you hadn't made it."

"I nearly didn't. If it hadn't been for these two.... Those Hounds are everywhere, and Siphons." Allie handed Ryan the sniper rifle. "Found this. I'm out of ammo, though."

Ryan focused on Ebony. "I thought the explosion killed you."

"It'll take more than a few fires and explosions to kill me now," Ebony said.

"Ando?"

"In hell, where he belongs. They wanted the perfect killing machine. They got one." She shook Ryan's hand. "Thank you. For years, I dreamed of giving Ando his comeuppance." She tied her hair into a ponytail. "How did you guys end up in here?"

"Takeshi died during our escape. Yamada wasn't happy and used the nanites to knock us out. We woke up in here. Gaz?"

"Ran off, saying something about going home."

Behind Ryan, Allie and Booth embraced.

"Booth, Sofia, Keiko. This is Ebony and Sam. We found them down in the lab."

"Sam. That's a better name than Dog," Allie said.

Ebony shrugged. "Dog. Sam. Whatever suits."

"How did you survive that explosion?" Cal asked Ebony.

"I wasn't where they thought I was."

"You didn't set it off?"

"That was Ando's doing."

The Nameless gathered up their backpacks and filled them with food and water before rejoining Ebony and Sam in the corridor. The warning lights still flashed, and the alarm hummed in the background. Before they left the power plant, Ryan wanted to raid the medical clinic. He was certain it held at least Potassium iodide, used for treating mild cases of radiation sickness. But first they needed to decontaminate in a washroom.

It didn't take him long to find what he was looking for. Ebony kept an eye out for hostiles as The Nameless threw away their clothes and scrubbed themselves clean in the showers. Finding clothing proved trickier. On the whole, Japanese people were shorter than Westerners. And Ryan, at six foot two, grumbled as he squeezed into the ill-fitting overalls.

"You look like a Dutchman trying to find clothes in the Philippines." Booth laughed.

"Yeah, yeah."

They located the medical clinic a few doors down. Ryan scanned everyone with the Geiger counter and was happy to find it only read forty counts per second now.

Cal handed out the Potassium iodide tablets and poured the remainder into her backpack.

"Something's been bothering me about the nanites," she said.

"What's that?" Ryan said.

"Well, they heal bullet wounds, cuts, and bruises. Repair tissue damage. Wouldn't they repair damage from radiation sickness too?"

"Maybe, but I'd rather cover all the bases. Just in case."

"What's the plan now?" Cal said. "Are we still going through with taking out their satellites?"

"It's the best idea we have, unless someone can think of something better?"

Ryan was met with shaking heads. It was a crazy plan, open to disaster, but if they could pull it off, it would save countless lives.

"Sofia, how much time do we have?"

"A little under two days. I need at least half of that to work with Avondale. Figure out their trajectories and maneuver them onto a collision course. Plus, we must be sneaky so that OPIS doesn't see us doing it."

Shadows of Ash

"Is that possible?"

"Yes. We can turn off the LK3 transponders. I'm hoping they won't notice. It's a risk, but what isn't."

Ryan rubbed his hand over the stubble on his chin. "Allie, where's the nearest airport?"

"Chitose. Near Sapporo."

"Private jets?"

"Definitely. I've flown in and out of there plenty."

"Good. It's settled then." Ryan looked at Ebony. "What about you?"

"I'm coming with you."

Sofia chuckled at something she was watching on her tablet, then handed it to Ryan. "You'll want to see this. All of you."

The screen showed another video from Touma Yamada. *"If you are watching this, you figured the way out of the power plant. I apologize for any stress or trouble that I have caused. I had to make Goro believe that you were going to die. As much as he struggled with his father, he still loved and respected him. To that end, I had to initiate this ruse. Yes, I'm upset at losing my son and Ando, but I need you for something bigger than all of us. Something that will make their sacrifice worthwhile. Contained on the USB is most of the information I have on Offenheim and some of the other members of OPIS. Take it and finish this."*

Yamada smiled and the screen went dark.

No one spoke for several moments. Ryan shook his head; his suspicions had been right. "Let's go."

Hounds prowled around the car park. As far as Ryan could see, there were ten of them. As The Nameless exited the building, the creatures' heads lifted, wolf-like snouts pointing into the air, sniffing. Their red eyes locked on The Nameless. Ryan lunged for the door as it swung shut behind Sofia, locking them all out. He cursed and pivoted.

Sam snarled and sprinted straight for the creatures. "Get out of here," Ebony screamed as she took off, slamming shoulder-first into the nearest Hound. It flew into the air for several meters before hitting the concrete, rolling, snarling, grunting.

Cal pressed the button on the key fob she'd found in a staff room. A Toyota SUV beeped, and its lights flashed. The Hounds howled and renewed their efforts to reach The Nameless, but Ebony fought them off with superhuman strength and speed. In a flurry of movements, she kicked and punched, grappling with first one wolf and then another, snapping their necks. By the time Ryan had ushered everyone inside the SUV and pulled out of the car park, only three Hounds were left. They had leapt on top of cars and surrounded Ebony and Sam. Both woman and dog had splashes of blood across their chests and around their mouths. Hound bodies lay at odd angles.

Ryan gunned the engine and squealed to a stop next to Ebony. "Get in!" he yelled as a cacophony of howls filled the early morning air. The Hounds on the cars answered the calls with howls of their own. Ryan didn't wait around once Ebony and Sam were in. By the sounds of it, Ando had built an army of wolf creatures and they were all loose.

They'd only traveled a kilometer down the road when Ryan slammed on the brakes. The SUV skidded to a stop next to a crashed Humvee.

Shadows of Ash

"What the hell are you doing, Connors?" Booth yelled, gesturing toward the pack of Hounds tearing toward them.

"Guns," Ryan said. He reached inside the crashed vehicle and grabbed two HK416s and one Glock 19 and passed them to Cal.

"Hurry!" Cal said.

***

Thirty minutes later they'd left the Hounds far behind. Ryan drove in silence, taking directions from Allie as they slowly made their way to Chitose Airport. Progress was slow but steady. Like the motorways outside Osaka, vehicles clogged the roads. They had to stop several times and push cars, and even the odd truck, out of the way. Several times, Ryan spotted other survivors in the distance. Some drove, some walked, while others were on bicycles. They were all headed in the same direction. Curiosity getting the better of him, he clicked on the car radio. A prerecorded voice crackled from the speakers. He translated for the non-Japanese speakers.

"Citizens of Hokkaido, please make your way to Sapporo. We have opened a center at Moerenuma Park. The government is providing you with food, water, and medical care. Please register so we can provide you with better care and put you in contact with family members. We are working on solutions. Do your duty for Japan."

The message repeated several times before Cal switched it off. "That's how they're infecting the survivors. Giving them nanite-contaminated food and water."

"I thought we stopped the second wave in Japan?" Allie asked.

"No. We stopped Offenheim from taking over. Yamada has other plans. Even more reason we need to succeed," Ryan said.

He drove on past crashed trucks and rolled vans. Piles of ash had been scattered by the wind and rain. Mutilated cadavers, their necks broken and licked clean, lay over a barrier as he pulled into the airport, scattering a murder of crows.

Allie pointed away from the terminal toward a cluster of hangars. Several FedEx jets were parked on the tarmac, next to a couple of cargo planes.

"Eyes sharp," Ryan said. He crashed through the barrier arm and, slowing down, entered the first hangar.

He whistled at the sight. Three blue and white jets were neatly parked, red carpets leading to open doors.

"No good," Allie said. "Those are Honda jets. Max distance thirteen hundred miles. If you want to reach Dutch Harbor on the Aleutian Islands, that's at least twenty-five hundred miles. We need a Learjet or maybe one of those FedEx cargo planes."

"Go with what your gut tells you," Cal said.

"Keep looking. I'd prefer a Learjet. Faster, more comfortable, better maneuverability in case we're attacked."

Ryan drove on. Each of the hangers had a different company's jets parked up.

"Try the hangar over there." Allie pointed to a second group of buildings. These hangars were much larger than the rest and had been painted in bright red and white paint.

Matsuda Industries was painted across the side in large black letters. A Learjet sat inside. As in the other hangars, a red carpet led to a rolling staircase and the aircraft's cabin.

"Perfect," Allie said. "Learjet 60XR. This will take us where we need to go."

As The Nameless loaded their gear, tires squealed on the concrete outside in the distance. Booth ran to the hangar doors and peered out.

"We got company. Japanese Defense Force. Three trucks."

"Where?" Cal said.

"They're at the first hangar, beginning a sweep."

Ryan cursed and threw his backpack to Allie. "Get her ready. Does it need refueling?"

"I'll check. Normally when the planes are in this position, they're ready for departure." She disappeared inside the luxurious plane.

"Ebony, when they come in here, let me do the talking," Ryan said. Ebony raised a questioning eyebrow but said nothing. He didn't need to say anything to his team. They were well-versed in keeping the peace when they had to. The guns were tucked away, out of sight but close enough to act if needed.

Cal threw Ryan a suit bag she'd found in the office. "Put this on. You'll look more the part." The bag contained a pilot uniform complete with white shirt and blazer. The arms and legs were a couple of centimeters short, but it was a much better fit than the overalls. Once he'd finished dressing, Ryan tucked the gun into his waistband and covered it with his shirt.

"Here they come," Booth warned. He jogged back and stood with the others.

The Defense Force soldiers entered the hangar, rifles raised, eyes alert. Ryan turned and smiled, holding up his hands.

"Whoa. Easy now, fellas. We're American citizens trying to get home."

The lead soldier stopped a few meters away. He raised his radio and spoke in rapid Japanese. Ryan only caught a few words, but he understood the gist. *We found some.*

He signaled Cal using sign language. *Stay alert. Fuel? Fully loaded*, she signed back.

At least that was something going their way. After hearing the radio instructions, Ryan had purposely taken smaller roads. Maybe they had just been unlucky. He had hoped for the best, but as the old saying went, prepare for the worst.

"Captain Jordan," Ryan said, holding out his hand. The soldier ignored him and kept his rifle trained on the group. Six more Defense Force soldiers arrived. They blocked the hangar doors and made a show of clicking the safety switches off. One of the soldiers, a sergeant, approached Ryan.

"Who are you and why are you here?" he said in English.

"As I was saying, my name is Captain Jordan. Inside the cockpit is Richards. We're trying to get back to the States to our families, using the company jet."

"You work for Matsuda Industries?"

"Yes, sir."

"And these people?"

Shadows of Ash

"Tourists who were staying in the same hotel. They were here for the big sumo tournament." Ryan smiled again, remembering the signs everywhere.

"Why are they wearing gray overalls?"

Ryan chided himself for forgetting a small but important detail. For a deception to be successful, it was best to base it in truth. He gestured at Ebony and Booth.

"We found these two trapped inside the nuclear power plant. There was a fire, so we went to investigate. It looked like a battle had taken place. You may what to check it out. Be careful, though, those things are everywhere." He paused and pointed to the Geiger counter. "I changed everyone into the overalls as a precaution."

The sergeant pivoted and conversed with the soldier behind him in hushed tones. The soldier walked back to the truck and spoke into a radio.

The Japanese sergeant flicked his eyes between the members of the group. His face was difficult to read. The soldiers had relaxed their pose, their rifles now pointed at the ground rather than at The Nameless.

"All civilians are to report to Moerenuma Park. Foreigners included. The radio transmission was extremely clear. Did you think you could just take a Japanese plane and leave?" the sergeant said.

Ryan bowed deeply. "I'm sorry. We meant no offense. We heard the transmission, but it was in Japanese."

"It was in English too."

"We never heard it, and as a result, received no instructions. So we took matters into our own hands. If you let us, we could be on our way and out of your hair."

"Impossible. You will accompany us and be processed. Transportation will then be organized."

"Sergeant. We're ready to go. Less paperwork for you."

"That is of no consequence to me Captain Jordan."

The soldier returned and spoke to his superior.

"It would appear that you were correct about the fire," the sergeant said. He clipped his heels together. "Please, come with us. We will take care of everything."

Ryan bowed for a second time. Behind his back he signaled for Booth and Cal to be ready. He ran through the odds in his head. The soldiers had grown bored while he and the sergeant talked. The Nameless had displayed a relaxed pose and acted like concerned tourists. Ebony had sat down on the stairs with Sam, patting his shoulders. Eight armed soldiers in total. Seven who'd be able to respond in seconds. One – the sergeant – would take longer. Ryan could take down two before they knew what was happening. So would Cal and Booth. That left a further two. As always, Ryan struggled with decisions like this. He was trained to sneak in and out of places, avoid entanglements at all costs. Killing fellow soldiers who were just doing their job wasn't what he had signed up for. Protecting and serving humanity, however, was. *For the many, we sacrifice the few.*

He rose from his bow. "Of course. I apologize for the misunderstanding." At the same time, he held three fingers at a right angle, behind his back, and drew the Glock. He fired at the two soldiers to the sergeant's immediate left. He hit them both in the throat. Blood sprayed out in a gruesome arc.

Shadows of Ash

Pop. Pop.

He swung his pistol back in the direction of the sergeant. The soldier behind him fired his rifle, hitting Ryan in the upper left arm and spinning him around and down to the ground. Booth and Cal fired at the remaining soldiers while Ebony burst off the stairs and vaulted over the prone Ryan in an awe-inspiring leap. She landed in front of the sergeant and twisted his neck with an audible crunch.

Less than five seconds had passed, and eight Japanese Defense Force soldiers were dead.

Without being instructed, The Nameless spread out. Cal checked Ryan's wound. The bullet had gone straight through the muscle and missed the bones. It hurt like crazy, but the nanites had already begun their work, repairing the damage. A few minutes later, it was just an angry red mark. Throbbing, but nothing more.

They brought the two trucks inside the hangar, stripped the bodies of ammo and weapons and loaded them into the vehicles.

The Japanese Defense Force trucks proved to be a goldmine of much-needed resources. Cold-weather clothing, more ammo, and food. They loaded it all into the Learjet 60XR and slammed the door shut.

The engines were whining awake as Ryan took the co-pilot's seat.

"That was ruthless," Allie said, flicking switches.

"Not our usual style, but circumstances called for it." He said a silent prayer for the soldier's families. "Flight path sorted?"

"Dutch Harbor course plotted. Get some rest. Five hours flight time." Allie smiled. "It feels good to be in the cockpit again. Send Booth up when you're ready. Now buckle in and please enjoy our in-flight entertainment."

Ryan grinned. He liked Allie and was thankful that out of all the people in Koya, she had survived and opted to come with him. "Thanks, Allie. We couldn't have done any of this without you." He left her there and took his seat next to Cal. Keiko sat with Ebony, Sam across their laps, in the seats opposite. The seats were wide and comfortable, covered in soft leather.

"Booth. Captain wants your assistance."

"Yes, sir."

"Try not to distract her too much."

Booth slapped him on the shoulder as he left the cabin. The movement caught Ebony's attention. She looked between Cal and Ryan.

"You know something. I ran away to Japan thinking I could leave my problems behind. Stupid selfish reasons. Now look at me. A freak."

"A freak?" Ryan said. "How so?"

"You've seen what I can do."

"How long were you Ando's prisoner?" Cal asked.

"Depends. What year is it?"

"Twenty twenty-one."

Ebony shook her head and stared back out the window. When she looked back, she had tears in her eyes and one tracking down her cheek. "I was a few hours away from being free. Ando drugged me. When I woke up, I was in a cell..." She looked out the window again. Sam whimpered and nestled his snout into her chest.

"When did they take you?"

"New Year's Eve. The Millennium."

Cal whistled and shook her head. For twenty years, Ebony had been subjected to the horrors they had seen down in the lab. How many victims had been cast aside, preserved in tanks, before they figured out the right formulae? Ebony had the appearance of someone in their early twenties, not a woman in her forties.

Ryan was eager to go through the plan with everyone but after the harrowing experiences they'd all had over the last few days, he left them to relax.

Cal kissed his hand. "You okay?"

"I can't help but think that Yamada was just testing us."

"Maybe. Does it matter?"

"This whole crazy situation. We've always been two steps behind. I'm tired of it."

The plane eased its way onto the runway and the engine noise rose several decibels as the jet shot forward. Within seconds, the Learjet was banking away and heading northeast. Ryan let his eyes wander over the disappearing islands of Japan.

He had come to this country seeking solitude and reflection. To assess the next stage in his life. After so long fighting with every available resource to help keep the world safe, he had been burnt out. A hollow shell. His family's sacrifice had been great – greater than most. For a year he had found what he sought but, like his mentor had told him many times: *"You can leave the spy game, but the spy game never leaves you."* Ryan had thought it corny and ridiculous, but John Stapleton, as wrinkled and chain-smoking as he had been, was right. It never left; that desire to do what had to be done. Now they had a new mission, a vital mission. One that could either save the world or doom it to an even worse fate.

"I'm tired too," Cal whispered. "For three years I dreamt of seeing you again. Explaining why and how we could win. Have we underestimated Offenheim?"

"I don't think so. We know what we're up against now."

"I hope you're right." Cal rubbed a hand over her head and rested it against his shoulder.

Ryan looked out over the Pacific Ocean again. Despite his doubts, he was glad to be heading home. He kissed his wife on the cheek. "Whatever happens next, I'm happy I got to be with you again. I hope we get to see Zanzi soon."

He looked across the cabin. Sofia was busy tapping on her tablet, scribbling notes into her notebook. He reached up and dimmed the lights, hoping to get some rest before the operation ahead.

TWENTY-FOUR

PORTLAND, OREGON

There was nothing in either the bedroom or the bathroom that could assist Zanzi to escape. The windows only had sheets of plywood screwed over them, but she couldn't get enough force behind her kicks to dislodge the timber, and she had nothing to pry them off with. No tools, nothing. She even looked inside the toilet cistern, checking to see if it was an old ballcock system that had a small piece of copper, but it was a modern system, the mechanism made from plastic. The rooms were bare, only containing beds, musty blankets, and discarded food wrappers.

Zanzi lay down, running through her mind all that she'd noted. The windows were out. What then? She eyed the hinges on the door but discounted them immediately – she had nothing to hammer the pins out with. The walls were sheetrock. A couple of well-placed kicks and she could make a hole large enough, but the biker standing guard would hear it. An idea sparked in her mind. Zanzi jolted up and went back into the bathroom. Yes. Above the shower was an extractor fan. It, like the drywall, was plastered in mold. She stood on her tiptoes and tested the ceiling. It was soft and spongy and gave way with minimal pressure. Thinking quickly, she grabbed the bundle of wet towels and placed them in the shower. Praying that the party noise would be enough to drown out her efforts, she punched the ceiling out around the extractor fan. Little pieces at first, then larger ones as her confidence at not being discovered grew. Five minutes later, she had a hole large enough to climb through into the ceiling cavity.

"Josie?"

The scientist stirred and rolled onto her side. She rolled her shoulder, testing it. She nodded, apparently satisfied that it had healed. "What are you doing in there?"

"Getting us out and finding Tilly. I need a lift." Zanzi showed her the hole in the ceiling.

"You'll get us killed trying to escape," Josie said.

"They're going to do that anyway." Zanzi tugged another piece of drywall down. "Cup your hands like this."

"Wait a minute." Josie pulled her away. "They'll hear you. What then? They'll rape us and possibly kill us."

Shadows of Ash

"We have to escape now. It's our best chance. Listen. What do you hear?"

Josie turned away and cocked her head. "A party. So what?"

"Right. They're drunk. Reactions are slow. We must do it now. Tomorrow, we'll be in that cage fighting Rabids. If we somehow survive that, the gang will continue to use us as entertainment until we're dead."

"I don't want to risk it." Josie made to leave the bathroom, but Zanzi grabbed her arm.

"Listen, Doctor. What the hell do you want? Yesterday you wanted to kill Offenheim and those responsible for Harriet's death. Now you're willing to wait while these animals do what they want with us?"

"After seeing their display out there, I'm thinking that maybe ReinCorp and Offenheim were right. The world needed a reset. To be rid of people like that." Her face softened, her mouth twitching into a firm smile. "They'll come for us. ReinCorp men. We just have to be patient."

"All the more reason we need to leave."

"I'm staying. They'll come."

Zanzi groaned and let go of the scientist's arm. "I had this friend in high school. She would come to school, always wearing thick make-up. The mean girls would tease her, and the jocks would call her horrible names – you know, the usual crap. I had suspicions why, but I never had any proof. She never invited anyone over, she always came to our house. Some days she wouldn't wear any make-up, and she would smile and be happy, make jokes, come swimming with us. But the make-up always returned, along with her sullen moods. Whenever I asked her, she deflected.

"After my brother died, I went to grief counselling. My friend was there too. It was only then I learned that her mother beat her. Blamed her for her father's suicide. The sad thing is, my friend believed her mother. Said she was the reason. Said she wasn't good enough. I found that heartbreaking. Offenheim killed billions of people. Innocent people. Your daughter. Now you're defending them?"

"Better ReinCorp than these creeps."

"You're being ridiculous," Zanzi said.

Josie turned away and faced the wall, ending the conversation.

Regardless of what Josie thought, Zanzi was still going to attempt escape. There was no way she was going to wait and see. Tilly needed her help. She owed the young woman that much. Tilly had helped her in The Eyrie with her chatter, with her stories, her optimistic character. Zanzi shuddered to imagine what the bikers were doing to her.

Using the walls of the shower stall, Zanzi climbed up into the ceiling like scaling a chimney. The air in the cavity was stale and had a slightly moldy odor. She knocked eddies of dust motes as she crawled over the ceiling joists. Using the HVAC system as a guide, she made her way across their prison and into the rest of the house. It was slow going and painful on her hands and knees. Zanzi paused at a ventilation grate and peered through. It was another room with captives, three that she could see. Two African American females and a scrawny white guy with blue hair. She wanted to call out a greeting and give them hope, tell them that she was working on a way to free them. But she didn't.

The next bedroom was empty. World War Two memorabilia adorned the walls and shelves, mainly German, with some Russian. Nazi symbols and helmets. Knives, and a uniform in a frame.

Zanzi moved on, hunting for the access panel. She found it next to a room from which loud punk music blared through the sheetrock. Singing and stomping reverberated as she slid the panel over and peeked out. The access opened into a hallway, the carpet stained and old. She risked a quick glance, looking for a back door or something similar, but found only trash. Beer cans and fast-food wrappers were everywhere. Lying against a doorway was a comatose man, a Jack Daniels bottle gripped in his hand. She moved the trapdoor back into place and carried on. It was tough going, moving over the sharp edges of the timber. She had to remind herself why she was doing it. Why she had to do it.

Grub was easy to recognize as he lay in bed. Traci, the woman the gang had tormented during the fight, lay with a thin arm covered in track marks draped across his tattooed chest. Then she saw Tilly. Tilly was handcuffed to the bedpost, both arms behind her head, her naked chest exposed. She was shivering, her eyes puffy from crying.

Zanzi pulled back from the ventilation grate and steadied herself, catching a sob that threatened to escape her throat.

Grub stirred on the bed and propped himself up on one elbow, roughly shoving Traci off him.

"Hey. What the fuck?" she grumbled.

"Get off me, dumb bitch." He shoved the junkie again and looked at Tilly. "I want to fuck this one now. She's watched; now it's her turn."

Tilly brought her knees up to her chest and shook her head. "Go away. I don't like boys."

Grub laughed. "Don't like boys? Lezzie then, is it?" He pulled Tilly's legs out straight and tried to crawl on top of her. "Traci here likes girls too. You can have both."

"Get off!" Tilly screamed, so loud dust rained on Zanzi from the rafters. She kicked out at the biker, which only angered him. He slammed his fist into the side of her head, dazing her.

Traci jumped onto his back, scratching and yelling obscenities. Grub hollered and threw the junkie off. She landed in a heap against the wall. Grub kicked her a couple of times.

"Stay out of this, bitch." He kicked her again, brutal blows that lifted the skinny woman off the floor. "No more meth for you, worthless whore."

Zanzi had seen enough. She jumped through the aging drywall. A fine mist of plaster rained into the room as Zanzi plummeted the eight feet to the bed. Despite her outrage, she had judged her entry well, falling directly onto Grub's head, first with the sheet of drywall, then her knees. He grunted and cried out as he hit the floor.

Zanzi rolled away and winced as the force of her drop vibrated up her legs and back. Quickly she scanned the bedside table for keys to Tilly's handcuffs and pulled out her weapon—the crossbow bolt.

Grub stumbled as he rose, throwing the sheetrock away. His eyes widened when he recognized Zanzi. "What the fuck? You?"

Zanzi breathed out, took two steps forward, leaned back slightly, and swiveled from her hips, aiming a roundhouse kick for his head.

Grub flinched away, taking the blow on his shoulder. "Fuck you!" he spat.

She ignored his curse and glanced at the other bedside table. There were the keys! She had perhaps ten more seconds before the guard came rushing in. She had banked on the fact that he had drunk too much, but was that going to be enough?

Grub was opposite the door. She was blocking his escape. Traci was nearest, on her hands and knees, gasping from Grub's attack.

"Traci, get up. We need you."

All the junkie could manage was a pitiful moan. She was down. Spent, with nothing left to offer.

Grub growled. He leapt at Zanzi, arms and hands outstretched like a Rabid hoping for a meal.

Zanzi twisted and ducked, rolling across the bed. She grabbed the keys and shoved them into her pocket.

The biker scrambled toward her. She whipped the crossbow bolt out of her bra and held it like a knife, eyeing up the side of his neck where his jugular would be.

"Is that your weapon?" Grub said, smirking.

"It's all I need."

The room shook with a tremendous explosion. Glass shattered. Metal shrieked.

People screamed and shouted out as rifle fire pounded over the party noise.

Grub staggered back and caught himself on the bed. He shook his head as if shaking the ringing from his ears. He unlocked the door and glared back at her. "I'll deal with you later," he snarled.

To Zanzi, the threat sounded empty, like he was saying it more as an assurance to himself. More people screamed as smaller explosions tore through the Outcast Mongrels' fortress. The bikers were answering the attack with gunfire of their own, but it sounded sporadic and messy compared to the controlled bursts of the attackers.

Zanzi unlocked Tilly and kissed her on the forehead, brushing her messy hair aside. "Are you okay? Did he violate you?"

"I don't think so." Tilly shook her head. "I mean, I don't know what violate means."

"Did he touch you where he shouldn't have?"

"Ew, no."

"Good. We need to get out of here. Whoever's attacking isn't going to differentiate between friend and foe." Zanzi pointed up. "Through there."

Tilly shrugged into her top and pulled it down over her waist.

The battle outside grew in intensity. The rifle fire was joined by shotgun blasts and Harley Davidsons' throaty roars as bikers fled. On a hunch, Zanzi checked under the bed and smiled at the stash of weapons. She discounted

Shadows of Ash

the AR-15s and AK47s. The Mossberg's were too bulky as well. She pulled out a silver metal case and flicked open the lid. Four Sig Sauer P229 Compacts gleamed at her. She took three, and all the magazines, cramming them into every available pocket. She double-checked hers was loaded and, with Tilly's help, moved the bedside table under the hole in the ceiling.

Traci groaned and tried to stand. "What's happening?"

"The bikers are under attack. Can you stand?"

Traci groaned again but managed to stay upright. "There's a tun—" She gasped and held her side.

Zanzi wanted to help her, but with her injuries – most likely broken ribs – she wouldn't cope with the crawl through the ceiling cavity.

"There's a tunnel," she gasped out, and moaned as she opened one of the drawers. She brightened as she pulled out a bag of crystal meth. Without hesitation, she opened it and swallowed a couple of chunks.

"A tunnel? What do you mean? For escaping?"

"It's where they hide this stuff." Traci wiggled the bag of drugs. "And in case the pigs raid us. Bull, the former president, made them build it." She swallowed another chunk of meth.

"Where is it?" Zanzi asked. She moved to the door and strained her ears, trying to determine where the battle was taking place. The gunfire had slowed, with only an occasional pop of rifles and boom from shotguns coming now. There were the distant sounds of screams and pleading before single shots rang out, silencing them. Whoever had attacked, they were executing, not taking prisoners.

Black Skulls? It had to be. Maybe they did care about Doctor Josie Lahm after all and had sent a squad to track her down. With the noise the motorbikes had made, it wouldn't have been hard. The Black Skulls must have waited until the bikers were drunk and wrecked from the party before attacking.

"The tunnel's in the middle, between all the houses. Behind the main bar," Traci said.

Zanzi nodded and looked back at Tilly. Her priority was Tilly's safety, and her own. Josie had made her choice, deciding to stay. It was too risky to try to help the doctor as well, but they needed her knowledge. Indecision twisted her stomach. More gunfire erupted, much louder this time. She sighed. "Let's go, then."

Traci bounced back to the bedside table. She yanked out the drawer and flipped it over. A key was taped to the underside.

"Grub thinks he's clever, but he's just an asshole." She smirked and unlocked the door. Zanzi stopped her with a tug on the shoulder. "I'll go first." She handed Tilly one of the P229s and showed her the safety. "Just point and shoot. Don't hesitate. These men will kill us. Okay?"

Tilly turned the gun over, feeling its weight.

"Careful," Zanzi said. "Keep it pointed at the floor, away from your body and me. Only bring it up when you see a bad guy."

"How can I tell if he's bad?"

"Assume they're all bad."

Zanzi dropped into a crouch and creaked open the door. The drunk guard had gone, leaving the hallway empty. She tried to remember the route back to the bar and the cage. That was their destination, but first she had some prisoners to rescue.

TWENTY-FIVE

SOMEWHERE OVER THE BERING SEA

The cockpit door banged open, jolting Ryan awake. He reached for his gun, habit dictating his actions.

"Easy, old fella." Booth grinned. "We're being hailed."

"Hailed? Who?"

"*USS Nimitz.*"

Ryan stood and shook the fuzz from his head. Ever since the first combusting incident on Koya, he couldn't shake the feeling of doom whenever he slept. After Yamada had knocked out The Nameless, his anxiety had grown.

Allie glanced up as Ryan entered the cramped cockpit. She held her hand over the microphone on her headset.

"I told them we're American citizens heading home from Japan."

"Did you use any of our names?"

Allie shook her head. Ryan sat in the co-pilot seat and eased the headset over his head.

"This is Captain Jordan."

"Jordan. OS Waugh from the USS Nimitz. *Your co-pilot has informed us of your point of departure. What is your intended destination?"*

"Good to hear your voice, Waugh. We had a hell of a time leaving Japan. Do you have any idea what's going on? It's like World War Three out there."

"I'm afraid I don't have that information, sir. Please state your destination."

"We're heading home to Portland, Oregon, but we have to refuel in Dutch Harbor."

"Stay your course. I have an escort to guide you in. Do not stray from your current flight path. Any move to do so and you will be fired upon. Understand?"

"That's highly unnecessary, OS Waugh. We're American citizens."

"Stay your course, Captain Jordan. F-18s will be there shortly. Over and out."

Waugh's voice was replaced with white noise. Ryan shifted in his seat and looked out the window. OS Waugh was true to his word. Screaming out of the clouds, two F-18s approached. They flew close enough to tip their wings and give him the thumbs up.

"Unknown aircraft. Keep on your current flight path to Dutch Harbor."

Shadows of Ash

"Wilco," Ryan said, giving them his own thumbs up. The F-18s moved away but stayed close.

Allie clicked off the radio and let out a long breath. "Holy crap. I thought that was it."

"Really?" Booth said.

"Can you understand why? With what's going on out there, I thought they'd just shoot us down. Protect our borders."

Ryan nodded. Allie made a fair point. If he was being honest with himself, he too had some fear, but OS Waugh had given no indication apart from a warning. "Booth, inform the others. What's our ETA, Allie?"

"Thirty minutes out. It's going to be bumpy. There's a storm brewing."

"Okay. We must keep up the charade, even on the ground. You can tell them your real name, but we can't – at least not until I know they're on our side."

"They're US Navy, though."

"Even so. Yamada told me that OPIS went deep. They had men and women in power all over the world. Everywhere. Until I know, we go anonymous."

Allie turned her attention back to flying the Learjet. She used the radio to inform their escort of any small tweaks as they began their descent into Dutch Harbor.

Allie's prediction was spot on; the private plane bumped and jolted as it dropped below the gray clouds and swooped over the Bering Sea, the F-18s mirroring their every move. Allie circled the runway, checking for any litter. A plane sat at one end, unmoving. Apart from that, it was clear.

Five minutes later, Allie taxied the jet to a halt outside the small terminal building. The two F-18s landed too and took up flanking positions alongside the Lear.

Ryan entered the cabin and looked at everyone. "Keep your wits about you. Stick to the story. We lost our passports in our escape from Japan and the Siphons. If they separate us, remember what we must do, what's at stake."

The Nameless and Ebony answered him with grunts and nods. He didn't want any more delays. They had maybe eighteen hours to stop the second wave. Sofia needed all that time. Ryan's job was to get them into the NSA spy station. Was anyone there alive? If so, were they OPIS?

Booth and Allie pushed open the door and the stairs unfolded in one smooth motion. Ryan waved at the two pilots. One had exited his aircraft, while the other stayed in his.

"Captain Jordan," he said as he walked down the stairs.

The pilot kept his pistol trained on Ryan. "Bring everyone out." The tell-tale thump of a helicopter's rotors echoed over the windswept bay.

Ryan turned and beckoned everyone out. They stood in a small huddle. Pre-planned by Cal, it was all about giving the pilots, and whoever was in the chopper, what they expected to see. The lie was that they were tourists, stuck in Japan, chased by creatures and the defense force when all they wanted to do was to get home. Huddling together gave off a non-threatening vibe, like they had a shared experience. She hoped it sold the lie.

The SH-60 Seahawk bumped to the ground a short distance away and disgorged six heavily armed men. Once

Shadows of Ash

The Nameless were surrounded, the F-18 pilot jumped back into his cockpit. The leader of the armed men – a colonel – slung his rifle and took off his helmet.

"Peter Booth." He laughed. "What the hell are you doing out here?" The colonel pivoted and waved the F-18 pilots away. The scream of their jet engines was deafening as they took off and banked southwest. The colonel signaled to two of his men. They entered the Learjet and began searching the cabin.

"Well, Booth?" the colonel said.

"Dudek." Booth shook his head. "I had a spot of bother in Sapporo, met up with these guys, and here we are. Can you tell us what's going on? One minute I'm enjoying the company of a lady and the next, she's a pile of ash."

"You haven't changed a bit, Booth. Still knocking around with that agency?"

"Nah. I'm an independent contractor now. Why all the bother?"

The colonel ignored Booth's question and turned his attention to Allie. "Don't I know you?"

"Not unless you fly United. I'm a captain, flying 787s."

"Maybe. I don't forget faces, and yours is something to remember."

The two soldiers sent to search the cabin returned with their stash of weapons and food and dropped them in a pile in front of The Nameless. The colonel pursed his lips together and ushered them inside the terminal.

Ryan was glad to get out of the biting cold and wind. He had never liked freezing temperatures and the wind from the Arctic was fierce. The soldiers directed them to a line of seats and ordered them to sit. Dudek paced in front while the remaining men grouped behind the seats.

"You lot have left me in an uncompromising position. You see, my orders are very clear. Keep our borders safe from harm. Stop unwanted persons from entering my country. The United States of America. You and you." The colonel gestured to Booth and Allie. "I know to be citizens. The rest of you is anyone's guess."

Ryan began to speak and Dudek held up his fist, silencing him. "And here's the real dilemma. I don't need to tell you what happened. You all witnessed it. My problem is that the president sent out a list of persons of interest. Traitors he believes have a hand in the events of last Wednesday." He turned and stared at Booth. "Guess who's on that list? Yes, that's right. You." He raised his rifle to his shoulder and swept it over The Nameless. "I'm guessing you two are the Connors. And that would make you Sofia Ortiz. Am I right?"

Ryan glanced at Cal. Eyes cast down, looking at the floor. He felt it too. Pain. Pain at being called a traitor. LK3 and The Nameless were the furthest thing he could imagine to traitors. For nearly eighteen years they had fought, bled, and grieved, while serving America, keeping her citizens safe. Yes, they had failed to detect OPIS and their grand plan. So had the other intelligence agencies. They had all been fooled. They still had a chance to rectify it, at least in a small way.

"Yes. I'm Ryan Connors," he said, squaring his shoulders. If he was going to die, then he would die proud. Proud of serving the many.

Colonel Dudek grinned and dropped his rifle. "Good. I'm glad I found you." The soldiers surrounding them began to laugh. Small and giggle-like at first, before it became uncontrollable.

"Wait. What?" Booth said.

"General Munroe out of MacLeod told us to keep an eye out for you. Said you might need some assistance. To bring you home."

"So there isn't a list?" Cal said.

"I'm afraid there is. But I've known Booth for years. There's no way this guy's a traitor."

"You're disobeying a direct order from the president?"

"Lady, have you seen what's happened out there? Planes falling from the sky. US Navy vessels drifting in the Pacific. The Atlantic. I've heard reports of soldiers dressed in black roaming the cities and towns, killing citizens. People killing each other and sucking on their bone marrow. It's chaos. Hardly anyone's left in DC, and the new president orders us to track down a list? Something didn't smell right. If Munroe vouches for you, then you're not traitors. I'll always trust a general over some paper-pushing politician. Now, what the hell are you doing in this frozen crab farm?"

Ryan relaxed his shoulders. "How did this Munroe know we were coming?" he said.

"You know the answer to that. Don't ask because it's classified."

Booth shook the colonel's hand. "It's all right, Connors. They're here to help us."

Sofia held up her tablet. "I was in contact with Avondale on the flight, told him our plans. He must've informed Munroe. He's the only other person who knows."

Cal and Ryan snapped their heads up. "Zanzi?"

"Avondale's not sure. Omstead is alive. Zanzi was taken to the mountains north of Sacramento, where her tracker went offline."

Ryan frowned. "Why didn't you tell us earlier?"

"I'm sorry. You were asleep, and then I forgot when I became engrossed in the coding."

Dudek clapped his hands. "People, focus. What do you need?"

"All right, then. We're going to need your chopper, and if you have any spare uniforms, that'll help."

Colonel Dudek shook Ryan's hand. "Anything you need. Where're you going?"

"Makushin Bay. Two hundred clicks southwest."

Dudek signaled to some of his men who brought crates from the Seahawk. For the third time in six hours, Ryan redressed. At least the gray battle fatigues felt comfortable. He holstered his Glock and shouldered his backpack and satchel. He left the rifles so he didn't weigh himself down with too much. *Light and breezy.* Ebony offered to stay behind with Sam and Keiko. Both Cal and Sofia accepted. If they stayed hidden in the terminal, they'd be safe enough. Better than storming into the unknown.

"Keep out of sight," Cal said to Ebony.

Like Ryan, Cal trusted the red-haired woman with her nanite-assisted abilities. "Use this if you have to."

She handed Ebony the sniper rifle Allie had found back at the power plant.

"I don't need that," Ebony said.

"Just take it, for my peace of mind."

Twenty minutes later, the pilot guided the chopper over the airport. Soon it was sweeping over the snowy hills of Amaknak Island. A dozen or so crab boats were tied up in the harbor, awaiting their captains. Captains that would never come. The Alaskan king crabs would be spared from dinner tables and fancy restaurants for now.

Ryan ducked into the cockpit and directed the pilots to their exact destination before turning and briefing the soldiers.

"We're heading to an NSA listening station. We may meet resistance. My team will try the diplomatic approach before we use force. These are still US citizens. I've instructed the pilots to keep trying to raise the station on the radio." The soldiers looked at the colonel before confirming they understood Ryan's instructions.

Cal, using sign language, said, *Are you sure about this?*

No. But let's play it out. Protect Sofia.

Booth leant against Allie and made sure she knew the plan. The hold fell silent as everyone escaped into their own minds, going through whatever rituals they went through before a mission. For Ryan, it was a drop into the unknown and the uncertain.

The pilots circled the NSA station before landing the Seahawk. The station was perfect for their needs. It had an array of large and small satellite dishes, radio masts, and microwave towers. The hold doors slid open and Dudek and his men spread out. Three went right, three went left. The Nameless hung back until they were given the all-clear. The station itself was protected by a high wire-mesh fence like at a federal prison, with razor wire on top. The gate was open a meter or so. A pile of ash sat on the guard's chair inside the small gatehouse.

The silence and lack of movement added to Ryan's sense of dread. Were they too late?

The soldiers covered each other and advanced deeper into the complex as The Nameless followed.

The main building was a squat concrete box. Having been here before, Ryan knew the real station was underground, beneath the utilitarian-looking structure. Inside was just as quiet and unmoving. The room was simple but filled with computer equipment and weather data-collecting machines. Human forms of ash sat in chairs and lay on the floor. Next to what looked like a cupboard was a frozen form, leaning back in its chair as though relaxing with a beer. A bunch of keys and a magnetic card lay on the floor. Ryan picked them up and handed them to Sofia.

The soldiers completed their sweep and reported back to Dudek.

"All clear."

"Very good."

Sofia moved forward without being asked, tablet in hand. She unscrewed a small keypad and attached a cord. "You would think the NSA had better security," she said as she swiped the card. The door made a strange hum before clicking open. Elevator doors slid open, revealing a spacious cargo area.

Shadows of Ash

"This is where it gets tricky." Sofia repeated the process on the internal keypad and was rewarded with buzzers. The swipe card failed. "Damn," she muttered.

"Problem?" Dudek asked.

Ryan shook his head. Even with no real planning and limited time, he had absolute confidence in his team. Booth acted like a goofball, cracking jokes, but his eyes were sharp and never missed a thing. His intuition was spot on most of the time. He could read a room, assess what the danger was and act accordingly. Sofia – anything mechanical or computer-based. She was the sort of person you wanted on your side: fierce and deadly when she needed to be, smart, sexy, and sweet the rest of the time. They all marveled at her technical skills. Cal – his rock, his second in command, loyal with the right amount of ethics to make the right judgements. Sure, he still struggled trying to figure out her reasons for her three-year absence, but as she had proven time and again since, she wanted to make it right. Allie – circumstances had thrown them together and she had shown her value ever since. The old members had not said it out loud, but they all liked her, all wanted her to stick around.

Yes, there was a problem. Not that he would ever admit it.

Sofia had pulled the panel off the inside of the elevator, exposing wiring and computer boards. She attached wires with crocodile clips and other cables that looked like the kind stuck into a router.

After another five minutes of cursing from Sofia, and with smirks from Dudek, the elevator finally dinged, and the doors shut. There were no floor buttons to press. The colonel had left two soldiers topside to guard their backs. The lift glided smoothly to a stop. Everyone tensed and raised their weapons as the doors pinged open.

Ryan had a sense of déjà vu. A group of Siphons snapped their heads around. They still wore the suits of agents, but their eyes were cloudy, and clumps of hair were missing. Instead of smooth skin, though, theirs was wrinkly and pruned like they had stayed in their baths too long.

They snarled, howled, and shrieked.

"What the hell are these?" Dudek said.

"Aim for the head, Colonel. They're hard to kill," Ryan said. He flicked off the safety and took aim.

TWENTY-SIX

SCAPPOOSE, OREGON

Lisa had seen enough. Enough of the Black Skulls disguising themselves as FEMA or National Guard. The Black Skulls drove into each town, announcing their arrival with broadcasts on local radio. At first glance, they looked and sounded the part. But their body language and mannerisms gave them away. The men were arrogant and openly leered at the women. The doctors administering medical care did so with a bored attitude like they really couldn't care less. Any of the Rabids they saw, the Black Skulls killed them and dragged their bodies out of sight.

Lisa and her team were parked up on the west of town, overlooking the main shopping district, observing the Black Skulls with binos. Reid had point, while Clough watched their six.

"Radio for you, Omstead. Someone called Avondale," Torres said, handing her the long-range radio.

Lisa frowned and clicked the talk button. "Avondale."

"Director. I found The Nameless, with a little help from Sofia. They made it out of Japan alive and have just landed at Dutch Harbor."

"Dutch Harbor? What's going on?" Lisa asked. "Hold on a moment." She waved Torres over. "Go and help Reid." Torres gave her a curt nod and jogged away.

"Okay. Go ahead."

"Sofia contacted me on an old secure network we set up some time ago. She said everyone is alive, including Cal."

"Cal? Are you sure?"

"Positive."

Lisa grinned. She should have guessed. The female Connors were just as stubborn as the male. For the first time in over a week she felt like something was going her way. The team was back together.

"Fill me in."

"They confirmed that ReinCorp, along with YamTech and Zizer, are responsible for last Wednesday's events. An organization she called OPIS. They also confirmed it was achieved with nanites ... and it's going to happen again. In sixteen hours' time."

"Again, how?"

Shadows of Ash

"Sofia said they use satellites and cell phone towers to broadcast the signal. At zero-six-hundred tomorrow, the second wave will hit – taking out more of us, I guess." Avondale went quiet.

Lisa sat back with a thud and ran her hand over her head. It was a lot to take in. She'd suspected maybe a fraction of it. When Monica had discovered the nanites, Lisa hadn't wanted to believe they were the cause. Now her most trusted operatives had confirmed it – operatives who were like family to her. It all fell into place, the degree of conspiracy this must have taken. Men and women in the halls of power, passing the right laws, covering the truth with secrets and lies, keeping the intelligence agencies in the dark. It was mind-boggling, but they had succeeded. It sickened her to even think of harming the president, but everything pointed to him being one of them. Part of OPIS. The people on that list weren't traitors; they were individuals who could expose OPIS before they completed their machinations.

"Director?" Avondale said.

"Yeah. I'm here," Lisa murmured. "Are they in Dutch Harbor trying to stop the second wave?"

"Correct. They plan to use an LK3 satellite, crash it into one of theirs. We have no way of knowing if it will work. I'm tracking down the target now, calculating trajectories."

"Good. Give them all the help you can. Call in any favors you need. I'll inform Munroe. This is priority one, Avondale. Understood?"

"Yes. Of course. Stay off your phone, Director. We'll just use radio from now on. Out."

Lisa craned her neck and stared at the cell tower on top of the hill behind her. *So you little bastards helped broadcast this catastrophe.*

She rummaged through their supplies. They had a small amount of C4, easily sufficient to render the tower useless.

It took her a few minutes to reach Munroe. He sounded agitated when he finally came on.

"Omstead, what've you got for me?"

"I've had confirmation that it was nanites and ReinCorp. To be more precise, an organization called OPIS."

"Who confirmed? Your missing team? USS Nimitz contacted them."

"Affirmative. They're in Dutch Harbor as we speak, trying to stop what they call the second wave. They're going to hit us again at zero-six-hundred tomorrow."

Munroe let fly a stream of expletives, including some words Lisa had never heard, let alone heard someone of his rank say.

"How's it going to happen?"

"From what I understand, they use satellites and cell phone towers to broadcast the signal. I'm putting forward that my team start blowing as many to kingdom come as we can."

"Get on it. I'll send some men out around here and inform the president."

"About that," Lisa said. Her breath whistled as she sucked in a breath. She respected Munroe. He was a brilliant commander, always putting the soldiers' abilities first. He wasn't weighed down by prejudice. If a soldier suited the mission, they went. Pure and simple. What she was going to say next troubled her, but it was necessary. "I think Ward is one of them."

"One of this OPIS?"

"Yes."

The silence dragged for so long Lisa thought Munroe had been cut off. *"Ward is up my ass with this list, giving it priority over everything else. I've got the White House calling me every hour for an update. Because of our history and the fact I know you have integrity, I'm going to give you the benefit of the doubt. I need proof, Omstead. Real proof. You, the Connors, and several other LK3 operatives are on that list. You're America's Most goddamn Wanted. Whether you're right or wrong about Ward, he's my Commander-in-Chief."*

"I know the location of a ReinCorp/OPIS satellite station. Can you send some bombers to take it out? It's in the Sierra Nevada's."

"Look, for old time's sake, if you get me ironclad proof that those corporate scumbags are responsible, then I'll bomb that complex so much it'll make Vietnam look like a bloody training run."

"Wilco, sir. Any news from Doctor Johnson?"

"She's got some new fancy equipment and is doing further tests. Go dark, Omstead. Do what you must do, but until you have evidence, don't contact me. Out."

It was harsh, but it was the right move. Any further contact would risk the enemy finding them. She half-smiled. Which enemy? She had so many.

She switched to her internal comms.

"SITREP."

"Citizens keep filing into the FEMA facility. No change." Reid's voice came through, strong and confident. Omstead glanced up, checking that Torres was with him. He was nowhere to be seen.

"Torres. What's your position?" The airwaves remained silent.

"Clough? SITREP." More silence.

Lisa checked her immediate vicinity as her instincts screamed a warning, raising the hairs on her neck.

"Reid. To me." She kicked open the door and slipped out, swinging up her MP5 in one smooth motion. It didn't take long for Reid to join her behind the SUV. There was still no sign of either Torres or Clough. It was as if they'd vanished into thin air. Reid was low and peering around the front of the vehicle when the headlights shattered into tiny fragments. Lisa flattened herself and scanned the bushes and buildings to her right. Logic told her that if they were being flanked, then that was the direction they would come from. A split-second later she caught the glint of something moving and rolled under the SUV as bullets sparked off the concrete. She returned fire to where she'd caught movement. The firing stopped.

"We have you surrounded, Omstead. Reid, you can leave. We have no quarrel with you."

"I'm staying here," Reid said. His eyes found Lisa's and he mouthed, *What the hell is going on?*

"What do you want, Torres? I guess you're the leader. Clough doesn't have the smarts for it," Lisa shouted. She kept an eye on the bushes and listened for any traffic noise.

Black Skulls would be trained to react and respond to any signs of fighting. She estimated she only had a few minutes to end this.

The response to her taunt was rounds hitting the vehicle, thunking into the metal panels.

"We can't let you stop wave two," Torres called back. "We listened in on your transmission. Our orders are clear: stop anyone who discovers our plans."

Reid frowned at her, shrugging. "What?"

She waved the question away and signaled for him to lay down covering fire while she lifted the back door and snatched the bag with the explosives in it. She shot at the bushes for a few moments, then reached in and started the SUV. The next move was the hardest: getting herself and Reid to the drainage ditch behind them, using the vehicle as cover. She fired another burst and wrenched the wheel as Torres returned fire. Neat round holes stitched across the windshield. She dropped the food bag on top of the accelerator. Sharp, sudden pain erupted up her leg. She twisted away and fired the remainder of her magazine. Gritting her teeth through the pain, she pulled the pin on a grenade and pulled the gear lever into drive.

"Reid!" Lisa yelled. The sergeant understood what was happening and rolled away as the SUV lurched forward, groaned for a second, then took off toward the hidden Torres. Reid and Lisa spun and peppered the building, hitting the partly exposed Clough. He crumpled to the ground.

It took a few seconds before the vehicle plowed into the bushes and exploded in a fireball. They couldn't tell if Torres was dead or alive, and Lisa didn't want to hang around to find out. Black Skulls would have seen and heard the fight and fire. Everyone would have. She stooped and removed Clough's ammo but left his weapons. She didn't need more weight.

They jogged toward the cell tower and away from the carnage. Lisa didn't look back; she was still trying to figure out how she had missed Torres and Clough being sleeper agents. *Getting sloppy.*

She ran up to the cell tower and stared at the main mast. A large access panel, securely locked, was a couple of meters off the ground. "Know much about these babies?" Lisa said to Reid.

"Sure. It was part of my training. Why?"

"I'll fill you in as soon as I can. I need to destroy it." She pulled out the C4.

"That'll work. Place it a little inside. You'll fry the whole system."

"No way for it to broadcast?"

"No way."

Lisa threw him the C4. "Hurry up. Do it."

She liked Reid. Respected the sergeant. He followed orders. Was exceptional at what he did, and from his actions a few minutes ago, loyal. He showed it again now. Using his Ka-Bar, he pried opened the door and stuck the explosive as far back as he could reach. He fiddled around for a second, getting the timer attached. "How many minutes?"

Shadows of Ash

"Two should do it," Lisa said.

Lisa and Reid sprinted for the tree line and ducked into its shadows. Branches slapped against their arms and legs as they weaved deeper into the woods. The boom of the explosion reverberated through the trees.

The ground started to slope downward, the trees thinning. Lisa and Reid found themselves in someone's yard. Trampolines and kids' toys were scattered everywhere; a slide with a neat child-sized form of ash. Lisa choked back a sob. No matter how many times she saw the remains of those lives snuffed out, it never got easier. There were so many. Fathers and sons. Mothers and daughters. Friends and lovers. Co-workers. The driver someone had flipped off that morning. The parking warden someone had cursed. Gone, all of them. Like the innocent child on the slide. As much as seeing the remains of the victims pained her, it also gave her strength. The strength to do what was right. Fight OPIS until either they were defeated, or she was dead, whichever came first.

Lisa gripped her MP5 tighter and charged around a house after Reid. Smoke from their burning SUV clouded the skyline, obscuring their view. It wouldn't take long before Black Skulls found their tracks and gave pursuit.

Reid stopped as the hill sloped away. "Up or down?"

"Up. There's more cell phone towers on this hill. We're going to take them all down."

"They'll catch up soon. A car?"

"Too noisy. Those." Lisa gestured at two mountain bikes leaning against the back verandah.

"Bikes?"

"Yup. Hurry up, soldier."

Reid grumbled but followed orders. Lisa stole a quick look at the wound on her calf. The pain had subsided considerably. Instead of blood and muck, it was red and angry, the skin healing over. Frowning, she checked her old wounds. Those too were all but healed. Nanites?

Putting the mystery of her accelerated healing out of her mind, she hurried on.

TWENTY-SEVEN

MAKUSHIN BAY, ALEUTIAN ISLANDS

Ryan bolted right and shot two of the Siphons in quick succession. His aim was to one side, but he still scored direct hits in the throat and jaw respectively. He adjusted and finished the creatures off with shots to the head. Dudek and his soldiers put the rest down in a matter of seconds and squatted to examine the Siphons.

"What the hell?" Dudek said. "I thought these were just someone's crazy story."

"We came across them in Japan. We call them Siphons."

"Because?"

"If they get a hold of you, they suck out your spinal fluid."

"Gross," one of the soldiers said. He stepped away from the creature that had once been an NSA agent.

"I heard reports of it, but thought it was an exaggeration. Why would they do that? It makes no sense." Dudek rolled an agent over. His red tie still hung around his neck. "Fan out. Even numbers. We're going to sweep this place. Move!"

The base was divided into four rooms with a communal central living area with kitchen and dining as well as a TV and armchairs. The biggest room at the end of a corridor had a slight kink like a dog leg and held all the computer equipment. In front of a multitude of screens was seating for two agents. The Nameless cleared the rooms on the left while Dudek's men went right. Ryan signaled for Booth and Allie to cover their backs. But before they could begin a sweep of their own, shouting and gunfire from the soldiers erupted, answered by the pop of handguns. Ryan knew that sound as intimately as his own breathing from the hours he'd spent on the firing range, practicing his skills.

"Connors. We need you," Dudek shouted. The gunfire ceased as quickly as it began. Dudek had pulled back two injured soldiers. A bright blue-eyed kid gasped as blood gurgled out of a wound in his neck. It would only be a matter of time before he and the other soldier bled out.

"We got live ones. Agents. They were hiding in the bathroom. Savage took the brunt of the attack." His explanation was met with more nine-millimeter fire. The bullets took out chunks of concrete, throwing shards into Dudek's face.

"Cease fire!" he yelled. "We're US Marines from the USS *Nimitz*, sent here under the orders of General Munroe."

Pop! "This is Agent Larsen. We have our own orders, Marine. Kill anyone who enters the base." *Pop!*

"Who gave that order? Let's get the general on the horn and see what he says."

"Secretary Ward. Sent specific orders days ago. If it weren't for those damn things, we'd be doing our jobs."

"Agent Larsen. My name is Colonel Dudek. I have no wish to harm a fellow American, even one trying to kill me for no good reason. Come out calmly and we can work this out. From what I've seen outside, there's been enough death."

"Tell me, colonel, why are you here? Why did you come storming into our base?"

Dudek gestured at Ryan. He had never specified what they were doing here exactly, and Dudek had never asked.

Ryan cleared his throat. "Agent Larsen. My name is Connors. My team and I were sent here to use your equipment to stop a second wave of attacks. At zero-six-hundred hours, we're going to go through the same pain. More will die. Perhaps billions. We have no way of knowing numbers. We need to use that room."

Cal glanced up at him. The second soldier that had been shot had stopped breathing. She grimaced. Her steely gaze told Ryan all he needed to know. The NSA agents in that room were not going to back down. They didn't care if they were on the same side. Americans, like them.

Muttering sounded from the bathroom, the acoustics of the tiles making it echo.

Dudek rolled his eyes and said, "Larsen. I'll give you one minute. Then we're coming in…"

The bathroom door smashed open as two men burst through. Ryan spun, ducking around one of Dudek's soldiers. He completed his spin, dropped to one knee, and sighted his target. The NSA agent was disheveled, eyes red and puffy. Black stubble covered his face, his hair wild. Both agents fired their pistols as they charged from the bathroom. The soldier Ryan had spun around grunted as he took a bullet to the thigh and upper chest. In seconds, the agents crashed into Dudek and his men like a tight end crashing through the defense. Dudek and the rogue agent collapsed in a heap, arms and legs twisting together as they fought. Ryan tried to get a bead on the agent, but the intensity of the fight made it impossible.

Booth shot the second one. His bullet entered the agent's jaw and exploded out the back of his ear. A piece of skull the size of a golf ball hit the wall, coated in brain and tissue. He was dead before he hit the ground. Allie kicked his gun away and trained her weapon on the rolling mass that was Dudek and his attacker.

Dudek grunted as he received a blow to the stomach. He brought his knee up into the man's groin and pulled the gasping agent to his feet. He grabbed the gun and twisted, snapping the NSA man's hand. He howled and lashed out, earning himself another vicious kick to the groin. He doubled over, tears streaming down his face. He fought no more. Dudek bent his hands behind his back and cuffed them. He was down to one soldier now, with two left up above. He grabbed the agent's throat. "Are there any more surprises?" he said through clenched teeth.

"Screw you."

"Screw me? You were the ones shooting at us."

Dudek lashed out again, this time striking the man's face. Once, then two more times. Each savage blow seemed to knock the agent's head back farther.

Ryan had seen enough. He signaled to The Nameless to leave Dudek to it. He hated seeing someone suffer at the hands of a tormentor, but they had bigger concerns. Sofia shut the door behind her and took one of the seats at the desk. She had the computers up and running in no time. She smiled as she typed in passwords Avondale had provided and brought up screens with satellite trajectories and maps of their current locations. There were hundreds.

"Cal, I need you with me." Sofia pointed at a screen. "These are NSA satellites. Keep an eye on them while I find LK3's. Also, this screen is for communication, and this joystick controls the position of the dishes. They can be moved to point to where you want."

Ryan moved to the bank of radio gear. It was all here – new technology and analogue. He switched it all on, sat down and waited for it to warm up. Sofia passed him a scrap of paper.

"Avondale's frequency."

"Thanks."

"We might have to put it through some relays due to the distance. Bounce it from one tower to the other. Enter the frequency on that keyboard and press that big yellow button. I can control the rest from my console."

Ryan followed her instructions and stood to stretch his back. The hours he had spent unconscious on the concrete floor back in the nuclear power plant were coming back to haunt him. Getting old sucked. One discovers new muscles as they twinge and knot, revealing themselves in weird and painful ways. Nowadays he had to be careful not to sneeze with his neck forward. The nanites may repair damaged cells and tissue from wounds, but they did nothing for aches and pains.

"Is there anything else I can help with, Sofia?" Ryan said.

"Nothing in here. Cal and I can take care of it. We may need you guys to check outside. I'm having trouble sending radio signals. It's like something is disconnected. Check the radio mast. It'll be the tallest aerial."

"I'm on it."

He waved to Booth and Allie. "Booth, stay here. Keep your eyes open. Allie, we're going back up. Comms are down."

"Can you do something about the TV signal? There's a Vikings game on soon," Booth said.

"What? You want to watch them lose again?"

"Like your Seahawks?"

"We have a Superbowl ring. Where's yours?"

Allie dug her elbow into Booth's ribs and rolled her eyes. "Men. It's all football and beer."

"Beer?" Booth said. "I'm an educated man. I drink whiskey."

Allie rolled her eyes once more and looked at Cal and Sofia.

Shadows of Ash

"Just ignore them. They're idiots," Cal said.

"I'm beginning to realize that. For a moment I thought they were going to start the whole 'all songs are about sex' discussion again."

Allie was learning fast. Ryan chuckled. "Don't start him on that again."

"What?" Booth was off. "You guys know I'm right. Take the song 'Bohemian Rhapsody.' It's about a guy who feels guilty for having sex with this other dude's wife, and he shoots him out of jealousy for being with the woman he loved."

Sofia sighed. She clapped her hands. "Let's move. We don't have long. I need those comms."

Nothing more was said. Since that stormy night in Tokyo, Ryan's life of solitude had ended. His period of mourning terminated. He never would have imagined the events of Wednesday when the people of Koyasan dissolved into piles of ash around him.

Dudek had taken the NSA agent into the communal area and bound him to a chair. The agent's eyes were swollen shut.

"We need to go topside. Comms are down," Ryan said.

Dudek lifted his head. "Take my two men if you need them."

As the elevator ascended, Ryan slammed a fresh magazine into his Glock. He wanted to tell Allie what he suspected: that Dudek's men had taken out the comms. Instead, he said, "Stay frosty."

The soldiers were waiting for them when the doors opened. "The colonel said to assist you, sir."

They led the way past the weather-monitoring computers and the ash forms of people once alive and doing their jobs.

The icy cold wind bit through Ryan's fatigues. He paused at the open door and grabbed one of the coats. He offered one to the two soldiers. They shook their heads.

"North Dakota born and bred, sir. This is nothing."

"North Dakota. How are those Fighting Sioux doing this year?"

"Top of the division last I checked."

Ryan shrugged into the coat and braced against the gale-force winds whipping around the base. He immediately spotted the radio mast. It was like Sofia had said: the tallest reached up at least sixty meters. It was secured with thick wire ropes that stretched out in all directions and was designed to be climbed. Ryan clicked on his flashlight and searched the top. A light covering of snow lay on the ladder rungs. Maybe it hadn't been sabotaged. He frowned. He had tested the soldier who claimed to be from North Dakota, asking him about the football. The team now known as the Fighting Hawks was still a sore point with some of the alumni. Any fan would surely correct him. Maybe the soldier didn't care? Maybe he'd decided to let it slide?

Ryan kept his hand close to his Glock, just in case. The soldiers looked bored and uninterested, but he knew that ruse. Allie walked up to the shed-like structure nestled under the mast and reached out to open the door. In that instant, the soldiers' body language changed. They stiffened and glanced at each other. Ryan kept his eyes on their gun hands.

Shadows of Ash

Was he being paranoid? He didn't know anymore. In times like these, it was difficult to trust anyone. Who was friend and who was foe? He would have liked to think that in times of an apocalyptic crisis everyone would band together to survive. Unfortunately, it was the opposite.

"Anything?" Ryan said.

"Everything's green, so there's power going to the mast," Allie said.

"Let's check the rest, and quickly. It's cold as brass monkeys out here," Ryan muttered. "You boys know anything about radio signals?"

The soldier from North Dakota shrugged. "As if. Technology's moved on, old man."

The second escort turned. "I know a little bit. Could be something inside – a switch or something."

"Spread out. Check all the dishes and masts. Make sure nothing has come loose. They get bad storms up here."

They separated. Ryan jogged to keep warm, going from dish to dish. They were grouped together with a panel of lights inside a metal box. Nothing was out of place, and everything was on.

Entering the weather station, Ryan shook off the jacket. He cast his eyes over the array of equipment. A screen showed a live feed of a low-pressure system sweeping down from the Arctic, and another from the Pacific. He scanned the data, reading the Estimated Time of Arrival. Dutch Harbor was going to be hit on two fronts.

"Over here," Allie called from across the room. She had pushed the rolling chair aside, careful not to disturb the ash pile too much. A bank of servers was above the desk, and one had been pulled out as though the now-deceased agent had been running diagnostics or repairs. In his death throes, he had spilt coffee all over the circuit boards.

"Shit," Ryan said. "How do we even repair that?"

Allie shrugged. "Maybe they have spare parts for everything. Would make sense, being stuck in the middle of nowhere."

Ryan glanced around and spotted what he was looking for, an old landline phone. The agents up here had to have some way of communicating with those below. Conveniently, the buttons on the phone were labeled.

"Sofia, we found the problem. Server board's been fried. Maybe you can reroute it or tell us how to do it?"

The tell-tale noise of safeties being clicked off sounded. "We have a new problem," Sofia murmured.

"Get down here now, Connors," Dudek spat.

Ryan spun as he drew his Glock. The two soldiers were grinning, rifles raised.

"Now, now. Don't do anything stupid. Colonel wants you alive."

Ryan cursed himself for not trusting his gut. At times, his desire to see the good in everyone led to moments like these.

He handed his Glock to the soldier and joined them in the elevator. He wanted nothing more than to disarm them. He knew he could. Back at the Lodge, they had trained over and over for situations like these. Confined spaces were difficult at best, but not many people attempted it, and guns gave people a sense of power. The soldiers' rifles were no use in the elevator. Allie stared at him as if waiting for the signal. He shook his head with the barest of motions. Not with Dudek down there with Cal, Sofia, and Booth.

TWENTY-EIGHT

PORTLAND, OREGON

Battles were messy. Not the ordered action people expected. It wasn't like the 1700s when the British and French would line up and shoot each other, launching cannonball after cannonball. Cease fire at two for a cup of tea and cakes.

No. They were chaotic and crazy. Bloody and noisy. People screamed. Not only in terror, but screamed out orders, each side trying to get the upper hand.

The Outcast Mongrel Motorcycle Club had the firepower, but none of the training the Black Skulls had. A single glance told Zanzi how the battle was going to play out: everyone dead. The bikers might hold off the commandos for a short while, they may even kill a few, but they'd be lucky to survive. Herself and Tilly included. If what Traci said was true and there was an escape tunnel, they had a chance.

They crept down the hallway as gunfire and shouts echoed around the bikers' HQ. Zanzi used the same key to unlock all the rooms as she passed. She was met with gasps and stares. One or two of the captives stared back blankly, their hair stringy and their skin raw from scratches. Limbs with bruised skin. Meth, she guessed. She had seen the photos of what the drug did. Addicts scratched their skin, thinking there were bugs underneath. The addicts cringed at the sight of Zanzi and shooed her away.

"C'mon, we can get out. Now's your chance," Zanzi said.

"Leave us alone," a girl said. A tattoo of a bulldog decorated her neck. Zanzi left them and urged Tilly to follow. Being an addict meant you wanted to be close to the source of your drug. Grub and the bikers knew this. Kept them fed. Kept them hungry. They demanded loyalty and got it, regardless of the danger.

Zanzi unlocked the final door. One of the African American women and the scrawny white guy with blue hair turned, eyes wide. The other African American woman didn't move.

"What's going on?" the one who'd turned said. "It sounds like SWAT are raiding the place. Are they raiding the place?" She laughed, nervous and shallow. "That would be a first – a black person wanting SWAT."

"It's not SWAT. Worse. These guys will kill you," Zanzi said.

Shadows of Ash

"Honey, you obviously never lived in my neighborhood." She laughed again. "White girl, come in here, tell me what's what."

"I'm Zanzi. We have a way out."

"Jacqueline. But call me Jacqui. Well, don't stand there staring. Let's go."

Zanzi couldn't help the grin that spread across her face. Despite the death all around them, some people had a way with words, a way to make you smile. Her group now numbered four. Blue hair didn't follow. He sat in the corner of the room, rocking back and forth. Nor did the second woman.

"What about her?" Zanzi said.

"Meth withdrawal. She's not going anywhere," Jacqui said.

Like the prisoners in the other rooms, she was too strung out. It pained Zanzi to leave them behind.

Traci guided them out a side door. The bar was twenty meters away. Problem was, standing behind it were Grub, Mutton, Axl, and several others, firing M4s, sweeping them from side to side. The Black Skulls had used an SUV to smash through the front gates. It had crashed into a row of motorcycles and become wedged. Bullet holes were everywhere like a chicken pox rash.

"Traci. Where's the tunnel exactly?"

"In the beer cooler. That shed."

Zanzi followed her gesture. To one side was a square shed, white, like an outdoor walk-in refrigerator. If they circled both houses to her right, it was possible they could reach it.

There was no more time to think. She grabbed Tilly's hand and took off at a run. They ducked under beer-stained clothes hanging on a crude line, jumped over engine parts stacked on narrow concrete paths, and over dead gang members with pools of blood leaking from head wounds. They kept as low as they could.

At the back of the first house, Zanzi saw a chance. A dozen or so Rabids had been locked inside another cage and were agitated, worked up into a frenzy. Maybe they could smell the blood. Maybe they could just sense the humans they craved. Several wildly rattled the wire mesh, so desperate to get out, the mesh was slicing into their ivory flesh. Saliva dripped from their clenched teeth.

Zanzi checked her perimeter. They were out of sight here. The battle was taking place at the front of the HQ. Something puzzled her; why hadn't the Black Skulls attacked from the rear at the same time? She shook away her questions and refocused on escaping.

"Wait here. I'm going to release those creatures as a diversion."

"Oh hell no. You mad?" Jacqui said.

"It sounds crazy, I know, but it's the best way."

"It just doesn't sound crazy. It is."

Tilly grinned. "You remind me of my friend Tenisha. She was sassy too. I think that's the word … sassy. Where does that word come from?"

"Your girl all right?" Jacqui said.

"This is Tilly, and she is," Zanzi said. She took off, not looking back. The suckers howled as she drew closer. The door was locked with a single padlock and a bolt. She glanced around for keys but saw only tools next to a partly dismantled Indian motorcycle. Zanzi grabbed a ball-peen hammer and smashed the lock. It fell to the ground as the suckers screamed and rattled the cage with newfound fury. They were hungry. Starving. Their need for spinal fluid had whipped them into an uncontrollable frenzy. Before she could second-guess her decision, she unlatched the bolt and sprinted, waving her little group toward the second house. Thankfully the Rabids ran straight into the battle, toward the louder sound. Shouts and screams replaced the shooting for a few moments as the opposing forces refocused their attentions. Zanzi had nailed the diversion, and she needed to use it.

She rounded the corner of the house and nearly ran into a biker. He was holding his stomach, blood pooling through his fingers. His skin was pale and clammy. His eyes focused on her, lids drooping.

"A little help."

Before Zanzi could answer, Jacqui brushed past her and slammed her fist into the biker's face. "Racist piece of shit. See that wound. That's a gut shot. You gonna die nice and slow like. And don't think you're gonna meet Jesus. No, you gonna see Lucifer himself." She punched him again as bullets thudded into the bricks above her head.

Zanzi yanked her down and scanned the vicinity. She didn't spot anyone. The firefight was still around the front of the house, and the high fence stopped any snipers. The HQ was in an industrial area – no tall buildings. Where did the shots come from? More bullets smacked into the house, pinning the group down.

"Under here," Traci said. "I hide from Grub when he's too rough." She kicked open the access door to the crawl space. Jacqui grumbled and muttered, but she followed.

It was a tight squeeze, and full of cobwebs and trash. Candy bar wrappers and beer cans. Old take-out boxes and the smell of rotting food.

Zanzi ignored it and crawled on, Tilly beside her. Traci opened a second access door. The beer cooler and their chance of freedom was only thirty feet away.

"Tell me about this tunnel, Traci." Zanzi turned to look at the strung-out girl who dipped her finger in the bag of meth again. "Where does it lead?"

"I don't know. I've only seen inside once. Grub told me to get something and not to try to escape. Said it was their emergency route or something. These guys feared the pigs big time. Mostly those DEA guys..." Her voice trailed off as she dipped her finger into the bag of meth once more.

"How do we get inside?"

"There's stairs and a trapdoor."

Zanzi looked toward the bar. Dead Rabids lay amongst bikers and Black Skulls. A few were only injured, and still trying to crawl toward the humans. Grub and his bikers were crouched behind the bar, reloading. Some bled from wounds.

"I'm scared," Tilly whispered.

"It's okay to be scared. It means you're alive. Stay close to me, okay?" Zanzi said.

As they watched, something snapped inside Traci. Maybe it was seeing all the blood and carnage. Maybe it was seeing her tormentors vulnerable, pinned down by armed men. Zanzi would never know.

Traci, screaming curses, burst from the crawlspace firing a P229. Most of her rounds went wide or hit the bar, but one scored a hit. Right through Mutton's throat. Grub whipped his head around and he gaped. The Black Skulls reacted and charged, their rifles cracking as they released three-round bursts. Traci's body jolted as bullets tore into her body – and those of the remaining bikers. First Axl and then Grub went down, holes blown out in their skulls, lifeless eyes staring at nothing.

Zanzi knew this was their chance. She hauled Tilly and Jacqui out and fired a couple of rounds at the commandos to keep them guessing as they ducked into the beer cooler.

Boxes upon boxes were stacked inside, leaving barely enough room to move. Like Traci had said, there was a trapdoor in the back room. With Jacqui's help, Zanzi lifted it and blinked. Lights flickered on. It was crude, but efficient.

The motorcycle gang had used stormwater concrete pipes, over two meters in diameter, to build a storage/escape system.

Rounds hit the shed. The sound echoed, rattling the metal siding. "Hurry," Zanzi said, and shut the trapdoor behind them.

"White girl leading me into a tunnel like she's some savior on the underground railway," Jacqui muttered.

The storage area consisted of several small rooms branching off from the entrance. Zanzi ignored them, but spotted what looked like bales of cannabis, cocaine, and crystal meth. One room had unopened boxes of electronics. LED TVs and laptops. Another held crates of ammo. She paused at the ammo room and cracked open a couple of crates. She grabbed some boxes of nine-millimeter rounds, cramming them into her pockets. Jacqui followed her and whistled when she found a case with more P229s. She took one and clicked in a magazine.

"Now I feel better," she said.

As they left the ammo room, a dull explosion rumbled above. Had the Black Skulls finally stormed through the back?

On they walked. The tunnel was clear of trash, swept clean, and well lit. It didn't take them long to reach the end – perhaps twenty minutes. Rough concrete steps had been cast, leading up to another trapdoor.

"I'll go first," Zanzi said.

"Damn right," Jacqui said.

Zanzi spent a few seconds waiting, listening. There was no sound from the other side of the trapdoor. Carefully she cracked it open. Darkness greeted her like silence in the night. Scents of oil and grease wafted in the still air, and there was no movement. Once they were all through, the light from the tunnel revealed that they were in a mechanic workshop, down in the trench where the mechanic can work on the underside of the car. The doors were down, and the windows shut. Vehicles in various stages of repair sat around the workshop, and a pile of ash was between two of them. Someone had returned and closed the workshop after the event.

The three escapees huddled in the back office to look out the grimy window. Gray smoke poured from the bikers' HQ, clouding the early morning sky. If they bothered to search the HQ, the Black Skulls would find the tunnel and follow it.

"What now?" Jacqui said. "Who the hell were those guys?"

"We call them Black Skulls."

"Did they cause all this?"

"I don't know. Tilly and I have been trying to avoid them. They're rounding up survivors and taking them to camps. There's something about them I don't trust. I've seen them wearing FEMA jackets, but more often than not it's plain black fatigues. They're ruthless, gunning survivors down." Zanzi checked her magazine and clicked it back in. "I have a friend on the other side of Portland. He can help. He has food and water. A warm place to sleep. But it's imperative that we're not observed going there. You're welcome to come."

Tilly hugged Zanzi, her arms squeezing tight.

Jacqui looked at the two women and glanced back toward the tunnel. "I was heading up to Seattle. See if my family were still alive. No one I knew was. All..." She pointed at the person-shaped pile of ash. "Everyone was like that. Did y'all feel that pain and black out?"

"More or less," Zanzi said. She wanted to tell Jacqui everything. Warn her what was really going on. She deserved to know. Or was ignorance better?

"Well, after I came to, I checked on everyone I knew. No one was left. I stayed home for a few days, too scared to move. Ate all my food. But you know what finally drove me out?"

Zanzi shook her head.

"Damn coffee. I ran out of coffee. I was in the store helping myself when the bikers showed up. Next thing I know guns are pointing at me and I'm in the room with those other two."

"If you take back roads, you might make it to Seattle. But like I said, you're welcome to come with us."

Jacqui smiled. Small at first, spreading into a wide grin. "Food and water. Hot shower?"

"Should be. Yes."

"Honey, you had me at food. Better be some coffee too. Look, I'm shaking from withdrawals." She held up her shaking fingers as if to prove her words and grabbed a wrench off a nearby tool chest. "Just in case."

They found a set of keys hanging in the office and used them to let themselves out. Jacqui offered to guide them, as she was a local. Zanzi glanced over her shoulder at the gray smoke. Whatever Josie had decided, she vowed to find her again and ask for help. Her knowledge of nanites was vital. If they were to have any chance at beating Offenheim, they needed her on their side. Josie understood how they were programmed, how they could be used against their masters.

Zanzi laced her fingers into Tilly's and followed Jacqui deeper into the wooded area, toward the Willamette River.

TWENTY-NINE

MAKUSHIN BAY, ALEUTIAN ISLANDS

Colonel Dudek was waiting for Ryan and Allie as the door of the elevator opened. He had his Beretta M9 pointing at Sofia's head. Cal, hands raised, stood to one side, two meters in front.

Booth was slumped against the wall, a scorch mark on his neck. Allie brushed past Dudek, crying as she knelt next to Booth. Ryan flicked his eyes over the mark. From this distance, it was hard to tell what had caused it. He just hoped the nanites were healing Booth.

"Ah, Connors. Thanks for joining us."

"Why are you doing this? We both serve the United States."

"Yes, I do. And there is your answer. You and your team are on the traitors list sent out by President Ward. To be taken dead or alive, like a good old-fashioned bounty."

"President Ward?"

"Newly sworn in,"

"I thought we'd already cleared that up?"

Dudek said nothing to Ryan. He took a phone off the wall. "Come on down." The colonel looked back to Ryan and pressed the barrel of the M9 harder against Sofia's temple. "I have orders to stop you and bring you in. Someone wants to see you and your wife badly." He grinned.

Sofia drove her elbow into his sternum and stomped on his foot causing the colonel to release his grip. At the same time, Ryan dropped, pivoted and swept out a leg. He caught the two soldiers completely unaware. First one tumbled over, then the next. As Sofia and Ryan sprang into action, Cal dove forward at the soldiers. She grabbed Ryan's Glock from the soldier's waistband and tossed it to him. In one fluid motion, he shot both soldiers in the head.

Bang!

Bang!

Dudek shot Ryan twice in the arm, causing him to drop the Glock. "You guys have balls, I'll give you that." He laughed, pulled out a wicked-looking cattle prod and zapped Sofia in the chest. Her body jolted and she fell. Ryan barely saw Dudek give Cal an electric shock. Her head jerked back, and she gasped and staggered, her eyes searching for Ryan's. She tried to stand up, but Dudek shocked her again, twice, in the chest. Next, he zapped Allie in the back. She slumped over Booth, twitched, and lay still.

Ryan grimaced at the pain and clamped his hand over his already-healing wounds. He was struggling to comprehend what had just happened. The Nameless, taken out in seconds. Defeated by a single man.

"You see, Connors, you're no match for me. I don't only serve the United States. I serve something greater. Something that's going to take us to the next phase as a species. Wednesday was just the beginning. For too long we've stood by and watched the weak and insignificant suckle at our teat. I traveled the world, saw the filth, and wanted better. I was given that chance. A seat at the table. Now we are just mopping up the dregs, tying up the loose ends."

Dudek holstered his M9. "I heard rumors that you could fight. Really fight. How about we settle this like warriors of old. With our hands and feet. No weapons. If you defeat me, you can finish what you came here to do."

Before Ryan could answer, the elevator dinged, and the two helicopter pilots emerged. They glanced around but didn't seem surprised at the carnage.

"Set the charges. I'll be done in a minute," Dudek instructed, waving them away.

The pilots did as he asked, pulling explosive charges from a bag as they went.

Ryan looked at his arm. The bullets had gone through the fleshy part of his forearm. Already the blood had clotted. The nanites were doing their job. Did the colonel know that he and the others had elite status?

He kept his eyes downcast and slowly flexed his muscles. Yes, he could fight. John Stapleton – his mentor – had trained him hard, breaking him over and over as he taught him martial arts. Brawling, wrestling. Anything and everything. Techniques to disarm and kill a man in a blink of an eye.

"A fight? Just you and me?"

"Just you and me, Connors."

Ryan loosened his shirt and took off his satchel, kicking it over to Cal. She was still gasping, her eyes blinking at him.

As Dudek had talked, Ryan had inched forward. He rose onto the balls of his feet and charged, jolting right at the last second. A lot of his fighting style was misdirection. Fool the opponent into thinking you're going to do one thing, then do another. Ryan jabbed with his right fist, stepped forward, and brought his left knee into Dudek's ribs. Dudek grunted and twisted at the savage blow. He fended off Ryan's follow-through jab and smashed a powerful right hook under Ryan's defenses and into his chest, just above the heart. Then he pounced with a left jab so hard it rattled Ryan's teeth. Points of yellow lights flashed in his vision. He shook his head, trying to stop the spinning. He staggered, trying to regain his balance.

"You're pathetic. Hardly worthy for me to fight you. That's the problem with you spy boys. Not enough real-world fighting." Dudek slammed his fist into Ryan again. Harder – if that was possible.

"Pathetic," Dudek said again, and punched him in the stomach and kidneys, brutal blows, full of hatred. Full of loathing and anger.

Ryan feebly hit him a couple of times, but the lack of oxygen in his lungs made it difficult. He gasped as each blow crushed his confidence a little more.

Dudek's grin was maniacal. "When I was a boy growing up in Detroit, there were plenty of kids like you. All flash and all talk. Parading around school, girls hanging off their arms. But when the chips are down and the enemy is bombarding you with everything they got, those boys are the first to die. Silent, apart from crying for their mamas. Pathetic." He smashed Ryan's kidney again.

The nanites might heal, but the pain remained, sharp and exploding. But Ryan was losing on purpose. He wanted Dudek to become overconfident, like Mohammed Ali's famous "Rope-a-dope." Take the beating. Infuriate the enemy. Take the punishment and rise each time to face more. He could hear John Stapleton's words clearly in his pain filled mind.

Defeat the opponent in their mind and they are yours.

Ryan gritted his teeth and rose first to one knee, then the other, before standing and glaring at Dudek.

"You're the traitor, Dudek. You and Ward should be on the list, not me." He feinted with a left jab and a right, bringing up a knee. Dudek blocked it all and crushed his forearm into Ryan's nose. Blood gushed out as the cartilage shattered, soaking his shirt in seconds. He dropped back down to one knee. He may be losing on purpose, but he was taking the worst beating of his life. His kidneys screamed at him as pain from the crushing blows pulsated through his torso.

"Pathetic." Dudek smashed a knee into his face, loosening teeth. Ryan slumped to the floor, his eyes fixed on Cal. She had her hand in his satchel. She had understood with perfect clarity why he had kicked it to her.

Dudek grabbed his knife from his discarded belt. "You see, Connors, you and your pitiful team of glorified hackers are no match for us." He stabbed Cal in the left knee, driving the blade in deep and twisting it. She cried out as tears flowed down her cheeks.

"Leave her. It's me you want," Ryan said.

"Tsk tsk. Wait your turn." Dudek twisted the knife again, bringing a scream from Cal. "I have some friends coming soon. I think I'll give your wife to them."

As the colonel tortured his wife, Ryan was reminded of what had inspired him to join the army. What inspired him to push himself. To become the best. The helplessness as bullies beat him at junior high. Tormented him. Stronger, more aggressive, they deserved his pity. He didn't get back at them for physically and mentally abusing him. No. There was no point in that. Bullies are always replaced with more bullies. For Ryan, it was enough to know that, now he was trained, he protected society. Protected people from the real bullies. The real evil of the world.

He struggled to stand on his shaking legs. "I said. Leave her alone."

Cal jabbed the taser under Dudek's chin. As electricity coursed through his body, he convulsed and went rigid. Cal zapped him again, holding the baton fast against his chest. Dudek began to froth from the mouth. The chopper pilots ran back into the room, drawing their sidearms. Too slow. Ryan shot them both in the chest.

Pop... Pop.

They looked at him with stunned eyes. Was it the fact he had shot them, or that Dudek was lying unconscious on the floor? Whatever the case, he didn't care.

Pop... Pop.

Two more nine-millimeter bullets left the barrel, this time entering the pilots' foreheads and blasting out behind their ears, taking with them blood, cerebral fluid and fragments of skull. Their bodies thumped to the floor.

Cal jammed the taser into Dudek for a third time, then a fourth.

Ryan gently pulled her arm away. "That's enough." He replaced the baton with his Glock.

She looked up at him. "You don't want to do it?"

He shook his head. Cal shrugged, and shot Dudek three times in the head, coating the carpeted floor with blood and brain matter.

"The nanites?" Ryan said.

"Not that advanced. They can heal tissue and bone, but they can't repair brain synapses or if you take a bullet to an artery." Her voice whistled with effort. "Here, help me with this." She tugged on the knife lodged in her knee.

Despite the nanites that flooded his system, Ryan's body ached and throbbed in places he hadn't experienced since his time at the Lodge. He checked to make sure Dudek really was dead. There was no sign of a pulse, and the holes in his skull hadn't begun to heal over.

Ryan helped Cal into the office chair before checking on the others. Thankfully Dudek hadn't known about, or compensated for, the fact that The Nameless had elite nanites. Sofia and Booth were alive. Breathing shallowly, but alive.

Allie was in worse shape, drifting in and out of consciousness. Ryan made as her comfortable as he could where she lay. They now had only eight hours to go through with their plan. Would it be enough? It had to be. There was no other choice.

The NSA agents had kept their watch station well stocked with food and medical supplies. Ryan spent a few minutes cleaning his and Cal's wounds, drinking electrolytes, and refueling with protein bars.

"Well, this went south fast," he said between bites.

"There you go again, Captain Obvious," Cal said. "I see that hasn't changed in three years."

"Nothing changed. Not even my love for you."

Cal smiled. "Still the romantic I fell in love with."

"I'm ashamed to say that I had given up hope and was beginning to believe that you were gone."

Cal lifted her eyes. "I'm sorry. I know it's going to be hard for us to get back what we had, but I want to make up for lost time." She smiled again.

Ryan tried to read her expression. It conveyed the right body language. Smile soft, lips curled slightly. Shoulders relaxed. Her eyes had crow's feet creases, but something wasn't quite right. Something he couldn't put his finger on. The computer beeped a warning, interrupting his doubts.

"Can you carry on with what you and Sofia were doing?"

"Some. We need to contact Avondale first."

"I'll use the radio in the chopper. Going to be tough with the approaching storms." Ryan grimaced and started to drag Dudek's body toward the elevator.

"Aren't you forgetting something?" Cal said.

Ryan looked at her blankly. "Help me out here," he said. "I just took a beating."

"The charges."

"Shit." He chastised himself for forgetting such an important detail. The pilots had set explosives during his fight with Dudek. Thankfully they hadn't bothered to hide the small C4 devices, which all had simple timers set for one hour. All he had to do was pull out the timers. Ryan put them aside. "I'll do a sweep upstairs too."

Cal waved and swung her chair back to the computer console, dismissing him with a shake of her head.

Ryan couldn't help but wonder what had driven a decorated soldier like Dudek to do what he had done. To forego his oaths and take on the manifesto of something else. It was another mystery to add to the ever-growing list.

THIRTY

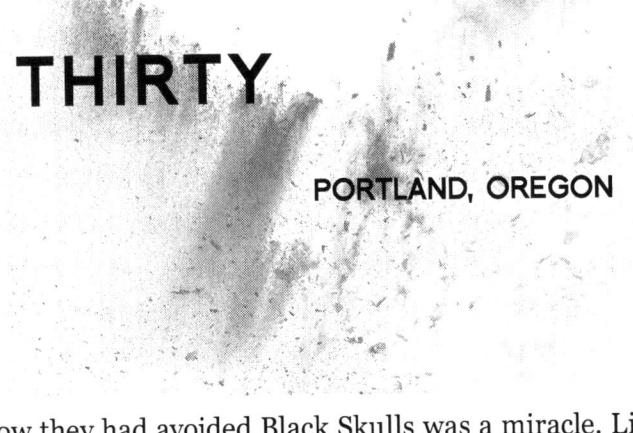

PORTLAND, OREGON

How they had avoided Black Skulls was a miracle. Lisa was drenched in sweat from riding the mountain bike. She and Reid hid in ditches with brush covering them, up trees, in sheds, inside drains – anywhere to escape the Black Skulls. The burning wreckage of the SUV and the cell phone tower was far behind. It was nearing midnight when they finally stopped on the outskirts of Portland.

"How much farther?" Reid said. "I don't know how much more of this seat my butt can cope with."

"A few more miles. On the other side of the cemetery."

Reid grumbled under his breath and adjusted his combat vest. Lisa was happy that the Rabids were sparse. They'd spotted a few walking up hills toward the cell towers. When she'd learned about the towers and satellites, she'd made up her mind to destroy as many as she could, wherever she went. As a child, she'd heard her grandparents talk about World War Two and the exploits of commandos. Destroying bridges, knocking out communications in Nazi Germany. She'd loved those stories. To her, anyone who fought fascism and for their right to freedom was a hero. Now it was her turn to fight a guerrilla war. To fight for not only her freedom, but everyone's.

She frowned as her pocket vibrated. It took a few moments for her tired mind to register it was the smartphone Avondale had given her.

"Avondale."

"Director. I found Zanzi."

"Where? How?"

"I've been keeping an eye out with the traffic cams and city cams. There was a bustle of activity over in Banfield, so I took a closer look. A battle. Those Black Skulls bozos and some bikers. I nearly missed her but caught her and two others a few blocks over before I lost them in Laurelhurst Park. I'm trying to find her now, but there are limited cameras over there. What's your location?"

"Near the Selwood Bridge. Plot me a course to intercept. We're on our way. Find them. And Avondale?"

"Yes, Director."

"Anything more from The Nameless?"

Shadows of Ash

"Munroe and the Nimitz *have sent men to assist. I'm still waiting for Sofia to contact me. There's a bad storm in the area that could be affecting the communications."*

"Okay. Good work."

Lisa slipped the phone back in her pocket and turned to Reid. "On your bike, soldier. We have a job to do."

Reid groaned but followed Lisa as they pedaled away. The cell phone towers would have to wait. They still had a little time. She had made a promise to find Zanzi and Harriet again. Keep them safe.

She had made many promises during her distinguished career. Some, she had no way of knowing the outcomes. She had held soldiers' hands as they died from blood loss after IEDs took their legs. Held sobbing husbands and wives when she told them the news of a deceased loved one. Each death ate away at her soul. She didn't want to add Zanzi to that list.

They made good time tracking through the back streets of Portland, keeping off the freeways and cutting through parks. Avondale directed them to the railway tracks and deeper into the city.

"I found her again. She's with two others. They're on electric scooters."

"Is there a girl, about fifteen?"

"Sorry, Director. No."

Lisa hurried on, the bike rattling and jarring as she sped along the gravel access road. The night was clear and crisp. The lack of ambient noise made her nervy, but also gave her confidence. Engine noise would travel, echoing through the still air. Still, she kept her eyes peeled.

On they rode, mile after mile, Avondale giving her directions. He phoned again.

"I think she's heading here."

"Of course. I should have guessed," Lisa replied.

"She's heading for Ross Island Bridge. If you hurry, you'll reach her before she crosses."

"How's our six?"

"You're clear for now. Those Black Skulls goons aren't exactly sneaky."

The bridge came into view and Lisa spotted three figures riding in the cycle lane. She pulled Reid back. "Stay here. She knows me. I don't want to spook her."

Lisa rode out into the middle of the freeway and turned toward Zanzi. She stopped immediately, shoving her two companions behind her.

"Zanzi! It's me, Lisa." She edged her bike forward a few feet.

"Lisa?" Zanzi had a pistol trained on her. "If it's really you, what kind of fish did I catch that day you first let me fly?"

"I think you called it a snapper."

Zanzi laughed, ran forward, and wrapped Lisa in a hug. "I can't believe it's you. Where have you been?"

"I could ask the same about you. Let's get off the road."

Zanzi nodded and beckoned the two women over. Lisa led them down an alley and into an open cafe. They left the bikes and scooters in the kitchen and sat down. Reid took up guard at the window.

Zanzi and Lisa looked at each other, grinning. "That's Sergeant Reid," Lisa said.

Shadows of Ash

"Tilly and Jacqui." The women greeted each other with warm smiles. Jacqui was clutching a hefty wrench.

"I have some good news and some you're going to find hard to believe," Lisa said.

"Ah. Okay." Zanzi frowned. "Well?"

Lisa started to speak but stumbled over her words. She had known Zanzi all her life. Watched her grow from a shy bookworm into a confident woman. How did she tell her that the mother she'd thought dead was in fact alive and well?

"Your father's alive and trying to stop a second wave. Also, your mother is with him."

"My mother? Cal?" Zanzi shook her head and scraped the chair out. "No way. No. I don't believe you. Why would you tell me that? We buried her!"

"It's true. Sofia confirmed it to Avondale."

"No. It can't be. She would never leave me. Stay away. Make me believe she was dead. That's not her. That's not the mother I knew."

"I didn't believe it myself. But why would Sofia lie?"

"Maybe Sofia's telling us this to mess with our minds. Maybe she's on ReinCorp's side."

"You know Sofia. That's not her. Not her style. I should know. I trained her."

"Maybe." Zanzi went to the window and looked out. Reid, Tilly, and Jacqui watched in silence. What was there to say? She had just learned that the mother she'd thought dead all these years was in fact alive and well.

After a few minutes, Zanzi sat back down at the cafe table and picked at the label on a water bottle. "You know,

I always had an itch in the back of my mind that wouldn't go away. Maybe it's the DNA we share, but as we buried her, held the memorials, and I watched Dad fall deeper and deeper into a depression, it felt wrong. I thought that it was part of the grieving process, so I threw myself into my studies and work. Now, here amongst the madness, the itch is gone."

Lisa reached out and took Zanzi's hand in her own. She loved her as if she were her daughter. "As soon as we get to Avondale's, we'll get them on the radio."

"I'd like that."

"Sergeant Reid, over there, and I have a mission of our own. He's up to speed. We need to destroy as many cell phone towers as possible before zero-six-hundred. The second wave is being broadcast then. We destroy the towers, no signal."

"A second wave?"

"Yes. The bastards are going to hit everyone again."

"Count me in. Once Tilly and Jacqui are safe that is, plus you'll need the extra pair of hands."

Lisa should have guessed. She knew she could always rely on the Connors.

"Huh," Jacqui said. "Whatever you white girls are planning, you can count me in. No one messes with my family without retribution, and besides, what is the second wave?"

Lisa sighed. "The day everyone turned to ash. It was caused by nanites inside us. An organization called OPIS broadcasted a signal which – now, I'm theorizing here – switched on a self-destruction program in the nanites, causing the combustion. At zero-six-hundred tomorrow, they hit the switch again."

"Nana-what now?"

"Nanites. Microscopic robots."

"Oh no, uh-uh. You telling me that I have tiny robots inside of me like some twisted sci-fi shit?"

"I'm afraid so."

"And you all knew about it?" Jacqui arched one eyebrow, looking at each of them in turn.

"Not until recently."

"What about the government? Don't we have the National Guard for situations like this?" Jacqui said.

"Have you seen them?"

"I've seen them. Telling everyone to report to the camps they've set up. Come get your food and medicine."

"We believe they're imposters. Put there by OPIS."

"I heard the new president on the radio telling everyone to stay calm and follow FEMA and the military's instructions. But I've never seen our military wear black. And I never trust the government anyhow."

"That instinct is why you're still alive," Lisa said.

"Who are you guys anyway? CIA?"

"No. Reid and I are US Army out of MacLeod."

"So how do I know you don't work for this OPIS?"

"Because General Munroe sent us out to destroy the towers. He's on our side."

"OPIS. Shit. What is it with rich folks? Do they have so much money they look at ways to mess with people instead? Nothing else to worry about. If you ask me, we need to go back to the hunter-gatherer days. Shit was simple then. Get up, get some food. Eat food. Sleep. Repeat."

"I can't ask you to put yourself in danger," Lisa said. "You should know that what we're doing, those soldiers dressed in black are more than likely going to try to kill us."

"Girl. You ain't never spent a day in my neighborhood, have you?" Jacqui grinned. "I'm coming."

The cafe fell silent. Out of habit Lisa checked her weapon and clicked the magazine back in. She didn't need to do it. She could tell by the weight of it roughly how many bullets she still had. The sound and feel of the action comforted her. Relaxed her.

"Heads up. I've got movement," Reid said from the window. The faint sound of engines cut through the night. "Two Ford Explorers. Black. Half a click. They're searching the buildings."

"Let's go. Head for the bridge and keep out of sight," Lisa said.

Within seconds, the group was making its way down the alley and out into the side street. No one spoke. Lisa didn't have to tell them to be quiet. They'd all experienced what the Black Skulls were capable of.

They drew closer. Lisa spotted two more SUVs heading for the Ross Island Bridge from the side streets. She berated herself for not insisting they keep moving. It was a mistake that could cost them dearly.

"Under there," Reid pointed.

The bridge had been in the middle of being repainted before the world had gone down the tubes, so the steelwork was covered in a lattice of scaffolding.

"Go!" Lisa said, desperation in her voice. Even though the bikes and scooters were silent, she had no way of knowing what kind of equipment the Black Skulls had. Thermal imaging cameras? NVGs? They could have anything.

Reid watched their backs as the ever-growing group began to climb. Lisa shook her head and passed the sergeant.

"It's going to be a long night."

"Just how we like it," Reid said.

THIRTY-ONE

MAKUSHIN BAY, ALEUTIAN ISLANDS

Biting cold wind stung Ryan's face as he dragged Colonel Dudek's body outside the NSA listening station. Before dealing with the dead Dudek, he'd found five more explosive devices set by the pilots, disarmed them and added them to his satchel.

He gritted his teeth and dragged the colonel farther away. His back ached. His kidneys were screaming. Dudek's punches had been like sledgehammers. Strong, powerful, and accurate. Bludgeoning blows. Ryan was sure he would be coughing up blood and probably pissing it too for the next week. Never had he put his body through so much. In the past week, he had been shot, exposed to radiation, and taken a brutal beating.

With one last heave, he dumped the body outside the security fence. Staring down at Dudek's face, he frowned when he saw a tattoo behind the colonel's ear. Three squares, each smaller than the last, connected by lines. It reminded him of the crop circles that appeared in corn fields. He shook his head. Another mystery.

Ryan left Dudek to the elements. He really wanted to dump him out in international waters. Traitors didn't deserve to be interred on United States soil and Dudek had given up that right when he had conspired to kill billions.

The wind grew in intensity, whipping around his legs and stinging any exposed skin. He jumped inside the chopper. It took him a few minutes to familiarize himself with the radio controls and enter Avondale's frequency. Sofia had mentioned something about relaying the signal. He shrugged. If he had one weakness, it was communications.

"Avondale. Do you copy. This is N1." Ryan repeated the call several times with no luck. He glanced north. The sky was darkening, losing the light of the moon as the storm tracked toward the island.

"Avondale. This is N1."

"N1. I read you. It's a bad signal. SITREP?"

"Alive but ops down. Radio busted. Motherboard fried. Request instructions. Over."

"Don't need radio. NSA station hardwired ... internet. Sofia will know. Over."

Shadows of Ash

"She's out. Tell me. Over."

Ryan could just see the computer genius in his chair, rolling his eyes. Avondale was brilliant at what he did, but like all geniuses, he hated explaining how to do something he considered to be as easy as breathing. Avondale had once worked for the NSA. While with them, he had hacked into terrorist networks, exposing codes and money trails. Highlighted targets for drone attacks. But Avondale wasn't a killer. After he had learned what his skills were being used for, it had been too much. He broke down. Folded within himself. Became catatonic. The NSA had locked him away in a Baltimore mental institution and pumped him full of sedatives.

Slowly, over three years, Avondale recovered and escaped. With nothing more than a smartphone, he hacked into the hospital computers, deleted his records, walked out, and found his way to LK3.

"The station will have backup servers. Replace the ruined with the new and reboot. Log into LK3 like normal. I'll see and take over remotely. Over."

"Wilco." He guessed that Avondale had some way to do that. He and Sofia always came through for them when they were on a mission. One fact he was certain of, he was glad they were on his side.

Sleet and snow began to fall as Ryan ran back inside the station. He filled in Cal and, after a bit of searching, found the drawers with server boards stacked neatly and numbered, just like Avondale had said.

The soldiers, in their haste, hadn't done a thorough job. Twenty minutes later, all the damaged servers were replaced. He picked up the internal phone.

Cal answered in seconds. *"Are we good?"*

"All done. Servers replaced. How do I reboot?"

"Red button next to the server deck. Press them so they're all glowing."

"Done."

"Is there a keyboard and screen nearby?"

"Right here. It's just showing white text like when Liam was coding."

"Good. Press Ctrl, Alt, Delete. Just like at home."

"You're kidding? I thought the NSA would have something fancy."

"That comes later. Right now, we're just booting up the operating system. Next, you must enter some codes. Lucky for us, I have the manual."

Ryan groaned and followed Cal's instructions. Fifteen minutes later, the system was up and running. Lights across the board.

"Are we good?"

"System's all go. Nice work. Can you get these bodies out of here?"

"Yes, ma'am."

It wasn't a pleasant task, but a necessary one. What made it difficult was that he was moving men who had served the USA. Those who served swore an oath. Swore to support and defend the constitution against enemies both foreign and domestic. And to obey the orders of the president and the officers above their rank. Had these men simply been following Dudek's orders? Were they innocent pawns?

Maybe The Nameless were the traitors after all.

Ryan shook away his doubts. He unequivocally believed in what he was doing. He always had. Sure, he had been born in New Zealand, but when he joined LK3 he became a US citizen. He swore to defend America. As the center of Western democracy, it was where he needed to be. Defend America, defend the democratic world.

He dragged the bodies outside and covered them with a tarp, making a promise to himself to give them the burial they deserved. Maybe he could get the *Nimitz* to come back and pick them up. Visions of fields of white crosses flashed through his mind. Crosses that he'd seen in France, Belgium, and Turkey.

Sofia was up and sitting at the console when Ryan got back down. She rubbed the deep purple bruises on her chest and looked up at him.

"You look as bad as I feel."

"Nice to see you up."

"Good job rebooting the system."

"Cal and Avondale were the brains. I just did the grunt work."

"Usual story, then?" Sofia grinned.

Ryan grinned back. "Are we going to make it?"

"It's possible. In short, I don't know. I'm in contact with Avondale. Together we can run the calculations, but I'm afraid we may be too late. See this." Sofia tapped one of the monitors. "This displays all the satellites above North America right now."

Ryan let out a low whistle. "There's hundreds. I mean, I knew there were a lot, but that many?"

"Most are inactive. Currently there are around nineteen hundred active satellites. And that's just the ones with transponders. Who knows how many orbit the earth, offline or redundant. Incognito."

Ryan looked at the screen. Two of the symbols flashed green, while three flashed red. "What are those?"

"Our two are green. We think those are OPIS's. Avondale highlighted them."

"There's no way of knowing for sure?"

"Maybe, with some research, some time, we could figure it out. Time, we don't have. We've already started moving ours to intercept. Six hours and seven hours—" She jabbed a finger at each symbol in turn. "—give or take, to impact. They're the satellites ReinCorp launched over the last few years."

Ryan paced, feeling desperation with every step. They were flying blind. It didn't sit right with him. Offenheim and OPIS had spent decades planning this. The ultimate long game. Carefully moving the pieces of the puzzle into place. With a conspiracy this large, OPIS would have had to do so much.

He tapped his finger against his chin as he thought. Part of the success of The Nameless was that they could think like their targets, enter their minds, anticipate their next moves. Like the spy game, everything would have two or three meanings. Nothing gained unless something given. Every detail thought about, leaving no room for mistakes. It made no sense to have three large satellites blinking like lighthouses in the fog. Or was it a ruse within a ruse?

"Sofia. To broadcast a signal with the amount of data required, it would have to be a large satellite, right?"

"In theory, yes, but also no." She shifted in her seat, rubbing her bruises again, gingerly. "Data storage is going off the charts with how it's stored. OPIS designed nanites. For all we know, they could have a satellite up there that is seemingly inactive when it's not." She shrugged. "I'm sorry. We have no way of knowing."

"Are the satellites with transponders registered?"

"They should be. I see where you're going." Sofia tapped furiously on the keyboard. "I'm getting Avondale to send me that data."

"Keep going with the original plan. If I can figure which satellites are theirs, we'll work something out."

"Flying by the seat of our pants as usual," Cal said.

"If the situation fits."

Ryan left them to it and checked on Booth and Allie. They were both awake and looking around. Booth rubbed his neck where Dudek's taser had zapped him.

"How do you guys feel?"

"Like I've been run over by a bus after a night drinking whiskey," Booth said, grimacing. "I'm just surprised I'm alive. Where's the bastard?"

"Dead. He's outside."

"What happened?"

Ryan filled them in.

Booth tested his jaw by opening and closing it. "Dudek clobbered me from behind, like a coward. By the time I'd recovered from the shock, he'd zapped me. He was fast, Connors. Real fast."

"I know. Believe me, I know." Ryan lifted his shirt, showing his old friend the fading bruises on his torso. "I'm sure he broke a couple of ribs too."

Booth passed Allie an electrolyte drink.

"I hate to break up this party, but we got a job. Allie, can you fly the Seahawk?"

"Yes. I started training with choppers before moving on to planes. I might be a bit rusty, though."

"Once the storm passes, do you think you could have a look. I don't fancy hiking back to Dutch Harbor."

She grunted. "If it means getting home, sure."

A dull thud sounded, followed by three more. Ryan snapped his eyes up to meet Cal's. They all knew that sound. In their line of work, it was a noise they were all too familiar with. Explosives.

"I thought you did a sweep?" Cal said.

"I did." Ryan held up his satchel and pointed to the timers.

"Signal's down," Sofia said. "I've lost contact. Radio's gone too."

That could only mean one thing. The pilots had placed explosives on the radio mast and some of the dishes.

Ryan cursed. How could he have missed those? He hadn't even thought about the outside. Of course Dudek would have ordered it. He'd been so preoccupied with the colonel that his normally analytical mind failed him.

"Booth, are you well enough to help me upstairs?"

"I'll survive," Booth said, getting to his feet.

"Sofia. What do you need?"

"Assess the damage. After that I'll need at least one dish pointing in the right direction. Preferably a big one."

"On it," Ryan said. He paused as he put on his jacket and shouldered his satchel. "Guys, I'm sorry. I let you down. We fought so hard to get to this point. Survived Yamada. An earthquake. Siphons. Those robotic spiders. We fought like the team we once were. The team I would like us to be again."

He looked each member of The Nameless in the eye. Cal coughed. "You have nothing to apologize for. I should be the one apologizing after what I put you all through. For what it's worth, I'm sorry. It sounds weird, but I did it out of love. I wanted to protect you all."

These were the moments Ryan lived for. Ordinary people doing extraordinary things. Not just for one another, but for all of humanity.

"I feel the same, Ryan," Sofia said. "You have nothing to apologize for. Let's work the problem and fix it."

"Agreed," Booth said. "C'mon, old man." He stood and went to wait for Ryan by the elevator.

That was why he loved this job. Working with these people every day gave him a sense of purpose. A sense he had missed for the past three years.

THIRTY-TWO

PORTLAND, OREGON

The Willamette River swirled below the Ross Island Bridge as the group climbed the scaffolding.

Zanzi clung to the metal tubing hauling herself up to the next platform. She risked a quick glance over her shoulder searching for the chasing Black Skulls.

"Keep moving," Lisa said.

Zanzi grunted and squeezed her tired body under the framing and up onto another row of metal planks. They climbed in silence, Lisa on point and Sergeant Reid bringing up the rear. Zanzi looked over her shoulder again. She couldn't help it. How the Black Skulls had found them so easily bothered her – if they were indeed looking specifically, or just doing a general sweep. Lisa had been careful and taken the group to a cafe out of sight. She shook away the thought and concentrated on not slipping.

Reid let out a short, low whistle, halting the group. The scaffold rattled and vibrated as bullets pinged off the scaffold above and below and the Black Skulls charged. Their heavy bodies shook the metal tubing with every step.

"Move!" Reid shouted, pushing into Zanzi's back. She grabbed Tilly's hand and ducked. More bullets bounced off the bridge.

Reid lay down suppressing fire, sweeping his MP5 from side to side. It wasn't about hitting the commandos, just about giving his friends time to escape.

"Here!" Lisa said. She had taken cover behind one of the central girders as the main arch swept down to a lower concrete pylon. Lisa covered their retreat, expertly keeping the pursuing Black Skulls occupied until Reid slid behind the giant beam of metal, sucking in air. "We got at least eight coming," he said.

"More this way," Zanzi said. She gestured with a flick of her head. "Five that I could see."

"Shit," Jacqui cursed. Zanzi didn't blame her. They had just escaped from the hell hole of the biker's HQ and run straight into this.

"There I go again following white people." Jacqui shook her head as she looked around.

The scaffold they were on stepped down, following the arch of the bridge support. Thin metal poles joined their section to the scaffold on the far side of the river, which the workers had been taking down. Zanzi noticed it too. Everyone did. They were trapped. If they walked back out, commandos from each side would take them out. They were too high to risk jumping into the river. Maybe the safety netting?

"They'll pick us off," Lisa said, seemingly reading Zanzi's thoughts. She ducked around the corner and halted the advancing Black Skulls with bullets of her own. "Go! Reid and I will cover you."

"Not without you," Zanzi said.

"We don't have time to argue. Take the others and get to Avondale's."

Zanzi groaned. "We should stay together." She checked the positions of the Black Skulls. She could make out their individual shapes now. They were cautiously advancing. The chasing pack was only a hundred meters away.

"We're all going, you fools," Jacqui said and started to loosen the nuts holding the swivel joints to the metal tubing with the adjustable wrench she'd had from the workshop.

Reid fired another burst grinning from ear to ear. "Do it. Head down, keep to the right, loosen as we go."

Jacqui moved quickly, undoing nuts in a precise manner as if she'd done it all her life. After she'd loosened each tube, she kicked it off and into the river.

Zanzi, Tilly, Reid, Lisa, and Jacqui moved in a tight knot with Jacqui and Tilly removing pieces of the loose tubing as they went. Lisa, Zanzi, and Reid fired round after round.

Reid and Lisa jammed fresh magazines into their MP5s. "Last one," they both shouted.

Zanzi helped Jacqui free the last piece of tubing and helped Lisa across the gap. Reid fired another three round burst and leapt across. There was a road below them now and the scaffold ended next to a portable construction building. Safety and warning signs covered the temporary fence surrounding it.

"Go," Reid shouted.

Zanzi managed to duck behind another metal girder as the Black Skulls rained down bullets. Reid cried out and tumbled, crawling behind a steel beam. Blood streamed from his side and leg. "Go," he said again. "I'll cover your retreat."

Zanzi shook her head. She wasn't going to leave him. No one left behind.

She hooked her arms under Reid's and hoisted him to his feet. "On your feet, soldier."

Tilly ran back to support the sergeant from the other side. They weaved their way between the workers' tools. The scaffold rattled and groaned. Shouts rang out as the tubing Jacqui had loosened collapsed.

Metal clanged.

Scaffold sagged.

Screams echoed.

Several Black Skulls fell into the river below and a couple thumped onto the road with a sickening sound like a wet sack, their cries fading as the nanites healed them. The remaining commandos fired, but the latticework of tubing prevented their shots from reaching their targets.

Shadows of Ash

Two minutes later, the tired group reached the construction office.

"Zanzi, Tilly, dress Reid's wounds. Jacqui, find us a car. Something silent, like a hybrid. Quickly." Lisa said. She pulled out her sidearm and aimed it back into the scaffold. The Black Skulls were moving carefully, testing each platform before stepping onto it.

Jacqui ran ahead, checking cars. Her figure flitted from one to another. It didn't take her long to find one with keys in the ignition.

The group crammed into a Toyota Prius. Reid struggled but took the passenger seat. Jacqui slipped behind the wheel.

"Keep it under fifteen miles per hour," Reid grunted, wheezing out breaths. "The petrol engine kicks in when it hits seventeen miles per hour."

Roaring V8 engines pursued the Prius, and headlights stabbed through the night like guards seeking an escaped prisoner. They nipped down tight alleys, ducked behind wheeled trash bins, parked behind abandoned cars. All the while the Black Skulls searched, their spotlights probing. Another SUV joined, and another, pulling the noose tighter. Jacqui was driving in circles. Whenever they thought they had an opening, an SUV would appear, and they were forced to hide again.

"How do they keep finding us?" Zanzi said.

"Like they're tracking us," Lisa murmured. She looked at Tilly and Zanzi. "One of you has a tracking device. It's the only way."

"In there," Reid said. He winced as he stretched out his right arm, pointing to a parking garage.

Jacqui pulled in and drove to the third level. She stopped in a space between two minivans and switched off the engine.

"Tilly and I will lead them away. There's no use getting everyone caught. It's us they want. They don't want you guys," Zanzi said.

"Maybe not before, but they do now," Lisa said. "I lost you once, I'm not losing you again. Like you said on the bridge, we have to stay together."

Tilly rubbed the side of her neck, just below her left ear. She looked at Zanzi and then at Lisa. "We used to have this cat called Pickles. He was lovely. All colors everywhere, and long whiskers that would tickle your face when you hugged and kissed him. Pickles and I used to lie in the sun and read together, but she was a fighter too. Any cat that came in the little cat door, and Pickles' tail would go whoosh and puff out." She rubbed her neck again, tracing the curvature of her spine.

"Why are you telling us that, Tilly?" Zanzi said.

The V8 engines roared through the parking garage, the sound reverberating off the cement walls and floor.

"Dad got sick of other cats coming inside and put in this special door. Pickles had to get a chip under her skin. Alba gave me one at The Eyrie. She said I was like a naughty cat that needed to be tracked."

Zanzi felt under Tilly's ear. She nodded at Lisa. "Tilly, we need to take that out. It's going to hurt, but you'll have to be brave for me."

Reid, gasping in the front seat, passed her his knife. Zanzi held it up and Reid heated the blade with his zippo lighter.

SUV engines roared.

Tires screeched.

Zanzi took a deep breath and exhaled slowly. She focused her mind, pretending she was back in the lab and just taking a sample.

Tilly bit into the fabric of her collar as Zanzi made a small incision and pried the chip out. It was the size of a grain of rice. She handed the knife to Lisa and pulled back her brown hair.

"Now me," Zanzi said.

Lisa found the chip. When that was done, she crushed both under her boot just as the Black Skulls' SUVs squealed up the ramp.

"Out, go!" Lisa shouted.

Zanzi scrambled after Tilly, following Lisa, Jacqui, and the hobbling Reid into the stairwell.

THIRTY-THREE

MAKUSHIN BAY, ALEUTIAN ISLANDS

Ryan hated the cold. The older he got, the more he disliked winter. One would think, living in the Pacific Northwest, he would've grown used to it. But there were subtle differences to cold. Some climates had damp cold, others a biting cold that chilled one to the bone. Some, like the Aleutian Islands, were just nasty. It was the kind of cold that if you got lost outside, you'd likely die from exposure in minutes. It got through the thick layers, seeped into your bones, and made you shiver.

The wind had picked up to gale force while he was downstairs and it whipped around Ryan, buffeting his thick jacket. He jammed his hands deeper into the pockets and stomped his feet.

The communications equipment was a mess. The main radio mast was a twisted wreck. The top third had fallen over and smashed onto the chopper, bending the rotor blades.

Booth scuffed his shoes in the thickening snow. "That's just great, man. That's just great."

Ryan agreed. The damaged chopper was a kick in the guts. After everything they had been through, now they had a long hike through unforgiving terrain to look forward to.

The pilots had been haphazard, placing the four charges on random dishes and aerials. The cell phone tower was unharmed, but all the dishes had suffered catastrophic damage. They lay in a heap of tangled metal. Wires and jagged shards of plastic peppered the snow.

Sofia had said she needed one dish, just one. They picked through the debris, turning over the twisted metal – some of which was still hot. Booth called out. He was lifting an intact dish. The wires connecting it to the transmitter housing had been severed, but other than that, it looked operational.

They set about rewiring it. Dudek had been confident of defeating The Nameless. If he hadn't, he'd have blown the station and flown away. He'd had no reason to be pedantic about explosive placement, to The Nameless' benefit.

"Where does this go?" Ryan asked, holding up the coaxial wire.

"In that housing. Haven't you ever set up a dish at home?"

"That's what the guy is for. I pay him money. He makes the TV work."

Booth shook his head and screwed the thick wire into the board. He gave it a couple of tugs before screwing the weatherproof plate back in place. "That should do it."

Ryan pulled the hood of his jacket tighter, trying to block out the howling wind. "How's that, Sofia?"

"All good. We're back in business. You'll need to get the dish higher and point it northwest at an eighty-degree angle."

"On it."

Looking around, Ryan could only see one possibility. The satellite dishes had been grouped together on a raised platform, which was now a tangled mess of metal. Off to one side was a strange, white, domed shape. He had seen larger versions at Air Force bases in Nevada, and giant ones on a mission in China. "We need to get this up there," he shouted over the wind, and gestured with his head.

"In this weather?" Booth grumbled. "I'll look for a ladder."

Ryan dragged the dish closer to the white dome, straining with the weight. He checked his satchel for duct tape, something he always carried. It had a thousand uses, and this was a perfect example.

"Ryan, do you copy?" Cal said. Her voice was faint as the radio hissed.

"Barely. Go ahead."

"I got activity on the radar. Choppers, from the looks of it. ETA forty-five minutes."

"Damn. Any idea who?"

"Identification transponders are off."

"That can't be good."

"Probably Black Skulls."

"Can you reach the *Nimitz* and see if they're from there?"

"Avondale is trying, and Munroe as well, but with this storm, communication is going to be difficult at best. I'm afraid we're on our own."

Ryan turned and gazed out at the Bering Sea. It was charcoal in color, boiling and swirling, whipped up by the storm. Did OPIS know exactly where they were? Had Dudek informed his superiors, or was he working alone?

As usual, too many questions with no answers. He stared at the damaged Seahawk. Surely it had some sort of transponder the Navy could home in on. Maybe he could alert the *Nimitz* that way? But first they needed to know who was friendly.

Booth returned with a ladder, and they hoisted the satellite dish onto the roof of the dome. Struggling against the wind and snow, Ryan used the entire roll of tape. As an extra precaution, they secured the feet with tie-down straps they'd found in the station.

"Satellite is up," Ryan said.

"Good. Now adjust the transmitter until I say stop," Sofia said.

It took a bit of wiggling, but they got the dish as Sofia wanted it. Ryan nudged his comms again.

"I don't fancy taking on Black Skulls if that's who's in the choppers. We have limited firepower. I vote we barricade ourselves until we complete our mission."

"What about the bodies?"

"I have an idea for that." He turned to Booth. "We'll have to set up a crime scene."

They dragged the corpses of the pilots, the four marines, the agents, and the Siphons into the weather station. They placed the bodies in a haphazard pattern, doing their best to make it look like a fight had taken place.

Ryan gagged as he cut open the stomach of one of the marines and pulled his intestines out. He lay the body of a Siphon next to it. He hated to desecrate the soldier's remains. It went against everything he fought for. But sometimes unpleasant tasks had to be done, and during times like these, this was crucial. "I'm sorry," he whispered to the deceased before moving to the next task.

"I don't think the pilots should be inside," Booth said. "It's not logical. Why would they be in here? And where's Dudek?"

"I dumped him outside the fence, near the Seahawk."

The two men stared at each other. After working together for so long, each knew what the other was thinking. Without a word, they dragged the pilots back outside to the damaged helicopter, placed their sidearms in their hands, and positioned Dudek's body a couple of feet away.

The scene wasn't in any way perfect, but to the untrained eye it looked convincing enough. Ryan hoped it would give them enough time to complete their mission. He glanced at his watch: 0315 flashed back. A little under three hours. Thunder and lightning cracked in the distance, masking the thumps of the two choppers' rotors. Ryan scanned the horizon, searching for them. With the snow falling in thick flurries, he hoped it would be enough to disguise their presence.

Allie was waiting for them as they exited the elevator. She opened a panel next to the call button and pulled a switch. It looked like an old-fashioned circuit breaker.

"Safety protocols. This locks down this level. We can't leave, and no one can get in."

"Perfect," Ryan said. Booth and Allie embraced, wincing slightly at their still-healing wounds. With everything that had been going on, Ryan had ignored his own throbbing pain. Now that he stood still, the pain returned in waves. He sat down next to Cal and Sofia and swallowed a couple of painkillers.

"How are we looking?"

Cal pointed at a screen. She had the station's cameras pointing toward the northeast. The choppers were now smudges against the strobing skies. "Let's hope your ruse works."

"It only needs to fool them for another couple of hours," Ryan muttered. "Sofia?"

"I'm not liking our chances. Avondale's tracked down all ReinCorp's satellites. They have over a hundred in total, including the three main ones. He's still working on YamTech. We focused on North America."

"What's this cluster here?" Ryan pointed on the screen.

"Weather satellites. Telecommunications for broadcasting sports, news, etcetera."

Ryan tapped his finger against his chin. He gazed at the screen. Sofia had a red line showing the predicted trajectory of the LK3 satellite and its collision course with ReinCorp's. They were going to be twenty minutes too late. There were dozens of satellites whizzing by that they had to avoid. Or did they?

"This is going to sound crazy, but what if we deliberately hit other satellites into theirs?"

"How's that going to work? There are way too many variables."

"Like a snooker shot, or eight-ball. We hit that cluster there and send it spinning off. We have a better chance of stopping the second wave that way. And we use our second satellite to take out the two satellites down here. If I'm reading this right. Ours are at a higher altitude?"

"Correct, but then we have no more satellites."

"So what? If it means stopping this madness, we must take a chance. I mean, that's what we all signed up for, isn't it?"

"A slim chance is better than no chance," Cal said.

Sofia sighed and rolled her shoulders. She had a chat window open, communicating with Avondale. She wrote their plan. His reply fired back in seconds. "Yes. Do it."

It was now a waiting game for The Nameless. Wait and see if the Black Skulls would buy their staged scene. Wait and see if they had any success with, quite frankly, a ludicrous plan. And wait and see if, by doing so, they managed to stop the second wave in North America.

THIRTY-FOUR

PORTLAND, OREGON

On they ran through the abandoned streets, around cars that had mounted the sidewalk and crashed through shop windows. Past motorcycles lying in the street with piles of ash next to them. Past bags of goods scattered by vermin as they scavenged for food.

Zanzi ducked into yet another alley and risked a peek over her shoulder. Sergeant Reid had volunteered to lead the Black Skulls away, back toward the river. His sporadic gunshots echoed through the empty streets. She said a prayer for him and hoped he survived. She liked the tall soldier. His movements had been methodical and precise as he dispatched the Black Skulls on the bridge, but she had detected warmth in his eyes. She had been around military all her life. Some soldiers had that hard look, like they had seen too much death, too much evil. They had become desensitized to it all. Those men and women didn't know how to switch off. It was with them all the time. Others, like Sergeant Reid, had something to live for, a life waiting for them after their service. Or perhaps he was just better at hiding the trauma. She brushed away her thoughts and refocused on the road ahead.

Lisa urged her on with a pull. "Don't stop." She pushed them harder, winding around strip malls, through parks, and deeper into the suburbs. After thirty minutes of running, she brought them to a halt.

"This is an LK3 safe house. I'm going to check the front," Lisa said. She disappeared around the side of the house.

Tilly and Jacqui gasped beside Zanzi, sucking in breaths. Sweat glistened on their foreheads.

"I'm sick of running from these guys," Zanzi said.

Tilly smiled in agreement, breathing hard.

"I'm ashamed to say that you guys are fitter than me. Flo Jo will be turning in her grave. And to think I was All State champion," Jacqui said.

"You ran track?" Zanzi asked.

"Yes, ma'am. Oregon State Champ three years running. Eight hundred and the mile."

The back door cracked open. "All clear," Lisa said. "Keep it down. We'll refuel and arm ourselves. We leave in ten minutes. Zanzi, with me."

Shadows of Ash

Zanzi joined Lisa in the garage. A gray minivan was parked inside. "We stocked the safe houses with these a couple of years ago. Best way to blend in. Look like your typical soccer mum taking her kids to sports."

"Smart. If we keep our speed down and lights off, we might just make it to the tower."

"That's the idea. Do you think Tilly and Jacqui will be okay? I'm reluctant to put them in any danger," Lisa said. She flipped the lid off a crate she had pulled out from the crawlspace and handed Zanzi an MP5, a combat vest, and full magazines.

"After what they've both been through over the last few days, if they want to help, then I say who are we to deny them that?" Zanzi sat down and loaded ammo into her P229 and checked over the MP5. She looked up at Lisa. "Tilly comes across as a bit weird, a little eccentric, but she's proven herself to be one resilient young woman. If it wasn't for her, we'd never have escaped The Eyrie. Those bikers were sick bastards, matching Rabids against innocent survivors, people so traumatized that when I tried to free them they were frozen stiff. Unwilling to move. Jacqui survived in that den for days, using only her wits. I don't think we're going to find a more determined pair."

"Good. That's what I'd hoped. Avondale said Black Skulls attacked the bikers' HQ?"

"I suspect it was to rescue Dr. Josie Lahm. She was with us. She was Harriet's mum, and for a time she was going to help me infiltrate the Eyrie."

"On your own?"

Zanzi glanced at her shoes, suddenly ashamed for her bold plan. At the time of making it, anger and hate had fueled her desire. As she had walked the halls with Tilly, she had discarded scheme after scheme trying to figure out a way to take down Offenheim, but her thoughts all had the same result. Black Skulls guarded everything. She would need help. That was obvious, but in the FEMA camp, Zanzi had nothing other than her plans. Perhaps now with Lisa they could achieve something. Together.

"I didn't know who was alive," Zanzi said. "I tried to do what my parents would have done. Lahm, I thought she wanted the same thing."

"She changed her mind?"

"I'm not sure. Maybe had doubts? The gang made us watch one of their cage fights. It was brutal. We witnessed the Rabids feeding on humans. Josie is a nanotechnology scientist. She helped OPIS develop the nanites. Her expertise was finding agents they could bind to, construct the nanites from, so they bind to our cells without our bodies rejecting them."

"I'd say she succeeded. We need someone like her," Lisa said. "With an expert of her caliber, maybe we could develop a defense. Where would the Black Skulls take her?"

"They've set up a FEMA camp near the Legacy Emmanuel Medical Center, but Josie said they were organizing a laboratory for her inside the center. Those Rabids out there weren't meant to be. Her job was to figure out why."

"Okay, good. We need her. Let's deal with this tower first – at least save this part of Portland from the second wave." Lisa pulled two duffel bags from the crawlspace. "Get the others and grab some food. We need to leave."

Two minutes later, they were crawling their way through the suburban streets of Hillsdale, heading for Marquam Nature Park. At its summit was a small cell phone tower. Zanzi remembered the behemoth towers that used to be around, eyesores in the beautiful scenery. Nowadays, cellular network technology had shrunk. The towers could be smaller, tucked away out of sight, barely noticed by passing runners and hikers.

Jacqui crawled along Terwilliger Boulevard, keeping the minivan to the middle of the road. Even here, people had been driving. Some cars had rolled to a stop on the side of the road in the absence of a guiding hand, while others had spun off the road and into the shrubs and trees. Several times Jacqui had to stop so that Lisa and Zanzi could push vehicles out of the way. She brought the minivan to a stop next to the trail head.

Lisa pulled them into a huddle beside the van. "Zanzi, you have point. Stay off the trail. Watch for hostiles – human and otherwise. Reid and I blew up a tower north of here. There's a strong possibility the Black Skulls have sent men to guard this one. We go in, set the charges, and get out. Nothing more. Am I clear?"

"Got it," Zanzi said.

"Tilly, Jacqui. You're our extra eyes. Don't take any risks. If I say run, run. Once we blow this tower, it's back to the safe house. If we get separated, go there. Okay?"

The two women nodded. Zanzi detected fear in their eyes and body language, in the way they shuffled their feet and continuously flicked their eyes about. She didn't blame them. She and Lisa had a distinct advantage – training. Ryan had said to her many times that sheer will went a long way.

Zanzi spent a few seconds adjusting her weapons, then darted into the forest. Apart from the odd hoot from owls, there was no other noise. What had really surprised her since their escape from the motorcycle gang was the lack of civilians. There either were none, or everyone was wisely staying out of sight, which seemed unlikely.

The trail steepened and soon Zanzi's tired muscles were burning. She first led the small team of women south, then west, to where several trails intersected before heading to the summit.

Lisa let out a low whistle and halted the group where the track finally split in two. "There's something I need to tell you. I think you should all know, and I won't think any less of you if you decide to go back to the minivan."

She looked at each of the women before carrying on. "Sergeant Reid and I saw something strange a few nights ago, and again last night. The Rabids, or whatever you want to call them, congregate around cell phone towers at night. Reid and I were tracking them, trying to figure out the reason. That was before we knew about the transmissions. I don't know if this tower is any different, but if those suckers get a whiff of us, they'll charge en masse. You can't hesitate for one second. Keep shooting until they fall. Understood?"

"I've never killed anyone before," Jacqui said. "But I guess they aren't people anymore. Unless we can switch off the nanites, make them human again?"

Shadows of Ash

"I'm not sure if it works like that, but I'm no expert. All I know is that we need to destroy the tower on this hill. If we save one person, then we've done our jobs," Lisa said.

Tilly stayed silent. She gazed at the horizon. Zanzi nudged her gently. "Understand, Tilly?"

"It's getting lighter. Sun's coming up," Tilly said.

"Understand?" Zanzi repeated. She had to make sure Tilly comprehended what she was getting herself into.

"No hesitating. I get it."

Zanzi stared at Tilly for several seconds before she was satisfied.

"All right. If you guys are sure, we'll carry on. Zanzi, you take Tilly and approach from the south. Jacqui and I will come in from the north," Lisa said.

The four women separated and crept slowly up the hiking track. Zanzi glanced over her shoulder to check Tilly was following closely. The summit was a few hundred yards away now, the tip of the cell tower peeking above the trees. She turned to Tilly.

"Don't be afraid to run, okay? If it gets to be too much, go. You're not a soldier. No one would think any less of you."

"I want to help," Tilly said. "I'm scared, but I'm always scared. Before you came to The Eyrie, I was afraid of everyone there. I'd seen a few of my friends die. Others just vanished. But then you came, and everything changed. So I want to help too, though I have no idea how we're going to do this."

"Tilly, I'm glad you're here. Remember how I showed you. Point and squeeze the trigger, watch the recoil. Just keep aiming for here." Zanzi pointed at her chest.

It was the stench that alerted her to their presence. A musty pong, like dirty socks. Zanzi crouched behind a fir tree and looked at the tower. At least a dozen Rabids milled around as if awaiting instructions from their boss. Was that it? Did the cellular network broadcast some kind of signal to them? That didn't make sense. Maybe they had malfunctioned during the combusting event and were now attracted to the tower. Zanzi surmised that was why they wanted cerebral fluid too. She ran through her options and tried to judge which Rabid would be the fastest. From what she had witnessed so far, they all ran about the same speed, as if hampered by an injury.

She nudged her radio. "Beta team in position."

"Alpha team in position," Lisa said. *"Numbers?"*

"Fifteen that I can see."

"Twenty-four here. On three ... two..."

Zanzi flicked off her safety and gripped the MP5 tighter.

"...One."

Gunfire erupted from the north. Immediately, the Rabids snapped their heads around. A few jolted forward as those closest to Lisa began to fall. Zanzi squeezed the trigger, letting go a three-round burst that hit the nearest creature in the neck and chest. Down it went, gurgling blood from its mouth and a gaping hole in its neck. She didn't have time to feel sorry for the woman it had been as the creatures spun toward her. She adjusted her aim and dropped two more, and a third.

Tilly shrieked as two of the Rabids charged from their left. She raised her Glock. Her hands shook as she pulled the trigger, and she missed with each shot. Zanzi swiveled and shot one in the gut. It lurched closer, howling.

"Breathe, Tilly!"

Zanzi went into a sort of trance. Aim, shoot, aim, shoot. Reload and repeat. In the back of her mind, the numbers nagged her. She had personally killed ten, and still they came, as if they were melting out of the forest, the trees giving birth to the sightless beasts.

"Zanzi!" Tilly screamed. Two Rabids had crawled over the bodies of the dead and howled as they pulled on her legs. Tilly was pulling the trigger, but instead of bullets, the firearm clicked.

"Reload!" Zanzi shouted. She shot another creature, ran, and kicked the Rabids in the head in turn. They snapped back and groaned, rolling over the blood-soaked earth, heads twitching as they sniffed the air. With their cloudy eyes, it was difficult to tell if they were looking at her or not. Zanzi shot them both in the head and pulled Tilly behind her.

"Watch our backs and this side. I'll watch front and my side."

"I can't reload."

Zanzi whipped out her P229 and flicked off the safety. "Use this," she said, handing it to Tilly, then quick as a flash she took a fresh magazine from her vest and jammed it in the Glock.

Zanzi saw Lisa and Jacqui were making progress from the north. They had made a dent in the Rabids' numbers now that no new creatures flowed out of the trees. Zanzi methodically killed the rest of the creatures in her target area and scanned for any new hostiles.

She listened out for the tell-tale sound of engines. Black Skulls were sure to respond.

The clearing fell into silence as Lisa shot the last Rabid. She gestured for Zanzi and Tilly to protect their escape route. They had planned it out. Up by minivan. Blow the tower. Back down via the steep track leading to the river. Disappear into the cluttered suburban streets and make their way back to the safe house.

"Explosives set. Move out," Lisa said over the radio.

Zanzi took one last look at the carnage, at the motionless Rabids. Some were still alive, somehow, pulling themselves over the grass on useless legs. It seemed cruel to leave them to suffer, but Zanzi knew there was no alternative.

Down she and Tilly raced through the trees, over logs and stumps. Leaves scattered as they ran, sometimes sliding down the steep banks. They hit the road and hurtled straight across and into the trees. If Black Skulls responded, the road was the most likely route they would use.

Kaboom! Kaboom!

The explosions cracked through the still night air, rumbling over the hills and the city. If anyone was alive in the houses and apartments nearby, they would be gawking in fright.

Lisa and Jacqui caught up to them at the bottom of another steep ravine.

"Good work, everyone," Lisa said.

Jacqui was breathing hard, hands on her knees. "And to think, last week I was happy reading and cuddling my cats. Now I'm running around with crazy people, blowing the bejesus out of stuff."

Zanzi took the moment to rest too. She had been on the go for days now, barely sleeping. Out of one dire situation and into another. What she wouldn't do for a warm bed and a hot shower.

The thumping of a helicopter sounded. Lisa jolted her head up.

"That's not good. Shit. An oversight on my part. Of course they would have choppers."

"Remember after headquarters? That soldier said they had thermal cameras too."

Lisa unfolded a city map from her combat vest. "Here, there's a mall. Go! Now! We can't afford for them to spot us."

Zanzi sighed and took off along the bottom of the ravine. She wondered if she'd ever rest again.

THIRTY-FIVE

MAKUSHIN BAY, ALEUTIAN ISLANDS

Cal and Sofia talked between themselves and tapped away at the console, attempting to sacrifice LK3 satellites by purposely smashing them into a cluster of weather and sports channel satellites, putting those on a collision course with OPIS. If they succeeded, the second wave would not hit North America, sparing the continent from more horror, more chaos. Give it a chance at survival.

The camera feed was crystal clear, showing both the area outside the station and inside the weather-monitoring building. White-capped waves pounded the jagged rocks lining the shore below, and the wind whipped flurries of snow about the rounded hills.

Booth, Allie, and Ryan watched two Seahawk helicopters land in the buffeting winds. Ryan had to admire the fearless pilots. In that storm, they guided the choppers to the ground and disgorged two companies of Black Skulls, just as expected. One investigated the damaged helicopter while the other headed toward the weather station.

"Cross your fingers they buy our ruse," Ryan said.

"They're just grunts," Booth laughed. "Above their pay grade to wonder why."

The Black Skulls inside the weather station crouched down next to the dead soldiers. One poked at the intestines with his rifle. He shrugged his shoulders and moved on to the living quarters. Ryan flicked his eyes to the monitor displaying the second company. They were sweeping the outside, darting through the downed equipment. Ryan wished he could tap into their comms system, to hear what they said – anything to give him a better idea as to why they were here. He could guess. Dudek would have reported in with his superiors once he'd made contact and found out where they were flying. It dawned on him then that Dudek's orders were to not only murder The Nameless but to destroy the station.

The agents inside had been unable to contact the outside world after they became trapped by the Siphons. It all made sense now. When neither Dudek nor his men reported in again, whoever was in charge had sent teams to investigate. Sofia and Avondale had assured him that unless someone had a code or heavy-duty cutting equipment, there was no way they could gain access down here.

Shadows of Ash

"They've finished their sweep," Booth said.

"Outside too," Ryan said. "But they're hesitating by our makeshift satellite dish."

"Do you think they bought it?" Allie asked.

"We can only hope. I figure that they don't know we're down here. They'll see the dish strapped down and figure it's from a previous storm. What worries me is the damage from the explosives, but it should be obvious it was the pilots."

"Let's assume they take the bait. Figure Dudek got caught off guard – it happens to everyone. What then?" Allie asked.

"Then we carry on with our mission," Ryan said. "If, and it's a big if, we succeed at this, we carry on. Destroying their communication center at The Eyrie is first on the list. I know I'm making a ton of assumptions, but that's all we've got. Assume they see the carnage and figure the soldiers died after a shootout with the agents and fighting the Siphons. I suppose it depends on how curious they are. Did we leave any trace upstairs?"

"No way. I cleaned up everything," Booth said.

Three Black Skulls broke away from the rest and walked back inside. They had no indication of rank. From the way they walked, Ryan could guess at staff sergeants and a lieutenant, or equivalent. They pointed to the man Ryan had gutted, and at the agent-turned-Siphon. Anyone with half a brain could see that the man's stomach had been sliced, not torn open. His ruse had been for the quick look, not closer inspection. He turned and looked at the countdown above the monitor.

They had a little over twenty minutes before the scheduled second wave.

"Sofia, Cal. How are we doing?"

"Calculating trajectories now. This must be precise. One millisecond out and the satellite will miss. That's even if it's the right one," Cal said. "I need at least ten more minutes. Can you distract them?"

Ryan glanced at the armed men climbing over the dome. One of the soldiers was testing the tie-down straps. He shrugged and slid back to the ground.

"If it comes to that, yes. Sofia?"

"I'm trying. All those codes I took off the general are useless so far. They're just spy satellites. Most pass over the Middle East, a few over Africa, and one over Indonesia. I'm making notes; they'll be handy later. Nothing to indicate that they have other satellites, other than what's registered. If only I could access their data core, I could tell you which ones fired the data stream at each of the towers."

"Keep at it. I know you guys can do it. We believe in you."

"If you believe, then you're halfway there." Sofia grinned. She was giving Ryan a hard time. She'd visited the Connors in New Zealand a few years back and had laughed at Ryan's mother's house, filled with inspirational quotes. She had them everywhere, printed out on colored paper and stuck to the walls.

"Any luck getting hold of Keiko and Ebony?"

"Safe and well. Holed up in a back office at the airport terminal." Sofia met Ryan's eyes. He saw her worry. The anguish. It was natural to feel that way; any parent would.

But he knew Sofia was focused. She understood what was at stake and trusted Ebony to keep Keiko safe.

Ryan stood and stretched his neck. He glanced over at the radar station and frowned. He could clearly locate the *USS Nimitz*. It had passed the headland and was now entering Dutch Harbor. Farther out to the west were two other ships. From their signatures, two destroyers.

"We got more ships incoming. What's the range of this radar?"

"Five hundred nautical miles, give or take," Allie said. "More US Navy?" She clicked the mouse and switched on a couple of blank monitors. One showed the GPS locations of all vessels in the area, while the other showed their transponders. The NSA station had a fully operational VTS – Vessel Traffic Service – like that used in busy ports around the world to track everything coming in and going out.

Allie furrowed her brow. "One helicopter carrier and a destroyer. Could be US. I'm not sure."

"It doesn't make sense to be US. Maybe Black Skulls. Cal, where was that ship you saw?" Ryan said.

"West, right on the edge of the radar."

"That explains it. Black Skulls."

Ryan paced back and forth, periodically looking at the screens and the cameras showing the soldiers.

"Cal, Sofia. How close are we?"

"We're making the final adjustments to our satellite. Avondale has done the math. Sofia is double-checking it. Two minutes. That's all we need," Cal said.

They could hear muted gunfire and small explosions.

"Connors. You need to see this. The Black Skulls are shooting up the weather station," Booth said.

Ryan groaned. Every step. Every step of the way, they were thwarted. They caught a break for a few hours and then *blam!* Something else.

The second company walked through the station, firing haphazardly at the computer equipment. As they left one room, they threw grenades to finish the job. None of it made sense. Was their superior cleaning house?

Ryan wasn't worried about the damage. Downstairs ran separately. Only the cables running to the dishes and comms ran through the top of the building. If the cables remained unharmed, they might just do it.

The Black Skulls halted their destruction and filed out. As the last soldier left, he placed small bricks of C4 in each room, switched on the detonators, and joined his men. Why waste all the ammo if they were just going to blow it up anyway?

Ryan thumped his fist on the desk. "They know we're here."

"No way. How?"

"They have to know. Look, they destroyed all the computers. Everything electronic. All of it. They know they can't get to us. So what's the next best option?

"Bring down the building. Trap us," Allie said.

"Exactly." Ryan nodded.

"Well, let's go stop those explosives," Booth said.

Ryan mulled it over. It was extremely risky, but perhaps their only hope.

"What if they want us to come charging out?" Allie stood. "Smoke us out. Maybe they know we can see them. They make a show of shooting everything, plant the charges and pretend to leave. We go charging out and they ambush us."

"What if they don't want us to charge; they just want to trap us?" Ryan said, shaking his head. It was too much. The Nameless was operating on fumes. Their bodies ached from exertion and their minds had dulled from lack of sleep. Normally he would figure out a plan, weigh up the options, and execute with no hesitations. He squeezed his temples with his thumbs.

"No, we stay put," he said. "The mission comes first. Saving the people of North America is our prime directive. If we die trying, that's the sacrifice we make."

"For the many," Booth whispered. He grasped Ryan's shoulder. "For the many."

The Black Skulls boarded the choppers. The last soldier ran to the dome with the dish and placed another brick of C4. He spent a few seconds getting it snug against the metal struts and jogged back to the Seahawk. Ryan could only watch in horror as the two helicopters lifted off the ground and banked away. The ground shook above them as the plastic explosives detonated in a concussive *kaboom*!

Concrete dust rained down as the shaking subsided. The monitors blinked, went dark, and switched back on.

"Please tell me you had enough time?" he said as he dashed into the console room, Booth and Allie on his heels.

Sofia had her head in her hands. "I don't know. I'm sorry." She rolled her shoulders back and stared at the screen. "Avondale was in the process of getting the cameras online. We saw briefly, but now..."

"What did you see?" Allie said.

"The OPIS satellite. We had a visual. Now I can't make any more adjustments."

The dark screen in front of Sofia blinked and sprang back to life. The HD camera showed an awe-inspiring scene. Planet Earth curved away below. The coasts of Alaska, Canada, and the Pacific Northwest drifted past. The sun was rising, bringing light to the Rockies, and thick storm clouds gathered over Nebraska and Kansas. In the top right of the screen, coming up fast, was the largest satellite Ryan had ever seen. It reminded him more of a module from the International Space Station than a satellite.

"That thing is huge," Booth said, voicing his thoughts.

The Nameless were riveted to the screen. Everything they had worked toward in the past eight days. Every Siphon they had killed in mercy. Every step they had taken over that mountain after the earthquake. Every horror they had seen in Ando's laboratory. It had all come down to a maybe. A slim chance.

A slim chance is better than no chance, John Stapleton had told Ryan. There is always hope – he had said that too.

"If anyone is religious, then it's time to pray to your deity," Cal said.

Closer the satellites came, flying at incredible speeds.

Five minutes until the second wave.

Ryan draped his arms over his wife and kissed the top of her head.

Four minutes.

Sofia groaned, looking at readouts on her screen. "It's going to miss. The speeds are different."

Shadows of Ash

Three minutes.

"For what it's worth, everyone, I'm honored to have served with you. If we fail here and perish, I want you to know that I couldn't have asked for better friends, for a better life, with all of you," Ryan said. He kissed Cal again and held Sofia's hand.

"You too, big sook." Booth slapped him on the back.

Two minutes.

The satellites were a kilometer apart. Sofia began counting down the distance.

To Ryan's eyes, it looked like they were going to miss. The LK3 satellite was spinning. With every rotation, the camera brought the OPIS monstrosity back into view. Every muscle in Ryan's body tensed as the last rotation began. Instead of revealing the satellite, the camera shook violently and shut off.

"What happened? Did we do it?" Booth asked.

Sofia and Cal tapped away at their keyboards. "The satellite is reading severe damage!"

"So did we do it?" Allie clasped her hands in front of her chin.

"I'm sorry. We'll have to wait and see," Sofia said.

Nobody moved. Their eyes were locked on the countdown clock.

Thirty seconds...

Twenty...

"Work you son of a bitch," Booth said.

Ten...

Zero.

Nothing happened. No pain. No agony of pressure build-up behind the ears, squeezing the brain like a vice.

No screams of terror. Nothing. The silence was bliss. The lack of pain, hopeful.

"Did it even happen?" Cal said.

"Checking with Avondale now." Sofia frowned, and typed in the message box again. "Damn it. He's gone dark. No response."

That was all they needed. Their computer genius dead. Without him, their task would become that much harder.

Ryan walked away from the group and went to the elevator. With the soldiers now gone, he wanted to evaluate the damage from the explosives. He flicked off the lock-out switch and pressed the door release.

The elevator cabin was full of chunks of concrete and debris. The pulley mechanism lay on the floor in a twisted heap. He gazed up the shaft. All he could see was darkness and dust.

The Nameless would need to find another way out.

THIRTY-SIX

PORTLAND, OREGON

Zanzi ran. For the fourth time in the last twenty-four hours, she found herself running for her life. Ever since that night at HQ, she had been on the run. From Black Skulls. From Rabids trying to drink her spinal fluid. From this OPIS. She was tired of it. She glanced at Tilly beside her. The young woman was panting hard, sweat dripping from her brow. Zanzi cursed herself for not insisting she stay at the safe house. Now she was in more danger.

The helicopter circled overhead, its bright spotlight searching for the fleeing saboteurs.

"Keep going!" Lisa said. "We need to get inside."

"There." Jacqui pointed at a department store.

"Not again," Tilly groaned. "Last time the smelly bikers caught us."

Lisa ignored her and pushed her across the road. Several engines roared in the distance, getting closer.

Zanzi gasped in a breath. Lisa was right. They had to get inside. It was the only way to escape the thermal cameras on the chopper. At least, once inside, they'd have a chance.

They entered the still-open doors. Barking replaced the sounds of the engines. Did the Black Skulls have dogs now?

Zanzi glanced at her watch. Thirty minutes until 0600, the scheduled time for the second wave.

On they ran, through displays of make-up and perfume. Through women's clothes and baby strollers. Up escalators and into the bedding section. Here there was evidence of looters – shelves ransacked, racks of clothing overturned. They ran through the outdoor section. All the cabinets holding knives and crossbows were smashed open.

The barking grew louder, appearing to surround the fleeing group. Tilly's eyes widened with each bark. The sound of boots thumping on the escalators joined the frenzied barking.

"This way," Lisa said as she burst through another door leading to a storage area. Boxes were piled high here, and some had been torn open.

As they weaved through the mess and entered the management area, a dozen surprised faces turned and gawked, mouths dropped open. Crossbows and pistols snapped all round.

Shadows of Ash

"Whoa. Easy now. We're friends," Lisa said, holding her hands up.

"Says the idiots leading those mercenaries right to us," a man with a thick bushy beard snarled. "Get out of here before you give away our hiding spot."

"You hear that?" Lisa lifted her finger. "Those dogs will sniff you out as well. You all need to move."

"Lady, we don't have to do shit," Bushy-beard snarled again. "Now get."

The thumping of the boots and the barking of the dogs intensified. Several pairs of eyes snapped around, searching for the direction.

"She's right, Jerry. We need to go."

"Shut it, Leslie. I told you that if you came with me, I'd give the orders. If you want to leave, I ain't stopping ya."

"You're a stubborn asshole," Leslie said, and looked at Lisa and Zanzi. "Follow me," she said. "There's a goods elevator back here. We can go down to the basement and out from there." Leslie glanced at the other survivors gathered in the staff room. "Anyone else coming?"

No one answered, their eyes looking anywhere but at Leslie. She shrugged, pushed through the crowd and out the door.

It didn't take long to reach the goods elevator, but the sounds of the Black Skulls chased them all the way. Gunfire erupted from the office. Shouts, screams, and cries of pain. Leslie stopped in her tracks, her eyes staring back.

"Keep moving," Lisa said. "We gave them the opportunity."

The noise from the battle subsided into muffled pops as the lift creaked its way to the basement.

The doors opened, and Zanzi took point, sweeping her MP5, searching for any hostiles. The basement remained silent. Hints of oil and petrol lingered in her nose. Like so many other places, even down here were forms of ash. People frozen in death, frozen in tasks they would never complete.

Leslie led them deeper, past the loading docks and bathrooms, through the electrical room, and into a room housing the air conditioning units. Dozens, stacked in rows, with large fans.

"We've been using this entrance to get in and out. Keeping out of sight," Leslie explained.

"Smart," Lisa said, bringing everyone to a halt. "You didn't go to the FEMA camps?"

"I did at first. I registered my name and posted pictures of my missing family and friends. I didn't like how they insisted on medical checks. I told them I was fine. When they wanted to give me an antibiotic jab, I guess I grew suspicious. Wandered around on my own for a couple of days before I met Jerry. We've kept out of sight, and earlier today I saw National Guard and army trucks rolling in. Jerry and I argued about going to them. He's paranoid. Said an event of this magnitude needed help from the government if it wasn't an attack by the North Koreans or the Chinese. Which makes more sense to me. Why would our government do this to us? This is America, not some commie country."

Lisa nodded. "Jerry has a right to be paranoid. If we escape, I can give you a few answers."

Shadows of Ash

"You know what caused it?"

"More or less."

Rifle fire erupted from the direction of the loading dock behind them, interrupting their conversation. Screams cut above the rattle of the carbines, only to be silenced seconds later. More dogs barked.

"Lisa. We need a car," Zanzi said.

Lisa turned back to Leslie. "What's directly outside this door?"

"An alley that leads back to the main street. Um ... Macadam Avenue."

The dogs were growling again as Black Skulls entered the electrical room. Zanzi grabbed Tilly's hand once again and kicked open the door.

Cool morning air, laden with moisture, chilled Zanzi's skin. Being a Portland native, she knew when it was going to rain. She'd felt the subtle changes in pressure countless times, smelt the faint salt as the winds brought the rain in from the Pacific.

Once everyone was through, they rolled a trash can across the door and locked its wheels in place. It wasn't perfect but it would force the Black Skulls to find an easier route.

They ran.

Zanzi looked at her watch. One minute until 0600.

They tore up the rubbish-filled alley and out onto the street. An SUV screeched to a halt twenty yards away. A lone Black Skull stepped out. He whipped up his M4 and aimed it directly at Zanzi.

Lisa stepped to her right and the commando lanced the concrete with bullets.

"Stay where you are," The Skull ordered.

Jacqui reached out and pulled Lisa back, then raised her hands above her head.

"I found them. I'm out front on..." The commando looked around, confused as to their location. "I'm out front. Five dissidents. Chicks too, if you believe that."

His radio crackled, but it was too garbled for Zanzi to understand what was being said. Instead, she watched the commando carefully.

Her watch beeped. The second wave was about to begin.

Lisa, Tilly, and Jacqui all turned and looked at her. She wondered if they understood. Had they done enough to at least save some people?

She tensed her muscles, anticipating the pain. It began like before, deep in her brain, and spread out, pulsing. But, unlike at The Eyrie, it subsided almost straight away.

Leslie gasped beside her, clutched her head, and dropped the Beretta pistol with a clatter.

The Black Skull grinned. "It's starting," he chortled, but kept his carbine trained on them.

Zanzi and Tilly eased Leslie to the ground. There was nothing else they could do. Leslie must have been dosed with nanites when she went to the camp. She shrieked and let out an agonizing wail. She smashed her hands against her temples, gasping with each passing second.

"Why aren't you suffering too?" the commando asked Lisa.

She ignored his question and crouched down to Leslie and the others who were doing their best to make Leslie comfortable.

"We can take him," Lisa whispered.

Leslie let out another pained howl and went rigid, her arms and hands locked in claws. Her skin turned ivory and erupted in angry red slashes. Her eyes snapped open. Gone were the brown irises, the dark pupils. Instead, they were cloudy. She clamped her mouth shut and struggled against Lisa, thrashing and kicking. Tilly choked and vomited, before crawling away from Leslie, now a Rabid.

"Kill that thing." The Black Skull ordered. He kept his rifle trained on Lisa's head.

"I'm sorry," Lisa said. She placed her pistol against the still-thrashing head and pulled the trigger, silencing the woman.

The Black Skull laughed before speaking into his radio. "Only one died after turning into a freak."

Zanzi looked away from the corpse and cast her eyes down the street. Nothing moved, and apart from the thumping of the chopper flying away to the north, it was silent. If they had been successful in saving anyone, she couldn't tell. She looked down at Leslie. All that effort for nothing. Now Zanzi had more questions. Why had they survived and not turned into Rabids like Leslie?

"You four, get in the car. The boss wants you alive."

He took a couple of steps forward and swung the rifle between them. The engine noise of approaching Black Skulls returned, growling down the street between the empty buildings.

"It's over for you guys. Why delay the inevitable?" the commando said.

"Why did they leave you on your own?" Lisa said. "Don't rats travel in packs?"

"Get in the car."

Tilly squared her shoulders and tilted her head back. She laced her fingers through Zanzi's.

"No," Tilly said.

"What do you mean 'no?'" the commando said. He squeezed the trigger, shooting Tilly in the fleshy part of her thigh. Tilly shrieked and dropped to her knees. Zanzi was stunned. Not at the commando's actions, but rather, at Tilly. At risk of injury to herself, the young woman continued to reveal facets of a complex personality. Gone was the timid mouse-like woman, replaced with an assured, brave fighter. She would need to be. Zanzi had no doubt that the worst was yet to come.

A silver SUV slowed to a stop. The door swung open and Milo stepped out. He glared at Zanzi before moving his stare to Lisa.

"Stand down, Corporal. I'll take over from here."

"Sir," the corporal said. He took a step back and hesitantly lowered his rifle to point at the ground.

Time seemed to slow as Zanzi glared at the commando. Milo walked up and stood next to the armed man.

"You were meant to disappear. Not run around blowing up towers," Milo said. Without hesitation, he removed a handgun and shot the corporal in the head.

Pop!

Brains and gunk sprayed out as he collapsed, falling next to Leslie's corpse. Milo stood over him and shot him twice more, once again in the head, and once at the base of the skull.

Shadows of Ash

"You have to kill the alpha nanite for him to die properly," Milo said. He pivoted, walked back to the car, and hopped into the driver's seat. "Well, come on. Don't stand there gawking. Director, nice to see you again."

"I wish I could say the same," Lisa said.

"Chill. I'm helping you this time."

Zanzi and Jacqui helped Tilly into the back seat of the SUV. A figure in the passenger seat turned and smiled. Zanzi was happy to see it was Josie.

"Who's this?" Lisa glanced at Zanzi.

"Dr. Josie Lahm, the doctor I told you about."

"I thought she ... never mind," Lisa said.

They tore down the vacant roads of Portland. Milo drove, squealing around corners, the SUV lifting onto two wheels.

"Where are we going?" Lisa shouted above the roaring motor. They sped down SW Macadam Avenue and crossed the Selwood Bridge.

"Industrial area south of here," Milo said.

"Why? Aren't you one of them."

"Yes, but I'm taking you to the faction I'm now part of. You can rest there. OPIS is hunting for you, I'll lead them away. Keep them off your trail. You'll have to trust me."

"Why should I?"

"They killed Amelia. My Amelia. Zanzi will explain."

Lisa looked at Zanzi, eyebrows raised.

"You can trust him. He smuggled Tilly and me out."

"They'll find us eventually," Lisa said. "We need to fight them. Better yet, set an ambush. I'm tired of running from these pricks. I'm tired of them finding us. It's time to even the score."

"You can't. Not yet. Hide for now," Milo said. He made a right turn and bumped over the railroad tracks.

"Fine. At least tell me where," Lisa said.

"An old paper factory."

Zanzi leant back into the cushioned seat. Lisa was right – they had to make a stand. They had to give themselves a better chance. With Josie back, they had the inside knowledge they needed to succeed. Maybe the faction would be willing to help.

THIRTY-SEVEN

PORTLAND, OREGON

As far as abandoned factories went, McLoughlin Print was normal. It had faded and peeling paint, stains on the concrete, and dirt-encrusted windows that hadn't been cleaned in years. Some walls had been tagged with graffiti, while others had holes from being kicked.

They dumped the SUV, and Milo guided them through an auto wrecker and a garbage and recycling center. It was all an attempt to mislead the dogs. Tilly hobbled on her injured leg, leaning heavily on Zanzi as they walked through grease and oil, through putrid water leaking from the mounds of garbage.

Zanzi remembered happier days when she had come here with her twin brother Liam to help make his short film for AV class. Liam had been obsessed with movies, especially horror. He had wanted to make his film about the vengeful spirit of a bullied worker who went berserk, killing off his tormentors. He had sold it to her as Portland's answer to the *Blair Witch Project*. She'd helped him film the background shots of the recycling center with its machinery squishing piles of trash.

Sadly, he'd never got to finish it, cut down by a coward and his bullets.

Milo pulled back a section of a chain-link fence and urged them through into the old paper factory. They stopped outside a rusty door. He spoke German into his radio and the door buzzed open.

They entered, and Zanzi craned her neck, scanning the space. A walkway ringed the upper floor. A smaller room with desks and typewriters lay opposite the main office up high. A clear view of the whole floor. Old, disused machinery was stacked against the pillars. Nowadays, it'd be deemed a fire hazard.

Two men and a woman, dressed in jeans and sports tops, waited in the center of the room. The woman had a red bandana holding back her black hair.

"Three. You only have three?" Lisa said.

"In Portland, yes. More elsewhere," Milo said.

The three faction members shook Milo's hand, and he conversed with them in hushed voices for a few moments, hands gesturing wildly, and pointing outside.

Shadows of Ash

"We have to keep moving. The choppers have been scanning the area with thermal imaging in a grid search," Milo said. As if to emphasize his words, the roar of a helicopter rumbled out of the morning sky, along with the sound of V8 engines. The faction members snapped their heads around at the sound.

"You led them here?" the woman with the red bandana said.

"Not on purpose, Mendoza. I told them to search north," Milo said.

The trio cursed and darted from the room. "We'll hold them off. Get out of here," Mendoza said.

Milo turned. "I can help you escape, but you'll have to trust me. I can't be seen with you."

"How many will be coming?" Zanzi said.

"Hard to say. We have teams of three. Maybe four or five teams."

"So fifteen?"

"Maybe. I'm sorry," he said, before sprinting after the other faction members.

The whole sequence of events had played out in a matter of minutes. So odd and choreographed, Zanzi thought it was a setup, an elaborate ruse to torment her.

Lisa glared at her. "I thought you said we could trust him."

"He got us out."

"Doesn't mean anything. It's all a game to the likes of him. Right. We're on our own. We stand here. No more running."

"No more," Zanzi said.

Lisa gave the orders. "Lahm, Jacqui, and Tilly. Hide in the office. Keep out of sight. Only fire on the commandos if they get up onto the gangway. Your handguns don't have the accuracy for long distances. Understood? Leave the bulk of the fighting to us."

She nodded at Zanzi. "You and I at the north and south, behind those pillars. Here, take this." Lisa handed the M4 to her. "You're a much better shot than I am. Wait until they're all in the factory. Choose your target carefully. Take out their leader first, then the next. Keep firing until they're all dead. Stay to your zone."

It was the perfect ambush site, with clear views. Zanzi paused and listened hard. Nothing, except the windows rattling in the wind. That didn't mean that Black Skulls weren't out there. Maybe they were being cautious. She hugged Tilly. "Be careful. Like in the park, okay. Pretend they're the Rabids, except these ones shoot back. Just stay out of sight. You're the back up."

"Okay." Tilly had dark bags under her red-rimmed eyes. They were all exhausted. They hadn't had a full night of sleep since The Eyrie.

Zanzi let her go and waited until she was hidden before making her way to her spot. She spent a few seconds getting settled. She needed spare magazines within easy reach but couldn't decide whether to place them in or out of her combat vest. In the end she did a combination.

Gunfire erupted from outside, short bursts. Silence, then more bursts. No shouts or screams, nothing. Then a single shot, quickly followed by two more.

Shadows of Ash

Silence gripped the printing factory.

As Zanzi waited, she tried to figure out how long it would take Offenheim's armed men to find them, if they bothered to pursue at all. She bet they would, going by what the commando had said.

"The boss wants you alive."

The boss – Victor Offenheim. He didn't accept failure. There was no way the commandos would go back to base empty handed. It was a lot to assume, but these men followed orders. Had they killed the faction? Would the Black Skulls sweep the buildings? Would the dogs follow their scent?

One minute went by. Then two. Three. No sounds other than birdsong and creaking timber.

Four minutes.

We should have run. No. I'm tired of running.

Tilly and Jacqui stood up and shrugged. Lisa waved them back down with a stare.

Five minutes.

Zanzi's ears picked up the faint sound of a dog whimpering like it was being held back from some exciting smell.

Eight minutes.

She heard boots scuff on the dirty concrete below. It was a short sound, but sudden and clear.

She glanced at Lisa who pointed at her eyes and held up three fingers, indicating three men had entered the factory.

Three was an odd number. Why three? Maybe the rest were in another factory. The trio swept the room. One stayed at the beginning of the row of machinery while the other two checked every nook and cranny.

Zanzi ducked down and looked through her scope. The commandos had no rank insignia, standard practice. No use telling the enemy who was in charge. She looked for body language, trying to determine who the others were looking to.

She lined up the crosshairs on the commando standing at the head of the row and waited for Lisa's signal.

Lisa held up a fist, then three fingers. Another three Black Skulls. The first group waited for their teammates, then gestured to the second floor.

Zanzi followed the commando on point and watched as he ascended the stairs. Her finger caressed the trigger guard. Doubts plagued her mind. Yet again, she was being asked to do something that went against her beliefs: she had been trained to kill in self-defense only. She swiveled the rifle, searching out the commando bringing up the rear. Yes, she had been trained in self-defense, but these pricks were going to kill them, sooner or later.

The factory creaked with the rising sun. A fraction later, Lisa shot the commando on point.

Crack!

He dropped like a defeated boxer, crumpling on the stairs.

Zanzi had run through her shots as she waited. Now she executed her plan. First, she took out tail-end Charlie, then the commando in her zone nearest the stairs.

Lisa shot her second commando with a bullet to the head.

The two remaining Black Skulls reacted with calm precision. They both ducked behind the heavy machinery while firing into the upper floor. Glass rained down, clinking off the concrete floor.

While Zanzi pinned down her last commando, Lisa jammed in a fresh magazine. Silence returned.

"Truce!" one of the commandos shouted. Like in the forest, his voice had a hint of a German accent. Faint, but there. "Hold up a minute," he called out. "There is no need for anyone else to die."

Silence. Zanzi didn't want to talk. Didn't want to listen to these guys. A sudden thought hit her. Where were the dogs?

"Am I right in assuming that those shooting at us are Zanzi Connors and Director Omstead? Am I also right in assuming that with you is Dr. Josie Lahm?"

Still no words from either herself or Lisa.

Zanzi was growing frustrated. How did they know who they were? She squinted through the gun sight, but the commando was just keeping his head out of view.

"Don't be afraid to speak. The boss wants to see you. He wants you all alive. He was very insistent on that order."

"If you want us alive, come up here and take us," Lisa said, breaking her silence.

"Well now. If you throw down your guns, we can." He chuckled.

Zanzi gripped the M4 tighter. She urged one of the commandos to slip up and expose his head.

Barking dogs broke up the conversation. A few at first, followed by a whole chorus.

"Are you coming down?" the Black Skull said.

"No," Lisa shouted back. She made a show of slamming in her magazine.

"This is ridiculous. We have you surrounded. You have nowhere to go. Your little insurgency and sabotage of the cellular towers is over."

"Fuck off!" Lisa shouted. She fired, peppering the machinery around the Black Skulls.

Zanzi glanced around. She saw no way out. They were surrounded – unless they went out the office windows? It was possible. Maybe.

As she finished that thought, the office windows smashed. Dark objects bounced inside. Immediately, thick gray smoke ballooned out. Zanzi was choking in seconds. She fired her carbine a few times, hoping to hit one of the Black Skulls, but the tear gas took hold, stinging her eyes and mouth.

She could do nothing but cough and gasp for air as Black Skulls, with gas masks hiding their features, ran up the stairs. Somewhere in her foggy brain, she remembered her own gas mask in her backpack. Struggling, she slipped it on. Now that she could breathe, and the gas had stopped stinging her eyes, she searched for a target.

The Black Skulls went into the office and dragged out Jacqui, Tilly, and Josie. Lisa managed to shoot a couple of commandos before one slammed the butt of his rifle viciously into her head.

Zanzi kicked her rifle away and lay flat on the floor. She wanted to keep on fighting but didn't want any harm to befall her friends. The commandos yanked her to her feet, ripped off her mask and shoved her outside. Zanzi half expected to see Milo standing next to one of the vehicles, arms folded and grinning at them, but he was nowhere to be seen. The Black Skull in charge pushed her to her knees alongside Lisa, Tilly, Josie, and Jacqui. A few feet away, the bodies of the three faction members lay motionless on the concrete, the backs of their skulls blown out, exposing what was left of their brains.

The commando in charge walked back and forth along the line. He would let out grunts and whistles every few seconds. "You're all expecting a big speech where I gloat and tell you how hopeless your little rebellion was, aren't you?"

"So what's this, then?" Lisa said. "I thought you said your boss wants us alive. President Ward is a close friend of mine. I don't think he would be pleased with this treatment." As Lisa spoke, taunting the Black Skull, her hand slipped in her pocket. For a split second, in and out.

"Ward works for us, you fool. Just another puppet," the Black Skull leader said. He placed his pistol against Josie's temple and pushed. "You disappoint me, Doctor Lahm. First, you run off and get captured by a motorcycle gang. Now, I find you with these people?" He grimaced before striking her across the face, drawing blood from the corner of her mouth. He hauled her to her feet.

"Put her in the car."

He walked along, placing his gun against the back of each woman's head for a couple of moments. Tilly began to cry, her chest heaving with sobs. She looked at Zanzi, her eyes pleading. The leader stuck his pistol under Jacqui's chin.

"It's a pity to kill you. All day I'm surrounded by pasty ivory skin. Sometimes I like chocolate, if you know what I mean." He jammed a taser into her neck and kicked her to the ground as she twitched.

Zanzi watched on in horror. She wanted to taunt him, to say something brave, but she had nothing. She was too spent, tired of it all.

"What about you?" The leader stood behind Tilly.

"Not her. Kill me instead," Zanzi said, her voice quivering. "Me for her. Just let her go. Offenheim will reward you for killing me."

Tilly's sobs grew louder. The commando grinned and tasered Tilly. Her body convulsed and slumped over.

"No!" Zanzi screamed. She bolted upright and charged the Black Skull. With superhuman speed, he dodged and smashed the back of her head with the butt of his pistol.

Pain seared in the corners of her mind as she rolled over and focused. The Black Skull stood over her, but his image kept jolting to and fro. Zanzi shook her head, trying to clear the pain and regain clear vision. She managed to get to her knees as an SUV pulled up. Milo stepped out and waved the commandos away.

"I'll take over from here. Leave us."

It was déjà vu all over again for Zanzi.

All, apart from the leader, saluted, hopped into vehicles, and drove away. Milo let out a loud sigh, turned, and raised his eyebrows.

"Is this violence and torture really necessary?"

"I'm just having a little fun," the commando said.

Shadows of Ash

"These are important prisoners, to be treated with respect."

"Of course, sir."

"Go back to base and get on with preparations. Wave two is being reset. We have ten days. Make sure every citizen gets food, water, and medicine. I'll deal with them." He pointed to the women.

The Black Skull saluted and drove off, with Josie in the back of the SUV.

Zanzi cursed. Josie was their best chance at unraveling the nanites mystery. Zanzi moved over to Tilly and checked her pulse. Slow, but steady. She cradled the young woman's head in her lap.

"You guys did well. Sorry I took so long. I had to make it look legit. I'll drive you to wherever you need to go."

They moved Tilly and the unconscious Jacqui into the second SUV and sped away.

The sun had risen above Mount Hood. Mixed with the gathering rain clouds, it painted the landscape in dappled grays, oranges, and pinks.

"Where to, Director?" Milo said.

"Head west. I'll tell you when to stop," said Lisa.

Zanzi pulled Tilly into an embrace. She let her eyes wander over the forested mountain in the distance. She wished none of this had happened. She wished that her whole family, Liam included, were walking the trails, sharing laughter around the fire at night. Not any of this. This nightmare.

"It will be okay."

"It will be okay," she said again.

She repeated herself over and over in her head as she looked at the empty streets.

"It will be okay."

THIRTY-EIGHT

MAKUSHIN BAY, ALEUTIAN ISLANDS

"There has to be another way," Booth said. "Why would they build all this, and add the lockdown switch, if they didn't have an alternative?"

"You're asking a lot of the government," Cal said. She shone the flashlight into the shaft. Hunks of concrete choked the space and tangled the mechanism. Ryan looked down at her. He had tried to climb out, but his way had become impassable after only a few meters.

"It's blocked. The building's collapsed over the shaft," he said. He clambered down and wiped the dust off his gray fatigues.

"Say what you want, but we always build contingencies." Booth began to pace in a circle. He stopped at cupboards and opened them, knocking on the back panels and listening.

"I hardly think another exit would be hidden," Cal said.

"Well, at least I'm trying. What're you doing?" Booth said.

"Guys, c'mon. Look, I know we're all tired..." Ryan paused as a hollow sound rang out.

Booth grinned and knocked again, getting the same hollow ring. Excited, he pulled out boxes of spare computer parts. He felt along the edges, pushing. The back panel popped open, revealing a narrow tunnel with a metal ladder.

"What did I tell you? You guys never listen." He kissed Allie and grinned at Ryan and Cal.

Ryan let him have his win. They all needed it. He glanced up the escape tunnel. It was clear of debris and dust. At the top was a metal hatch, a glowing keypad next to it.

Seeing a clear way out gave Ryan renewed hope. Normally they planned everything, had alternatives upon alternatives, back ups, anything they could think of. They never went in blind.

He turned to Sofia; she was still on the phone to Keiko. She smiled when she saw him looking and hung up.

"They're safe. The *USS Nimitz* is anchored in the harbor. For now, they're keeping out of sight. Ebony moved them to a cargo hangar. The Black Skulls shot up the jet and all the other planes on the runway." She glanced at her computer monitor. "Still no word from Avondale. What's the status of the Skulls' ships?"

"Keeping in international waters at present, two hundred nautical miles out," Allie said.

"Bearing?"

"Southwest. They're circling."

The presence of the Black Skulls' ships concerned Ryan. One thing he was certain of, the US would not allow them to enter American waters without reprisals if they showed aggression. They had to contact *USS Nimitz*.

Sofia let out a whoop which sounded celebratory, with a hint of relief. She reached out, clicking on the loudspeakers. "Avondale."

"Hi guys. We did it!"

"We succeeded?" Sofia said.

"Second wave blocked from North America."

Ryan clasped Cal's shoulder. "Anywhere else?" he asked.

"I'm still gathering data. It's night in Europe, so could take a while."

"Can you get hold of *USS Nimitz* for us. Let them know we're here and friendly. That we have some deceased Marines too. Explain about the Black Skulls."

"Could take a little while."

"Thanks, Avondale," Ryan said. He turned slowly, looking at all The Nameless. "Thanks everyone. We risked everything, and we succeeded. It's a small victory, something we can savor for now."

Booth disappeared from the room briefly, returning with a couple of bottles of scotch and a stack of glasses. He passed them out and poured everyone a drink. For once, no words were spoken, each lost in their own thoughts. Ryan accepted a top-up from Booth and sank into one of the office chairs. Weariness descended on him and his body begged for sleep. But from the way his mind still raced, he knew sleep would be tough. He glanced around the room. At the blood, brains and skull fragments smeared on the floor and walls. At the signs of his fight with Dudek. The tipped-over chair, his satchel still lying in place with the taser baton dropped next to it. The Nameless had fought tooth and nail for this mission. They deserved this respite.

Booth chuckled, breaking the silence. "'Summer of Sixty-Nine' is definitely about sex." He was answered with a chorus of groans. "What? C'mon. You have to give me that one."

"No way. It's about nostalgia. How you look back at your youth and wish you were there again," Allie said.

"I'm with Allie," Cal said.

Sofia murmured her agreement.

"For once, I think Booth's right," Ryan said. "Sixty-nine is a metaphor for the innocent sexual encounters of youth."

"Ugh. You guys." Cal shook her head and downed the rest of her scotch. "What's our next move?"

Ryan unfolded a map of the island. "Thoughts?"

"Sleep," everyone answered.

They were right. As desperate as he was to carry on, to get back home to Portland, to find Zanzi, and to fight OPIS, they all needed rest.

"We take shifts. Two on watch – one monitoring the VTS, one monitoring the other comms."

Shadows of Ash

"I'll take first on comms," Sofia said.

"I'll do VTS," Cal said. "I'm too worked up to sleep right now."

The Nameless dispersed. The NSA station had small sleeping quarters next to a bathroom. Booth and Allie headed straight for the nearest bunks and rolled into the covers.

Cal pulled Ryan into a hug and kissed him on the lips. "Get some rest. You look like shit."

"Speak for yourself."

She laughed. "Don't beat yourself up."

Cal had always had a way of knowing what Ryan was thinking, what he was feeling. She knew his thought processes as well as her own. She had proven that when she had tricked them all into going to Koyasan. Keiko had been the bait, and she'd drawn them all in like moths to a flame.

"I can't help but feel we've failed," Ryan said.

"Even if we have, we're still breathing. With that, we can still stop them."

"How? At every point we've been a step behind."

"Get some sleep. We'll debrief and plan, really plan, our next move."

Ryan slipped into his jacket. "I need some fresh air first."

He left the group and climbed up the ladder. He opened the hatch with the code Sofia had given him and found himself in a shed. Two snowmobiles sat under tarpaulins. That was something. At least they wouldn't have to walk kilometers back to Dutch Harbor.

"Wait up. I'm coming too," Cal called out.

Ryan and Cal climbed the hill next to the weather station. The storm had subsided. On they walked, over rocks and scrub, leaving a trail of footprints in the dusting of snow. They wound their way up the steep hill, following a narrow trail. The sea below surged and broke against the mussel-filled rocks. The landscape was barren, no trees or shrubs, something that always disturbed Ryan.

Ryan sucked in deep breaths as he made for the summit. A lone granite boulder stood guard. Next to it, someone had built a cairn. He wondered if it was a monument to someone lost at sea or just a record of how many times someone had made it to the summit. He leant against the weathered boulder and gazed east, thinking of his daughter and his lost son. Cal nestled herself against him, and he wrapped his legs around hers.

Together, they silently watched the sun rising above the horizon like they had done countless times before.

"What is it?" Cal said.

"What?"

"You have that look like something's bugging you."

"I just ... no it's nothing."

"Ryan, we were married a long time, I know it's not nothing."

"I'm trying, Cal. Trying to understand but I keep circling back. The way you responded at Yamada's mansion, laughing when Offenheim's men found us."

"It was an act."

"For whom?"

Cal stood and folded her arms. "Offenheim has spies everywhere."

"But the game was up, everything was revealed."
"Not everything."
"What does that mean?" Ryan clenched his jaw. Normally Cal was forthcoming. He wasn't used to this side of her.
"All Offenheim wanted was for me to spy on Yamada. Find out his plans. I saw a way out and took it, so I fed him false information and moved into position to bring you guys in. When Offenheim's helicopters showed up, I had to keep the act going."
"Making him think you'd been captured."
"Exactly."
"And the German speaking yakuza?"
"After the codes that Sofia and Booth had."
"That important?"
"Yes. They would've been concerned that LK3 would figure out their plans with them."
Ryan pushed up off the gray rock and turned away from his wife. His mind was still whirling, trying to grasp at something nagging him. It hit him like a ton of bricks. "The death squads in Koyasan. I saw you there and the men clearing the university mentioned orders from a woman. You?"
"I couldn't break cover. I had to bide my time. Yamada was aware of the situation and sacrificed his men."
"He knew your plan all along?"
Cal grabbed his elbow and turned him around. "I needed Yamada to bring you in. He approved because he needed The Nameless as you found out."

Ryan saw a flash of a scowl, like Cal was uncertain of her answer then it was gone. She kissed his cheek. "I understand that you're cautious," she said. "That everyone is. I was in deep. Once we get home I'll submit to a debriefing."

In LK3 if an operative had been captured by the enemy then returned, a debriefing was standard procedure. From what Ryan had witnessed it was a grueling and sometimes torturous affair. Two weeks ago, having Cal here with him was but a dream. Could he let her go through that?

"I think that's for the best," Ryan said. "I'm sorry."

Cal guided her husband back to the rock and sat down. They stared at the ocean for a few moments.

"Do you remember when I told you I was pregnant?" Cal said.

"Yes. We were having a cup of tea and watching the sunset over the Pacific."

"And do you remember what you said to me at that moment? I know I'll never forget it." She clung to his hands. "That's what kept me going during my darkest times with Offenheim."

Ryan blinked away his tears. "I said, 'And so, the sun is setting on our first act. Tomorrow it will dawn on our second. It's junctures like these that I know I'm doing the right job.'"

"That's why we must keep going. We're doing the right job. Doing the right thing. For us. For everyone."

Ryan held his wife tighter and returned his gaze once more to the sun rise.

Shadows of Ash

He thought of all the people he had killed. All for the greater good, to keep the free people of the world free. He thought of all the atrocities he had witnessed. In the Congo. In Romania. In Mongolia. All over the world. Human trafficking and slave rings. The hollow looks of the victims still haunted him every night.

"Do you think Liam is looking down at us?" Cal whispered. "It's weird, but I feel him here." She pointed at her chest.

"I think so too," Ryan said. "Like he's guiding us. You know, some cultures believe that when you die, you become part of the world again. That your soul becomes part of the fabric of the universe itself. That they guide your choices. That's why we sense loved ones we have lost."

"I like that. I feel him every day. Maybe because he was made from us, with our DNA. I feel him, not just here, but out there. That's why we must carry on. Not just for Liam and Zanzi, but for all humanity."

"God, that sounds clichéd."

"Maybe. But as clichéd as it is, it's true," Cal said.

"I miss Liam so much. I can't help but think, did we do enough? Train him enough? We taught him survival skills and weapons. Martial arts. And still he died. Too young, with so much before him." He brushed a tear and looked away.

"He did everything we taught him, and more. He sacrificed himself and saved lives," Cal said. "He may not have sworn the oath we did, but he lived up to our values. Arthur Price would be proud."

"Your dad? He said as much at the funeral and at yours. We need to contact your parents."

"We will," Cal said. "You should've seen them when I joined the Army, swelling with patriotism. Our daughter they said, protecting this great country. For the many."

"For the many," Ryan repeated.

He breathed deep, filling his lungs with the chilled air. It stung as it entered, but he didn't mind. It reminded him that he was still alive. Unlike in Tokyo when he had thought he had nearly lost it all. He'd sunk to the lowest he had ever been. Thought his life had lost all meaning. Lost all purpose.

The sun finally broke above the horizon, kissing his skin.

Maybe now, for the first time since the birth of his children, he knew what his purpose was. To stop not just one madman, but a whole organization of madmen. Maybe that was his destiny.

He sighed and enjoyed the moment of reflection and peace.

EPILOGUE

Victor Offenheim stood at the expansive window that stretched from floor to ceiling, staring out over the Sierra Nevada mountains. Their snowy peaks reminded him of the Austrian Alps. He longed for those mountains. He longed to be back in his ancestral lands. To walk the fields and meadows. To feel the crisp air on his skin. He had fought hard for this new world and now his enemies were thwarting his vision.

He pivoted and threw his glass against the wall, screaming at the empty room. No one had foreseen what The Nameless had achieved. In all the scenarios they had run through, all the think tanks they had employed, no one had figured they would crash a satellite into an OPIS satellite. It had only been one, but it had been enough to stop the second wave in North America.

Not for long. They would reset and do it again.

His gaze settled on the bank of monitors arranged around the boardroom table. The four founding families and five of the six secondary families were present on the video conference. Yamada had shown his cards and cut himself off from OPIS. Offenheim. Prendergast. Ibrox. Santander.

Offenheim clasped his hands behind his back and raised an expectant eyebrow.

"Well?"

"We are still correlating numbers. Estimates put the figure at seventy percent success after wave two."

Offenheim stared at the speaker. Robert Prendergast was a Welsh mining and shipping billionaire from an ancient family; his wealth and power went back centuries. He was tall, his eyes steel blue. Offenheim nodded. Prendergast always delivered.

"Ibrox. What about your sector – Africa, Australia, Oceania?"

"Too difficult to say at this stage. We have billions of hectares of land to cover, thousands of tiny islands. It'll take months."

"A rough estimate?" Offenheim said through clenched teeth. Ibrox had jet-black hair, combed back, and an amused look permanently locked in place. Another whose family was from old money.

Shadows of Ash

"We estimate seventy percent in the major cities. As we speak, our teams are coordinating to mop up the dregs."

"Good. Keep me informed."

"Victor. I understand you're upset, but it was your sector that had the issue. We've always worked together to achieve this goal. Now, when you need us most, you have the audacity to be angry?"

Offenheim slammed his palm onto the table, rattling the monitors. "We all had people involved to stop these pesky insects. That, Santander, is why I'm upset."

Santander. Red hair with faint Asiatic features, a genetic oddity from the steppes of Kazakhstan. Her territory was by far the largest, from Moscow to Beijing, including India. Almost half the world's population, and some of its remotest areas. She grinned. "Estimated success of sixty-five percent. If we wait two weeks for the reset of wave two, this will give my staff the time we need to reach everyone liked we originally planned."

"You will all have your time. Has anyone else encountered problems?"

"Some," chorused the replies.

"As expected," Offenheim said. "Carry on as planned."

Offenheim pressed a button on his remote, ending the video conference call. The Nameless. Pesky insects that needed to be made an example of.

His retribution would be swift and deadly, but first, he needed to consult the manual. He spent a few moments calming himself, relaxing his muscles. He wasn't used to failure. Offenheim checked that none of his servants were present outside the boardroom before activating the switch, a panel hidden in the armrest of his chair. A keypad panel popped open on the bookshelf and he quickly entered the code.

A door hissed open and he stepped into the secret room beyond.

Peace immediately descended over him. Two of the walls were covered in banks of servers, blue lights blinking. These servers were separate from any others in The Eyrie. They contained valuable data on OPIS. Victor ignored the servers. Instead, he focused on the other end of the room, his shoes clicking on the polished floorboards. A simple desk made from English oak sat against one wall. Placed on top was a thick, blue-dyed leather-bound book, with the Offenheim family crest stenciled in gold leaf on the front cover. Next to the desk was a shrine. Candles burned next to a photo of his parents, and a larger one of his mother. Offenheim picked up his mother's photograph and kissed it, looking longingly at her blonde hair cascading over her shoulders. Behind her, the mountains of his home beckoned. He remembered his last conversation with her before cancer took her. She had begged him to wheel her to the roof so she could breathe the mountain air one last time. See the snow-capped peaks.

"Do not despair, my son."

"How can I not, Mother. First Father, now you? We were meant to stop this."

"Death comes to us all, even those who seek to stop it."

"I'm afraid that this won't be enough, that we will never see our vision."

"You're close, son. Keep going. Be strong."

"Yes, Mother."

They had watched the mountains for an hour, enjoying the serenity without speaking.

"It's time, son. I'm ready."

"Must you?"

"The pain is too much, even for me. Stay focused, Victor. Soon you will see the Austrian Alps again."

He had taken her back to her room and held her hand as the doctor administered the drugs to end her life. Years later, the grief of her loss still haunted him. She was the family's strength, its guiding beacon. Now he was alone. Offenheim sighed, kissed his mother's photograph once more, and opened the leather-bound book. Before she had died, Edith Offenheim had left instructions. Instructions on what to do if and when he met obstacles. She had been a brilliant strategist. What worried Offenheim was Milo. He knew Milo had helped Zanzi escape The Eyrie, and again he had been present when they had escaped the Black Skulls a second time. Could he use Milo to discover more of the faction? Three faction members were dead. Victor understood there were more scattered around. Parker – his head of security – had a lot of work to do.

Offenheim continued to read his mother's thoughts. He smiled to himself. Milo may have gone rogue, but Offenheim still had a way to bring him back to the fold.

He placed the book carefully back on the table and kissed his mother's photograph once more. As he left his sanctuary, he pulled his phone from his pocket. Enough of the games. It was time to clear the field of threats. A smile tugged at the corners of his mouth. Maybe he would get to play after all.

***

END OF BOOK TWO

THE STORY CONTINUES
IN
MASKS OF ASH

AUTHOR'S NOTE

This series started as a seed of an idea while I traveled through Japan in October 2017. I had spent the morning hiking a pilgrim trail up Mount Koya near Osaka. When I reached the top, I was in awe of the breathtaking scenery. Mountains, lakes, trees, and wildlife. It was simply serene. As I often do, I daydreamed, and I thought ... what would happen if some apocalyptic event occurred and I survived, only to be trapped? How would I get home? Could I?

The more I thought about it, I knew I had to turn it into a story.

Also, as a teenager I was fascinated by stories of World War Two and the espionage that went on. The level of planning that went into D-Day. How mistakes, bluffs, and double bluffs turned the tide of the war.

I wondered, could a secret group of powerful men and women bring about the apocalypse?

After taking all those ideas, the story grew into what you've just read.

I hope you enjoyed it and want to read more. I would be grateful if you would leave an honest review. I'm sure you've heard it before but reviews really are an author's bread and butter. They help in so many ways.

Thanks again,
Adrian

Want to keep up to date?

Join my Facebook group: Guardians of the Apocalypse.

You can contact me on:
Email: adesmithwrites@gmail.com
Website: www.adrianjonsmith.com

Made in the USA
Columbia, SC
12 October 2024